MW01600369

JESTER

R.C. ALLAN

For my parents.
For the strangers.
For the bold.

THE REALM OF GALIA

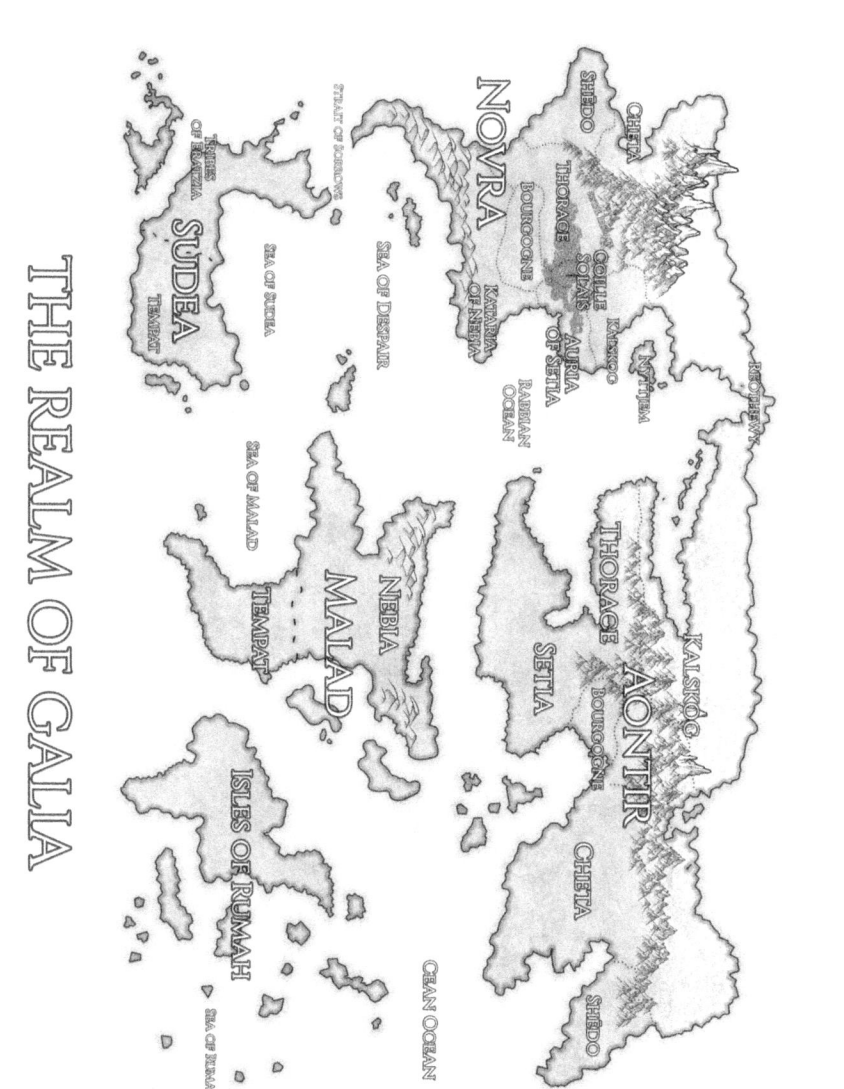

NOVRA

REOTHEWY

CHETA

NYTTJEM

KALSKOG

SHĒDO

EISTAL PASSAGE

COILLE
SOLAIS

AURIA
OF SETIA

THORACE

BOURGOGNE

RABBIAN
OCEAN

CEAN
OCEAN

KATARIA
OF NEBIA

SEA OF DESPAIR

STRAIT OF SORROWS

From dreams it was born,
Lightning from heaven.
Thought turned to force, in three parts leavened.

The woman did listen,
The man desired,
And the eunuch in the shadows sought to acquire.

Visions to dreams,
And dreams to power,
The desires of men draeda devoured.

—*ORIGINS OF DRAEDA*, SETIAN ARCHIVES

PART I

CHAPTER 1

Tazio sprinted along the rampart, fleet as the wind.

"Stop, you fool!" shouted a guard blocking the turret entrance.

Tazio cut right, left, then leapt from the rampart, winking at the guard as he sailed toward a flagpole protruding from the turret. His fingers screamed as he grabbed hold with one hand, and the crowd watching from the courtyard below gasped.

"Fear not!" Tazio called down. "I won't die! At least not yet!"

Buoyed by their cheers, Tazio pulled himself up and used the stone crevices to scale to the tower roof. The guard he'd evaded nodded as he caught his eye. Nothing a little coin couldn't do to enhance a show.

Tazio stood and caught his breath. The great plains of Bourgogne rolled to the horizon beyond the castle walls. Just past the dry moat, his clan's camp teemed with life. Danuiin children scurried around blazing campfires, troupes rehearsed their acts gleefully, and flutes trilled through the air. During Lughnassa, the summer solstice festival, his clan chose one lucky city in Novra where they would perform their most dazzling acts—and *this* was his performance.

Tazio turned back to the eager audience in the courtyard below, legs trembling from the bloodrush. No matter how many times he'd vaulted, the nerves always had their say.

Bourgogne sprawled for miles in front of him, its seven emerald-crested towers arresting him, piercing the sky like giants standing above the gray-brick city. Golden wheat plains and scattered forests surrounded it, and the Luxen Mountains sat in verdant abundance to the west.

Ah, the Bourgognese know how to live.

He hopped to the edge of the roof nearest the courtyard and spread his arms. A cluster of dirty children at the front of the crowd gawked at him. Tazio remembered being like them, in awe of vaulters, knowing it would be his path as a performer in the clan, heart racing as he'd watch them plunge from towers.

"You there, children!" Tazio let out from the roof, pointing to the pack of street kids. A plump, brown-haired one's jaw went slack, and he pointed to himself. "Yes, you! Unless you've lost your tongue."

"I haven't!" the boy spat out.

"Tell me then, should I jump or am I a bump?" Tazio asked.

"It is too high!" one younger boy with red hair and freckles shouted, looking terrified for Tazio.

"Perhaps, but so are the stakes. And you, what's your take?" Tazio asked.

"If you don't jump, I will!" the brown-haired boy shouted back.

"Very brave! To you, I submit. Come, take my place, given you've triumphed over me!"

"Uhm, well. My mum needs me home soon!" the boy replied, and the crowd roared in laughter at his sudden change in sentiment.

"Well, your bravery has made me doubtful of my own skill!" Tazio said, turning to leave.

The crowd played their part, booing and chiding Tazio to jump as he walked away sullenly. Then he stopped, crouched, and sprang into a backflip. He came down hard on the tile, foot slipping. A collective breath gripped the courtyard as he fell in a scramble over the edge. But he hooked his legs around the iron flagpole, saving himself from the fifty-foot drop. Dangling upside down, he grinned, and the crowd's horror cut short. Wild cheers applauded his daring play as their anxiety transmuted to jittery joy.

Reward always waited on the other side of fear.

He worked himself back up to the roof as the crowd urged him on. Riding the excitement, Tazio squared his toes to the edge, then leaned forward like a felled tree. His stomach tightened as he flipped twice, legs

4

bent at the waist, coming down like lightning onto an angled landing fabric set up on stilts below. It absorbed the fall and flung him back into the air. He flipped and landed. Roaring applause drowned him, ale surely playing a part in the enthusiasm. Tazio moved through swarming admirers, suppressing a blush as a group of adoring ladies batted their eyes his way. The dirty, brown-haired leader of the street kids pushed through the crowd nearby, cutting Tazio's intrigue short. "Amazing! Though after seeing it, I could have done the same!" the boy exclaimed.

"I don't doubt it," Tazio replied, giving the kid a friendly pat on the shoulder. In the same swipe, Tazio made a deck of cards appear in his palm. "Pick a card, lad."

The crowd went quiet as the child reached for a card, hand trembling.

"Good. Show your friends there and put it back in the deck."

After Tazio felt the card find its place in the deck, he threw it into the air. Cards scattered, then exploded into flames, drawing gasps. Amid the blaze, Tazio snatched a card from the flurry—a card with a jester on it. The only one that did not catch aflame.

He dangled it before the boy.

"Was this your card?"

"Yes..." the boy trailed off, eyes wide.

"Excellent choice, lad. A rare card. He who chooses the jester can expect turbulence and trickery. But fortune is found among the chaos. Be wise and find the wit to win, young lad."

Tazio flicked his wrist, and the card disappeared before the boy's eyes.

"I can't keep it?" the boy asked.

"Of course you can."

"Well, you've made it disappear!"

"You already have it, my boy," Tazio said, turning to walk away.

"He tricked me!" the boy shouted.

Tazio looked over his shoulder. "Check your sleeve."

Before the boy could check for himself, his friend wrestled it out, brandishing it in awe. Tazio bowed, and the crowd sent him off with fervor—and so did the maiden with the eyes of a fox. Touch her though, and he'd be hunted like a fox.

Might be worth it.

Tazio put the fantasy to bed as he walked across the drawbridge from the bustle, nodding to Den and Kaitra, his cousins, and weapon acrobats, who were entering the throng. Their beloved act was throwing axes to give haircuts against a wooden board. Tazio was always surprised what people would do for free. Though the haircuts turned out quite fine compared to the typical barber hackwork. Throughout the year, his clan traveled the new kingdoms of Novra to delight commoners and nobility alike, but Lughnassa stood apart. Food tasted better, fire felt warmer, and Tazio relished it. Near one of the many campfires, his father, Grady, ladled stew, smiling gently as he uttered prayers, a circle of protection over man and meal.

His father was a strong man from all the acrobatics, but his face sparkled with kindness, and his soul was gentle—sometimes too gentle.

"Brilliant! Even I believed you on that fake fall," Grady said as Tazio approached.

"What can I say? I live to please."

"Supper?"

"Wouldn't dare miss a ladle from you," Tazio joked, never willing to let his father off for ladling his wrists as a boy.

"That's my boy," Grady said, prodding him with the clean end of the ladle.

"Performing tonight?" Tazio asked.

"Wouldn't dare miss it!"

His father had taken to tightrope in recent years, yet another arrow in his quiver. Tazio couldn't help but respect his father's ever-expanding fire for performance, but it also made his gut turn. Uneasiness that had lain roots in Tazio's soul felt ready to push out that summer. Not ready to go there, he let the greens and blues of the turning sky steal his gaze.

"Something on your mind?" Grady asked.

"Nothing noteworthy."

"Any note will do."

"I'm not sure it's a note you'll want to hear."

"About time you squashed all that uncertainty about your path. There's a place opening up to lead a troupe, and you're fit for it."

"Yes, you've made that abundantly clear."

"Oh, come now, I'm not so terrible, am I?"

Probing had been his father's favorite side act recently. But for Tazio, it was more than not wanting to perform. Ambition churned beneath the surface like a restless, caged animal.

"Of course not," Tazio replied.

"Even at your age, people follow you, Tazio. We need leaders. Especially talented ones."

"I understand, Father, but I'm beginning to tire of tricks and wit."

"They're your gifts, boy."

"I'd rather not go into this now." Tazio's tone put his father's eyes to the ground. "I'm sorry."

"Son, I'm not sure how to reach you. But know that I only want to help you. You'll just have to look for a way to get beyond yourself."

His father reached out in the Danuiin way, taking Tazio's hands and embracing him before returning to his duties. Tazio didn't like when he let himself be so sharp, or when he wounded his father. But frustration reared quickly when his father prodded away.

Maybe I'm ungrateful. Leading a troupe is a fine thing to do.

He had to be sure before abandoning that path—it might crush his father's spirit. All around, his people were dancing, eating, enveloping themselves in jubilance. Just beyond the circle, his cousin Peader watched his troupe leader, eyes tight with focus, as he learned fire-juggling. Tazio tightened at the sight, unable to bear the thought of pouring in years to train for another act.

He stood from the fire to find his mother's tent. Their family's plaid flap marked the entry, and he folded it back to find his mother sitting sewing garments in her plush chair, a fur draped over her lap. She curled her blond hair around an ear, and her soft face, reflecting an open soul, greeted him. His father always joked that, "Catoria is the most beautiful woman without a king." And while she was, it was her soothing presence Tazio loved more than anything.

"Tazio."

"Mother." Tazio hugged her.

"Am I the most interesting event you could find tonight?"

"You're always the most interesting thing I can find."

"Oh dear. Have you been wandering around like a lost boy, staring into great *Etria* for answers?"

"Is it that obvious?"

The wrinkles by her eyes gave the answer. "Well, what is it?"

No one could pierce through the seriousness Tazio hid from the world like she could—her bright blue doe-eyes flecked with silver and white, colored like his own, making audience for his doubts and dreams.

"Father brought up the open role again."

"Did he now?"

"He did."

"And?"

"I feel I want something else."

"And what would that be?" Catoria asked, eyebrows peaked.

"When we travel to different regions, I see soldiers and wonder what it would be like to war. Or merchants, they have commerce. They're seizing the world. I sometimes feel we're so removed, so much so we're not even a part of it."

His mother sat silently, nodding gently in consideration. "I understand."

"I wish understanding settled this feeling inside me, but it doesn't go away."

"Maybe it's there for a reason."

"How can you disagree so easily with Father?"

"I'm not here to convince you to take any particular path. I only want what you feel is right."

"Sometimes I wish our people were a bit more driven. I feel I'm rowing upstream against our entire lineage."

"We prefer to be content. You've always been more voracious."

"Then why does Father force a path onto me?"

"He simply wants to help guide you out of confusion. We can't truly control anyone's direction, and he knows that too. He just knows your talent and wants to help."

"It's pathetic I don't know what I want. Though one thing I do know—I don't want to lead a troupe." A rush of relief poured out, but the sadness in his mother's brow made him wince. "I'm sorry."

Catoria reached out and gently took his hand.

"Tazio, you have to have the courage to do the thing you're afraid to do—even when you're afraid. We only discover the answer when we move into fear. Just know that no matter what you choose, we'll be the wind at your back."

The fire crackled in the center of the tent as his mother's words wrapped him in warmth. Fear eased away with the rich smoke drifting through the hole in the tent's canopy, greeting the three moons of Aontir above, all aligned in a perfect triangle on the summer solstice.

"I love you, Tazio, as your father does. Enjoy tonight. You've always loved Lughnassa. These problems can wait."

"Thank you, mother." Tazio kissed her gently on the temple, and as he walked out of the tent into the camp, a few children darted by with spools of yarn toward the solstice portal ceremony.

Tazio walked to the central campfire. Already, man, woman, and child were attaching yarn to a wicker portal erected some twenty feet high. Taking a thread of his own, Tazio attached it and joined those standing in a circle around the portal.

Across the fire, the youngest Danuiin child who could stand lit her yarn cord with a chirp of joy, and all followed. Flames crawled up the yarn and gathered in the center, the summer breeze urging sparks into a blaze. The portal burned against the night sky, a marker of the passage from summer to fall—when the veil between *Etria* and the worldly realm was thought to be thinnest.

Amid the silence, all searched for what spoke inside them, grasping for wisdom, kindling the ancestral tradition that predated the exodus from the old world to Novra more than a century ago. From the blazing portal, solace spoke to Tazio, and he let go of the hands of the two beside him, stepping out of the circle. The meadows beside the river bending around Bourgogne called to him, and he lay down, letting his eyelids drift closed. Half-present, he swam in the muffled sounds of celebrations coming from camp and within the castle walls, a sense of peace breezing over him. In the distance, a light thunder gurgled, and he smiled at the thought of being rained on.

I'll apologize to Father later. Never feels good biting at him. Mum is right, he only means well by me.

His heart swelled as he thought of them. He was no easy lad—even he struggled to understand his own desires. To have such patient parents was a gift from *Etria*—one he shouldn't forget.

Low rumbles moved through the soil from the thunder, and Tazio put his hand to the soil. The thunder was growing. Tazio sat up, shaking off his dreaminess as he searched the horizon.

The hairs on the back of his neck prickled as he stood slowly. There were no clouds far off, yet the soil trembled beneath his feet, growing in intensity. A horn from the castle wall tore through the night. Alerts chained together across Bourgogne's castle wall—then Tazio saw what the horns warned of. From the nearest hill outside the castle walls, with the three moons set behind them, a torrent of cavalry poured forth, their shadows stretched out long in front of their charge from the pale back-light. Thousands of foot soldiers broke over the hill behind the riders, their battle cries blending with the beating hooves. Those on the edge of the camp saw what storm had come, and scattered screams grew into frenzied panic.

"Run!" Tazio screamed as he sprinted toward the camp.

His chest burned, legs throbbed, throaty pleas swallowed by the cacophony of mayhem as the cavalry pounded through the low river, water spraying, gaining on the camp with each stride.

"Everyone, run!"

The cavalry tore into the outer edge of Danuiin camp, flattening man, woman, and child under the chests of their plated stallions. Tazio reached the side of the camp closest to the city walls, about three hundred feet away from the charge.

He sprinted toward his family's encampment, hurdling over tent wires, slamming into those he knew, their faces blurring by, twisted like ghouls. Reaching his parents' tent, he tore open the entrance. Nothing but a heavy void stared back. His palms grew hot, feet like bricks, until a scream snapped him back. A torrent of people surged toward the draw-bridges that were open for the festival—when war was supposed to be forbidden.

Tazio bolted out of the tent toward the drawbridge, looking over his shoulder at the dark column of riders gaining with every step, swords glinting in the moonlight as blood sprayed from sharp steel. He turned forward to focus and slammed into someone, tripping, falling, clawing at the dirt to steady himself. A desperate, curdling groan tore out of him as the consequences of his carelessness threatened him.

The riders were fifty paces behind. The thought of losing his parents made his vision grow red with horror. Hundreds of Danuiin crammed onto the drawbridge, and he saw his parents among the mass forcing its way into the gate. He shoved his way into the crowd as volleys of arrows came down from the ramparts onto the attacking riders.

Twenty paces. He screamed at his parents, desperate to get their attention. Ten paces. The grinding chains of the castle gate cut through the air.

No.

His people screamed as the gate slammed shut, and with it, the hope of escape.

"Mother! Father!" Tazio screamed, shoving through as hard as he could, the mass of people straining under the force of the riders crushing into them, hacking down the defenseless, plowing people over the edge into the moat. Ahead, Grady shielded Catoria, both enduring the horror in calm acceptance of their reckoning.

"Mother!" Tazio cried, the sight of their helplessness splitting his heart open.

"We love you," she mouthed back, like the moment was carved out of eternity for them.

"No!" Tazio shouted, chest tightening under the harsh truth this was, in fact, his last moment with them. He reached toward his mother before an armored stallion crushed into his back, tearing him back to reality, the force hurling him off the bridge toward the moat below. The sky spun, rhyming with the dizzying violence cutting his life apart. Down, and down, and down he fell, knowing death had found him, knowing it had found his parents, knowing it had ruined him, until he slammed into the crooked pile of those who had fallen before him. His breath shot out, eyes flickered and rolled back as he hung onto the last thread of consciousness, where from some distant, unreachable place, he could hear death laughing at his naivete—at his stubborn disbelief that it could have chosen *his* people, on this sacred night, in this sudden way.

How foolish.

Death makes no exceptions for a foolish street clown.

CHAPTER 2

TAZIO'S EYES CRACKED OPEN, head throbbing as moonlight from the three moons inflicted like searing metal. As he sat up woozily, his wrist rolled off the gaping neck of a corpse.

"Peader?" he groaned, seeing his cousin staring blankly back at him like a dead animal.

Tazio gagged as he remembered where he lay, the stench of flesh thick in the air, flies swarming. Bile pushed up his throat as he scrambled crookedly over the moat of corpses, retching as he searched for an escape from the pit of horrors. But he stopped. An arm thrust through the gnarled limbs caught his eye, the unmistakable patterns of his mother's shawl upon it. Hand shaking, he peeled back limbs, revealing his mother, her last moments of terror frozen on her face. A wound gored from her collarbone to the center of her chest, and Tazio tore his shirt, covering it and bringing her face to his chest like she'd done just hours before.

A hole opened in Tazio.

This wasn't how it was supposed to be. She wasn't supposed to die like this. And his father.

Between the tears, Tazio cackled.

"Of course. One parent isn't enough, is it?" he muttered.

He lay Catoria down, holding his breath as he fumbled through the mess of man, woman, and child to find Grady peering up at him. Death, unlike all trials before, managed to strip his father's gaze of its kind wonder. He clutched his father's still body, hoarse, slow breaths pouring out as tears welled in his vision, chest rising and falling, the slow wind rolling across his face, an intoxicating numbness settling in his blood. The thought of ending himself, or running straight at the Thoracians drifted to mind. It would be easy to be done with it all, everything stripped away anyhow.

But from the drawbridge above, the chatter of soldiers shot fear through his veins, instincts taking over as he dropped prone, watching as the soldiers sauntered by. When they'd passed, he began to drag his mother across the sea of bodies, tug by tug, struggling to preserve her innocence, but failing as her corpse fought every slip and fumble.

Near a tent by the drawbridge, he put her down next to a few tethered horses, calming them as he secured her across one. He turned for his father and saw the newly hung banners snapping by torches along the rampart. They bore a falcon with a snake in its talons—the mark of the Thoracians.

Lord Falkone did this, King of the Thoracians. A forbidden war on the solstice of peace.

Tazio returned with his father, heaving him across the horse's back, keeping an eye on some nearby soldiers celebrating over ale. Tazio mounted, and his horse whinnied in protest.

"Ey!" a soldier shouted as Tazio spurred, ducking as a lance whirled by. He galloped, the river and valleys disappearing in a blur until he reached the tree-lined hills at the foot of the Luxen Mountains, stopping only when the woods were dark and the wilderness swallowed him.

The hoot of an owl.

The stirring of branches under the summer wind.

Tazio dismounted and untied his parents, collapsing as he hoisted them off. Exhausted, he sank into the mud, the pinch of twigs some distant pain. But the sight of his mother's face lodged in the mud beside him sparked duty. So he rose, and in the precincts of the night, built the pyres they deserved, time bleeding by in a fever, a growl curling through the air behind him in the dead hours.

Tazio turned to see a group of wolves.

"Fuck off," he growled back, staring death into the eyes of the pack leader.

He wished they'd attack, but of course, fate didn't grant him that request, his fearless abandonment scaring even them. But they did stay, observing like sentries as he folded his parents' arms, placing them on the finished platform. Touching the point between their eyes, the eye to *Etria*, the One, the All, he muttered a prayer, then struck flint, watching the kindling take, flames growing from a flicker to a roar as his parents melted before his dead-set eyes.

This time, no tears came.

Instead, the fire lit a fury, its heat consuming the old, forming his resolve as he stood unmoving, until his parents turned to ash, the name Falkone burning in his mind, hoping soldiers might see the smoke signals.

I don't give a fuck if he's the great conqueror. I'll cut him into a thousand pieces.

—

Morning sun glanced through the trees, a ray nicking Tazio's eyes as he stirred awake. His legs ached, but his mind was clear. With heart mettled, he stood from the mud with focus. With one last glance at the pyre, he turned toward Bourgogne.

Life into ash. Ash into life. Vengeance.

—

The next morning, with the mist of dawn clearing and the sky yellowing, Tazio rode down from the hills. In the meadow just beyond the river, he paused, seeing Thoracian soldiers burning the Danuiin camp, killing survivors, and looting anything of value. Tazio let his horse go free in the fields and used the brush to conceal his approach.

As he crawled through the fields until he neared the edge of camp, he looked through the grass at the nearest group of soldiers. The thick wooden branch he carried felt just right, ready for its deed—its gnarled, heavy end whispering murder when he first lifted it off the forest floor.

The soldiers' pewter armor was harsh, sharp angles and years of battle-torn wear giving a menacing ruggedness. Unlike armies that polished and refreshed their kits for dignity, the Thoracians enjoyed wearing the scars of battle, the most legendary warriors donning an alarming patchwork of dents and cuts.

His club wouldn't do much against armor, but it had assured him faces weren't made of steel.

The three soldiers bantered in a circle like idiots, helmets off as they stood off duty. Tazio crouched behind some smoldering tents, then darted behind a cart with corpses piled high in it.

"At least we're not on head chopping," said one soldier facing away from Tazio. "No one likes lopping kids and women—well, women ain't bad with a little taste before," The others reveled in the sadistic joke as the sick comedian took a swig out of a wine flask.

Tazio slid around the edge of the cart, taking a deep breath to calm his shaking.

Go.

Now!

Tazio burst out, swinging his club with every ounce of fury. It cracked into the first soldier's temple, sending him limp into the dirt. Another went for his sword, fumbling with shaky hands as Tazio swung again, the club cracking his jaw. Teeth splintered, and the man staggered over, gurgling on shattered teeth.

The third, helmet now on, hacked at Tazio with a shortsword. Tazio evaded with a desperate forward roll, then turned and crunched the man's knee inward. The Thoracian screamed and fell off balance as Tazio rose, poised to deliver a final blow.

"You fucking sick bastards," Tazio said, afraid of the hoarse darkness in his voice.

The man heaved his armored elbow into Tazio's ankle, and tackled him over, driving his elbow into Tazio's face, beating him relentlessly until his steel gauntlets ground Tazio's skin to the bone.

The soldier stood, picked up his sword, and lifted it.

Tazio raised his arm in desperation, knowing it would only delay the inevitable when a cool, curt voice cut him short.

"Enough."

"My Lord!" the soldier replied. "With due honor, this *scum* attacked us."

"An astute observation. If a piss-poor Danuiin can catch you three by surprise, you're likely more useful dead. Perhaps I'll have you killed for incompetence," said the mounted officer, brown eyes gleaming with vicious calm from his helmet's eyeslit, and angry brown locks falling freely down his shoulders.

"After you give him a good beating, throw him in prison. A few years in there and he'll wish we hadn't been merciful."

"Forgive me, Lord Sieg—"

Lord Sieg unsheathed his sword and tossed his sword. It landed point first in the dirt before the recalcitrant soldier.

"Yes, my Lord," the soldier said.

"Also—my sword there—polish it until you can see your ugly face in it. If it passes muster, I may let you and your idiot friends live."

Sieg wrenched his stallion around in a cocky arc and galloped off.

Tazio rolled onto his stomach in an attempt to escape, spasming in pain in the process.

"Where you going?" the offending soldier cackled, grabbing Tazio by the hair and turning his face to a stack of decapitated bodies. "Next time, you lose your head like your brothers. You were lucky this time."

Tazio coughed out a delirious laugh, much to the soldier's disappointment. "Thanks for the advice," Tazio sputtered through a bloody grin, a tooth rolling out for effect.

"Ahh, a cheeky one, are you? How's this for a smart mouth?"

The grunt raised his boot.

Mud dripped.

Darkness.

CHAPTER 3

THE THICK SMELL of excrement clawed at Tazio's throat as he groaned awake.

"Ahh, pretty Danuini's up," a man croaked from across the damp torchlit cell.

Every muscle screamed in protest as Tazio shifted, a cacophony of pain from yesterday's beatings. Tazio made out the silhouettes of three men sitting chained to a wall a few feet away in their tiny cell. A fourth sat against a gate that divided their cell from the others.

"Cork it, filth," another man with a low, grizzly voice said, rising from his seat to strike the one who'd taunted Tazio.

"I'm Ulrich," he said, sliding closer as the other man gasped in pain. "If any of you touch the boy, I'll split you in half with mah bare hands."

Tazio recognized Ulrich from town—a huge, earnest man who worked the forge. Grady went to him for parts to keep their wagon in shape whenever they visited Bourgogne. His peppered-gray hair was cut crudely short, as if with a dagger, and his gray beard was coarse and thick.

"Don't know if we're lucky or not for being tossed in here," Ulrich said, "Suppose it's better than dead."

"Lucky isn't the word I'd use to describe it," grunted one of the other prisoners.

"Why'd they lock you in here?" Ulrich asked Tazio.

Tazio's normal wit escaped him as it never had, blunted by the previous two days.

"Clubbed some soldiers," Tazio muttered, his voice like a shadow of itself.

"Can't see why you'd do that," Ulrich joked.

The smallest of the three chained on the wall cackled at that, and Tazio managed a faint smile, sensing Ulrich was trying to introduce some cheer.

"Keep your head up. The hard part is over," Ulrich said, leaning away, patting Tazio's shoulder with his soot-stained hands.

Red and coral light flickered off the walls, shadows dancing in the stones like cruel entities. Tazio coiled into a ball, the crusty garment of blood on his skin cracking as he shut his eyes.

Tomorrow will be better. It must be.

But a darkness slid into the cell like a whispering fog, making his neck tighten.

Or perhaps it would be worse.

→

Days bled into weeks in the dank cell.

Tazio and the other prisoners grew frail on thinned pottage.

The man who'd jeered at him on the first day was beheaded along with a few others from the cells. But the Thoracians eagerly refreshed the stock with Bourgognese types. And after seeing the latest batch of criminals, Tazio realized his crime paled in comparison, the minor status of it granting him a few extra days of life as the Thoracians cleaned up the more gruesome criminals first. Tazio certainly didn't fancy the idea of being beheaded, but a life of torture seemed worse in some ways.

But the axe hadn't come yet.

After a few weeks of dark isolation, they were rounded up and put to work building barracks, repairing destruction from the battle or whatever other tasks amused the soldiers. The work was relentless, and whatever food they got provided scant sustenance to match the brutal labor.

Soon Tazio was hunched, crooked, sick and pale, his wounds infested, twitching like a mute as soldiers beat him.

In-fighting among the prisoners dwindled to non-existence as their strength waned, so the guards did their best to break them down further, clubbing or hacking them down as others gawked in fear, the broad, armored soldiers contrasting the filthy, emaciated prisoners in a demented display of dominance. The lack of effort required was pathetic, and the soldiers seemed to thoroughly enjoy the disparity.

Following a beating in the cell one day, Ulrich whispered to him, "You know, you remind me of my boys. Don't know if they survived or not. Sent them into an alley when the battle broke out."

Perhaps in softer days, Ulrich's kindness would warm him, but instead it felt like hot water on ice-burned hands.

"I don't know what's worse—if they're actually dead or wondering and never knowing. They could be alive right now, but are they? Are they suffering? Beggars and maimed? Maybe it's better if they're dead, you know? But I can't know. That's what kills me."

Tazio listened hollowly.

"I'm sorry, Ulrich. I truly am."

"I'm sorry, I'm rambling, aren't I?" Ulrich said.

Tazio opened his mouth, but the words curdled in his chest. Why provide the brittle promise of hope, ready to shatter at any moment?

"Sometimes all we can do is ramble, ey?" Tazio replied.

"Yes, I suppose so."

"I think they'll be fine," Tazio said, the words grating his throat as they came out.

"Hah! That hopeless little speech did make me feel better. But only because of the struggle you went through to bark those words out."

"Damn, I wish I could do better for you."

Ulrich reached over, bringing Tazio closer by the shoulder.

"It's okay. I have a plan," Ulrich whispered. "It will take time though."

"What is it?"

"When the time is right, I'll tell you to act. Promise me you'll obey."

"What's that supposed to mean?"

"You know, stubborn would be an understatement to describe you."

"Born this way, I can't help it."

"Just promise me."

"I'm with you, I promise."

"Good."

"Well, this cell isn't so bad after all is it?" Tazio joked, the vision of escape making him lighter.

Maybe hope is worth the risk.

"Best inn in all of Novra if you ask me," Ulrich patted the dank cobblestone floor sardonically.

"Oy, you two, what's with all the smiling?" a Thoracian guard barked, sensing a departure from the normal glum mood around the cells.

"We were just appreciating our little home. Maybe you'd like to join?" Tazio asked.

A hock of phlegm from the soldier hit Tazio square in the face, and he fell backwards laughing.

"Shut up, or I'll come in there," the guard threatened.

"Come, come, we'll welcome you with open arms," Ulrich added.

A wild, tiny laugh worked its way up in Tazio that they'd aggravated the guard.

They can beat us, but now, it'll only fuel us.

→

The next morning, Tazio awoke to the familiar feeling of urine hitting his back. He thrashed off the floor and jumped at the guard pissing on him through the iron bars.

"Funny seeing you squirm like a caged rat! Want me to come in there and piss on your face? Can't get it from this angle!" the guard taunted.

Tazio let out a crazed scream.

"Come closer and I'll bite your face off!"

The man backed off a bit.

"Scared, are you?" Tazio taunted.

"Fuck off," the guard said, tying his fly.

"Don't play coy. Come closer. I'll give you a little kiss. Maybe a little nibble." Tazio clicked his teeth a bit and the guard flinched.

"Back off, Tazio," Ulrich said from behind.

"You best listen to your big friend," the guard said. "Well, he's looking quite frail these days, isn't he? Food must not be to his liking."

The bones in Tazio's hands hurt from gripping the bars so hard. But he refused to be like the poor bastard, who, close to the point of death, stopped fighting the torment—just lay there dead one day, the guards pissing on him.

Cut off my head. Beat me to a pulp. But I won't die from a broken will.

Sunlight spilled through the stairwell as another guard opened the hatch above and clambered down the stairs.

"You lot are being moved out," the new one said, "Wish we could have spent more time together, but I'm sure you'll enjoy our frontlines."

The prisoners groaned. Tazio could hear some scuttle their asses backwards away from the cell doors as if they could hide.

"Outside! Now!" the piss guard yelled to the lot of prisoners, unlocking gates and beating resistors.

The sun stung Tazio's eyes as he and the procession of scraggly prisoners creaked up the stairs into the courtyard. They walked past the gallows where a few men still hung. One prisoner with rotting, sallow skin eyed the high beams of the scaffold erected in the courtyard, probably considering if they were going to be hanged.

"Chipper up. They can't conquer Novra without a few thousand slaves to carry the load," Tazio said to the man.

Whispers of Falkone's continued conquest through the south had made their way even into the ghastly prison chambers. As if actual torture wasn't enough, propaganda about their string of victories drove the stake even deeper for all the prisoners.

"Uh huh," the man said, realizing Tazio was right but looking broken regardless.

They slogged past a lineup of Thoracian cavalrymen. Ahead, a transport wagon swallowed prisoners as guards crammed them into its tiny door. A few crude slits were hacked along the top of the wood, and seemed the only access to air.

Tazio stopped shuffling, refusing to go closer, feeling the world closing in on him as he imagined being inside the suffocating cart.

"Move it, piss-head," hissed the piss guard, jabbing Tazio in the back with a club.

Tazio considered wrapping his chains around the man's neck and spending his final breaths draining the life from his eyes. But he could barely manage standing.

A dull crack on his head stopped his fantasy, bringing him to the floor, hot blood spilling down his face. The soldiers picked him up by the armpits and dragged him to the transport. One of his shoulders nearly tore from its socket as they shoved him in like a cork through the small door.

He landed limply against a heap of men all coiled in a mess.

Immediately, another man landed on top of him. Then another. And another. It was cramped. Hot. Disgusting. An even deeper nightmare than the cell they'd just left.

"Ulrich?" Tazio wheezed, hardly able to breathe, hearing his own desperation.

"I'm here," Ulrich responded, voice dampened by the dungeon.

The back door slammed. The padlock slipped shut. Prisoners scraped and groaned on each other in discomfort. Tazio's breathing raced, and he couldn't stop his panicked wheezing as the cart lurched toward whatever fate they'd soon encounter.

$\rightarrow$

Two sharp thuds hit the outside of the cart.

"From the trees! From the trees!" a Thoracian soldier screamed from outside the cart. "Fall in!"

Panicked, wordless muttering from prisoners picked up as the mass of limbs ground in response to the chaotic energy outside. Tazio shoved a leg off his chest amid the tangled pile. Darkness. Heat. Putrid, sweaty skin. Battle yells ripped through the air outside, and the men inside the cart cried and cursed and screamed. The suffocating darkness pressed in on Tazio. Sharp light cut the face of a man standing with his mouth shoved against the slit, groaning and wailing stupidly as he sucked air as if it would provide him freedom. Tazio thrashed and shoved to get untangled, adding to the growing panic. Ankles and shins squirmed out of the way as he bit, scratched, beat. On his feet, with just enough room, Tazio squirmed over the pile of men toward the man peering out one tiny slit.

22

"Move," said Tazio, and the man flinched like an animal at the sound of a human voice.

Tazio looked out as Ulrich stumbled up beside him and put a hand on his shoulder.

"What do you see?" Ulrich asked.

"Only the sky. The slit's cut upwards. Fucking bastards won't even give us a view."

He jammed his ear to the hole and heard a soldier scream and fall into the side of the cart, gurgling. Thoracian officers yelled out commands, but mostly the disordered screams of slain soldiers filled the air. A horse pounded by, and Tazio heard another body tear open at the end of a blade, accompanied by a wail that sent shivers through him. Swords pinged, and more waves of hooves thudded in and out, solemn battle yells accompanying them.

Tazio's hands began to sweat.

"The wall is hot, Ulrich."

"Course it is. 'Nough men in here to sink a ship."

Tazio put his eyes to the slit again and saw a small trail of black smoke drifting to the sky. His eyes widened.

"The wall is on fire," Tazio hissed to Ulrich.

"What?"

"Hey! What's going on out there?!" one man wailed in Tazio's ear, grabbing him nervously.

Tazio lashed out with a reactive elbow, catching the man in the jaw.

The man's limp head snapped back unnaturally, and Tazio recoiled at his base reaction, tripping as he stepped away.

The stench of smoke crept into the cart, and screams intensified as men realized a fire was consuming the cart. One man beating his head senselessly against the floor, already hopeless. Most piled atop each other, the already crammed cart now stacking into a diagonal pile that reached the low ceiling on the opposite side.

"We have to do something now!" Ulrich shouted, as he and Tazio fought in the pile.

"We're doomed!" one man screamed.

"Shut up! Shut up!" Tazio screamed back, noise and heat constricting his ability to think.

Men who couldn't make it the one or two enviable feet farther from the burning wall wailed as the inferno crept across the floor. A lone hero hurled himself at the burning wall in a desperate attempt to break it. His hair and clothes went up in flames as he dropped to the floor after a few desperate kicks. Soon the pile had stacked tight to the ceiling, Tazio and Ulrich in the middle of the pile, and then Tazio felt the cart's axles loosen as the cart tilted slightly off axis.

"The cart is on a hill. We can tilt it over!" Tazio shouted to Ulrich, close to asphyxiating. "We can tip it! We back into the fire and slam into the pile. Jump to the top of the pile!"

"Go!" Ulrich replied.

Tazio crawled over men who gladly traded their position to get further from the fire.

Flesh and smoke filled Tazio's lungs.

Sweat poured down his face.

Now near the small space that had cleared near the blazing wall, he grabbed the hair of two men who were writhing beside him, staring into the fire, doing anything they could to move an inch here or an inch there away from the fire.

Tazio pulled them out of their fits and peered into blistering eyes.

"The cart is on a hill! We can tilt it!" he shouted, praying they'd understand as his feet and back began to roast.

Each nodded back from a distant place of hope.

"Tell the man next to you! Tell him!"

After a few agonizing seconds, Tazio gave the order, "Now!"

He and Ulrich got up, pulling two others up with them. About five or six others stood, and they all took a searing step backwards, then slammed into the pile of bodies.

The cart creaked.

And for a heartbeat, the cart hesitated, then lurched over.

"It worked!" Tazio shouted.

Tazio's stomach dropped as the cart tipped, and the world began to spin—bodies tangling, wood splintering, fiery embers searing his skin as the cart battered downhill and men were turned to dolls bludgeoning each other with loose limbs. When they jolted to a stop, the impact punched Tazio's breath out. Pinned at the bottom of the gaggle, he couldn't draw breath. Fighting to do so, his face felt ready to explode.

Men kicked and groaned around him as they fought to free themselves from the tangle. One man pushed off Tazio, jamming a hand into his eye in the process. More feet stomped down on him, and with each progressive step, the pressure lessened on his chest until he saw what they were going for—a hole in the side of the cart—a doorway to freedom that had split open. Relief eased over Tazio as he drew his first unlabored breath.

The raging fire hissed with defeated smoke as men poured joyously out of the cart. The man who'd been beside him for the charge was pulling men out at the exit. Determination lined his gaunt, ashen face as he poked his head in and saw Tazio. Melted skin covered his arms, but the joy of freedom burned brighter. Tazio pushed himself up and took the man's hand, trembling as he crawled out of the broken hole into fresh air.

A lush forest stood in front of him. They'd rolled down a ravine and landed in a thin creek.

"Where's Ulrich?"

Tazio turned back to help Ulrich and any others who remained.

"They're done, lad," the man said, stopping Tazio.

A look of hopeless abandon spread across his face, and he scrambled away.

"Ulrich!" Tazio shouted into the cart.

A delirious groan drifted amid the hissing embers. Tazio went back into the pit of horrors. His eyes adjusted, and there before him, lay Ulrich—wood and iron splintered through his stomach.

"Ulrich," Tazio said, trying to hide his horror. "We're free, Ulrich."

He came close to him.

Ulrich's eyes, stark white against his melted, ashen skin, held little trace of the strength they normally did.

"We have to go," Tazio said, looking for a way to help, but not knowing how to lift him in his melted, punctured state without killing him.

"My children, Tazio—Svaen and Laena. If you ever find them, tell them of the depth of my love for them. How I fought to stay alive for them."

"Please, Ulrich, we're leaving now. You're coming now!" Tazio's voice cracked, his hands hovering over Ulrich's ruined body, unsure how to comfort him without hurting him more.

Yells ripped through the air outside, and Tazio whipped around to see if he'd soon have a sword in his back.

"I'm perishing, Tazio." Ulrich's eyes fluttered, the light in them fading like embers in the rain.

A cold knot gripped Tazio's gut. His chest ached, the tears burning behind his eyes, refusing to fall and show Ulrich he believed him.

But Ulrich was right—and it cut deeper than any blade.

"You can't die, Ulrich. You're the only friend I have. And your kids. You can't leave them."

The reasons sounded weak as Tazio said them.

"I can't come with you."

"No, stop." Tazio was frozen, staring down at his only friend left on the earth expiring before his eyes, like a shadow dancing away at dusk.

"This is the escape we dreamed of Tazio. Go!" Ulrich's eyes burned with agony.

"I won't go!" Tazio shouted, the injustice of it all enraging him.

More men screamed outside, his fellow prisoners probably put to the sword.

"Go, you fool!" Ulrich shoved Tazio in the chest.

Tazio stared in shock at him.

"I told you a time would come when you had to obey. This is it," Ulrich said.

Tazio's face hurt from fighting back tears.

"I'll never forget you, Ulrich."

"Enough with the sob stories. Go you damned idiot, and let me die in peace."

Tazio's chest stung from holding back tears, but Ulrich's cheer pulled out a painbent smile on Tazio's face.

"Fucking hell, Ulrich."

Ulrich pushed him one more time.

"Go, lad."

The cart was still in that moment—as Tazio wondered how he could leave the man who'd saved his life there to die. His mouth opened to protest again.

"Go!" Ulrich shouted, the veins in his throat bulging.

His heart tremored, sorrow charging through him as he climbed out of the cart, the only man in Novra he cared about already fading into a memory.

Tazio wiped away the hot tears that had rolled free in a stream down his cheek, cruel reality sobering him as he climbed free of the cart and saw what was unfolding. At a hundred paces, a group of warriors in midnight-colored cloaks closed in on his fellow fleeing prisoners. One drew a bow on horseback and put an arrow in the back of one, sending him onto a pile of rocks.

Ulrich's final words echoed in his mind, as the sound of hooves snapped him back to reality—three other warriors, seeing Tazio, galloped down the hill toward him.

Tazio slid off the wagon, knees buckling the moment his feet hit the ground. His vision swam with tears and smoke as he clawed at the dirt, looking for anything to defend himself with. His fingers brushed against a jagged stone, and he staggered to his feet, legs trembling as he readied to fight—even if it was a hopeless case.

The warriors rode up, thin one-handed blades drawn, circling him on their horses, ready to end the task. But their heads snapped uphill toward two others that were trotting down, and they paused at ten paces.

Wolf-fur adorned the collar of their cloaks, and beneath the tie at the neck they wore thin leather armor. Unusual in an age of iron and steel. They had fine features and strong stature, and their blue, silver, and white eyes with huge pupils were intoxicating, like you could fall into them if you stared too long. The three men looked him up and down.

Their glares made Tazio realize he was covered in burns and blisters. Blood and ashen bile dripped off his face. His feet stung as dirt worked its way into melted flesh.

The two men who now rode up were older. The eldest wore his hair long and thick to the chest—he was mid-aged, with a strong face and dignified features. He said something in a tongue to the others that Tazio had never heard. A language that sounded primordially familiar.

They could be Daemonae.

His parents had warned him of the Daemonae. They were the first people to cross the ice bridge more than a thousand years ago to settle Novra. They'd defended the northern passage until it melted, stopping all other nations from crossing until the last one hundred fifty years when the other powers had sailed the rugged Rabbian Ocean with new technologies. Known for raids, brutality and a shadowy distance from the rest of the nations, they were likely the last people anyone wanted to encounter.

"You're alone?" the oldest asked in the common tongue, his voice strong and calm like a wide river.

"Yes."

"Thoracian slave?"

"No."

"I see," the man said, smiling. Tazio fought his urge to like the magnetic man.

"I saw what you did to the others. I'd rather die than make idle talk."

"They ran."

"Something against running?"

"We don't respect those who bend to fear," he said, his horse whinnying as a chill evening wind bristled the woodlands.

"I'll walk then. Since you have an aversion to running."

"Witty fox. Wounded one, though," he said, taking a sheep's bladder from his saddle and throwing it to Tazio, who fumbled his stone as he caught it. By the time he grabbed his stone again, ready to fight, they were already walking away.

"Hey, I'd rather die! Fight me!" Tazio screamed, but only one offered a final departing glance of pity. "What are you looking at?"

They slid away before his eyes like a dream coming to a close. Now only the trees stared down at him.

"Or you! What are you looking at!" Tazio screamed at the trees. "I can't take this anymore!" He collapsed onto the ground and pounded the dirt, pain that had taken a seat for the time being coming center stage. "This life is too much to bear," he whispered into the soil.

He scraped himself from the cold dirt in hysteria and hobbled deeper into the forest, stumbling until the sun retired, and the moon and stars took its place. The breeze chilled his wounds, the rush of survival wearing off as he cracked the bladder open. Thirsty beyond imagination, he gulped the water desperately, the cool liquid soothing his hoarse throat. But quickly after the refreshment, his tongue burned and throat tightened. Panic wriggled in his chest as he gagged and spit out the rest of the liquid.

But it was too late. Quickly, his limbs grew heavy, and he crumbled over with aches gripping his belly.

"Bastards!"

His eyes began to grow heavy, like they were one step behind his thoughts. The grove of giant trees swayed in a liquid dance, stars twinkled and breathed in the sky like gems of peace from some distant realm sharing their subtle wisdom. His body began to grow warm and indistinct. Sounds deepened. Soon, as if from nowhere, heavy, warm tears rolled from out of his soul and down his cheeks. A slack, faint smile unfurled in acceptance of the release of pain. Breath like it were the distant hush of someone else's. Faces dancing in the flickering moon-washed branches, his mother and father speaking through leaves and shadows. Time melting away as his thoughts became one with the world. Or perhaps came *from* the world.

He closed his eyes and floated.

Off the ground.

Weightless and beyond.

Surrendered to a calm, blank abyss. Free at last.

CHAPTER 4

A CIRCULAR, thatched roof came to a point above as Tazio stirred awake. Thick, earthy aromas drifted around a simple, circular hut, escaping through the hole at its peak. Tazio sat up, and the burns on his back split in protest.

"*Fean!*" he yelped.

"*Iliya ech tuetasa,*" a woman said from behind him.

Panicked, Tazio moved to escape, but she gently pressed him back down. She was mature, with long, white hair well past her shoulders. Her pristine compassion melted Tazio's fear, making him glad for the first near-peaceful awakening he could remember.

She stepped back once he was calm and walked out the flap of the hut.

Furs, rugs, and blankets lined the floors, and incense sticks burned nearby. Linens saturated in an oily balm covered his feet. The mixture smelled like animal fat and herbs and made his feet tingly and numb.

The tent flap opened and the tall warrior who'd thrown him the sheep's bladder came through with the woman behind. He moved with dangerous grace, like a man could level anyone, but chose restraint.

"You slept well," the man said.

"If you could call that sleep."

"I wish I could sleep that well."

"Interesting place. I'm wondering why I'm here."

"A fair question. I thought it best to let you heal."

"I mean, *here*. Why am I alive? From what I recall, you left me for dead, but nevertheless, here I am."

"Most would say you should be thankful."

"Most aren't too bright."

"Well, I can put you down now if you'd like."

"I wouldn't want to cause you any more strain."

"You're no strain at all, I assure you."

"But why take me at all?"

"I told you we respect bravery."

"And the bladder?"

"A small taste frees the spirit from the body's grip."

"That's one way to put it."

"It's intense, yes, but was necessary in your state."

"Are there any others?"

"Other prisoners?"

"Yes."

"I'm afraid not."

Ulrich's white eyes, stark against his ashen face, flashed through Tazio's mind.

"Seems to be a theme recently," said Tazio. "How long have I been here?"

"Three nights."

The woman interjected, and the pair spoke in their native tongue, the language rhythmic and full of song.

As Aeon spoke, Tazio's mind buzzed with his father's warnings— whispers of Daemonae cruelty, tales of raids and dark rituals of incest and human sacrifice. The Danuiin hadn't been their victims before, but they'd also avoided the Aroinn forest where the Daemonae dwelled. Equally confounding was why the Thoracians decided to take a caravan near the lands of the Daemonae.

Fools, the lot of them.

Tazio never fully trusted his father's warnings, though. When they'd travel, Tazio would speak to locals, and many regarded the Daemonae with a kind of reverence. They lived off the Aroinn forest and were indomitable warriors. They were certainly condemned for living a freer life, and in that sense Tazio felt sympathetic to them, given the Danuiin shared the plight of prejudice.

"I'm Aeon," the man said, putting out his hand. "And Morvudd is the one who mended you."

"Tazio."

They shook, and as they did, Aeon held his other hand out to the side, open to the sky, and Tazio balked. The Danuiin were the only people he knew who used that greeting—the upturned palm a sign both hands were free of deceit.

"Do you greet everyone this way?" Tazio asked.

"Yes."

"My clan does the same."

"Then we share at least one thing in common."

"Don't speak of my people," said Tazio, the mention of them making his heart burn.

"Do you wonder if you were supposed to end up in that cart?"

"That my parents were killed, and I was burned alive so I could end up here?"

"That despite the paths of life being beyond our control, we find the path we need."

"Then I called forth the death of all those I love so I could find my path?"

Aeon's gaze lingered, something unreadable flickering behind his eyes. "When you've regained your strength, we'll discuss more."

"I think I'd rather know what you mean *now.*"

"I admire your fire, but don't take my kindness for openness to disrespect," said Aeon, standing. "As you recover, the village is yours to explore freely. You have my word that no one will harm you. *Bennaich.*"

"*Bennaich?*

"Blessings upon you. Our common greeting."

"Ah, I see. *Bennaich* it is."

Aeon smiled and pushed the flap open, his long, midnight cloak the last thing out as the wind breezed in. Just outside, he looked back, nodding one last time to Tazio, the look in his eyes carrying a weight Tazio couldn't quite figure out.

He pulled the blanket up to cut the chill, the raw ache in his back a reminder that he was still alive. If they'd just left him there, hate would have been simple. Pure. But now it tangled with something dark—Tazio wished Aeon had left him to rot in the forest.

At least then it would have been easier to hate him. To hate all of them.

→

Tazio was pleasantly surprised with how well his feet had healed over the last two weeks. Though being cooped up in the tent, he was beginning to crave some fresh air. The feeling of staying beyond his welcome had also become an unwelcome nag.

Tight spaces... had enough of them for one season.

Tazio sat up, and just then the flap of the tent cracked open and Aeon came through.

Goodbye, my time alone.

"*Bennaich*, Tazio."

"*Bennaich.*"

"Please, sit." Aeon indicated to a stool near the fire.

"Very well."

Tazio sat and Aeon kneeled beside him, taking his ankle into his hand and inspecting the burns on his feet. Tazio tensed, not used to such contact, and particularly taken aback by the rugged man acting so gently.

"I believe you're ready."

"For what?"

"For a walk."

→

Tazio tied the last loop on the light, padded boots Aeon gave him and stepped out of the hut behind Aeon. It was the first time he'd left the hut and the lush woods hit him fast. The scent of the dense dawn. The croak of some animal echoing from a faraway place. Daemonae walking about the large dwelling of huts, Tazio had spied through the flap before. The village was larger than he expected, probably a hundred or so dwellings in what looked like a spiral, his dwelling on the end of the last arm of it.

"By Novra, even if my feet weren't ready, I'm damn well ready for this walk," Tazio said, feeling alive at the taste of fresh air.

"The flesh shouldn't hold us back."

"Tell that to the other poor fools in the slave cart with me."

Aeon walked ahead toward the heart of the camp, cutting through the dwellings. Daemonae of all types looked at Tazio. They all shared the same still presence and penetrating depth Aeon and Morvudd did, like it was a type of soul. The entire camp seemed positively mirthful and peaceful—far different than what he'd heard from the outside about *'those savages.'*

Tazio nodded at a group of beaming children who chuckled seeing him walk gingerly on his burned feet as he hit a patch of sharp rocks.

"You'll get used to it," Aeon muttered.

"Oh, I'm used to the chuckles. Danuiin after all."

"The rocks."

"Ah, yes."

They walked through the center of the camp where a large communal fire pit burned steadily. Women fed their children around it, some sewing and mending leather. One burly man skinned an animal Tazio had never seen—some kind of mix between a buck and an antelope.

"Come, you'll meet my wife. It's not healthy to be totally alone."

Aeon walked Tazio toward a group of stately women commiserating.

"Tazio, this is Daere, my wife. *Maiise ciarad.*"

Daere's dark red hair fell around a porcelain face rich with authority. Her beauty was that of a queen's.

"*Righ làidir*," Daere said to Aeon before bringing her lips to his. As far as Tazio could tell, the tone sounded like they were sweet greetings. She fit comfortably between his arms, but was quite strong herself.

"*Bennaich*, Tazio. Welcome to Coille Solais," Daere said, turning to Tazio and bowing her head cordially.

"*Bennaich.* Should I call you Daere?" asked Tazio in the common tongue.

"It is my name." Despite it being a joke, Tazio still felt reverential toward her.

Hell, I can barely look at her, she's so damned beautiful.

34

"Thank you for taking me in here," Tazio said. "And Coille Solais?"

"The name of this village. It is our pleasure. We don't take any and all here."

"As I've been told," Tazio smiled, tightening a bit as she measured him.

Aeon may have spared me, but not all are convinced in a day.

"Aeon tells me you showed great bravery," Daere said. Even in the common tongue, she was elegant and forward.

"Well now I've made a reputation I'll have to uphold."

Daere smiled. "Not the worst reputation to uphold."

"Indeed, not."

"Come," Aeon said, "I want you to meet my daughter—wherever that free spirit is."

"It was an honor to meet you, Daere," Tazio said, giving a performer's bow.

Daere seemed to like it, offering a crease of the eyes. "And you, Tazio."

He and Aeon walked through the village into the thicker part of the woods. The Aroinn, this place was called. Most of the world knew little of the woods given that the Daemonae raided and killed virtually anyone idiotic enough to pass through.

The woods were seemingly alive, like they breathed around you. But also quiet and composed in steady evolution. Ahead, a golden buck paused in the middle of the path they walked on, and eyed them.

Aeon put his hand out and paused.

"A good omen, that is," Aeon said.

"Is it now?"

"Very much so."

"What does it mean?"

"When a buck calmly crosses your path, we see this as a message to trust our inner peace. To be gentle toward guiding our strength. Not to push, but to let life pull us."

"Hm."

"Animals are connected to us. Do not discount their presence. How they speak to us."

The buck sauntered off in no rush and Aeon continued down the path.

"Pardon me, Aeon, but I've been wondering since I arrived—can I ask something without fear of offending you?"

"Yes, Tazio."

"It's simply that, on the outside. Well, my people, we've traveled across all of Novra performing for all types. And the Daemonae are the only people our clan avoids and the only people nearly everyone fears. And fear might be an understatement."

The reality was that most people thought them savages. That just didn't feel like the right way to lead in.

"People fear what they do not know. We defend these lands with a strong sword because a plague has spread across all of Novra." A tension Tazio hadn't seen before rose in Aeon. "*Drochaid deigh*. The ice passage in the north. Over a thousand years ago, we crossed it from Aontir—to escape famine and sword in the old world. Daemonae defended the passage into Novra until the age changed, and the ice was not passable anymore—turned to water in the middle. But since Novra was invaded by the powers of Aontir, our people have been culled and cleared like vermin."

A somber silence was broken only by the crunching of their footsteps.

"Were there more Daemonae before?"

Aeon stopped walking.

He took a deep breath and looked up to the canopy to the sky. Sunlight filtered down around him, dotting the mulch.

"We call this time *Am Dorsa*. The dark time. Our clans used to roam from the Rabbian Ocean to the tundras west of Aroinn. To the plains and northern icelands where the nations you call Thorace and Bourgogne and Kalskog and Setia now settle. When my father's greatest rival united the southern Daemonae clans, I was forced to unite the northern clans and wage war against them. While we won, this war ended the lives of too many of our blood."

The wind rustled through the trees carrying sorrow on it.

"What happened to the southern clans?"

"The right to lead is determined by valor. Many you see here today chose to follow me and join the north. Those that refused were killed— such is our way." Despite it being their way, Aeon sounded stricken, like the memory was a raw wound that never quite healed.

"And then the other nations arrived," Tazio said, realizing the awful timing of having a civil war just before having to fend off an invasion.

"Yes. Deeper into the forest. Higher into the mountains we had to retreat. And the Aroinn is what we have left." Aeon turned to him, sadness swirling in his eyes. "*That* is why they call us savages. *That* is why we cut down any who wander here. Do you understand?"

"I understand, Aeon," Tazio said, unable to hold Aeon's gaze, too overwhelmed by the sorrow it provoked in him. This man he barely knew, but that gripped his soul, lorded over by existential threat.

There was a chasm between how the world spoke of these people and who they really were. And of course the world's fear of the Daemonae had only increased given they were secluded deep in the mists and dews of the crisp Aroinn forest.

They're not savages. They're surviving. Beaten into a corner of their own land.

The injustice disgusted him. The plight that infested Novra lands. The shelter the Daemonae sought from the whole dilemma. It all made sense. Of course they'd kill anyone who came close. Everyone was against them. And from the little Tazio had seen and felt, despite his hesitance, the Daemonae seemed to live in sacred harmony with each other and nature.

It was the other nations that were brutes—all engaged in an endless war between kings who wanted supreme rule and merchant city-states who demanded coin rule the world—two hands of the same tyrant, both hungry for dominance, both slaughtering opponents of their worldview.

"We'll find a way," said Aeon, putting a hand on Tazio's shoulder. "Come, Anya is nearby."

Aeon turned right off the path and Tazio heard the thwack of an arrow hitting bark as they walked through a few more trees.

Then Tazio saw her.

Anya.

By Novra.

She notched an arrow and pulled back a fine bow, shooting without hesitating to aim. She had stripped her animal pelts to shoot, and her figure was full and sensual. A warrior beauty. The chord twanged. The arrow drove deep into her target tree just a hair beside another arrow.

Tazio's heart stuttered at the grace of it all.

Feeling their presence, Anya turned to them, intense focus drawn in her eyes.

A gleaming wonder.

Eyes of ice-blue and white as the Daemonae's are.

Her gaze was defiant—a pristine valor. Her shining blonde hair tied into a braid that hung long down her back, and a small, coiled vine entwined in her hair like a crown of the lush green woods.

"Anya," Aeon said, walking to her.

"Father." Her voice was like silk frayed by hardship. She put her bow down and put her furs on.

"Will you kill the poor tree?" Aeon asked with a fatherly smile.

"I rotate when they start to cry."

"Surely they appreciate it."

"This is Tazio, the one I told you about."

Anya looked at Tazio.

"*Bennaich,*" said Tazio, doing his best not to choke on his words.

"*Bennaich,*" she returned. Her voice was smooth and assured, and her blessing certainly held a few pricks in it.

"Tazio has endured a rugged way."

Anya looked Tazio over once more, as if deciding whether Aeon spoke the truth about him. She was a hand shorter than Tazio, but her glare was mighty.

"Is there anything else, Father? Otherwise I'll be back to my training."

"Always more training. Tazio and I will leave you to peace."

No doubt she'll be a tough one to win over.

"You'll have to teach me how to shoot a bow like that," Tazio offered.

"Some things can't be taught," she said back.

"Come, Tazio."

Aeon led them away from Anya, who immediately began shooting arrows again. They went deeper into the ripe woods. Normally Tazio could find his way back to nearly anywhere he'd been, but at this point, he'd be wolf's bait if he tried getting back alone.

Eventually they stepped through the edge of the forest into a glade with a stream running through it. Bugs and birds flitted about the grasses, and the autumn sun just cut the chilled air, bringing warmth to Tazio's face.

Aeon walked over to a fallen tree and sat down.

"I come to this place to free my mind of burdens," Aeon said.

Tazio sat beside him. "A fine place it is."

"Are you afraid here?" Aeon asked.

"In this glade?"

"With our people."

"Not afraid, no. Though it almost feels like a dream each day I wake up. Like I'm supposed to be here, but I'm not sure how I ended up here."

"When I was about your age, my father sent me to find a wife among the other tribes. When I met Daere, I stayed with a tribe in the south for some time. Each day I lived with them, I grew more restless. They never fully embraced me. So I understand your restlessness. But I don't intend that same feeling to occur here for you."

"Thank you."

Though I'm not sure I should stay.

"What you survived. You don't have to speak of it." Aeon looked at him with rugged calmness. "But know that I have felt some pain like it. Not the same, but close enough."

Ulrich's charred face and the screams of his fellow prisoners rushed through Tazio's mind, and he looked blankly away from Aeon, trying to push the pain out.

"I've seen terrible things in my life," Aeon continued as they both stared parallel out into the glade. "I turn to the winds of *Etria* to carry them away."

The glade seemed to breathe before Tazio, like it was alive and speaking to his heart. His gut clenched. Memories he'd already tried to forget—the blood, the screams, Ulrich's eyes—all rushing into the chambers of his mind. He swallowed hard, but the pain fought to be free.

Embarrassed to be vulnerable in front of Aeon, Tazio turned to reply with something. Anything.

But he stopped before he could embarrass himself. Aeon stood still, eyes closed, powerful in his stillness. Energy seemed to push out from him as he took long, controlled breaths through his nose, letting them swell and fall through his chest.

It only seemed appropriate to follow the lead, despite the discomfort. As Tazio closed his eyes, the sounds of the glade intensified. The tension and pain he felt before intensified, but he allowed the images to well up.

The pounding hooves of the Thoracian cavalry. The spray of blood cast by their blades. The hopeless faces of his parents. The burning pyre he'd built for them carrying them away in ash. The guts bulging from Ulrich's stomach. With each breath, the serene spirit of the glade lifted the pain a touch, like a kiss of peace. When Tazio finally opened his eyes, Aeon was no longer there.

"Aeon?" Tazio said, standing from the log. "Aeon!"

Tazio scanned the perimeter. Aeon was nowhere to be seen. He ran to the center of the glade, where the small creek flowed through, finding nothing, worry intensifying that this was the moment they'd ambush him.

No, it's a test. Calm down.

He ran toward the camp, trees blurring, forest twisting. Every shadow a figure, every rustle a deathblow.

"Tazio," he heard Aeon cut in, as if right beside him.

Tazio's eyes snapped open and he fell off the log where he and Aeon had been sitting.

"I was just..." Tazio looked around, flummoxed.

"What did you see?"

"You were gone. I was running after you."

Aeon nodded as if he knew the significance.

"What does it mean?" Tazio asked.

"I won't abandon you, Tazio."

"I'm not afraid of that," Tazio said, standing up, realizing he was sweating. "I don't need your pity."

Aeon stood.

"Not pity. Trust."

Aeon took a step closer and gazed into Tazio's eyes like he read the codex of his soul.

"You are *Anam Teine*. Fire soul."

CHAPTER 5

TAZIO PUSHED out of his tent into the camp and out to the woods, resolved to abandon the place. The experience with Aeon earlier had shaken loose feelings he'd buried deep. Behind him, a woeful chorus drifted through the woods from the main campfire, haunting flutes, drums, and droning horns giving Tazio chills.

"Ah, *fean*, I have to see it at least once before I leave this place," he muttered.

He slipped through the woods to find a place to watch without being seen. But the trees and tents were too thick, so he scaled a tree and watched from the canopy.

The entire clan was gathered there, probably a thousand, dancing and singing around the massive fire. A chill wind brushed life into him, coaxing him toward them.

"What the hell am I doing? I was about to leave, and now I'm going to walk in there and dance like a fool?"

Near the fire, Anya moved like a siren, and Tazio's blood stirred.

Hard to win over. Also hard to leave.

Tired of being stuck between wanting to run and to join them, he let consideration finally elevate into decision. Already, as he slid down the tree and walked through rows of dwellings in the village, he felt relieved. Soon, firelight and song bounced into the sky about fifty paces away. But the sense he was an intruder in their life grew. He'd met Aeon,

Daere, Morvudd, and Anya. And he was only sure that Aeon and Morvudd were accepting of him. Others surely knew of his presence in the village—he'd been wandering around like a mute idiot now for a while.

"Join us?" a girl's voice said from behind.

Tazio whirled around. A girl about his age with a spritelike face stood smiling before him. Lush blonde hair fell long over her shoulders and her skin glowed translucent, bringing out the same ice-blue eyes streaked with white the Daemonae shared.

"I really shouldn't," Tazio said, glad it was dark enough to hide his face, which was red with embarrassment.

"Don't be scared. If we wanted to eat you, we'd have already boiled you over the fire," she joked with an impish grin.

"Is that right?"

"Come," she said, her hand floating out to his with subtle invitation.

After a moment's hesitation, he took it and she walked him toward the fire. As they rounded the final row of huts that ringed a lush glade glimmering in moonlight, the current song wound down. The weight of the silent forest hung in the air as translucent flicker moths flitted about. The Daemonae circled around a blazing fire, slowing from a dance.

Aeon's wife, Daere, whom Tazio had only met once, stepped out of a line of women. All their heads were bowed except hers. She held her hands up, tilted her head back, and began a song that poured across the night sky, its silver, sorrowful tones lifting Tazio's heart into a serene, weightless place. Others layered in low tremoring chants, and the hairs on Tazio's arms stood on end as the harmonies combined, the choral ascension calling like a home from another world. Then, like river ice breaking, the tribe moved into a slow dance like an echo of the Danuiin.

Tazio edged into the outer ring around the singers at the center. A few stepped aside to let him in. The sprite-like girl took his hand and a man beside him took the other, and their circle drifted into motion. The pace quickened as they raced by the inner circle that moved in the opposite direction. Joy seeped into his seriousness as faces and fire and trees and night blurred together, and the collective momentum pulled Tazio's arms outward as the tension holding them together stretched and stretched. The world blurred by, and whatever welled through him, he finally allowed to flow, the pain of isolation spilling out. Deep, freeing laughter poured out of him for the first time since his parents passed, and the hot fire warmed him, purifying even the burning memories of the slave transport. The spinning dance came to a rest, and people danced freely to drums and chanting. Men, women, and children dove across the fire. Dancers linked arms, and bounced and spun and flipped. A group of performers broke into dance and juggling. A trio posed, suspending each other with arm holds, flipping off each other's shoulders and backs, and Tazio's mind fought to determine whether it was merely chance that the vaulting was so similar to the Danuiin. Beguiling women and lithesome men embraced like classical art, alive before his eyes. Time bled by until Tazio was breathless and exhausted from his trance. He felt one with them, one like he was with his own people.

Tazio looked for Aeon, who was across the fire speaking with Anya. She stood firm, fire in her eyes as she spoke to Aeon about something tense. Tazio's heart stopped as Aeon caught him staring and motioned for him to come over. As he approached, Anya stood more rigid, if that was possible.

"*Bennaich,*" Tazio said.

"*Bennaich,*" Aeon replied.

"I've spoken with Anya. She will help welcome you into different circles and show you the ways of the Daemonae. If you so wish."

Tazio listened carefully, aware of obvious resistance to the idea from Anya, and not wanting to engender hostility by taking Aeon's side.

"I'll let you two speak. Enjoy the eve, Tazio," Aeon said, exiting the conversation and leaving a glaring hole.

"Don't worry about having to entertain me," said Tazio.

"Trust, I'm not."

"Well, anything is appreciated, but I'm all too familiar with being burdened by my father."

"I'm sorry for what happened to your clan."

"Don't be sorry, you didn't kill them."

Anya chuckled reluctantly.

"Truly, I don't mean to be a burden. In fact, I'm looking for some solace right now anyway. All that dancing stirred me up good and well."

"Enjoy your solace. I'll be on my way," Anya said, bowing.

Tazio watched her slide away, drunk on her visage, hoping he'd not botched the introduction. He chuckled at how quickly a beautiful woman could scatter memories of pain.

The clan hummed around the fire still, but after the wide influx of emotions the night brought, he followed his urge to be alone, letting the woods take him. He wandered through the lush trees and took to a quiet rock cropping at the top of a hill. He lay back and the night sky's starry eyes stared down on him, shimmering like a mirror of his catharsis, the heavens a sanctuary for his soul. Whenever he stared into the black expanse, he wondered if others were as stricken by the vast unknown above.

How were we placed here atop this earth, suspended in disbelief as to what holds us floating here?

Some feet crunched on the woodland floor nearby, interrupting Tazio's musings.

Surprisingly vexing to find some solace in the wild.

Tazio stood up.

"You know, I'd almost given up hope you'd ever join us at the fire," Aeon said.

"You don't seem the type to give up hope."

"Had to fight off a few ready to sell you to slavers."

"I can respect the lust for coin."

"*Anam Teine,* your dancing was lively, like one of our own."

"I know a jig or two."

"Sian certainly thought so."

Tazio laughed. "*She* brought me into the circle. Don't quarter me."

"Fortunately there is no law against love."

"Love might be a reach."

"You're moving well," said Aeon.

"Fully recovered, I'd say."

"Very good."

"I should be able to depart soon."

"Is that what you want?"

"You've opened your home too long."

"You're mistaken. We don't take outsiders. Either you're one of us or not."

Tazio's mind heard it, but his heart doubted it, despite Aeon not being the type to speak wastefully.

"I'm still not sure why you spared me. Or took me in."

Aeon looked toward a clearing in the canopy to the night sky, his profile lit by pale moonbeams.

He likes the sky as much as I do.

"Few stand against us in battle. When you did, I saw bravery. But we've killed many a brave man. It was your eyes," Aeon said softly. "Blue and white—like our own. Your people. The Danuiin. They're a clan of our people."

The words crashed against the shores of Tazio's mind, a sudden heat blooming in his chest—rage, confusion, grief—all tangled together in a mess. How could his parents have kept this from him? Why hide a truth that pulsed through his very veins?

"Why didn't you tell me earlier?" Tazio asked.

"Do you think you'd have believed me without first suspecting it yourself?"

"Who says I did?"

"You'd be a fool not to. We share so many practices. And the soul knows before the mind does."

"Why then? My people, they spoke evil of the Daemonae. Why didn't they call themselves Daemonae?"

"The Danuiin chose to leave us to live a roaming life. To perform. When Novra was invaded, they could not accept a path of violence. This caused a crack in our clan, but unless it's a challenge for power, we don't control the paths anyone takes. But they are Daemonae by blood. Their branch is Daemonae Raichiin."

Confusion sharpened to anger, like a splinter driven deeper.

No—they must have hidden it for a reason.

"I'm sorry if this comes as a weight for you," Aeon said.

Tazio looked out into the dark woods, overwhelmed, searching.

"You are welcome to leave. But you are also welcome to stay," Aeon said. "And know that I want you to stay."

"But them?" Tazio pointed toward the village.

"You will have to prove much, but with time they will see what I see." Tazio listened to Aeon's calm, broad voice as the forest swayed in the night.

"I don't want to prove anything to anyone."

"I understand."

He surmised the branches his life could take, knotted with tension as he tried to feel which was the right path.

"Why would you want me, Aeon? I'm a dead weight compared to your warriors."

"A raging fire burns inside you, *Anam Teine*. Right now, you're simply on a suffocated path."

The words stung. Tazio wanted to break down at the precise power of Aeon's observation.

"When I don't know which way to go," Aeon said, "I put each potential way above an open hand. And I ask myself which path feels like an open sky. Free. Alive. And which feels tight and restrictive. The one that stirs me to the expanse, I follow."

A throng of firebugs stirred in the trees, glimmering hope amid the doubt in Tazio's veins.

"Feel for the answer, *Anam Teine*. You will know."

Aeon seemed to sense his desire for solitude, and faded into the trees.

Stubborn resistance to the simplicity of Aeon's mystic approach itched at him. So instead, he thought about the different paths we could take, details of staying or going running through his mind, questions appearing here and there, broad visions of who he strove to be drifting in, fears and doubts nagging, until his mind was like tangled yarn.

"Okay, Aeon, I'll give your little soothsayer's trick a try."

He closed his eyes, eyes flickering as he drove his mind to focus on the questions—on his palms, on shutting up every distraction that shoved its way in. Soon, he was a tangled mess of confusion, both hands hot in the cool night air.

Breathe.

And he did. Until soon, he was calm, his chest drifting in serenity. One path did feel tight, suffocating. The other—light and open, like the breeze brushing his skin.

His heart pounded. Could it really be this simple? To trust in an answer that swam above his palm—an undeniable impulse. Fear clawed at him, but the pull was there, waiting to be followed. He bucked against the tension, afraid, incapable of reasoning to the conclusion he felt rising from the query. But somehow, knowing it had to be done—to test this tug of his heart and see if it could guide him. It was not the answer he expected, but somehow it was right.

Tazio opened his eyes, resolute. The forest swayed in celebration of his release.

Tazio turned to Aeon.

"Did you know the answer before I did?"

"Only you could find the answer."

"Thank you, Aeon."

"For what exactly?"

"For the gift of showing me the way to my heart."

CHAPTER 6

"Anya's training seems to be paying off in some measure," Aeon said from behind as Tazio hurled a lance into a stump.

"If you count lancing a log from thirty paces."

"Very much do. Are you ready?"

"Yes."

"Good. Come then. And try not to look like a doe ready for the slaughter."

They walked through the camp in silence as the morning sun cut through the late autumn air. Daemonae milled about their morning duties and Tazio nodded to those he'd met in recent weeks around the fire and otherwise. This time, all looked away—one mother even shooing her child as she looked at Tazio.

That doesn't ease the nerves.

Over the last month, Aeon had taught him the basics of their language, and Tazio added rudimentary Daemonae to the five tongues he already knew. Four he'd learned so he could perform across Novra in native dialects, and the common tongue which his people spoke. His parents insisted that cultural exposure was essential to being the best performer one could be—to understand a culture was to embody it. But they didn't need to push very hard on that point. Tazio would devour texts on different people from the books his parents had fed him. That combined with the vast oral, musical, and theatrical traditions of the

Danuiin sharpened his creative edge, and being with the Daemonae was certainly resparking his cultural curiosity.

As he learned Daemonae, the rhythmic words and phrases ran vibrantly through him, plucking at the strings of his soul. The language came from the heart, rather than the mind, and as his fluency increased, it was like his body got lighter, his mind freed by its buoyancy. When he and Aeon spoke at length, Tazio felt he was floating, even when he couldn't catch every word.

They reached the ceremonial chamber of the village, and Aeon stopped to mutter a phrase through the tent flap Tazio couldn't understand. A muffled voice from inside responded.

"Do not permit fear," Aeon said to him, opening the tent flap for Tazio to enter.

"Doubt it is, then."

Aeon smiled.

"Go on."

Then I'll be alone for this.

Tazio stepped inside. Thick smoke swirled in front of Divacius, who sat on an elaborate wooden stool with flora and fauna carved into its backrest, wolves' heads making up the posts. Divacius was the *Mistagea* for the Daemonae. Tazio had never spoken to the solitary mystic, and knew little about him other than that the *Mistagea* was considered the Daemonae's highest *draedic* practitioner.

Tazio sat down on the small stool opposite Divacius, anxious to properly signal respect.

"*Anam Teine,*" Divacius said, his voice throaty and coarse.

Divacius looked at him—or through him, felt more accurate. Tazio's innards felt tangled. Divacius had bony features pressed against taut skin, thick gray and black eyebrows standing over blue and dark gray eyes with lines of black streaking them, and his pupils nearly swallowed the rings of color. Tazio wondered why some Daemonae had more black and gray in their eyes, and thought it might have something to do with age or position, warriors and leaders tending to have more. But many of the older women had pure blue and white eyes, and it didn't add up.

"Two months have passed and you've sunk more deeply into our clan," Divacius said.

Tazio waited for him to continue, learning with time to not jump in or push forward while conversing in Daemonae. They communicated patiently, letting their thoughts rise naturally to a point.

"Aeon brought you here, pulling you out of the current of the world. An *old child* born new from fire—*Anam Teine,*" said Divacius, eyes unwavering. Then he closed his eyes, muttering as if conversing to some other voice. "But you're still half old-child. And you must choose, *Anam Teine*—at some point, every Daemonae must seek and find their way."

"What must I seek?" asked Tazio, kicking his voice, which was tight and dry, back to life.

"*Etria*. We listen, and *Etria* speaks," said Divacius, waving in the air with his hand. "When you find *Etria* and experience *daemonia*, you will then be a true Daemonae."

Divacius locked eyes with him, and Tazio grew heady and disoriented, his vision morphing like cream spilling in a stew, the world bleeding around Divacius. But he pushed through, not daring to break eye contact, which the Daemonae considered insulting.

"Will you seek?" Divacius finally asked.

"Yes, I'll seek."

"Yes, a new child, *Anam Teine*. Tomorrow, you will seek."

→

Atop Stùc Naom, the treacherous peak where all Daemonae sought *daemonia*, Tazio took a long breath through the nose to quiet his mind, pulling his awareness out of the body into a sphere around him like Divacius had told him. His mind wandered and fought the exercise like an ill-trained dog.

Exercise? Divacius wouldn't call it that.

This is impossible.

Shut up!

Thoughts bolted here and there, and he attempted to let them flicker by, but with every attempt at focus, they grew more obnoxious, like his mind was toying with him, like it knew he was trying to escape its clutch and was fighting back like a petulant bastard.

"Ahhh!" shouted Tazio off the cliff as his eyes snapped open.

The immense view of the Aroinn woods and the tundras west and north of them stretched out before him. Eagles coasted above the valleys, and the horizon churned with broiling storm clouds. It was beautiful, and witnessing something beautiful while angry added to his frustration—just another distraction from finding the entrance to the state of mind Divacius spoke of.

Tazio closed his eyes again. His stomach rumbled in protest from three days of fasting. Stillness seemed impossible as his body fought for attention, back aching, feet tingling, legs stinging. He forced himself quiet for another few moments.

Nothing but freezing storms, hunger, rage, tears, and haunting memories. But not stillness, no, anything but that. This is miserable. Pointless. Why am I even doing this?

"Shut up! Shut. Up!" Tazio screamed at the incessant thoughts, breaking from his sitting position and gnashing his head back and forth like a lunatic. "Fean, I'm losing it. Come on. Everyone before you has done this, and you think you're a special exception to the cosmic rule?"

He sat back down hard and gripped his crossed legs, again drawing deep breaths. A sense of calmness began to sink in, and he pulled calmer breaths, extending them, deepening them.

Thunder crashed from the clouds, tearing away his focus. His eyes snapped open again seeing lightning veining across the dark, churning sky.

"I sit here for two days in the cold listening for *Etria*? For *daemonia*? This is absurd! Fuck this!" he shouted at the sky as he stood up.

He fumbled for a rock nearby, throwing it as hard as he could off the precipice, nearly blowing his shoulder out and immediately regretting his ridiculous impulsiveness, shame following for failing to maintain his composure.

"What the hell am I going to do if I don't make this happen?"

Tazio realized he was talking to himself far more than usual, witnessing his mind cracking but unable to stop it, fear that he wouldn't pass the trial coiling up inside. Going back to the village without passing this would destroy him.

I could just never return—flee somewhere far. Surely they wouldn't miss me.

A vision of his mother and father peering into his eyes on the bridge came forth, arresting him. He slumped forward into the mud on his hands and knees.

The sounds of hooves clattering on the drawbridge, of steeds whinnying, bones splintering. A lifetime of love gone in an instant as the world spun and he fell to darkness. And failed.

Failed to save them. Failed to do anything to stop the massacre of my own people.

Thunder boomed again, and with it came a vision of driving a knife into Falkone's chest, bloody and brutal.

"When you get a vision of your future, latch onto it," Divacius had rasped to him the night before. *"Close your eyes, find the thread of energy, and feel it weave its way into your soul. Hold onto it. Let it pour its life into you."*

Traeda—threads of energy. The entrance.

He closed his eyes and the vision of killing Falkone came forth as threads of colorful energy in his mind's eye. Like it was playing out in another realm. He held the vision with focus. Rage and frustration boiled up, but this time he used it, using its hot energy to focus instead of fighting it. The clear vision changed into shapes and colors, more abstract until the vision coiled into a ball that shot from the sky of his vision into his forehead, snapping him off his hands and knees, sending him careening through the air onto his back, fierce as the energy surged through his veins. He fought to ride the ferocious charge without losing himself, his anxious mind racing to control the process, but refusing to grasp. But he let the tumbling waves thrash him as he leaned into the raw energy, screaming in the face of the storm from deep in his gut, joining the chaos of the gales. One with the world. One with *Etria*. The All. The ether pumping everywhere around everything. He could barely breathe, his mind stripped free of thoughts and worries, heart ripe with possibilities. He opened his eyes and heavy breaths shot out of him. The ground vibrated beneath him, brush and grass on fire, little licks of current passing between them. The world was pungent and lucid, the clouds roiling, lightning striking, thunder applauding his unification with allness. Bursting with strength, he spread his arms wide as he took in the endless view rolling out before him. All the pain. All the wrestling. It was worth the hell and loss and tears and doubts for this moment of transcendent power.

"This!" he shouted across the vast basin, feeling as if his voice boomed into the firmament, pushing past the horizon, filling all at once. "This is *daemonia!*

→

Tazio trudged deeper into the Aroinn forest following his descent from Stùc Naom, still burning from the previous night as rain rolled down his body. This section of forest was alive with *bithael*—luminescence that ran through the veins of plants and made the woods glow at night. Aeon told him of badgers, foxes, rats, and many other creatures who fed on the *bithael* in roots, ferns, and wildflowers. With only a hunting spear to protect himself, but alive with the taste of *draeda* pumping through him, Tazio was eager to return to the village and learn more about the experience from Divacius, so he moved quickly to return before daybreak.

The child moon, *Chalaiach*, rested above *Mathiach* and *Leanach*, the Mother and Father moons, signaling the deep of night was coming. In the Aroinn, in the period before dawn, when the *bithael* dimmed, the woods were completely dark aside from the light from celestial bodies. And this time, as the forest darkened, Tazio felt a warm wind bring a feeling of predation with it, every tree standing like a foe.

A branch cracked nearby and he twitched. Fear sprang up and grappled with the confidence he'd felt on the peak just hours ago.

He whipped around.

Shadows and faint outlines of roots and trees and boulders stood vaguely, light swallowed by the giant trees as he searched for threats. His chest tensed, hands gripping the spear until they stung. He screamed into the trees expecting to draw something out, but nothing moved.

But there is something.

He breathed and leaned into the feeling he'd felt on the peak, letting the *draeda* run through him. He drew it from the space around his body, and sprinted away toward camp.

A branch cracked—Tazio spun aside and turned. A huge beast loomed above him, a chilling roar accompanying its arrival. Currents of life force from the animal flared in Tazio's vision. Raging force surged through his body, and he thrust his spear toward the beast. The impact drove him ankle deep in the mud, the beast wailing on the end of the spear. Tazio's muscles burned from the power of *draeda* until the final breaths poured free of the animal. He dropped the corpse to the forest floor.

"Good, *Anam Teine*," Divacius said from behind.

Tazio spun around.

"Divacius?" Tazio fought to regain his breath, and was shocked to see Divacius stalking him.

"You did well."

"What the hell are you doing watching?"

"There must be a witness to this trial."

"Fucking hell," Tazio said, nauseous from the spike of death threat.

"All must go through this."

"That beast. What is it?"

"It is a *cath madad*. They live in the Aroinn. Creatures of mystery and power."

It had the features of a dark wolf and a panther in one, its open, yellow eyes set in the wide profile of a cat, but its features carved with the blocky brutality of a wolf.

"And you knew it would hunt me?" Tazio asked.

"Not certainly. Some are found by great wolves, or direcats, or boars. We believe they sense a new connection to *draeda*, and test this bond. It is part of everyone's journey."

"And if I died?"

"If you died, you would not have found *daemonia*."

"So you weed out the weak ones?"

"They weed themselves."

"Charming."

Tazio felt sickened by the prospect of people being mauled for failing. Most Daemonae were twelve when they did this, and he was nineteen.

Tazio rested his arm on a tree, his energy sinking into horrendous weakness as he came down. His vision began to close in and he felt Divacius lift him up.

"Don't worry. It's normal. *Draeda* cannot be used without consequence, especially when killing is involved. But with time and discipline you can learn to wield its power."

"I think I see now—why my parents left the Daemonae. Why they obscured my name. Hid the connection," said Tazio as delirium closed in, "This power. It's dark."

"This power will save the Daemonae. The world is closing in, crushing us out of existence. If we don't defend ourselves, there will be no more Daemonae."

The reasoning worked doubt into Tazio, and he had not the energy to spar with Divacius.

"You did well, Anam Teine. Come, let's return. You experienced much," said Divacius, supporting Tazio as they walked back.

This power was not something to be trifled with. Perhaps my people knew better to split from these people. What did they know that I don't?

But he remembered what reward peace had given them—life was not a child's game. Power ruled. And now he'd tasted it. Falkone wouldn't hesitate to use this power. Or any of the killers cutting their way across Novra.

Why should I?

"When you learn how to wield *draeda*, you will understand why we use it," said Divacius as they reached the edge of the village.

Coille Solais.

His new home.

Morning light streamed through the village, providing little warmth but much comfort from the darkness he'd just endured.

And he noticed something. Now, the faces of the Daemonae beamed back at him with acceptance and love, while before they measured him. They stood outside their tents bowing their heads as he and Divacius walked up the main thoroughfare. Before he was an outsider, but now he was one of them.

One in place.

One in blood.

One in Etria.

"Yes, Divacius. I will learn."

And I will destroy Thorace.

CHAPTER 7

Vibrant greens, yellows, blues, and reds; birches, ashes and willows; aspens, elms, cherries, and oaks—all streaked by as Tazio tore through the forest on horseback behind Anya. Wind whipped his hair and made his eyes water. It was the first real ride he'd had with Lasair, the black stallion Aeon had bestowed on him.

"Lasair means 'flame.' Rather suitable for you, I'd say," Aeon had joked when introducing Tazio to Lasair. "Though we named him before we even knew your soul would come here."

Lasair's red undertones shone as Aeon walked him into the sunlight. "He is yours now. And you are his."

The beast had stared into Tazio's eyes with a restless power—the same power Tazio so often felt. When Tazio stroked his neck, Lasair huffed, calmed, and looked at Tazio like he knew Tazio understood him.

Aeon had demanded Anya teach him the ways of the Daemonae, otherwise he'd be useless to the clan, and this hunt was the first major test. From the day Anya began training him, she did her best to remind him he was an outsider. After their first conversation, she spoke to him only in Daemonae for a few days, even though she knew the common tongue. And the fact that he respected and admired her, and found her gorgeous, made her distance that much more frustrating.

After his first experience on the holy peak of Stùc Naom, Tazio had briefly lived under the delusion he'd be able to use *draeda* easily and anytime. But Divacius emphasized that daily practice and mastery of the mind were requisite. Without the practice, the power waned, and use of it was unreliable. Using force of will and drawing on *draeda* was not free—it taxed greatly and was, therefore, used sparingly, most relying on it only in moments of dire demand, or to practice their tolerance for how it left the user vulnerable and demanded recuperation.

Debates had flared over thousands of years to uncover why certain acts left practitioners drained, and the general consensus was that acts of murder, especially against humans, brought the worst effects. But in spite of that, the Daemonae relied on *draeda* in battle as it was a huge help in the face of lower numbers. That in combination with their lethal silence, knowledge of the Aroinn, their absolute unity and trust, and their intelligence made them formidable in most cases.

Ahead, Anya glanced back, seeing Tazio struggling to keep pace with Kade, Dyvyr, and Bruic—three young warriors—as they followed her, increasing speed.

"Yah, Lasair! Yah!" Tazio whooped, focusing on not losing his own head to stray limbs as Anya urged forward her powerful brown and white mare, Iteal.

A branch lashed Tazio's face and he let out a yelp, then a chuckle.

"All well back there?" Dyvyr called back, far too cheerful.

"Golden!" Tazio shouted back.

Breathe.

Tazio returned his thought to the place he'd found before they started the hunt. They called it *àite lùtha*—the familiar place—where Daemonae went mentally to anchor a tangible feeling in *Etria*. An anchor in the ether they could return to in stressful circumstances. It was also where they felt and saw their energy body, or *analuth*.

Anya had been teaching him about the *analuth* and other concepts to deepen his understanding. Seeing in *Etria* was like seeing another world with the mind's eye, most intensely with the eyes closed. But once that connection had been made, a practitioner could see hints of threads and energy in the real world, like a shadow of color humming through the physical eye.

The *analuth* was the part of the self that existed in the beyond, in *Etria*. For every physical body, there was an energy body, the *analuth*.

When in the conscious state of *daemonia,* one could see and feel their *analuth,* and the *analuthae* of any living being nearby.

Draeda, the fundamental energy of *Etria,* flowed through all things, all connected in vibrant color and beauty by threads—*traeda.* A body, while appearing like a form, had distinct energy threads making it up, like yarn. Threads would spill off powerful energetic beings like rippling flames. And *draeda* could be used with a power called force of will, or *feantoiil.* That's what Anya was going to use shortly, and what he was here to learn as a part of his training.

Anya blew a bone whistle.

"She found the prize!" Kade shouted with goofy glee as he galloped beside Tazio. Kade was a good lad. One of the only who'd warmed to Tazio from the start. The others were still mostly cold.

"And I'll be the first to have it!" Tazio shouted as he accelerated past Kade.

Tazio cut toward Anya, Dyvyr and Bruic, closing ground, pushing Lasair, feeling the connection Anya told him existed between all living things in *Etria.* He remembered learning to ride with Anya as he surged up next to Lonn, a rambunctious, fiery one who clearly had an eye for Anya.

What available man in the village with a pulse didn't?

The Daemonae learned to ride bareback as children, developing a deep connection with their horses. "Be careful," Anya had told Tazio as he climbed onto Lasair the first day, "he's still half-wild and only knows how to walk or gallop." Then, she slapped Lasair's hind hard, Tazio halfway on, a question hanging on his lips as it tore off, laughter spilling from Anya as the beast rocked him at full gallop. With nothing but the mane to hold, Tazio lasted ten strides before careening off to Anya's pleasure.

Lasair cut to the right hard and bounded over a fallen tree branch. Ahead, a pack of fifteen or so giant boars pounded the dirt. Tazio pulled near Anya now. As she chased the boars, a look of silent confidence and joy flowed over her face, the picture of sheer focus and calm sending chills down Tazio's arms. Her pupils were huge and the blues and whites and grays swirled and mixed as she went deeper into channeling *draeda.* Life was like an elevated elixir running through Anya, and the freedom in the way she rode, hunted, and flowed with the world stirred wonder in Tazio.

Tazio gripped Lasair's mane tighter as Anya pushed straight up the middle in pursuit of the lead boar, a freak beast. Dyvyr followed her too, then turned with iron in his gaze. He was the best archer in the clan, and his gangly agility made him look weightless when he rode, absorbing every stride like he was floating above the horse. Kade cut to the right, his loose and chaotic style making Tazio smile, letting every bump take him where it would.

Boars snorted and squealed, thrusting themselves at their horses as Anya toyed with the lead demon. The huge *torc mòr,* a boar near as tall as a horse, had a gruesome ridge of a back, its bone structure jutting and wide.

Anya let out a low, forceful song. Not like the ones at the fires. One from the bones, a warning to the animal of its coming destiny.

She raised her spear like an ill omen, and with terrifying speed, she hurled it.

The lead boar crumpled and squealed as the spear lodged deep into its side. Its tusks dug into the ground and its body twisted into a heap.

Kade hurled a spear too, downing another boar.

The precision of the kills snapped Tazio's focus into place.

He raised his spear and channeled *draeda,* his arm feeling huge with power. The boar in front of him cut to the left just as he went to throw, and he nearly fell from the miscue.

Lasair kept pounding forward, tracking the boar fearlessly, and Tazio drew back again, searching for the moment between blurring trees. His vision narrowed and he hurled his spear with shocking speed. It lanced the boar through the shoulder blades—an incredible feat considering the thickness of those bones, but nevertheless a miss off the kill spot. Humiliation burned in his cheeks as the boar locked up, crumbling to the floor, its squeals an agonizing contrast to the clean kills of the others.

"End him now!" Anya yelled as she galloped over, drawing a long dagger and throwing it to Tazio.

"Go on!" Dyvyr demanded.

The boar squirmed and thrashed, and Tazio moved quickly around it under their glare. He jumped on its back, clenching its coarse fur and wrestling to slice the blade roughly across the thick pad of its neck. Hot blood spilled over his arms. With it, the shame and the drain of the *draeda* poured out too, turning his strength to emptiness as the ethereal energy left him.

Anya and Dyvyr loured at him.

"Forgive me. I don't have the aim."

"Don't apologize to me," Anya said, holding her hand out for the dagger. "Apologize to *torc mòr*."

Tazio tossed the dagger to her as the disappointment from her eyes cut deep. As she rode away, Tazio felt alone. A man in the valley of the endless trials standing over him.

"Have you never missed a throw?" Tazio shouted as she rode away. "You've been hunting these lands since you were a girl!"

Anya stopped her horse.

Ah, fean, you damned idiot.

Anya turned over her shoulder and walked her horse slowly back to Tazio.

"You're right about one thing. They're *my* lands. *Always* my lands." Anya spurred her horse and galloped away.

Rage boiled inside Tazio, but he didn't dare explode in front of them, pride checking him.

"It's okay, lad," Kade said, riding up after the others left. "She holds us all to a high standard. Just don't mess up again." He let out a chipper laugh.

"Encouraging."

Kade rode back to the others about fifty feet away, where Anya was putting her hand to the forehead of the boar she'd killed. She muttered a prayer of thanks, her face serene, alabaster skin rich.

Tazio calmed himself and put his hand to his *torc mòr*. He was supposed to feel a connection and mutter a blessing, but his rage interfered. He could feel it cooking him hot, making the *draeda* rise again inside him.

They don't know the horrors I've endured. They think I'm just a soft street kid. A broken branch of their tribe.

"Tazio," said Anya, who had ridden up.

"What." Tazio said, realizing the world had been dark and closing in as he went deep into thought.

Her thin eyebrows furrowed, as if reading him.

"What is it?" Tazio asked again, seeing she looked concerned—or even afraid.

"The others will return the kills to Coille Solais and stay behind. We ride alone now."

"To where?"

"You'll know in time."

→

Icy wind bit at Tazio's face, freezing his breath into brittle clouds as Anya led them into rock croppings at the foot of the Mora Mountains —a behemoth range that rose until they scraped the skies in the far north. Few who entered Mora ever returned, either swallowed by their peaks or gutted by Kalskog icemen looking to convert foolish men into vital supplies. Those that did were *changed*. Tazio gripped his reins tighter remembering a man in Auria who thrashed in the streets, blabbering about visions of burning worlds and storms of lightning.

Anya walked their horses into a cutout and dismounted.

"We go on foot from here. Stay quiet and follow," Anya said.

As if she hasn't already bound me in a pact of silence.

In the five day journey since they hunted the boar, Anya hardly looked at him. But when she did spare a glance, the cold air seemed to warm instantly. The whites and grays of her blue eyes cut through Tazio, her seriousness a rich tone that complemented her beauty. A chord seemed to stretch between them, stilling the tundra, stealing their words as they'd stutter like fools until Anya would break away and harden again.

Tazio sensed it was because he represented what she loathed—an outsider. And here he was, learning of their ways. It wasn't fair, considering he was actually Daemonae. But he understood that feelings are often more powerful than logic. So deep in Tazio's heart, he nurtured the dream that she'd shed her fear and warmed to him.

Maybe the draeda is getting to my good senses. But who isn't a little off kilter?

The night before, Tazio caught her watching him drift to sleep.

Or so she thought.

61

The next day, while skinning a rabbit, he let her watch, sensing she was lingering on him, feeling she was trying to figure him out. And when he did catch her, and time had stretched to its limit, he met her gaze. And though she'd turned quickly, a small break in her composure, nothing brought him greater joy than to see her curious. Her resistance only made him want her more. He had to break through to her—since the first night he'd seen her, she'd gripped him. Never had he met a girl so confident, yet so graceful. So cunning and so deep. Someone who demanded more of him just by her mere existence. And of course, the fact that she was Aeon's daughter made him that much more unstable around her, closing up, wishing he could show her who he really was, but failing time and time again to build a bridge to her.

The most satisfying chinks in Anya's iron edge of a will came when she'd give a nod of approval or go silent when Tazio would outperform the expectations of her training. Over the days of riding, bowhunting, fishing or tracking, Tazio reckoned he had to have earned some respect.

Joking with her sometimes pulled a laugh, but he'd only encounter another wall the next moment. With her friends she was cheerful, humorous, the center of attention, and he wished she'd just be to him as she was to others.

Let's keep the game fair, why don't we?

Young Daemonae men would posture, flirt, and gift rare pelts, flowers, or the occasional *vortae* mushroom to her—its three intertwined columns twisting into a splayed glory.

Still haven't figured out where those grew, but she certainly seems excited by them.

And Anya would charm them back. But she never committed to any of them. Only a smile or touch of their arm before drifting away like a wild fox to solitude. Maybe she hadn't chosen a mate because she longed for a greater role in the clan. She was made to lead and she certainly carried herself that way—not boastfully, but with assurance. Anyone had the right to be a warrior for the Daemonae, and she was revered as one. Few women actually embraced the path as the standard was strict. Physical capabilities were rigorously examined, and not because the men believed women were inferior, but because of the obsession with utter reliability of every warrior in battle—everyone supported one another, and even men who couldn't pass the mental, spiritual, and physical tests were forbidden from combat.

Nevertheless, she was still alone. The path to her was open, albeit full of jagged obstacles. But that made the pursuit invigorating.

Tazio's foot slid on a slick patch of ice.

"Damn," he muttered, heart spiking as he steadied himself.

The path ahead grew even more rugged. Ahead, Anya reached a jagged wall that loomed over Tazio, daring him to falter again. Anya gave a quick look back before ascending.

Well, at least she's checking I'm not dead.

"Aeon's probably the only one keeping me alive," Tazio muttered under his breath.

By the time Tazio was twenty feet off the surface in pursuit of Anya, he was happy the rock was sharp and sticking out in flat sheets, the grips proving reasonable enough to find. Anya made her way quickly toward a small crevice that sank into the wall about twenty feet up.

Add climbing to the list of things she's used to put me in my place.

But while Anya was cold, it was hard to deny she had a gift for teaching the Daemonae's practices. Bearing her stifling was something Tazio could live with in order to learn the secrets of the Daemonae. He loved the way she stretched him to his limits, pulling potential out of him he didn't know was there. His indefatigable attitude seemed to push her harder too.

She had to enjoy at least that.

A sheet of rock snapped beneath his foot, cutting his thoughts short. The foot that broke the rock slammed into the wall and his knee jammed, sending him backwards off the face into a tumble. His shoulder hit the wall, sending the world into a spin as he let out a scream, bouncing hard off the rocks until he slammed into the ground groaning.

"Are you dead down there?" Anya shouted from above after a few moments.

Her voice bounced down the rocky outcroppings into the unending tundra.

Tazio tested his limbs. His back hurt like hell and ribs throbbed. Breathing was difficult, but nothing felt fatal.

"Much to your disappointment, I'm still alive," Tazio shot back with a crooked grin.

"We're supposed to be climbing up!"

"Oh, is that right?"

"Yes, I thought it might be obvious, but I'm having doubts!"

Tazio chuckled and his ribs protested. Spurred on by her flippant jabs, he got up and started up the face again, this time moving methodically and without stupid, romantic dreams.

"I was about to start a fire you were taking so long," Anya said as he crawled over the edge.

"Would have been a nice touch. I didn't know you were so caring."

"Your face is bleeding."

"Not sure how that could have happened," Tazio wiped blood from his face.

Anya laughed, her bright almond-shaped eyes creasing and sending warmth through him.

"Oh, you can laugh? Incredible," Tazio said.

"Don't get accustomed to it."

Tazio smiled to himself as Anya reached into her pack to pull out a thick rope made of thistle fiber.

"This goes around your waist," she said, looping it around him. In the process, she pressed against him in the tight confines of the ledge.

She pulled the rope around, made a strong knot, and tied the trailing end of the rope around a reasonable looking rock, securing herself on the line too. As she finished tying the rope, her gaze lingered on Tazio. A flicker of curiosity softened her usual steel. Heat crept up Tazio's neck, and he clenched his jaw, desperate to fight down the blush spreading across his cheeks.

Fucking hell.

He looked away to the horizon, and the fifty-foot fall reminded him what they were actually here to do as the silence lingered.

"From here, I'll climb first and establish a hold above," Anya said.

"Don't fall, I've already tried it. It's not nearly as fun as I thought it would be."

"Is that right?" she said, starting up the wall like it was walking in a field.

About twenty paces above, she crawled over the next ridge and disappeared, then peeked back to wave him up.

Gusts of wind lashed and pulled Tazio off the wall. Holds became thinner and his hands lost all feeling from the frigid wind. At the top Anya put a hand out for him, pulling him up onto a long, thin ridge that was the peak of this particular range.

It spilled over into a wide, high valley that stretched east and west off the backside. At the northern edge of it, the mountains rose again, the pattern repeating as far as he could see, each valley and peak stepping higher and higher like stairs until clouds veiled the jagged steps hundreds of miles away.

Anya stepped gingerly to the east along the top of the ridge, which was fifteen paces or so wide. As they crossed a small crevice and rounded a large boulder, Anya ducked back and put her hand against Tazio's chest, stopping him.

"Be calm. Look around the edge," she said, pointing around the rock's edge.

Tazio edged up and looked around. About fifty paces away, a massive black eagle about twenty feet tall sat perched on a boulder, taking in the tundra. It cocked its head toward Tazio and his knees shook as he pulled back behind cover.

"Fean, what is that thing?"

"An *iolair mhór*."

"Great eagle?"

"Your Daemonae really has gotten better, hasn't it?"

"Was that a compliment?"

"Oh, shut up."

"I'll never forget it."

"We're here for this task."

"For the eagle?"

"Yes."

"Would be absurd to be here for any other reason, wouldn't it?"

"Be serious. As we walk toward it, be calm and feel the presence of the *iolair mhór* in your *analuth*," Anya whispered.

Tazio nodded.

"Close your eyes and begin your connection to *Etria*. See your *analuth*," Anya instructed.

Tazio closed his eyes and felt *daemonia* come across him after a minute or so. His energy body glowed.

"I'm ready," said Tazio.

Anya nudged him forward around the boulder first. Immediately he saw and felt the *iolair's* threads—strong and palpable as they danced off it, even in his regular vision.

Slowly they crept forward. With each step, the energy pumping off the eagle pushed waves through Tazio. His whole being spiked. The *iolair* could rip them to pieces in an instant.

I have to trust Anya.

He slowed his breath as they approached a rock about twenty paces away from the bird, their last vestige of a shelter. Anya came close and whispered.

"When you're ready, meet its gaze. When you feel the connection between you and the *iolair*, cast out fear and separateness in your heart. Become one with its *analuth*. Not it there and you here, but one together. This bond is called *anamea*, the bridge between man and animal. Empathy will bind your threads as one, but if it senses doubt or separation, it will not bond with you."

"I'm bonding with it? What the fean does that mean?"

"Quiet. All you must do is subdue that part of you which reasons against separateness. Find the threads the *iolair* has coming off it. Feel what it is and allow it to feel you. As you sink into the connection, you will feel its energy merge with you."

"What's the worst that happens?" Tazio muttered to himself.

"It kills you for invading its presence," Anya said.

"Thank you for that answer. That was more of a musing."

"I'd suggest you close your eyes and find the threads from its energy body, not muse." Anya said.

The threads off the eagle swirled around the mountain top off its energy body, the whole scene in his mind's eye swirling like an abstract form of liquid light and color.

Control the eagle, he heard a voice say.

Subdue separateness, said a second thought coming on the tail of the other.

"Did you hear that?" he asked Anya.

"What? Focus."

Tazio allowed his own *traeda* to stretch out and bond to the eagle. When they touched the bird's threads, a massive vibrancy pumped through him. Raw, primordial force. He nearly forgot to breathe until Anya spoke.

"I can sense you're bound. When you're calm, open your eyes and look at the *iolair*. Do not divert your gaze," said Anya.

Tazio eased his eyes open and looked at the eagle.

"Now, walk toward it. And not through words, but through intention, communicate your peace," Anya continued.

Tazio pushed tides of comfort and peace to the *iolair* as he walked toward it. It didn't move. Anya crouch-walked behind him.

"When you feel it's right, place your hand on her, and feel whatever comes," Anya said when they were about six feet away.

He inched closer to the eagle, fighting to relax the tightness screaming for him to protect himself and break away from the massive creature. At a foot away, the eagle focused on him, its head cocking as it took him in. Now he fully understood how helpless he was. Its talon was bigger than his torso. Its beak could carry a *torc mòr* with ease.

Whatever this bond Anya was pushing him toward was the only thing left to trust in.

He pushed out fear, respecting it, allowing himself to sense what the *iolair* felt. It shifted as he got closer, its massive talons cracking through stone and mud as it craned its head toward Tazio.

Tazio carefully inched closer, every muscle tight as he reached forward to close the final few inches. As his fingers touched the smooth, black feathers of the *iolair's* belly, each the size of his arm, wild energy tightened into a focused core. A current surged between them—raw, primal, terrifyingly intimate—as if their souls spoke in a language that defied words. Feelings, intuitions, expanses and valleys, shapes and sounds, scents and movements poured through Tazio like he was merging with the senses of the *iolair*. Then, energy expanded from Tazio's heart, exploding to infinity in a wave of color. Tazio's head snapped back, breath ragged, core chattering as Anya braced him from behind.

"Tazio, are you with me?" Anya whispered, her closeness comforting.

"Yes."

"You are fully bonded now. Until the bond is broken by you or her," said Anya, "You can look away from her if you want."

Anya's voice sounded foreign and muted as if spoken through water. He stood on his own, in awe of the lucidity of the world around him—at Anya, who looked as sharp as crystal and glistening with color.

"I look different to you now, yes?" she asked.

"Yes," said Tazio, flummoxed.

"Your vision is blended and enhanced by your bond."

"I feel alive... this power, it's..."

"I know."

Tazio looked across the tundra. Every object was sharper than a dagger's edge, even at staggering distances.

"If you want, you can now act in unison with *iolair*," said Anya.

"I'm not sure I understand."

"Now that you are bonded, your thoughts, your feelings—they're intertwined."

"I can feel that."

"I'm sure you can. Your eyes are as big as the sky," Anya said, chuckling. "This also means it will act on your behalf—as long as you are in tune with it."

The *iolair* stretched its wings over them, spanning some fifty feet across. Tazio took a step back as fear entered his heart. The sharpness of his vision flickered.

"Don't let fear and doubt enter your mind, or you'll lose the bond," Anya said urgently.

Tazio drew deep breaths and let the fear drift into the wind as the *iolair* closed its wings and looked down at him.

He felt an urge to reach out with both hands to the eagle.

It presented no resistance as he reached up to stroke its belly. Warmth radiated from underneath its outer coat feathers. This time he felt calm and it cawed lightly, which seemed a funny reaction for such a raucous creature.

An impulse to fly it came through him, and he moved closer to mount it.

"Are you mad?" Anya hissed as he crawled onto the eagle, using its massive feathers as holds.

Sensing Tazio's hesitation after hearing Anya's question, the eagle reeled on him, lifting its giant wing, screeching, and launching into flight.

Tazio careened off the bird onto the sharp peak, tumbling off the steep precipice, gripping for whatever he could as he fell. His palms tore against outcroppings until the rope at his waist yanked to a hard stop. Above he heard Anya grunt, and he could feel her struggling at the end of the rope.

"Tazio!" she shouted as he dangled from the rocks, groaning, his freezing hands barely holding him from a fall that would surely test their resolve.

"I can pull you up now!" she shouted and began pulling him up.

Using her help, he moved up rock-by-rock.

Finally halfway composed on the cliff-face, he saw the *iolair* strafing through the sky.

It leered at him with a freedom of will that brought out a grim laugh of respect.

"You're an impudent one. I get it," muttered Tazio.

He climbed the rest of the way and came over the edge.

"Are you insane?!" Anya shouted.

"Aren't we all?"

"No! You tried flying the beast!"

"Was it not you that urged me to have it act on my behalf?"

"Maybe hunt a fox or doe! But fly? You could have killed us."

"I didn't know there were specific rules to this!"

"You should know!"

"You told me to follow my instincts!"

"Instincts, yes! Not idiocy!"

"I was just trying to focus so I didn't lose my head. Have you seen the size of that bird?"

"Exactly. You nearly killed us!"

"If you expect me to take vague instructions and turn it into clear action, you're the idiot. I've never experienced *daemonia*, or *anamea*, or any of this!"

Anya looked away.

The wind blew brisker.

"I didn't mean to get so carried away," Tazio said, feeling compromise was necessary. "All this is new to me. It's huge. Tremendous even.

Like I've discovered a new life that was always inside. But an idiot must be given a few mistakes, or he'd be a sage instead."

Anya didn't take.

Tazio looked away, feeling raw.

They stared out to the horizon where the great eagle coasted above the tundra.

"Carried away is right," said Anya.

Tazio looked over. The slightest smile shimmered beneath her focused brow—the kind of gesture loaded with subtle jest. Then she looked over.

They broke into laughter, their chuckles soaring off the cliffs as the stress of the moment let out and all the tension of the day and week and weeks let free like a gust.

"You surprise me," Anya said as they came down.

"No one's tried to fly the damned bird?"

"Only one other fumbling idiot. You may know him."

"Let me guess. Kade."

"Hah! Kade wishes he had the balls of a *torc mòr* to try it. Or maybe the brains."

"I'll take that as a compliment."

"I slipped there, didn't I?"

"Really losing your edge, you are. I may have to tell your father."

"It was my father."

"Who tried flying it?"

"Yes."

"Not bad company. Did he fly it?"

"Of course not!" Anya gave him a gentle shove. "He failed too. And warned others not to try it. He fell down those cliffs like you and almost died from it. Since then, we've used ropes."

"Good man."

"Foolish man."

"We're going to have a great time on this topic, him and I."

"Oh, *Etria*. You know, I thought you'd lose the connection and the *iolair* would reject you."

"Well, I guess I'm not so untalented after all."

"I'm still holding my final judgment on that."

"That doesn't surprise me."

They were staring at one another now. The conversation had run its course, and Tazio's heart lurched, his mind racing between alternatives.

"We should go," said Anya.

"You know," Tazio jumped in, "you surprise me too."

"Why is that?"

"Because I know there's more behind that facade you maintain."

The cliffs seemed to swallow Tazio's words in their jagged cracks.

Too much, too quick, you fool.

Tazio held his lip as Anya searched him, taken aback. Churning clouds snaked around the peaks behind her, the rugged backdrop a wild chorus for his heart.

Anya looked back out to the horizon and took a breath.

Tazio wanted the moment to linger forever, feeling he'd found a way to her in the slightest, but fearing it would slip away.

"You know, despite almost dying, I'd say this experience was beneficial, even pleasurable in a self-flagellating kind of way," said Tazio, easing in and attempting to change courses.

"Yes, *anamea* is a raw beauty. And unlike *feantoiil*, it will not drain you," she said, her mood back to the serious depth she often rested in. "In *anamea,* man and animal are both connected to *Etria* independently, so both draw power and share it in the bond. As we master the connection, animals learn to trust us. But *anamea* will hamper your ability to use *feantoiil.*"

"Are we controlling them?"

"No, guiding, asking. If they sense dark intent, despotic control, hate—they will not follow. And they may turn on you. The beauty of *anamea* is that we learn by letting them instruct us as well. Great lessons rest inside their souls."

"Hm."

The beauty of it. Of her. Of all of it. The whole thing made Tazio quiet and serious.

"*Anamea* is not about power. In fact, all of this—it's a way of life."

Anya's cheeks were rosy from the cold, her fighting spirit softened, and for the first time, she shared that warmth with him.

"I understand," Tazio said, sensing the reverent feelings moving her.

"Somehow I believe you, *Anam Teine.*"

"I may not be Daemonae Aroinn. But I am Daemonae Raichiin."

The glimmer in her eye acknowledged his bridge toward unity.

"Thank you, Anya."

"For what?"

"For all of this," he said, nodding to the horizon. "I don't know how my clan ran from this life, but it's like rediscovering the truth of who I am after being held prisoner from it." As he finished uttering it, Tazio couldn't help but grow dark at how his parents, his whole clan, had buried these truths in a giant scheme.

"We should get down before night falls." Anya placed her hand on his arm.

The touch.

The invitation in her eyes sent waves through him.

Back along the precarious ridge they walked, this time close enough that Tazio could feel the heat off her.

But that couldn't stop his mind from wandering.

From fighting the thought that he was just one more fool descending into hopeless love with Anya. The brilliant flower of the Aroinn.

But isn't life more full when hopelessly in love, than without hope at all?

CHAPTER 8

THEY'D RIDDEN HALF a day since descending from the *iolair's* nest. Pines grew thicker. The lush woodlands were two days away.

Anya turned around in her saddle. "I want to show you something."

"Tell me it's another giant eagle," Tazio joked.

"You child."

"Is that a smile I see on your face?"

"It could be."

She's beginning to like me.

Anya kicked her horse into a trot and they weaved through the trees. She picked up into a gallop and Tazio chased after her, whooping like an idiot, getting a rare laugh out of her.

After a few more turns, Anya reared her horse at the opening of an impressive canyon.

"This is it. The real test," she said sardonically as she hopped off her horse before the crevasse.

"After that eagle, I can only imagine what horrific thing awaits in there."

"Trust me, this one will really scare you." She lingered on him, her ice-blue eyes enchanting.

"I'm ready for the fear."

Tazio hopped from his horse, his feet coming down without a noise.

"It's natural now, the silent feet?" She pointed to his feet.

"Suppose it's in the blood."

"Come."

Tazio followed her into the shadowed crevasse. As they stepped in, the wind whistled behind, and soon they were sheltered by the rising walls. About a hundred paces up, the sky poured through the cracked earth.

"Just a bit further," Anya said, her voice bouncing off the quiet walls.

Tazio felt her reach out and take his hand as the cliffs closed above and enveloped them in darkness.

"Come," Anya whispered.

Tazio strained to see in the dark until he saw an azure glow spilling around the next bend.

"What in the hell?" Tazio asked.

Anya pulled him into a cavern that was carved into the belly of the cliff. In the middle, a pool of water glowed a murky blue, bubbling as steam rose off it.

"It's beautiful," Tazio murmured, entranced. "How is it glowing?"

"*Bithael*, like in the woods. These waters renew anyone who bathes in them."

"Bathes?"

Anya laughed.

"Yes, have you ever had one?"

"Rarely."

"Well you should enjoy this then," Anya whispered, eyes coy as she turned and let the furs slip from her shoulders.

Tazio froze, blood rising.

"Don't look, you animal," Anya said.

Tazio turned. Behind him, her furs hit the floor.

"Mm," she sighed as she slid into the pool. "It's wonderful. Are you going to come in?"

Tazio hesitated, then dropped his pelts.

"Your back..." Anya said.

In the rush, he'd forgotten. He turned quickly to hide them.

"Oh!" Anya's eyes widened.

"Oh, damn!" Tazio said as he covered his parts. "Then *you're* allowed to look, are you?"

"I'm sorry—I meant to look away. But—your scars."

Tazio slid into the water, burning with shame, glad the cloudy water hid him.

"I've never seen them, but I can only imagine how ugly they must be."

"*Anam Teine...*" Anya's voice echoed softly. She waded toward him, ripples and blue light shimmering on her skin. "My father told me he'd found you burned raw."

Her fingertips traced the ridges and valleys of his scars, each touch sending a whisper of compassion.

"It's nothing," Tazio said, pulling away.

"Please," Anya said, gently holding his shoulder from the side.

Now his heart was pounding, and he was having to suppress his lower instincts, though not successfully. Despite the outrageous discomfort at having her see the burns, he couldn't coax away the silk that she was, choosing to close his eyes and feel her touch.

"How have we ended up here?" she asked.

"You tell me."

Anya kissed the back of his shoulder, her lips gentle and full. Tazio turned and looked down at her—into the innocent radiance that shone in her eyes. Into the allure of her defiance, and the beauty of her soul.

"Did you always hate me?" Tazio asked.

"I never hated you."

"Then, what?"

"I was afraid of you."

"Please don't be afraid of me, Anya."

"Not you. What I thought you were."

"And what is that?"

"The end."

A chill crept into Tazio's veins, the words hanging ominously in the air, threatening to shatter their closeness.

"The end of what?"

"The Daemonae. *Am Dorsa*—the Dark Time."

Tazio's stomach lurched, the words *Am Dorsa* striking a primeval chord.

"What does that mean?"

"I didn't mean it. I don't know what it means."

"Was it a vision?"

"Yes... and a feeling that hasn't left me."

Fear tore the warmth out of Tazio, shattering their fragile joy.

"It's okay, Tazio," Anya said, coming closer to reassure him, seeing the change that had washed over him. Her eyes shone, open and calm, as she placed her hand on his chest. "Your heart is running."

Words fled. Her gaze beckoned him. He wrapped his hand around the small of her back, gently pulling her in. He leaned in, heart thundering as his lips lingered before hers, heart calling for her to close the gap. Desire urged him to close the distance, but he held, placing the power in her hands. And she chose, her lips meeting his, gentle and full. Heat surged through his blood. The pain of the last few years faded to nothing for a few eternal moments as they merged in bliss. Her tongue was sweet, her moan a plea for more, their unity so strong the *bithael* glowed brighter in the cave. The warmth of her kiss drew him deeper. But from the edges of his mind, shadows crept in, tearing Tazio from the present. Faces flickered in his mind—of his parents, of Ulrich, of the bloody corpses of his people.

You are a curse to those around you.

Tazio pulled away, eyes burning.

"Anya..." Tazio whispered in her ear.

"What's the matter?"

"Please don't let me hurt you."

"I've tried to keep you away, *Anam Teine*. But I'd rather burn from you, than to burn without you."

CHAPTER 9

THE CLEAR WATERS of the creek beside Coille Solais reflected Tazio's face back at him. After so many lessons and days blurring together, he'd only see himself rarely in the last year.

Dirty blonde braids hung by his face. His nose and jaw had sharpened, brow grown heavier, and the softness in his cheeks melted away. The thought of youth brought back the sting of his helplessness at Bourgogne. He winced, then let the memory trickle away with the creek as he traced the burn scars on his feet. The horrors at Bourgogne had mostly dimmed. His heart beat for the Daemonae now.

"Tazio." Anya walked up and hugged him in a crouch from behind. "We're starting."

Anya led them through the winding woods, silken and quiet under the evening hum. Flowers breathed sweet scents, birds trilled bright songs, and bugs hummed as the world awoke into springtime.

In the months that followed Tazio's experience with the *iolair*, he and Anya had fallen deep in. What started as a duel evolved with the blooming spring into an intense exploration of each other's power. *Daemonia* opened the confines of one's soul, and now they'd seen each other stark and raw. Conversations beneath canopies and in sun-splashed glades became more frequent, aiding their closeness.

Anya eventually told him why she'd initially despised him. Given the rigor and strain placed on her by herself and others to hold the standard as one of the only current female warriors, and certainly the best one, she felt belittled by the task of training him. While it stung, Tazio understood.

Anya squeezed Tazio's hand as they entered Coille Solais, merging with others at the main fire. All were assembled for council. The last Daemonae filtered in, and expectation hung in the air as they waited for the council to speak.

Aeon stepped forward and everyone quieted.

"*Bennaich*," he muttered with a bow.

"*Bennaich*," the village echoed.

"Three days ago, I sent Barabal to track the Thoracians in the southern woods. He found that their army was moving toward Coille Solais. In the past, they always moved south of the Aroinn, but they seem emboldened by their string of victories throughout Novra."

"Will they march on Coille Solais?" Dyvyr asked.

"We don't know if they know our exact position or if they intend to go to war. The *bardeiin* has spoken, and we consider it wise to cut this weed now, before it consumes our lands. We cannot afford inaction. "

Murmurs.

"Then this means war?" Dyvyr asked.

"Yes. But waiting would also mean war. And with their numbers, we'll be crushed if we delay. If we move before they're organized, perhaps we can gain an advantage."

"Why not send a threat? They might consider changing their path," said Kalan, a well-respected warrior, his calm face open and ready to bear whatever may come.

"We considered this. But the Thoracians know us well. This is not the first time in thousands of years that we've warred with them—or the first time they've violated our lands. We crossed *reòthewy* into Novra to seek peace and freedom from the wars of Aontir. That ancient feud seems reborn again—perhaps some of you feel it stirring too."

Tazio's eyes darted from face to face as the appeal scattered around the fire. The posture of most stiffened, chests swelling in defiance.

"Unless anyone can provide another reason to stay, and present this case to the *bardeiin* council, we must fight. Tomorrow."

Aeon stood firm.

No one protested.

"Tonight—eat, cherish your kin, sharpen your blades, and savor this peace." Aeon bowed the lowest Tazio had seen. "*Bennaich.*"

"*Bennaich,*" the gathering muttered, then solemnly trickled away.

As Tazio stood, Aeon crossed to him.

"Tazio," Aeon said.

"Aeon."

"Come, let's walk." Aeon led them through the paths near the main village. "Are you prepared to fight tomorrow?"

"I don't have a choice."

"You're right. It would be dishonorable. But I know Anya has prepared you well. She speaks highly of your progress."

"She does, does she?"

"She does."

"How things have flipped since I first arrived."

"Yes, you two have certainly warmed to each other."

"Yes, I intend to do well by her, Aeon."

"I know. That's not what I'm here to speak of. The night before the first battle I ever fought, I still remember it clearly. All the feelings mixed together made me sick."

"I've certainly lost my appetite, but I feel ready."

"Where your appetite lacks, your confidence might compensate. But be wise—war brings horror in ways you can't imagine. Your training will help, but it can also kill you from the illusion of safety it attempts to provide. Please, do what you must to stay alive."

A deep softness rested in Aeon's eyes.

He sees me like a son.

Tazio had sensed it before, but with the raw suspense of battle on the horizon, the full truth was borne on the wise leader's face. Aeon couldn't hide it, brow creased, eyes drawn with focus. Aeon's struggle made Tazio's neck tense in anticipation of facing Thorace. Fear and readiness, sorrow and determination, pain and the pleasure of unleashing rage against them rushed through his veins.

"There is something left to be done," Aeon said. "The last part of what will bond you to us."

"Why does that not surprise me?"

"Good lad. Tonight."

Tazio followed the elders of the *bardeiin* council on horseback. The *bithael* put the midnight flowers on full display as they serenaded pollination partners. After a few miles, they pushed through the soft branches of the forest edge into an open glade.

In the center, seven huge stones lay in a ring, each about fifteen paces long and five feet tall with flame flowers crawling about. Each of the elders, four women and three men, including Aeon and Daere, climbed onto a stone.

"*Anam Teine*, take your place on the center stone," Daere said, holding her hand out, her red hair the color of blood, amber streaks reflecting the luminescent flowers.

He stepped onto the center stone, wondering what could be beyond the power Anya had already taught him.

"Tazio, you have learned of *Etria,* the All," said Daere. "Of *daemonia,* the conscious state; of *draeda,* the substance of *Etria*; of the *analuth,* or energy body; of *feantoiil,* the force of will which channels *draeda;* of *anamea,* your bond to animals. You will continue growing in these paths in this life and beyond. But there is one more power that binds the Daemonae together. *Ceanlinne*—a 'bonding pool.'

"You are familiar with *traeda* and how they spool off and entwine all things. From these threads, it is possible to latch onto each other, and onto paths and visions of the future, bending a thread of fate as we wish. In the case of the Daemonae, a thread that brings our will together as one, uniting us in a common purpose and multiplying our collective power. The first pool we know of was formed by Cathmor, one of the original discoverers of *daemonia.* As his power grew, he formed the first pool with his wife, Deirdre, then his apprentices, then his clan. Pools, he found, could only be formed by those wanting to join by the volition of their own heart. Perhaps this was a natural protection by *Etria* against unjust control by practitioners. We brought you here to invite you to join our path."

No turning back now.

"I am."

"Then the seven *bardeiin* will bring forth our common thread in

Etria. As you sink into *daemonia* with us, you will sense it. From there you must choose to bind yourself to this thread. Is this clear?"

"I think I'll sense the method."

"Your words are true. Let's begin—time demands it of us."

The *bardeiin* seven raised their arms, chanting in an ancient, unfathomable tongue that carried a longing to return to a place Tazio felt he knew. Around them, *bithael* cast a multicolored glow across the glade. Leaves kicked up, and branches groaned at the glade's edge.

Tazio closed his eyes, the rising power pulling at the seat of his mind. A cool wave rolled down his spine, chills spreading as he tilted his face back to the stars in surrender.

When he opened his eyes to his inner vision, *draeda* danced in the atmosphere. The *analuthae* of the seven elders shimmered in a tapestry of color and form and threads weaving the shape of their bodies. From the crowns of their heads, threads emerged and rippled in the wind. The elders brought their palms together at their chest. The threads pulsed, converging above Tazio in an orb of light. Then, the orb unfolded into seven lines, weaving around him, a living lattice of power.

Tension prickled at his temples. His heart sped, colors flickering as resistance clouded his focus. But then, from immeasurably far, but immediately present, as if from the edge of his soul, a primal roar erupted, banishing fear from the chambers of his mind.

Colors ignited and the ether sharpened again. Every particle in his body thrummed with vibrance. He spread his arms, surrendering to the threads of the elders around him. They welcomed him, sensing his presence, and in a flash, they united with him.

A vision burst in, transporting him.

Body gone.

Visions snapping through his awareness.

Aeon's face floating before him, vast and resolute, carved with the painful longing to save the Daemonae.

Gone.

Masses of Daemonae charging into battle.

Gone.

An incomprehensible flood of dark waves pouring over the great Mora mountains into the Aroinn.

Gone.

Tazio's heart seized like it was gripped by a vise.

A scream tore out from deep within, this time the same guttural death howl that came when he found his parents in the sea of bodies at Bourgogne.

The world inverted into a murky realm.

Inky purples and blacks polluted his vision. Darkness slithered over him, thick and suffocating. The inky fluid seeped into his feet, coursing through his veins until it bled from his pores. Panic surged, wild and uncontrollable. He gasped for air, but there was none to breathe in this realm. Nothing could stop it. Pumping through the doors of his heart until it choked his pulse to a near stop. Unable to move or breathe or scream. Eyes ready to burst as it squeezed out of their whites, light surrendering to that last point until all flipped again and he was back in *Etria* with the others. All the breath he had fought to breathe exploded out of him with gale force. He called for the elders, reaching for them as the floor disappeared out and he plunged into a dark realm, falling into a pool of mercurial liquid. He swam, desperate to surface until he stepped onto a ledge of smooth, obsidian stone. In the distance, lightning tore through the gray sky, splintering a lone oak into flames. Energy tore into Tazio and he flew back like an arrow shot from a longbow until he struck a wall.

The realm snapped shut.

He fought for breath, heart beating like a scared rabbit. He sensed the *bardeiin* elders around him in *Etria*, feeling them more intimately than before—their thoughts, and feelings too.

"Anam Teine," Daere's voice echoed in his thought. *"You've seen what Etria needed to show. Our thread, our wish and will, is to keep the Daemonae alive at any cost. We cannot know exactly what must be sacrificed to bend a thread this way—only that we can bring it closer to reality if we devote ourselves to it with everything. Do you accept our traeda cumanta? This is your last chance to turn back."*

"I saw... so many visions. Things I don't know the meaning of."

"We cannot know the meaning in an instant, Tazio."

"There was darkness," Tazio said, gaze a thousand miles away. *"There was—"*

"Tazio," Daere snapped. *"Those visions are for you alone. Only use them to make this choice."*

82

Tazio took a deep breath, fighting to pull his gaze to the present as the visions rattled through his mind. He put his palms out, feeling for which path was more free. And despite the fear, his heart beat strong in one direction, hesitating in the other, signaling him to go forward. Jaw set against lingering fear, he looked at Daere.

"I accept," he said resolutely.

Threads from the *bardeiin* speared into his crown, flooding every fiber of his being before coursing through the stones to the ground, out the stones and back to the elders. Colors turned to light, the energy threatening to tear him apart, sending him flying through a dimension of force, mind gone, reason exiled in ecstasy.

To where life was one with *Etria*—with *daemonia*. *Traeda cumanta.*

Bound to their common thread. One with their purpose. Alive with a fire to save their people.

No. My people. No longer am I alone. No longer am I helpless. I am one.

One with the Daemonae.

CHAPTER 10

TAZIO SAT on horseback with Anya and the other Daemonae soldiers in her *anead*. Their unit hid on the flank overlooking the path the Thoracians had traveled on a few minutes earlier. Silent to the ear, but clear through the *traeda cumanta,* Anya's words reached Aeon about a mile away. Their eyes all bore the same inky veil, channeling *draeda,* readying *feantoiil* to enhance their killing abilities. Bruic, Lonn, and Kalan led smaller *aneads* under Anya, their whispers channeling in the *traeda cumanta.* Tazio realized he was wringing his spear shaft, and he rolled his shoulders to try and loosen up. It didn't help.

Being selected for Anya's *anead* wasn't surprising considering she'd trained him, but nevertheless, it was an honorable appointment, and he didn't want to botch it. More than anything, he didn't want to lose her.

Kade breathed quietly beside Tazio, giving him a wink as they waited—until yells and steel broke the silence, reverberating over the hills. Anya tensed in her saddle as the intensity of the *draeda* rose in the *traeda cumanta*—then, an ugly, sharp drop. Grief slammed into his chest. Tears appeared in the eyes of the others, and Tazio knew he'd experienced the first severance of a life from the pool. Anya looked back, holding his gaze for a long moment before turning away suddenly.

"Now!" she hissed, spurring her stallion and leading the *anead* over the hillcrest they were concealed behind. Tazio could hear the horses breathing hard as the soft wooded hillside absorbed the noise of the descent. They broke onto the main path, and ahead, Tazio saw the flank of the Thoracian column exposed, facing the main Daemonae charge surging from the opposite side.

A sharp sting of bloodlust shot through Tazio, his stallion's hooves drumming courage into him as he surged forward in a wave of fury.

A Thoracian on the rear column sensed them closing in and shouted an alarm. Crossbowmen turned in haste and loosed a sloppy volley. One arrow cut through Anya's hair, burying itself in a young warrior's throat, one Tazio had dueled many times.

"*Gheibh iad bàs!*" Anya screamed, hurling her lance and pinning two men together who were stupid enough to be in a line.

Power shot through Tazio's muscles as he channeled *draeda*. His spear felt light despite its heft.

He drew back, finding the still spot between the horse's stride.

He released. The spear drove through the air and skewered a Thoracian pikeman to a supply cart. Relief and disgust mixed in his veins as the man squirmed.

A second Thoracian unit froze in horror as their *anead* closed the gap. A haunting call rose from Anya, summoning the *anead* into a frenzy. Tazio swung his bow from his back, nocked an arrow with the others and dropped another foe, numb to the violence, driven by the act.

Keep going.

The rest of the Thoracian unit retreated to rejoin the main column as Anya drew her longsword, blade glinting under scattered light from the canopy. Tazio drew his blade with the others in a chorus of sliding steel as Anya gave the signal to split into three groups. Anya charged the center and Tazio followed. The Thoracian company of armored pikemen stepped forward to face them, their unit leader screaming to arrange them for the assault.

From the hands of his fellow riders, two lances flew past Tazio, each drilling a pikeman. Tazio charged the right edge, then changed course at the last moment to draw the soldier's long pike awkwardly across his body.

Tazio cleaved the pike in two and opened the man's throat in a spray, carrying momentum deeper into the Thoracian ranks. Deep-seated rage erupted from Tazio, heads felled, bones crunched, Thoracians trampled like summer wheat. Screams turned to begging as pleas were drowned by Tazio's roars.

Soon, their *anead* left a gaping hole in the Thoracian column. The rest were cleared in sweeping motions as Daemonae in the east and west hills swarmed in. After fifteen minutes, only a handful—spared intentionally—were left to carry their tale of rout in the Aroinn.

A somber hue settled over the woods.

Tazio leaned back in his saddle and looked at the battlefield. Daemonae rode about calmly, reassembling amid the field of fallen Thoracians. He thought of his parents, and that Falkone still roamed the battlefield somewhere.

Tazio pulled his reins and trotted up to Aeon and Anya. With the rage of battle draining away, a stirring compassion moved through him for a man whimpering on his knees in front of Aeon, who towered over him like a king, the column of dismembered Thoracians a sobering backdrop.

"Tell your commander to stay east of Coille Solais, or it will be more of the same," Aeon said to the man, before kicking him away.

"How many did we lose?" Anya asked as the man scampered away.

"About fifty, maybe more."

Anya held still, but Tazio knew that despite the overwhelming victory, the number hurt, being more than a tenth of their force.

A look of panic came over Aeon's face and he reeled around.

"Anya! Follow, now!" Aeon shouted, spitting soil as he broke into full gallop.

The rest of the *aneads* tore after him, riding hard through the undulating woods. Threads began dropping out of the pool at an alarming rate, Tazio's heart wincing every time. Soon the smell of smoke choked in the air as the *anead* covered the distance to Aeon's army in a fever, charging over the hillside that spilled into the village. It crawled with Thoracians gutting homes, torching huts, and hacking down women and children.

Tazio's stomach dropped in horror.

Aeon roared and charged straight in, the rest of his men in chase. A volley tore Daemonae from their saddles. Aeon's haste left his unit exposed. Aeon, now separated from his men, carved through Thoracians, his blade a whirlwind of steel and bone and grief. But already, the swarm of Thoracian men was plugging the gap Aeon had cut into the horde.

Tazio drew all the *draeda* he could, channeling it into *feantoiil*. He cut a pikeman in two at the collarbone, then took an arrow to the shoulder, rearing back on his horse, crushing a man as he fell off, chaos fueling him, time disappearing as his blade turned countless men into a gurgling mess. Unable to bear the thought of losing another father, desperate rage lashed out. Then, he saw Anya, fear clouding her eyes as she surveyed the battlefield.

"Anya!" Tazio shouted, but she couldn't hear him.

Tazio parried a pike away, put the man behind it down, and climbed back on his horse. His guts gripped as he pieced together why Anya had frozen.

The Thoracians planned this...they knew Aeon would lose himself and overcommit.

"Retreat!" Anya screamed, pulling hard on her reins.

"We can't abandon him!" Tazio shouted back, pulling himself out of the daze.

"I said, *retreat*!" she screamed, hacking her way backward as Aeon pushed deeper into the fray—alone.

Tazio's eyes darted between Anya and Aeon, gripping his reins in indecision. Another pikeman charged and Tazio parried and downed him.

"Aeon!" Tazio screamed, throat hoarse, unable to find him in the sea of frenzy.

More Thoracians swarmed Tazio. More Thoracians fell.

"Aeon!" he screamed, rearing his horse.

Kade, on horseback, plowed through a wall of men to reach Tazio. "Tazio! *Baothaire*—fool! Let's go!" Kade screamed.

Tazio's vision opened again, and he reeled, in anguish as he followed Kade out of the fray toward the hillside where they'd charged in. Atop the hill, Bruic argued with Anya.

"You've abandoned them!" Bruic shouted.

"Hold your tongue, Bruic. I've done what I must. Look!" Anya thrust her sword toward the churning battle. "Do you think any of our own will survive that?" A look of hopeless acceptance spread across Bruic's face as he looked at the broiling battle. "Do *not* tell me I've abandoned my people when my own father will perish," Anya finished.

In the distance, Tazio finally sighted Aeon plowing deeper into the sea of Thoracians.

Engulfed. A lone warrior churning through an army. A sheer force, but a waning one—like a wheel spinning to an inevitable stop in Tazio's heart.

A looming figure on the opposite hill—black armor, spear in hand —caught Tazio's eye.

Falkone. It must be.

Tazio walked a step closer to the battlefield, in a trance as he watched the man take the spear and find its balance in his hand.

"Anya," Tazio muttered, hearing the words from another place, not sure if she even heard.

The ominous warrior spurred his horse forward, cutting into the fray, target clear. At fifty paces, he drew back and sent the spear. It sailed over the screams of battle, a single silent line.

When the spear struck Aeon, he collapsed in pain, clutching the protruding shaft, then the neck of his horse, life draining from his body.

"No!" Anya's scream split the air. Men fell silent. The trees seemed to hold their breath. Then the Thoracians turned toward them.

Aeon slid from the horse and crumpled on the forest floor.

It had to be a dream. Aeon could not die. Not like this. Confusion and reality collided inside him. No final words or duels like he'd read in stories of great battles. Just the sight of a simple, routine kill of the man who'd saved him. The man who'd given him a new life. The man he loved like a father.

Falkone cut into the group around Aeon, circling like a beast inspecting prey. The men jeered Aeon, gaining strength as Falkone grabbed him by the hair and whispered something in his ear. Around Tazio, the Daemonae worked their steeds restlessly, horses whinnying as they fought the urge to intervene in the cruelty. But the sea of Thoracians stood between them like a taunt.

Falkone yanked the spear from Aeon's side, holding it like a bloody warning, pointing it at Anya, then yelling a command.

His men rumbled toward them.

Tazio turned to Anya, the struggle on her face gripping his heart.

"*I will kill him,*" Tazio said.

"We must go!" Bruic demanded.

"They killed Aeon," Tazio said, pointing his sword at the charging horde. "They killed all of them!"

"Don't be a fool." Tears fell from Anya's eyes.

She tugged her reins, peeling away, the others following. But Tazio paused. Hate boiled up from a dark pit, urging him toward the Thoracians rumbling up the hill toward them. He raised his sword, pointing it directly at Falkone.

"I will find you! And I will kill you!" he roared.

He knew Falkone heard the message. He could feel it in his guts—the man's gaze locking onto him as he galloped. Vengeance screamed through Tazio's core, begging him to charge, to end it all in death or victory, every drop of blood yearning for vengeance, calling, calling.

Do it now!

But his love for Anya also gripped him, her pain more potent than his bloodlust, her safety of greater concern.

"Damn!" Tazio yelled, tearing at his reins and galloping away.

Lasair's hooves pounded beneath him, the forest he'd made his home now another memory he'd try to forget. Wind brushed the leaves in a song of sorrow, whispering tenderly. Trees consoled him, the spirit of the woods doing its best to comfort.

"No!"

Tazio galloped harder, heart shut to the offering, the flame of vengeance roaring inside him. Fury was invoked. Not even *Etria* could hold him from Falkone.

Tazio drew his sword, ready to strike.

"It's me." Anya put her hand on the hilt of his sword.

She'd awakened him before he fell from his saddle.

They were in a familiar part of the forest in the dawn light, and Tazio's body felt like it had been sucked of all life. Every movement felt ten times heavier from the dark drain of coming down from the *draeda* fueled frenzy.

The recent battle settled on him like a fog. Anya and the others seemed under its spell too, a rare slouched posture taking them over as they wound into the *clathain,* the glade where Tazio had bonded to the Daemonae the night before. As they came out of the forest's edge, Daere and her guard stood with about thirty others. Some were mounted, most wounded, all bloodstained.

"Anya," Daere cried.

"Mother," Anya said, dismounting.

They hugged as if neither had expected to see the other ever again.

"Are you all that remain?" asked Daere, looking at the rest that came with Anya.

The downcast look they gave back sent a sadness over her normally unperturbed countenance.

"A terror has happened." Daere waited for her next words, until a strength, rooted in years of wisdom, took over. "We have no time to delay at our most vulnerable."

"What do you propose?" Anya asked.

"Mora."

"The great mountains?" Bruic interjected.

"I advise we stay near the tundras," Anya said. "The Thoracians will have no interest in hunting us there. In a few years we can return to the forest and launch raids."

"There are other considerations."

"What do you mean?"

"We must find the Daemonae Atram."

"No one has even seen them in a hundred years."

"Then we shall be the first."

"Is that not wishful thinking?"

"The Atram know of power even beyond what we do. They'll know how to rebuild our people."

"I don't think it's wise."

"If I were seeking your counsel, I would ask for it," Daere snapped.

Anya looked stunned.

"So we'll run?" Tazio asked, chest tightening at the cowardly plan.

"I will not explain again," said Daere.

"Before we embark on an endless journey into that frigid hell, do we not deserve an explanation? For why we're running from those who *slaughtered* us?" It was the first time he'd defied authority since he'd been with the Daemonae, but the time for calm submission had passed. "I won't hear it. I can't. Falkone, the Thoracians—they just butchered our people. Twice if you count the Danuiin at Bourgogne. Those we love lie in pieces just miles from here, and we intend to flee to the Mora Mountains?"

Daere endured his questioning with great patience, and finally walked slowly to Tazio.

She took his hand gently into hers and hugged him. "Your fire burns beautiful and bright," Daere said.

The unexpected tenderness of it cracked him open, melting Tazio into her like a child. The specter of his rage fled, revealing the deep hole left in him from deep loss.

He fought to hide his sorrow in front of the others, but it was too strong.

"Aeon. He's dead," Tazio sobbed. "He's *dead*."

"I know, Tazio. He loved you, even if he did not say it," Daere whispered as she held his head.

"I saw him. I saw him die. Right there in front of me. Speared down like an animal."

"He still fights in *Etria*, and is always with us," Daere continued.

Tazio could feel the tightness and pain behind her strength.

"Your pain must be tenfold to mine," Tazio said, pulling away.

The chasm in her eyes revealed the truth, and she let a solitary tear roll free. The truth of it sobered him, turning his sobs to heavy breaths.

"You are right, Daere. As much as my rage drives me toward it, we cannot fight," he said, pulling away softly. "*But I must.*"

"Don't be insane, Tazio," Anya said.

"Insane?"

"Yes, insane!"

"The only thing that's insane is for me to avoid my responsibility!"

"What will you do against the entire army?"

Fury bloomed in Tazio. "I won't fight them today, but I will find a way. Before I came here, I vowed to kill Falkone. I ran once. And here we are. In the same pattern—a pattern I will not allow to repeat." His heart felt it would tear between his desire to stay and go. "You all welcomed me as your own, taught me like a child, reshaped my soul—and for this, only in *Etria* can you feel what I feel for you. I do not want to leave you.

91

My heart and soul ache. But I am sure I cannot go north to Mora. If the Daemonae are to rise again, the Thoracians must fall—and I must go."

The glade grew still. Then, above, a pair of ravens attacked a hawk, their caws echoing through the glade. The hawk struggled but broke free.

"I understand, Tazio. You must do as *Etria* tells you," Daere said.

"How can you say that?" Anya asked.

Tazio fought back the urge to weep. They had adopted him when they could have discarded him to the dead, but they didn't. The softness behind their prestige found a way to welcome him when he was but a shell.

"Please Anya, don't let us leave like this," Tazio urged.

She turned, tears already pushing out.

Anya ran and hugged him.

The pain of the world disappeared as they sank into each other.

Tazio's heart ached for her. Each day she'd grown more beautiful to him, and he wanted to pour out his love for her. But he feared that sharing it would kill the seed before bloom. It needed time. And less cruel circumstances. But the hope it was there somehow urged its beacon into the dark moment.

"Anya."

"What?"

"I don't want to go."

"Please don't speak like we'll never see each other again," Anya whispered, burying herself in Tazio's neck.

Tears warmed Tazio's neck. The ravens patrolled their glade. As the Thoracians hunted them, bugs hummed, and clouds drifted to their next glade. Until Anya pulled away, gazing at him, her eyes in havoc.

"Anya," he whispered, then kissed her, quieting the pain their embrace would soon stop.

"Tell me we'll see each other again," Anya whispered.

"We'll see each other again," Tazio said, heart straining as doubt cracked through the promise.

Anya leaned her head on his chest, and over her, Tazio saw Daere watching with tears in her eyes.

"Forgive me for being so forward," Tazio said to Daere, embarrassed for having embraced her in front of everyone.

"Love needs no forgiveness. It only pains me that it has become yet another casualty of this day."

"Then we share that pain."

Daere walked toward Tazio, and the remaining Daemonae came together to embrace. Tazio held onto them, fearing it could be the last familial embrace he might ever feel, knowing he would have to harden himself to survive the path ahead.

As they pulled apart, Anya lingered when the rest of the group began to trickle away. She took his hand, her mystical beauty almost too painful to behold. Already, she seemed of another world, like a dream fading away.

A gaping pit in his heart opened at imagining a future without her.

He painted her face as vividly as he could into his memory, tracing her angelic face, sinking into her eyes, transfixed.

"Why didn't we have more time?" asked Tazio, breath drawing tight.

"I'm sorry I was such a burden to you in the beginning."

"You're disappearing right before me. I can't endure it."

"I'll always be with you—in *Etria*. When your heart is troubled, find me. I will be there, Tazio. I will be there."

She put her cheek beside his. Her tears were still warm. His whole body stung, demanding he never let go, but knowing the time had come.

He liked to think they pulled away at the exact same time, like they both knew that holding on any longer would be more difficult than parting. But the truth was that he pulled away before her to prevent her the agony of having to part first.

She hung onto his hand for a second more.

Her last touch.

Then she walked away, pausing at the forest's edge to look back one last time.

Another clan turned to ash. Another family broken.

Tazio's heart snapped shut like the jaws of a wolf.

Vengeance.

PART II

CHAPTER 11

ON THE ELEVENTH day from the Aroinn, Tazio crested a hill beneath a steady evening rain. The dirt-packed trail crunched beneath Lasair's hooves. The route had taken him from the Aroinn through the Vestian valleys that rolled to the sea. Auria now stood before him, the great Setian merchant nation's lone city in Novra.

As Tazio began down the descent toward the sea, he saw a goatherd drawing water outside a humble hut. Looking for refreshment, Tazio dismounted, aching from days of riding.

"Ciao." Tazio said, approaching with a gentle smile.

"Ciao," the old man replied, his face lined by a hundred seasons. His hound nosed at Tazio. "*Perdono.* He does most of the seeing these days," the man said.

Closer now, Tazio realized the old man's eyes were veiled with blindness.

"*Perdono, Signore.* I come from a desolate place. Could I bother you for some water?"

"Where have you been?"

"The Aroinn."

"A terrible battle was there, was it not?"

"I passed south of it," Tazio lied.

"Come closer," the man said.

Tazio felt it rude to reject him, and walked forward, letting the man

read his face. "Handsome and cunning lines. You're no Setian, though."
As his fingers neared Tazio's eyes, he recoiled.

"A fire roils inside you. Even without sight I see it."

The dog stared at Tazio, its eyes yellow and uncanny, like the old man watched through them.

"Forgive me for the trouble, Signore. I'll be on my way."

"No, please, refresh yourself. The world needs your fire. But controlled, lest it consume us all," the man said, handing him the bucket.

"That seems rather sweeping, doesn't it?" said Tazio, giving a stiff laugh and setting the bucket down.

"I only say what I see," said the man, grabbing a wooden staff and walking away with a limp toward his cottage.

"Thousands passed through here into Auria. Do you tell each of their future?"

"Only if there is something to tell," the man said without breaking his slow, sure stride.

"Everyone has a future, though, yes?"

The man paused and turned on his cane.

"Yes. But not everyone has one worth warning them about."

"What are you saying?" Tazio demanded.

"I've told you what I sense. Take what you will."

"Grazie, Signore."

"Ciao," the man said, walking away to his stalls, his dog circling him dutifully.

The cool water replenished Tazio. The man's prescience, on the other hand, made his skin itch. He mounted, rejoining the stream of travelers heading for the *Gran Parete,* the infamous one-hundred-foot-wall that had never failed a siege.

Beyond it, Tazio could see the Aurian Senate behind another wall, perched on a high cliff that fell into the sea. As a child, when they performed here, Auria's grandeur had struck him. Now, seeing one of the last strongholds that might resist Thorace stirred him with hope. Auria could win—but also, it could fall.

Tazio remembered his father telling him of the ancient feud between Setia and Thorace—one that came from the old world to the new. The Setians crossed the Rabbian Ocean a century and a half ago, the Thoracians followed fifteen years later. Early battles ensued, and the Setians fought viciously, concentrating their effort on this port. The Setians had always relied on trade, so it made sense they risked it all for the central port closest to the old world. After tens of thousands perished, the Thoracians understood the message, and settled for the interior. Distracted by war with Setia, they lost much of the habitable lands to other nations.

Setia was the first nation to become a city-state, a point of friction with feudal powers. Setia was known to overthrow kings and emperors, launch shady trade networks, and convert nations into city-states. Over thousands of years, the tide had pushed and pulled, but still, the war went on.

A salty breeze licked Tazio's skin as he neared the gates. Setian guards stood watch, their blue, black, red, and gold armor gleamed with elaborate, floral patterns. Setia and its city-states, richer than any nation from trade, made no secret of its wealth. Many resented its exuberance, especially the austere Thoracians— but still, everyone bought its wares. In one form or another, Setia has had a piece of every coin.

Past the outer gate, Tazio rode through the middle city beneath the upper quarter of merchants, guildsmen, and minor nobility. People here walked with lifted chins tilted and furrowed brows, as if to look busier than their neighbor—all groveling to reach the upper sanctum while snuffing their more unfortunate neighbors in the lower quarters— apprentices, sailors, builders and the like.

Where the middle quarter blended into the lower, Tazio tied Lasair to the rail beneath a worn sign.

Il Sussurro—The Whisper.

Seemed like the right place to stir up some work.

A mangy man stumbled out, flashing a greasy grin as Tazio drew his hood up.

Tazio pushed the heavy door open. Tavern chatter bounced off the walls. No one cared who he was or what he wanted, the anonymity easing Tazio's shoulders.

He made his way to the long wooden bar, which wore the signs of age, more splintered than charming. He slid up to a spot at the bar and waited for the gruff, portly barkeep to take note.

"*Perdono, Signore,*" Tazio said in Setian.

"Seh," the barkeep grunted.

"I'm looking for work."

"No work here," he replied, already turning.

"*Signore*, I'm looking for more... *serious* work," Tazio said with a low voice.

The big man looked down his round nose.

"Over there," the man said, pointing a thick finger toward the hearth.

A skinny, pale man sat hunched in conversation with a Nebian in a rust-colored cloak. His gaunt cheeks drew inward toward a wiry brown goatee, and his whole look was crooked. The Nebian's skin was as dark as midnight and his eyes too, sclera and all. Together they looked, without a doubt, like the most dangerous pair in the inn.

"Grazie. I'll pay when I have some *numa*," Tazio said, but the man didn't seem to bet on it, already onto the next customer.

Tazio waited for the conversation to end, watching as two Setians eyed the Nebian.

Nebians were rare in Novra, hailing from the northern part of Malad in the old world, the continent island off the southern coast of Aontir. Known for being secretive, they were prized as assassins.

The Nebian slinked toward a back exit.

Tazio moved through groups of singing drunks as a minstrel performed for them, walking up to the skinny man.

"*Perdono*. I've been told you might have some work," Tazio said to the skinny man, who was even more sickly up close.

"And I should care, why?" the man said, his voice like it had been worn thin from years of combating pub noise.

"I've got skills that would put that Nebian to shame."

"And I've got two cocks."

"That makes us both special, doesn't it?"

"Heh, certainly aren't lacking in balls," he said, gesturing for Tazio to take a seat.

The man stunk of backhandedness. For all Tazio knew, his first assignment would be gutting someone for a few silvers, but it was a risk he had to take. He needed a way to find the levers of power, and it wasn't going to happen scrubbing slop in an inn, and he certainly wasn't going to land a position under a politician like some rich merchant's boy.

"Know your way around a blade?" the man asked, flicking an eyebrow up as he hunched toward Tazio.

And there it is.

"They call me *Stiletto*," said Tazio.

"Hah! Well, *Stiletto*, I've got a slice of something for you."

→

Billows of fog blew across the street as Tazio stood diagonal to the opulent stone flat he was meant to watch. Oil lamplight flickered off damp cobblestones. The target hadn't appeared like Otho said he would, and Tazio grew restless. Several city guards had already passed by, and he could only lurk so much longer before getting nipped.

A man, medium-height with long black hair, stepped out the front door across the street, checking both ways before linking away. Tazio stalked him, breaking off at the next split, and sprinting down a side passage, stepping in front of the man at the next street.

"*Perdono*, do you know the way to the closest inn?" said Tazio.

"Seh," the man said.

Tazio lunged forward. A look of terror spread across the man's face as Tazio jabbed him.

"Shut up!" Tazio hissed, pounding him into the ground and clipping him in the throat to stop his screams.

He pinned the man down, searching him until he found the leather-bound ledger Otho told him to retrieve. As he grabbed it, the man muttered under his breath, his eyelids fluttering. His eyes snapped open, dilated to near blackness, and the man shoved his palm into Tazio's chest, sending him flying into a wall. A flash caught Tazio's eye, and he ducked a dagger as it lodged in the stone beside his head.

Tazio closed his eyes, searching for his center, dropping into his familiar place as he channeled *draeda*. With eyes closed, he saw the man was emitting huge waves of *draeda*, bright threads pulsing off him, in particular, radiating from a point on his chest.

The man charged with a second stiletto drawn. Tazio ripped the one in the wall out, bursting off the ground and hurling it back. The man parried, but was thrown off balance. Tazio grabbed his arm, twisting him by the shoulder and slamming his head against the stone.

The brutality of it shocked Tazio—killing Thoracians was one thing, but he didn't even know this man. He bent down to feel his neck. He still had a pulse.

Tazio searched his satchel for keys.

Nothing.

He ran his fingers along two chains around his neck. On one was the key to the ledger. On the other was a thick, golden chain with an amulet that drew him in like it was whispering to him, warping his vision like the dream realms of *Etria* did.

"*Fermati!*" a guard shouted from the end of the alley, drawing his *cinquedea*, a wide-throated blade built for close quarters.

"Damn," Tazio muttered.

He snatched the ledger, wrenched the keys free and bolted, weaving between alleys to lose the guard, feeling drained as the *draeda* ebbed. He mixed into a scattering of people walking on a main street and pulled down his hood, betting on the deception of normalcy to blend in.

The guard spilled out of the alley and ran by.

Tazio's heart steadied. Ducking into another alley, he used the key to unlock the ledger. Inside lay a ciphered scroll. It would have to wait. He closed the ledger and jumped the wall into the rendezvous garden Otho had told him about.

"Impressive, *Stiletto,*" said Otho, mocking Tazio as he dropped in.

"What the hell did you send me into?" Tazio hissed.

"You said you were better than the Nebian. I guess you weren't lying."

"What did he use on me?"

"Not sure what you're talking about."

"He was strong—*ridiculously* strong. He sent me against a wall five feet away with one strike."

"Hm, well that explains how he dealt with the others," Otho toyed with his wiry goatee. "Well, I'm sure glad you made it back."

He tossed a satchel of silvers over.

Tazio caught it midair and cracked Otho's jaw in the same breath, sending him reeling into a small cherry tree.

"What's in the ledger?" Tazio demanded.

"You're playing with the wrong man," blood dripped down Otho's lip as he pushed himself awkwardly off the tree.

Tazio pulled his poniard and pressed the thin blade across Otho's cheek. His oily skin glistened from the blood tracing the dagger's edge.

"Unless you want your guts to feed the plants, you'll tell me what the hell is going on," Tazio demanded.

"Two lovers in a moonlit garden—how charming," a smooth, sardonic voice drifted through the air from behind. Tazio froze, and right as he went to turn and fight—"I wouldn't advise it," the same voice said.

Tazio turned, and a rapier's point hovered at his throat. The man pressed, pricking Tazio's throat until he fell pathetically onto his ass.

"Hand it here," the man said.

Tazio surrendered his dagger.

The man chuckled.

"No, no. Not the poniard, although it is a charming little blade," he said, his dark, assured voice stirring through the air. He wore a fine, dark green cloak with elaborate floral gold trim and black gloves, and a hood concealing his face.

Tazio pulled the journal from his cloak, tossing it the man's way. And at the same time, he lunged forward to tackle him at the legs. But before he could make the move, the man stunned him with the flat side of his rapier, and Tazio fell sideways, vision spinning.

"Cheeky boy." The man tucked the journal away. "Considering you couldn't touch me if you tried, I'll let your little act slide. Though I can't say I wasn't impressed with what you did to our little friend in the alley over there. Otho," he said, pointing his dagger at Otho, "where'd you find this one?"

"Il Sussurro," Otho muttered.

"Not the normal Sussurro rat."

"No. But didn't expect him to turn on me."

"Bold, we can give him that."

With few means of escape, Tazio wanted to use *feantoiil* again, but exhaustion gripped him from the chase.

"Well I'm awfully charmed you retrieved this ledger. We just got word as to who stole it. Didn't think a random boy off the street from— where did you say you were from?" the shadowy man asked.

"Didn't say," Tazio replied.

"That's right, didn't say. Well, I didn't think some random boy from nowhere would get it back for us. The man you stole from was a good thief, a good fighter. I watched the whole thing. Not a single dog sniffed you leading up to it—well, except me of course. But I don't count. Actually, I've always felt more like a cat. Anyhow, I digress." He pushed back Tazio's collar with the tip of his rapier.

Tazio pulled away.

"*Calmati.* If I wanted your throat cut, you'd already be draining on the stone. Where is your *talùth?*"

"My what?"

"Don't be an imbecile."

"I don't know what you're talking about," Tazio insisted.

"Search him," Neri said.

Otho patted Tazio down, but came up short.

"Are you talking about the necklace the man wore?" Tazio asked.

"Not his—yours," the hooded one said.

"I don't have one."

"I'm sure you don't." The hooded man came uncomfortably close, then broke away, muttering to himself in deliberation before returning. "I'll keep this brief—I have a proposition." He lowered his hood, revealing a disposition almost as shadowy as his cloak. A stark, askew nose met a sloping browline that hooded deep-set, cunning brown eyes —the kind that held sorrow deep beyond their cheery intrigue. Black hair fell thick past his shoulders and his jawline was blocky and irregular like his nose. His face was clean-shaven, skin deep olive, and overall had the look of someone who always had some plan churning beneath a veil of nonchalance.

He tossed a satchel. The *numa* clinked, working its persuasion.

"You can go on your way, and live like a rat doing odd jobs until you get your neck opened from a misstep. But you clearly have potential. So let's we use your proclivities for something a bit more valuable?" he asked with a twinkle in his eye.

A silence spread across the shadowed garden.

Almost have him.

"Then I'll go," Tazio said, moving to the side of him.

"Are you sure?"

"Never been more certain."

"Fair enough. But know, if you leave now, you'll never get this offer again."

Tazio paused, smiling at this man's desire to win him.

"I've never done too well with authority," Tazio said.

"Perhaps you're dimmer than I imagined. Listen, boy, you won't be a grunt like this poor bastard." He pointed at Otho, whose face twisted at the jest—denigration seemed a cornerstone of their relationship, and Tazio couldn't help but chuckle.

"Humor me. What will I be?" Tazio asked.

"Now if I told everyone what I was planning, I wouldn't be very effective at what I do, you see?"

"I'm not everyone," Tazio said.

The man walked over to him and held out an empty palm. With the flick of the wrist, a card appeared.

That's even smoother than me.

Embossed in gold leaf, a snake with three heads coiled around stone —the same emblem the man in the alley wore.

"You'll be powerful. And rich. But I will warn you—nothing comes without a price."

A loose shutter snapped against the wall from a stray wind.

"What does that mean?" Tazio asked.

"We deal in shadows—in secrets that shape the world." He flicked his hand, making the card disappear. "I can tell you want something. I'm not sure what yet, but you burn for it. If you're smart, you'll know that I'm the doorway to it." He drew his hood up, face barely visible. "I don't pass out an invitation to every street rat I meet. Even Otho will never get this offer. Sorry, Otho, it's just the harsh truth. As for you, *Stiletto*, do make it quick—I have important matters to attend to."

Desire and fear ran through Tazio like two stallions as he stared where the man's face should be, finding only the dark portal of the cowl. He wanted to know more before plunging in, but knew he'd heard all the man would offer—the bastard hadn't even introduced himself.

This is the connection you've burned for. Since Bourgogne.

This is what you've suffered for.

Tazio stood transfixed, hating the idea of submitting to the man, hating he was caving under the force of the offer.

Then Anya's words drifted into his mind, "Find me in *Etria.*"

He reached out, searching for her, heart vibrating across a thousand miles, feeling vaguely that she was there.

"Anya?"

"Tazio?" Her voice was a distant echo.

"I have to make a choice. I don't know which way to go, but it all feels dark."

"Open sky or closed fist?"

Light bounced off the wet cobblestones as a flash of Falkone's spear impaling Aeon flashed through his mind.

"Anya?"

The thread wavered, then cut, as the shadowy man walked away ghostlike. Tazio's veins tightened, Anya's reminder provoking courage as he searched for which path felt more open. Again, the path he feared most felt right. In some odd way, the fear called him forth, a vague promise the harrowing unknown was the way to go.

Through the fear.

"Wait," Tazio said.

The man stopped and looked over his shoulder, lantern light revealing a wry curl on his face. He knew he'd won, and it made Tazio's stomach turn over.

To get the blood I want, deeper into the pit of vengeance I must go. Already the waypoints are marked with doubt, but forward is the only way.

"I'll do it," Tazio said, the words drifting to Neri like a phantom contract.

The old goatherd's omen crept in.

The world needs your fire. But controlled, lest it consume us all.

Tazio gritted his teeth, burying the warning. Fire was all he had left —control could come later.

"Knock, knock—the door is open. I knew you were a smart lad."

CHAPTER 12

Neri.

Shadow, or more precisely—devoid of light. An appropriate name considering the way he'd sprang on Tazio in the garden the night before.

Buildings crunched against each other as Neri led them through the tight alleys of the lower quarter, a light rain slicking the grimy streets. Sailors mixed among brothels, bazaars, and a flurry of dialects traded in the messy, variegated stone streets as seagulls cawed overhead. Faces here were glum and drawn, too stressed to pretend like in the middle quarter.

The night before, Tazio had tossed and turned in his hovel of a room at Il Sussurro in anticipation of where Neri would take him. So he abandoned the idea of sleep and walked the city, visiting the *Coliseo*, failing to snake past the guards into the upper quarter, and drinking Setian *vita*—though that was a stretch, given it was a tea imported from the isles of Malad. Made from a pale, red flower, it made his whole body tingle, and his vision sharp. The downside was the comedown, but the solution was elegant—once you start, don't stop.

Keen way to drive a habitual purchase.

They rounded a corner a few blocks from the main port. A disheveled drunk with a beard drooled as Neri's horse stepped over him. A group of street urchins giggled and pointed at the drunk, and one flicked a rock that clinked off his head. He didn't stir, and the kids chuckled and ran to their next ploy.

Farther from the port, oddly enough, large estates appeared. Though the courtyards of most were littered by tents and hovels. A scraggly man came out of one and tied his pants hastily as a worn woman burst out and shoved him, demanding payment.

"Never seen a whore?" Neri asked over his shoulder.

"I've seen whores. Usually a bit more discreet though."

"Salt and whores. In Auria, both are cheap, and both are common.

"Noted."

"Though I'd stick to salt. You can sweat out salt, but you can't sweat out the grips."

"The grips?"

"Best to just keep your drawers on."

Tazio took one look back at the whore who, seeing him gawking, gave a lewd smile.

As he and Neri turned a corner, a looming wall stretched out about five hundred feet long. No other wall in the district was as imposing. Halfway down it, they entered a gated archway into a mossy courtyard.

A fellow with a playful mirth greeted them.

"*Bondia*, Neri. Who do we have here? Don't worry, *ragazzo*, Neri is twice as untrustworthy as he seems. I'm Leone," the man said, his narrow eyes shining.

His charm cast a wave of ease over Tazio, and Tazio liked how clearly he mirrored his name. His hair was sandy-gray blonde and thick like a lion's mane. He also wore a thin mustache and goatee, all of it adding to his demeanor.

"Evening, Leone, always a joy," said Neri.

"You know I live to serve."

Tazio smiled at their jabby respect for one another.

They dismounted and left the horses with Leone.

As they walked toward the main door of the refined stone building before them, the sounds of the city street recessed in the palatial front courtyard. It stood five stories tall, one taller than any other, constructed of a finer, darker stone than the region's traditional rough limestone, and surely the largest estate in the sector. It was intricate, but not ostentatious, and had classical geometric flourishes, balconies, and stained glass windows with abstract patterns, arched entries, and floral iron lanterns. Moss and vines crawled the walls all the way up to two towers at the ends, six floors tall. Archers stood watch there.

Not bad.

They walked through a row of hooded sculptures toward the entrance of the building. The statues loomed overhead, reminding all who entered they were being watched.

The copper front door stood twenty feet tall, and a language of abstract symbols adorned it. Tazio's father had taught him to read texts and music in languages beyond those he spoke, but he'd never seen anything like it. Though one inscription in Setian lay above the door:

BEHIND THE VEIL, *the tale is made.*

THE INSCRIPTION STIRRED thoughts of what the Guild would shape him into. Neri withdrew a key and worked it into the door, his green velvet cloak shimmering in the rain as he did.

"Welcome to the Setian Merchants' Guild," he said.

The copper door swung open, and a wave of warmth and chatter washed over Tazio. Tazio felt he'd stepped into the heart of darkness, the ornate embellishments dripping with candlelight. Younger members moved with haste, focus in their gait. Older ones progressed smoothly along, comments to each other tucked behind a palm or a duck of the head. All wore cloaks and tunics of varying colors. The interchange reeked of power, all its players weaving a patchwork of information and power.

Tazio pointed to the elaborate reliefs of traders, merchants, and wars carved into the wall. "What do these mean?"

"Historical tales of the Guild and Setia. Dates back thousands of years. You'll learn of it all soon."

They climbed to the fourth floor and walked down marble hallways to a bedchamber. Six beds lay inside.

"This is where you'll sleep. You can leave your things here," Neri said.

Tazio dropped his satchel at the last empty bed. At the foot of it sat a wooden trunk so polished he could see himself in the silver latches.

"There's a dark green tunic and a formal black cloak inside that trunk. Put those on—we're just in time for dinner."

"They're mine?"

"Completely and utterly yours."

Neri stepped outside into the hall as Tazio opened the wooden trunk and picked up the dark green tunic, testing its smooth fabric between his fingers before putting it on. It fit perfectly, like it was tailored for him, the fabric soft and pliable, with stretch to accommodate its fine fit.

Folded crisply beside was one black and one blue cloak, and a pair of fine leather boots. He slipped the black cloak on, and a feeling of comfort came over him. The velvet was thick, its weight grounding him and bringing a sense of prestige. The fabric gleamed with beauty, so much so he was afraid to scuff it.

Neri walked back in the room.

"These garments, they're incredible," Tazio said.

"We're not the world's finest merchants for nothing."

"Fair point. And the other beds?"

"You're not the only bright one in Novra. Those belong to your fellow *apprentici*," Neri's eyes creased ever so slightly in enjoyment of his little quip.

"Is this a school?"

"Partly so."

"Not what I expected."

Neri chuckled. "The list of surprises will only grow. Now, before we proceed, you must tell me one thing. Are you of the Daemonae?"

"What?"

"Don't play dumb."

Tazio's gut tightened. The truth would put a noose around his neck. "I'm not."

"You look more guilty than a petty thief." Neri stepped closer, his voice dropping into a coarse whisper. "We'll be working together on initiatives that require trust. The only way I can grow you, is to know you. Your past cannot be a liability. So, tell me, are you Daemonae or not?"

Tazio's heart raced as Neri glared at him, brown eyes beneath tilted brow waiting for him to crack. It seemed like Neri knew—but maybe he was bluffing. Maybe he could press his own bluff. But if Neri knew and Tazio lied—death.

"Not how you'd imagine," said Tazio.

"Well, stretch my imagination."

"I'm Danuiin."

"Your clan faced great cruelty."

"Yes."

"The report was not favorable for your people."

"That's a vast understatement."

"But you were exposed to the Daemonae. You act just like them. Look the part, too."

"I was captured. Turned to a slave. Eventually our transport was raided by the Daemonae and they spared me."

Neri stared at him, his face in calculation. "But Tazio is a Setian name, not Danuiin. I thought you may have taken it as an alias, but it's your given name?"

"The Danuiin elders had obscured the past—that the Danuiin are actually a branch of the Daemonae. They've been distancing themselves from the Daemonae for the last two generations. When the Daemonae found me, they knew I was Daemonae Raichiin because of my eyes."

"Yes, we're familiar with the connection between the clans," Neri nodded as if the missing pieces of the story were clicking together. "We also know of the battle at Coille Solais. Word is nearly all the Daemonae were killed. But we wondered if that was crafted in the Thoracian rumor mill."

"I killed Thoracians with my own hands. I saw them maul our people. Innocents. So no, it's not rumor."

"Usually 'sorry' doesn't offer much in these kinds of conversations, but I am sorry for your losses—in both cases."

Tazio felt Neri actually cared—this shadow of a man who could seal his fate in an instant.

"How did you know I was Daemonae?" Tazio asked.

"The way you used the power only Daemonae know—in the alley."

"Then our power is rare?"

"Unique, in fact."

"Unique?"

"Unique."

Neri seemed slightly perturbed by the fact Tazio was Daemonae. Why, Tazio didn't know yet.

"Come," Neri said, walking out in a breeze before Tazio could continue questioning him.

Neri led them through the labyrinth of hallways, just ahead of Tazio, keeping just ahead, dismissing conversation. They passed libraries, reading rooms, studies, crafting workshops, blacksmithing yards, private offices, dorms upon dorms. The Guild was spectacular.

The hallways grew increasingly packed as they went downstairs and filtered out of the main lobby toward a huge open doorway with golden light spilling over the mulling crowd that walked through it. Wafting out of it were the smells of a sweet, salty, and rich feast.

Tazio merged into the room beside Neri with hundreds of others finding their seats. Others near Neri recognized and deferred to his presence. As they made their way inside, thousands sat at long, polished marble tables in an absurdly grandiose ballroom. Vaulted arches held the ceiling afloat, glowing candelabras lined the perimeter, and grand chandeliers bloomed down the center. Rich reds, blues, and golds created a warm depth, and the Setians' love of elaborate frescoes appeared again and never failed to impress. These were mostly scenes of sweeping landscapes.

Professionals and apprentices of all types assembled and chatted, taking a seat according to the color they wore. Deep green, sapphire blue, blood-red, black, brown, purple, and white. Like Tazio, other apprentices wore black.

Servers in brown shuttled dishes to each table, hurrying back and forth—seafood and meat pastas, roast pork, pomegranates, bread, potatoes, carrots, curries, berries and cake graced the slab tables. Tazio's mouth watered. The masses filed past, eager to eat, a few bumping him innocuously along the way as they chased their hunger, too.

Neri stopped at a table of apprentices, and got the attention of a strong, friendly-looking lad with short brown hair, a good red beard, and a round, open face. He still had a hint of boyishness and appeared around Tazio's age.

"Alessandro, this is Tazio. Be an *amico* and warm him to the group, seh?" Neri requested.

"Of course, Neri," Alessandro replied, then turned to Tazio. "I'm Alessandro. Quite the spread, ey?" he said merrily, offering a handshake.

"Never seen anything like it, frankly, and I've seen my fair share," Tazio said, shaking Alesso's hand.

Alessandro smiled, squinting with merry cheeks, a charming contradiction to his oxen build. "I almost shit my drawers a few days ago when I first walked in, too," he said.

Tazio laughed. "Anyone call you Alesso for short?" Tazio asked, feeling like they'd been friends forever.

Alessandro paused for a second, as if it were a slightly tense thing for Tazio to ask.

"I'm sorry—I just thought it was a good nickname," said Tazio, "Alessandro it is."

"No—Alesso is good," he said seriously. "I just haven't been called that in a while, and now you're the second person to ask. But the next person who tries me is going to get it!" He held his fist up like he was ready to pummel someone.

"Alesso it is," Tazio said, watching to ensure he truly liked it.

"Oh, you'll like this—here come the rats," Alesso said, nodding to a group of students crossing the room.

The lad at the front of the group had deep brown hair cut tight to the head. He was medium height, broad-shouldered, and walked with stiff assuredness—dire and cold. His face was rugged and had the simple gaze of those who endured bitter winters. Though he felt gruffer than the normal northern bear. Northerners usually had long hair to fight the cold though, so Tazio guessed whether he hailed from the north.

The second was a skinny blonde lad with choppy hair. His light green eyes moved to and fro, alert, and he moved like power was ready to rip out of him at any hint of provocation. Definitely the kind you don't want against you in a fight, mostly because he'd take it too far, too quickly.

The third was a girl who moved slowly and coolly with a taste of underlying danger. Based on her jet black hair parted up the middle, long by the sides of the face with a knot at the back, she was Shēdo. The Shēdo migrated across the Cean Ocean from the far east of Aontir, settling on the western coast of Novra beyond the Venustian mountains. Only through the long western passes there could you reach the Shēdo. Her face was square, flat, with wide features, and she had a muted meanness that Tazio didn't feel like seeing the loud version of. And where the second lad seemed outwardly unpredictable, she seemed the type who felt no shame killing you in your sleep.

"Evening," Alesso said as they walked up.

"Evening," the first lad said bluntly, snubbing Alesso as he piled his plate with food.

"This is Tazio, he just arrived," Alesso continued.

"When did you arrive?" Tazio asked.

"Last week."

"I'm Tazio."

Tazio offered his hand across the table, and the lad looked at it like it was foreign, then shaking reluctantly. Scars lined the boy's hands.

"Corso."

Tazio offered his hand to the jumpy blond kid.

"Luca," the next one said, his slightly bulging eyes resting on Tazio, sending a message of pain deep within them, whether he knew it or not.

"Kage," said the Shēdonese girl, shaking Tazio's hand. One side of her face was slightly lower, but not in an off-putting way, more asymmetrically captivating.

Tension in the air radiated off the three of them. Tazio didn't know why he'd expected the other apprentices to all be friendly, but it was clear now that Neri was bringing in some afflicted types.

Guess that makes me afflicted too then?

Out of the corner of his eye, a pretty girl caught Tazio's attention. She bobbed down the aisle in a state of thoughtful wonder—like she was half-absorbed in some thought. Her hair was wavy and to the nape, deep brown with red undertones, and her rich caramel skin glowed.

"Eye hooked on something?" Alesso said, punching Tazio on the shoulder. "Don't worry, you and everyone else."

"Shh." Tazio said, seeing her approach.

"Alesso," she said, walking up with a radiant smile. "Oh, are you the last of our group?" she asked when she saw Tazio, her amber eyes lighting up.

"Me?" asked Tazio.

"No—him." She pointed past Tazio.

Tazio turned and saw he was the last one on the bench. His face turned red as he heard Zara giggle.

"Fair play. You call him Alesso, too?" Tazio asked.

"It's the obvious move, isn't it?" She dropped onto the bench with disheveled charm. "My name is Zara."

"I'm Tazio."

"Well why don't you two get a room?" Luca said.

"Well maybe we will. Would that make you jealous, Luca?" said Zara.

Luca looked like he'd choked and Tazio suppressed a laugh.

She has spice doesn't she.

"Splendid place, isn't it?" Zara said to Tazio and Alesso, now that Luca had been efficiently castrated. "Apparently it was one of the first buildings constructed when the Setians came here from Aontir."

"You our Guild history professor or something?" Alesso joked.

"Would be easy enough to teach a simple mind like you," Zara shot back.

Alesso turned red and smiled, knowing he'd been had.

Tazio couldn't hold back the laugh on that one. "You don't blunt your words much, do you?"

"Only when they're worth blunting."

"Fair enough."

A clear note rang through the air off a crystal calling glass, cutting them short. The auditorium fell silent as Neri stood on a platform in front of other seemingly important Guild leaders, all wearing the same dark green velvet capes, told apart by their custom embroidery and crests over the heart.

"Tonight, we welcome a new class to the Guild," said Neri, and the chamber sang with the chime of silverware on crystal.

Neri slid a dagger from his cloak and gave it a twirl until it balanced on the point of his finger. The chimes continued like the crowd knew what was coming. Casually, Neri nipped his dagger out of the air by the blade and flung it through the air. Thirty paces away, it plunged into the roasted pig's head at the center of Tazio's table.

More clinking and hurrahs broke out in appreciation.

"A bit excessive, no?" Alesso said.

"There's a small scroll there—on the hilt," Kage said.

No one else moved, so Tazio reached for the scroll.

"Please, read it for the hall!" said Neri from the platform.

Tazio cleared his throat and began:

"ALL APPRENTICI OF A CERTAIN BREED,
All capable, able to exceed.
Forged by past hardship,
Life sharpening their trip,
Creed to be metaled,
Their purpose to be settled.
In the family of our Guild,
Of your future, be thrilled,
But please, do not get killed!
Sodalitati gratam!
Welcome to the Guild!"

THE HALL ERUPTED into thunderous applause, and Tazio swelled with joy as thousands of faces welcomed them all like a family.

Family?

He shoved the thought down, the hope of it too painful to nurture.

Neri brought order again with his ringing glass.

"Zara, from the dunes of Kataria.

"Alessandro, from the plains of Bourgogne.

"Kage, from Shēdo.

"Corso from Kalskog.

"Tazio of the Danuiin.

"Luca from Auria.

"We welcome you all! Over the next two years you will learn, struggle, and grow together. But for now, grow your stomach. Some of you look like dogs who haven't eaten in a month!" Neri finished.

The crowd applauded a final time. Tazio and the others turned to the feast in front of them and they all dug in. Eating briskly, Tazio lost himself in the sumptuous flavors, going on one journey he was actually happy to be on.

"Nice poem," Corso said to Tazio bitterly.

Tazio grinned to himself but let it pass.

"Something funny?" Corso asked.

Tazio leaned back off his plate, losing his appetite. He looked around with a cheeky smile. "Usually I laugh when something is funny. What about you?"

"Don't play games with me, you bitch," Corso said, getting a chuckle out of Luca.

Tazio chuckled with them, then broke into an insane laugh louder than theirs. That made them confused, *very* confused. Like toying with children. Or hecklers at a performance. Tazio was all too used to it.

"Good chicken, isn't it?" Tazio asked, pretending nothing was amiss.

"What?" Corso asked.

Tazio leaned across and grabbed a chicken leg off Corso's plate, then crunched a bite through bones.

"Chicken," Tazio said.

Corso froze.

"You have some chicken in your teeth, by the way." Tazio capitalized on Corso's frozen state, driving the wedge. He could feel Luca and Kage waiting like hounds, ready to bite for their master.

Tazio let the tension linger, smiling as he chewed more bones.

"Well, you two seem to be getting off well," Alesso broke in. "Any idea on what we're learning for our first day?"

"Hopefully not combat," Zara commented. "Clearly there's some pent up male rage around here."

"No rage here, just thought Corso looked like the sharing type," Tazio said.

Neri appeared at the table. "Food meeting muster?"

"Wonderful, Neri," Zara replied.

"Awfully quiet, Corso. Food doesn't compare to Nyttjem?" Neri asked.

"It's fine," he grunted, staring at his plate.

"Well that's good—it's the last meal you all will eat for two days. So enjoy it!"

"What?" Luca asked, exasperated, chicken skin hanging from his lip.

"I'm kidding, of course," Neri said, letting out the kind of laugh that made Tazio guess whether Neri was actually insane. "Tomorrow, the fun begins!"

"Wonderful," Alesso muttered as Neri walked away.

The tension put a sour taste on the feast for Tazio. He was embarrassed he'd gotten so hot, but if he didn't cut these types like Corso off early, they could grow into a real problem. And Corso was definitely looking to be a problem. Tazio didn't know if Zara and Alesso would commit to being on his side or not, but it was definitely obvious the other three were like leeches on Corso.

Dessert came, and Tazio cooled off. A closing chime signaled the end of dinner, and the room stirred into motion, the crowd filing out. Tazio walked through the arched hallway out of the dining room with Zara and Alesso.

"Anyone figured out what the colors of the cloaks mean?" Zara asked.

"Rank and type, surely," Tazio replied.

"I know that, oh wise one. I mean, specifically."

"Gotta get myself a green one then," Alesso said, eyeing a group slithering by in green.

"The power does seem to wear green."

"Though the blood red types seem equally as intriguing if you ask me," said Zara.

From nowhere someone slammed a fist hard into Tazio's ribs.

Tazio whirled around and found Corso staring narrow-eyed at him, eyes cold with a quiet rage, a storm waiting to break. Tazio's whole body tightened in readiness. This Corso was a common tyrant, but Tazio had dealt with worse.

"Embarrass me again and I'll turn you into pulp," Corso grunted, coming close enough Tazio could feel his hot breath. Tazio took a step in.

"You're a funny one," Tazio said, pressing his nose into Corso's,

Corso huffed and recoiled, and Zara shoved in-between them, Alesso tight on her heels. Over Zara's shoulders, Tazio could see him wrung with anger.

"If you do this now, you've lost," Zara said to Tazio as Alesso held Corso back. "Don't mistake the Guild for measuring us solely by how we fight."

Tazio felt the sting of rage fade as her wise interjection worked its powers. His vision opened back up to the crowd inspecting the tussle. Their measured glares imparted the realization that Zara saved him from a catastrophic blunder. Corso dropped posture, perhaps realizing the same, turning like a wolf reluctantly knowing he'd lost his prey.

"Interesting one, isn't he?" Alesso said.

"Not here to fuck around, that's for sure," said Tazio.

"Gives me the chills, and not just because I'm from the dunes. But Neri is no idiot. Everyone's here for a good reason, I'd say," Zara said as Corso slunk off like a beaten wolf.

"Well! This is all way too serious. How about we blow our *numa* on a game of *rischio*?" Alesso asked.

"Nothing like a good gamble to blow off some steam," Zara agreed.

"*Rischio?*"

"It's a dice game. Only known Alesso for two days and I already know he's an addict," Zara said.

"It's what gives me my charm. And it's how you'll lose all your money to me," said Alesso.

"Hah! Well, you clearly don't know much about the Danuiin," Tazio said, winking and giving Alesso a friendly jab.

Alesso pulled a bag of dice from his pocket and gave them a shake. "Let's find out!"

CHAPTER 13

THE NEXT DAY, Tazio shuffled past a massive wood door into his first session, craning back to take in the ancient-looking carvings—simple shapes, crevices, and lines that ran off the door into the masonry like stone vines.

The wood-paneled classroom on the fifth floor was lined with floor-to-ceiling bookshelves, and a long, polished oval table of dark redwood dominated the room. On the table, in front of each seat, lay a curved dagger, a chalice, and a letter. Corso was seated, testing his dagger's weight, inspecting it before planting the handle end down and spinning it under the tip of his finger. Tazio picked his up. It was cool in his palm, snake scales carved into the bronze hilt, and the short blade was fat and curved. Alesso balanced the point on his pinky finger, and Zara inspected hers closely. Luca flipped and caught his; Kage rolled hers across her knuckles, twirled it, and snatched it.

Not bad.

Neri dropped a thick maroon leather-bound book on the table, snapping them to attention.

"I see you're amused by the *sacrapugiae*. They're only sacred ceremonial cutlasses passed down through the centuries. So breaking them shouldn't be an issue."

Varying guilty looks lined their faces as they put them down.

"In this volume is the cursory history of the Guild. Throughout the term, you'll learn its inner workings more precisely than the people you'll gut."

Neri may have used humor to deliver the message, but it only teased Tazio's suspicions that they'd be killers soon enough.

"The information in here is practical and historical, but most importantly it outlines rules and customs that unite us," said Neri, walking to a window overlooking the courtyard. He pushed aside garnet velvet curtains and cracked a window that overlooked the rising hill Auria sat on. Bells rang the final tones of the ninth hour as birds crossed the cloud puffs from the previous night's rain.

"Auria is our home in Novra, but our roots are in Setia. Setia still supports us from the old world. Our origins help us learn from those who tilled the rugged path before us," Neri said as a breeze kicked through the window.

He walked back to the table. Neri's shadowy, distant persona still dominated, but the intimacy of the instruction made Tazio keenly aware of the privilege of learning from such an influential man.

"But before I go into our history, something is required of you—of every member of the Guild. You've already taken the liberty to play like children with those cutlasses, but you may have glanced at the envelope." Neri eyed them like they were miscreants.

Everyone picked up their cream-colored envelopes.

Fine, raised lines ran diagonally across the envelope, the intricate texture evocative of the Setians' obsession with prestige.

"The first rule of the Guild is that you never reveal the functions of the Guild beyond what is known publicly. Second, you never act in a way that could expose the workings of the Guild or undermine its mission. The world knows we're powerful, that we educate apprentices, but it does not know the extent of our purpose. This knowledge is reserved for members. As far as the public is concerned, you're receiving an education in merchandising, trade and politics, combat, fine art, and other curricula of a wealthy merchant or royal family."

"Bit of a new topic to us, ey?" said Luca, fidgeting to catch the eye of Corso, who ignored him.

"The third rule is that murder of a fellow member is punishable by death."

The air got stiff.

"Well now, don't look so glum," Neri said.

"Does this happen frequently?" Kage cracked open the question they were all probably stewing on.

"Let's just say the rule has helped dampen the issue." Neri grinned. "The fourth and final rule is that you must take an oath. Once taken, you're a member for life, and will fulfill your duties and serve the interests of the Guild." He held his hands out as if what he'd run them through was, in fact, not that serious, but just a routine nothing. No stakes or tension. Just another day of initiations.

But it didn't feel that way.

"And if we don't take the oath?" Zara asked.

"Well, if you were foolish enough to do so, this moment would be your last chance to *exeunt*. Right now you don't know enough to be dangerous, but keep in mind that you'll be watched down to the last detail. And, of course, you'll be dispatched if we sense any untoward behavior. Your choice."

"Doesn't seem like much of a choice," Corso muttered as he sat back in his chair.

"Now, now, I understand some of you want to run, or fight me. Or maybe you're weeping a bit on the inside—I've seen it written on the faces of hundreds of apprentices before you. But I'll ask you this one thing—was I not clear when we first met that there would be no turning back?"

Everyone but Neri looked a bit more gripped.

"This is a step we all take. To turn back is folly, and the path ahead is ripe with glory," Neri said, breathy and full of wonder. "You can't even imagine the world that's about to open up for you. I'd advise you heed the gain, and abandon the fear."

Everyone traded subtle glances, as if checking for confirmation from one another. For Tazio, the past was in ashes, there was only one way forward.

"Unless you speak now, I will take your silence as a commitment to go forward," Neri said. No one muttered a word. "Good. Now take your *sacrapugia* and open the curve of your palm."

"This dagger? Open my palm?" Alesso looked dumbfounded.

"Yes, Alesso. Was I not clear?"

"It's just. Well—damn, alright."

"As the blood drips into the chalice," Neri pushed ahead, "if you're in agreement with the questions I prompt, you will respond, 'I do'."

Tazio picked up the blade and tested the edge against a fingernail, then set it to his palm. The cutlass smiled a wry, curved grin up at him, as if it taunted its newest servant. Knowing it was too late to reconsider, Tazio gripped the handle and drew it sideways, watching as blood poured over the cutlass into the chalice, growing heady as crimson sealed his submission to the oath.

"Do you understand all that has been told in this rite?" Neri asked, backlit at the end of the table, eyes hard to see under his brow.

"I do," they said.

"Do you swear that you are not, nor ever have been, an enemy working in conspiracy against the Guild?"

"I do," they said.

"Do you swear to follow the four principles that bind us?"

"I do."

"Do you accept this oath and agree to be bound to the Setian Merchants' Guild and all its duties?"

"I do."

"Then you are oathed!" Neri threw his arms up in joy. "With unity and reverence I, and all the honorable members of the Guild, welcome you." And he bowed.

Tazio put his dagger down and bandaged his hand with a cloth beside the chalice. The room settled. They'd crossed the threshold. There was no turning back.

"Are we ready for some history?" Neri asked.

"Some light learning to follow our sacrificial oath?" Tazio retorted.

"Always good to keep things in balance."

"I think I'm going to pass out," said Alesso, blood running into his chalice.

"Apply pressure. You'll be fine," said Zara.

"The Aurian Order was established in Novra 154 years ago," Neri started, "after Setia developed the necessary technology to cross the Rabbian Ocean. Masts were redesigned for more flexibility using wood from the far islands of Rumah. Keels were strengthened to withstand the violent seas. All of this allowed us to be the first to sail to Novra. In 2733, the first year the Setians arrived, the cornerstone of the Guild was laid facing the old world as tribute to the passage. Considering that even the Senate hall was only approved and built by the Guild afterward, that should give you a sense of where the Guild ranks in power."

"When did the Thoracians come?" Tazio asked.

"Thoracians?" Neri looked disgusted that Tazio would change the subject to them. "Fifteen years later. If it weren't for the Thoracians intercepting some of our early ships near the Straits of Malad, it might have been years—maybe decades—before they crossed."

"We might have had a few more cities than Auria then," said Luca.

"Yes, but it's of little concern. We still own the purse and prefer to operate from a single stronghold."

"The Guild in Aontir dates back over two thousand years when Setia was a great empire. But the tyrant, Emperor Enrico Valus, was the lever that threw the Setians over the edge. Edoro Ennius, a noble opposed to Valus, brought a council of five nobles and five merchants together to build a fail-safe against tyrant rule." Neri emphasized his points with flowery gestures. "To collect information about royal workings, influence the court strategically, and leverage collective economic power to negotiate with nobility and work political intrigue. But nobles are hard to trust, and they leaked the names of two merchant members in the council. To send a warning, Valus had them killed for sedition. Whoever did leak the information was not bold enough to reveal the others' identities, so the remaining members knew they had to build a tighter system. Soon enough they had routed out the traitors—who, by no surprise, were nobles. The council was changed to five nobles and fifteen merchants. Small wonder the merchants were more motivated to overthrow Valus. Establishing a new society based on the rule of trade and commerce was in their interest.

"As the founding members thought of ways to increase their posture and protect the coup, they grew their vision beyond the confines of the upper classes, and determined a school should be born—to increase power through numbers. But who to recruit? Yes—merchants' apprentices, masons, jewelers, craftsmen, artists, soldiers. But also, another type of candidate was needed. A rare candidate. A battered soul burning with desire and equipped with natural skill." Neri's eyes were full of vehemence, chest swelling as he recounted the story.

"They sought candidates across Aontir with pain behind them and a thirst for opportunity ahead—those who would go through the Guild and be taught the finest skills to protect the Guild against tyranny from within and without. Each year, the numbers grew, public opinion swelled, and but ten years later, the plan was hatched, and Valus overthrown. Rightfully put to the sword in his castle by Edoro and his finest apprentices. From that day, the first generation of Setian society you know today was born—Senate rule and a Guild-funded bank to drive commerce. Setia is the only nation like this, and we stand to die by it."

"Thorough," Kage said.

"Thank you, Kage," Neri replied.

Tazio wasn't sure Kage had meant it as a compliment.

"How many members are there?" Zara asked.

"For the purpose of protection, we can't reveal that. Just know we have a hand in every place."

Tazio wondered if that meant the Daemonae, too.

"And what's your role in all this?" Luca prodded.

"I'm the Head of the Guild in Novra. I devise the plan for how the Aurian Guild operates—strategy, politics, and commerce. And of course, I am head of apprentice education."

"That makes us rather valuable, no?" Zara asked.

Tazio loved how she'd surface even the boldest questions.

"Yes, you are fundamental to the Guild's future," Neri replied, then turned to retrieve an intricate wooden case from the shelf behind him.

He placed it on the table.

"Inside this case, something awaits each of you. Something with immense power," Neri cautioned, clicking the latch and swinging the box open. "A gift you could say."

He pushed the box to Luca, whose eyes shimmered with lust.

"We call them *talùthae*—*talùth* in the singular. Take yours out and hold it, but do not put it on."

Luca reached forward to draw out his *talùth*, inspecting it, hooked by its allure. "It's—beautiful," Luca murmured.

"We craft *talùthae* as part of our dynasty," Neri said.

Kage took the box, jumpy with desire in a break from her normal stoniness.

The box made its way slowly around to Tazio, who was last. Six slots were cut into the velvet housing. Names were carved on gold placards below each amulet.

The one with Tazio's name beneath it haunted him. The center of the stone was a swirling blue, deep as the skies above the Aroinn, a door to elsewhere. Flecks of silver, gold, and white drifted like wandering stars in the stone, endless depth and layers, colors appearing and disappearing as if it breathed.

Tazio pulled out the *talùth* and placed it in his palm. It sat snugly in his palm—like it was a missing piece that had come home. Warmth spread into his veins, feeding his soul, the *talùth's* power making the room spiral, his skin-crawling at it pulled at him.

Neri's voice snapped Tazio back.

"You all joined not knowing the extent of what you would discover here, yet you each crossed the threshold," Neri said. "Your *talùth* brings you power from beyond. *Draeda*—an energy captured inside the *talùthae* by an ancient method dating to the *antiquo tempore*."

"What do you mean it's captured?" Alesso asked. His eyes never left the stone, transfixed.

"You'll learn soon enough. Some things must be learned through experience alone."

A knock rapped on the door to the classroom.

"Right on time," Neri said.

"Signore, your attention is needed," said a somber-looking assistant.

"Pietro will collect your *talùthae*. More to come. Off to your next class," Neri said.

He bowed his head and left them, his absence leaving a hole of energy. The others looked drained as glum Pietro collected their amulets. Some even looked agitated, like they'd been deprived of a newfound joy. And while Tazio knew of the power of *draeda* as the Daemonae had taught him, he'd assumed only they knew of this power. It was strange though that none of them wore *talùthae* or mentioned them. The *talùth* felt good—*very good*. If the Setians wielded this power, then Tazio's bet was already paying off, and the Guild was the right place to be—at least to reach Falkone.

Tazio breathed through the pinch in his gut.

There was no clear path to Falkone—only the stark truth that each step must appear by moving toward the mist—and that forward was the only way.

CHAPTER 14

TAZIO'S LEGS strained under the pose he and the others had been holding for an excessive amount of time. They stood atop pillars in an interior garden with one foot pressed to the opposite knee, palms overhead, grunting as they struggled not to topple. The drop was just high enough to make Tazio wary of falling. Tazio stifled a laugh as Alesso swung his arms to stay balanced, Kage stared mercilessly at a single point on the wall, and Zara countered the slightest twitches in her balance. Fiona Corsica, their professor, looked from apprentice to apprentice as she balanced too. A kind but comical smile crossed her face as Luca bobbled and cursed.

"Be like a calm pool," Alesso mimicked something Fiona said earlier in the class and got a few snorts and chuckles.

"Composure," Fiona urged, her thin, flat lips pursed. She had round, ice-blue eyes flecked with white, a small cleft chin, and an airy mysticism that hinted at Daemonae origins. It would make sense given she was teaching a course on *draeda*.

"And stop," Fiona said.

Everyone exhaled in relief, and Luca lost his balance, falling off his pillar. The others laughed as he groped and clawed his way back up the column, cursing the whole way.

"Balance comes from the mind more than the body—it is a state of tranquility," Fiona said, sitting on her own and crossing her legs.

"I'll show her balance," Alesso whispered to Tazio.

"Thank you for that kind comment, Alessandro."

"Fean, you heard that?"

"These exercises develop many attributes, including heightened awareness," Fiona said, wincing at his informality. "The previous exercises were designed to bring balance. Now, we'll begin work with our *talùthae*. When you are ready, please put your *talùth* on beneath your tunic, in contact with your skin."

Fiona passed the same box around that Neri had used and everyone collected their *talùth*. Tazio slipped the necklace over his head, and the linked chain and amulet lay smoothly on his skin. His pulse quickened as it warmed, stirring a storm in his blood.

"Already, you may feel an intense connection to your *talùth*—this is normal. Place your palms up, close your eyes, and begin breathing through the nose. Follow my pattern," said Fiona, leading the class through progressively deeper breathing exercises, bringing Tazio back to his time training with Anya.

It also reminded him he'd neglected his discipline of finding his familiar place. Since being swept up in his exodus from the Aroinn, already the connection to *Etria* felt weaker and harder to access. The lessons Anya and the others insisted on—daily practice, bringing all thoughts into relation to *Etria*, moving from it—the habits demanded attention, but he'd ignored them.

The tenor of the garden deepened as the class focused and Tazio's connection to *Etria* intensified. Colors and threads came into his mind's eye, but he held back, worried the others would sense his more advanced state.

"Good, that's enough for now." Fiona said, bringing Tazio back to the tranquil garden, like the prior minutes had been a dream.

"Can someone share what they experienced?" Fiona said.

"I'm ready for a nap," said Alesso.

"Quite normal," she replied, looking disappointed at his lack of seriousness.

"My *talùth*. It was *hot*—almost alive?" Zara said.

"Yes. Its presence is palpable and *draeda* is a living force."

"A point. Pushing and pulling where it rested on my chest," Corso said.

"Yes, this point is called the *anima pontem*—the soul bridge where your energy body connects to the *talùth*. Inside the *talùth*, there is *draeda*. For now, the *draeda* stored inside is moderate in power, and has been stored by an *artifex*, our highest master craftsmen. The breathing exercises we just used help us to center our mind so we can feel the innate connection to the *talùth*.

"What is *draeda* made of?" Corso continued.

"*Draeda* is intangible to the eye, but tangible to other senses—here," she said, pointing to her forehead, her heart, and then moving her hands around her. "It moves about all things and is concentrated in a being's soul. For thousands of years, *artifexae* have known how to capture *draeda* to be repurposed by practitioners, allowing them to increase strength, focus, and also to use the qualities of animal spirits. But there are downsides. It is taxing, and dependency-inducing. Each use requires more *draeda* than the use before to achieve the same potency."

"Ahh, well I've kicked *opia* before, shouldn't be an issue," Luca joked.

"This is *not* a joke, Luca," Fiona chided, and Luca's face turned white. "The *talùth* is a bridge to power. But it can also take you somewhere you may not return from."

Fiona's words hung over the class like a brewing storm.

Then their beliefs are different from the Daemonae's—like another branch of the practice. Perhaps Fiona isn't Daemonae after all. But why did Aeon and Anya never mention this darker aspect?

"How is it refilled?" Zara asked.

"A lesson for another time. For now, *artifexae* will refill them as needed. Just come to me or Neri as needed. This will also help us introduce *draeda* slowly, and know if there is a dependency developing."

"Is there another way to use *draeda* than with a *talùth*?" Tazio asked.

"Another way?" Fiona replied.

"Yes, another way to access *draeda*."

"The *talùth* is the way," she searched him with her gaze.

He couldn't tell if she knew what he was truly asking, but Tazio wanted to know what the Guild knew about the Daemonae.

"But is it the only way?" Tazio pressed as innocuously as possible.

"This is the only way we practice."

With that, she turned away, her vagueness unsettling.

"Let us proceed with bonding you to your *talùth*," Fiona said. "If your mind is not clear, it will be harder to find this connection and use the *draeda* inside. Today, you will bond for the first time to your *talùth*. Over the next semester, you will become experts. The response to the first bond is usually rigorous, but know that whatever you experience is what you are supposed to experience. It is written into the fabric of *Etria*."

Her speech didn't seem to ease the tension in the room.

"Please, enter your breath. As you feel the tug from your *talùth* connecting to your chest, we will use a priming incantation to expand the connection and cross the bridge into *Etria*. When this happens, you will feel an energy from within you pour into the *talùth* and vice versa, like an exchange. Do not fight it."

Tazio closed his eyes. Everyone breathed into the exercise, the energy intensifying as the room swirled with the ethereal wind of *Etria* he'd felt move his soul so many times before.

"Repeat the following phrase. Allow the words to pass from the place above your eyes, through your heart, and into the *anima pontem*: *Corde aperto. Animum aperiam. Mens aperta. Utraque via draeda fluat per pontem animae.*"

As Tazio finished the words, the floor fell out. His vision flipped into a realm of colors like the cosmic backdrop of the stone. The class was gone, and a wave of sorrow and isolation rushed over him just before energy shot through his chest from the *talùth*, and, from a knot in his chest, a gnarled oak sprang, the tree splitting in two. He screamed as the growth tore his chest open and writhed into a million branches to infinity.

"Choose wisely," a voice whispered from all around—*his* voice, but *not* his voice.

His eyes throbbed, breath quickened, chest stretching like he'd be torn to pieces until his energy burst down the path of one tree, immeasurably fast, until he jarred to a stop in an inky realm of grays and blacks.

The floor was wet, thick black muck sliding around his ankles. Ahead, a shadow rose from the horizon, growing until it swallowed the gray sky and came down like a wave over him. Tazio turned and ran, stumbling through the liquid, spitting out its indiscernible bitter taste. He wanted to cry, to die, unable to turn and face it, the whole realm oozing *threat*. The sheer feeling of it, the weight of it in every pore as he fought to stand and run again. A mist curled over his shoulders, wrapped beneath his armpits, threatening to strangle him.

You can't escape.

The muck around his legs grew into sludge, every step like lead.

He breathed, but could not inhale.

"Face it," a voice boomed, shaking him with urgency to turn and face the immeasurable darkness.

Drawing from the courage in his heart, he strained to turn his head around and face what pursued him. Sensing his defiance, the mist hissed away, revealing someone in the damp darkness. Someone Tazio recognized—in the same brutal armor he wore when he'd lanced Aeon from his horse at the battle of Coille Solais. Falkone. Bigger and bigger with each step he took, he grew. Or perhaps Tazio shrank smaller and smaller until he was a crumb that Falkone pinched between his fingers and plunged into his mouth. Ugly teeth and the breath of murder pouring over Tazio as he fell into his jaws, arms flailing, digested by the abyss. Falling without end for what felt like days, he finally jerked to stop, his spine nearly breaking. Then, like a drowning man yanked from a river, a vast force tore him free and threw him down the other path of the tree.

He flew a thousand leagues away in an instant, ethereal blur stretching his organs to near implosion until he slammed into a field of wheat. Somehow painless, he stood, and saw Falkone. Standing in the plains of Bourgogne, a fire blazed thousands of feet high, consuming the horizon as malevolent laughs poured out of Falkone. Tazio shielded his face against the heatwave, sweat pouring out as his skin cooked.

"You'll die!" Tazio screamed.

The vision snapped to the size of a marble, heat vanishing—but Falkone remained, towering over Tazio. Then, from the marble, the Mora Mountains drove to the sky between Tazio and Falkone, relief pouring through Tazio as the wall they'd created. But as fast as they'd risen, Falkone shattered them, shouldering the range over. Tazio stepped back as great sheets of ice and rock crumbled, and Falkone razed the mountains.

The vision snapped to a marble and exploded again—the monster

Falkone was gone, but millions stood around Tazio, all bowing on their hands and knees.

"What are you doing?" Tazio shouted, people looking at him as if he were insane. Then he saw the massive force of the Thoracian army. Tazio's heart pounded in shame as he watched in horror. He wanted to become less than nothing, to implode and tear himself apart for doing whatever he did, but felt he had to do.

A sword appeared in his hands.

And he watched himself, from above himself, drive it through his stomach to pierce the core of his guilt, death the point. But death did not work, and he was shot back to the realm where the oak gnarled out of his chest. Excruciating pain gripped his chest again, the axis of his life balancing on these two branches of his future.

Choose.

The voice was insistent.

Choose.

The voice was a breath.

You want this power. You need it. Your parents slaughtered, your people defiled. Your honor defiled by Falkone. Take the gift. Confront Falkone. Kill him!

His muscles felt like they would tear from the tension ripping through him. He closed his eyes, attempting to hide from the decision in this dream realm. Behind closed eyes, he saw Daemonae children screaming under Thoracian blades; Aeon surging through the sea of men again; Falkone's spear lancing Aeon to desolation; deathly ash pluming out the canopy of the Aroinn. He saw the beaten caravan of Daemonae drifting out of Coille Solais, blood caking their reins, and Anya disappearing out of the glade.

Tazio groaned in pain, eyes wide as he stared at the tree tearing out of him. The branches croaked and the backdrop of the starry realm shimmered in response, colors flaring with each flicker of pain. Both paths felt rife with confusion and darkness, the future squeezing its threats onto the present.

But the pain of deliberation became too much, and Tazio threw his whole being down the path that led to the gray and black realm, knowing that bending the knee was worse than the indescribable darkness he felt in that gray realm. *Draeda* tore through him at the instant of his conscious choice. Springing from the floating flecks around him, the sphere turned to fury, consuming the branch on the right, the remaining branch shooting back into his chest, its endless roots pressing into every tissue until he felt he'd burst in a dazzling firestorm of energy. His back arched, eyes rolled back, arms splayed as the sphere of visions snapped closed, and Tazio saw he was back in the pillared garden with the others. Tazio gasped for breath, looking around wildly, and saw Zara's eyes snap open across from him. Alesso, Corso, and Luca, too. All their eyes were black, color only remaining in small streaks. Luca vomited wildly on the floor.

"What the fuck was that?" Luca coughed out.

"I don't know," Alesso said, catching his breath. "Fean."

"My eyes. Are they black too?" Tazio asked.

"Yes," Alesso replied.

Corso stood up and walked toward Fiona, who hovered above Kage, whose body shook like a broken bird.

"What's going on here?" Tazio asked.

"Dunno," Corso grunted.

Dark rambles, cruel laughs, and horrific cries shook out of her, until her limbs slammed to the floor. Her eyes snapped open, and one clear phrase came out. "A shadow rises. Unstoppable. *Unquenchable.*"

Fiona's head cocked, dismay settling in beneath her brow. Sensing Tazio's gaze on her, she looked at him, then to the door. A knot twisted in Tazio's stomach.

"What the fean does that mean?" Alesso asked as Kage began to thrash again, raking her nails against the stones.

"Luca! Get a healer, now! Hold her flat!" Fiona shouted. "The rest of you, help me hold her down!"

"What *malae* is this?" Luca asked, barely able to pull his eyes away as he stumbled off.

Tazio rushed over to help Fiona and Corso pin Kage down as she bucked and thrashed, black eyes flickering.

"What do we do?" Zara asked, stricken.

"Just hold her!" Fiona demanded, raising her hand to the sky. "*Surge, surge, redi ad pontem. Nunc!*" she shouted, then drove her palm into Kage's chest.

Dark liquid spewed out of Kage as she coughed and writhed, then fell limp. Fiona pushed in and rolled Kage onto her side. When the dark shroud faded from Kage's eyes, her gaze was haunted. Empty.

Luca burst into the room with a Guild healer.

"Class is dismissed. *Dismissed*, I said!" Fiona shouted, shocking them out of their stare. Even Corso was cracked out of his icy shell. Tazio stripped his eyes away along with the others, trying to put it out of mind.

"*Khara*, what just happened?" Zara asked as she, Alesso, and Tazio made their way into the rush of the hallways. They walked quietly for a while until Tazio broke the silence.

"Did you two go to another... realm?" Tazio asked.

"If that's what you would call it," Zara replied.

"Yes," Alesso nodded in confirmation.

From the stupefied look on their faces, Tazio got the sense they didn't know how to process what they'd experienced either. The sinking feeling he'd been given two paths that both felt horrific ran through him again.

"I wonder what Kage saw," Zara said.

"Dipped a little too far into the *draeda* bucket. She'll be fine," Alesso said, trying to lighten the mood.

"I was definitely in some kind of realm like you said, Tazio," said Zara.

"Well, if the classes continue at this rate, I'm not sure we'll make it through the day," Alesso said.

"And we're set to learn combat later?" Zara asked.

"Fean, I thought balancing on the pillars was hard enough," Alesso said. "We'll probably be dead before I can put you two to the sword."

"Don't know if I can even hold a sword right now," Tazio said, looking at his shaking hands.

"Scared, are you?" Alesso patted him and Tazio could feel the shakiness in Alesso's arm, too.

"Are you worried?" Zara asked, looking at Tazio.

Tazio's father's words echoed through his mind. *There isn't room for worry, son. Once you push over the edge, you have to let go. It's the only option. Otherwise you'll miss your landing, and then you'll really be worried!* The sea breeze brushed against Tazio's face, as he peered down at the landing sheet, the gaping distance making him wish he'd never chosen to be a vaulter. Everything around the landing sheet tunneled, a stray wind blew hard, and Tazio teetered between fear and courage.

"My father once told me there's no room for worry once you've jumped in," Tazio said to Zara. "Our only option is to go forward."

Zara nodded, the tension in her eyes softening. Tazio hoped he'd provided her some comfort—because his words, while true, did little to relieve the doom churning like a tide beneath his courage. Sorrow gripped Tazio. His father's whispers of encouragement were ghosts of the past now.

They walked the halls, footsteps clicking on cold marble. They'd leapt into a void, and Tazio could feel them falling, limbs flailing in darkness. But this time, he couldn't see the landing sheet below—he could only hope there was one to catch them.

CHAPTER 15

TAZIO STOOD with the rest of the apprentices in a sparring arena at the center of the Guild. It sat on the ground level, with five stories of hallways and windows looking over it, and was about one hundred by fifty paces—cavernous compared to the other courtyards Tazio had seen. Sculpted warriors lined the perimeter, vines crawling the walls around them while they witnessed centuries of *apprentici* in training. They bore all manner of weapons, perhaps a taste of what was to come. Dummies, beaten and scarred by endless blows. Targets, chewed by endless arrows. Movable blocks and platforms with chipped edges from being rearranged.

The entire group seemed a bit beside themselves at lunch. Corso, Kage, and Luca seemed bent on pretending they were unfazed, but Tazio could tell the bonding experience had made them on edge, too. Dark bags under the eyes were hard to hide.

This class was with Leone, the charming groundskeeper Tazio met the previous day while entering the Guild with Neri, and Leone had just finished running them through their warm-up. The soft red clay beneath Tazio's feet gave perfectly, sending pleasure through the pads of his feet, inviting him to spring.

"For the next game, your feet must remain planted. The objective is to force your partner off-balance," Leone said, giving Alesso a playful shove.

Alesso tried shoving him back, but Leone used his weight against him and kicked him over into the clay.

"Exactly how I drew it up," Alesso said from the dirt, most of the class chuckling as Leone helped him up.

"Now—let's begin," Leone said.

Grooves in the clay from previous spars shaped the edges of fighting rings. They paired off—trying force, using the foe's momentum, pulling back at the right moment—all probably having played some version of the game as a child. As Tazio and Alesso tussled, they busted into laughter as they punched and pushed.

"Shut up, Alesso," Tazio hissed, trying not to be caught, but thoroughly enjoying himself.

"This may seem like a joke," Leone snapped, "but from what I can tell from the way you're moving, you two may be the jokes."

"So serious," Alesso whispered.

Leone whirled around and slid up to Alesso's ear, hovering so close Alesso surely felt his breath.

"What was that?" Leone asked, seriousness and jest wrinkling the corners of his eyes.

"Just having some fun here," Alesso replied, looking astonished that Leone could get to him so quickly. Leone swiped his legs out from under him, sending him to the floor again.

"Excellent work! For a bunch of idiots!"

"Bloody fean!" Alesso groaned from the floor.

"The objective of the next game is to slap the shoulder of your foe without being struck in return," Leone said. "First to three strikes wins. Tazio. Corso. You two face off. Everyone else, circle around."

As the circle closed, Tazio felt his blood begin to rise. Corso stared back with frigid calculation in his deep-blue eyes.

"Touch shoulders to start," Leone said as they faced off.

Corso wrenched Tazio's shoulders, glaring needles, chest swelling like a bull. He was a few inches shorter, but his muscles felt like knotted rope as Tazio gripped back. Overpowering him with strength wouldn't be easy.

Leone dropped his hand. "Begin!"

Corso shoved Tazio hard and went straight up the center at Tazio with a punch toward his right shoulder. Stepping back, Tazio parried the blow and Corso stumbled forward off-balance. As he fell, Corso lunged for Tazio, wrapping him around the neck and bringing him to the clay.

"Stay on your feet!" Leone shouted, breaking them up.

"You're lucky he's here," Corso growled in Tazio's ear before Leone yanked him off.

"I thought that was just a friendly hug," Tazio said, playing off the immense pain and dizziness making the arena spin.

When he finally rebalanced himself, Corso curled his lip into an ugly snarl. His frame radiated a coarse confidence, like he'd seen the pain of some dungeon. Tazio circled, testing Corso gingerly as they started again. Corso dove in with a big hook, and Tazio ducked it, counter-striking toward his shoulder. But Corso blocked it away. As Tazio shifted to prepare for his next move, a searing elbow split across his temple, sending him backwards.

"Done dancing like a girl?" Corso taunted.

Tazio sprang from the ground and put himself inches from Corso's face, vision red. "Done cheating?"

A cruel satisfaction wrapped Corso's face as Leone spread them apart.

"Play for points, *per favore.*"

Luca snickered and Tazio wanted to put a fist in his teeth too.

"I'd be happy to show you how to lose to a girl," Zara added as they circled again.

Tazio heard Alesso chuckle, but any trace of jest had left him. After they touched shoulders and pulled away, Tazio shrugged his shoulders, pretending to loosen up, then bolted forward, cutting left, then right, to find an opening to Corso's right shoulder. He lunged forward, eyes locked onto the exposed shoulder, and just before his strike found purchase, Corso's fist slammed into his cheek, pain exploding as his head snapped sideways and the world tilted sideways. Corso pounced, his forearm crushing Tazio's throat. Tazio grunted, panic flaring as Corso drove his fist into his shoulder and won the duel. Even after the point was scored, Corso pressed his forearm harder into Tazio's throat.

"Enough!" Leone shouted.

Tazio's vision opened up as Corso let off, and he twisted Corso's wrist until he wailed. Tazio drew back, ready to strike Corso's nose, but Leone stunned Tazio from behind, then locked him in a hold.

"Let me go!" Tazio demanded.

"Calm down," Leone whispered.

"I'll calm down when the game is fair!"

"Fair?"

"Are you blind? He cheated!"

"He won, Tazio."

Leone released him and took a step away. Corso snickered at the outburst, and Tazio loathed that he'd lost his head—giving them the pleasure of seeing him upset.

"Did I say any of that broke the rules?" Leone asked. Tazio held his tongue. "Did I?"

"No!" Tazio boomed, sucking the air from the room.

"Then all of you take this as a lesson. You're training for combat, and combat is not fair. It's not like tales you've been told about honor, chivalry, and all the petty rules of engagement," he said, waving his arms dramatically. "E *cazzo*—it's shit! Do what you have to. The rules always bend in favor of the snake."

Delight subtly pricked its way across Corso's face.

Tazio's fists tightened, nails digging into his palms as the bitter sting of failure ate at him. He hated losing—but he hated the idea of bending his principles to Corso's level even more. *If I'd known the rules could be bent, I'd've twisted him into a knot. But that would only make me the same as him.* Violent urges screamed in his veins, demanding release, impelling him to break Corso's smug face into bone and pulp. But a faint whisper of restraint tugged at him, cooling his heart as his veins threatened to explode.

Do not stoop down. Victory will come another way.

Tazio exhaled, deep and low, knuckles white as he pressed his nails into his palms. Bloodlust would only hurt his ambitions. That's what Corso wanted—to muddy his reputation early in the game.

"Corso, you're on latrine duty for the next week," Leone said, "You may have won this game, but your hands deserve to be as dirty as they just were."

Corso blinked like a stupid cow in response, as if he knew a punishment was coming, but was happy nevertheless.

"That's it for today," Leone said.

Tazio made for the hall.

"Tazio, wait!" Zara shouted from behind as he entered the hallway.

Tazio quickened his pace, wanting to be alone, ducking between passersby. But Zara grabbed his shoulder.

"Please, come with me," she said, bringing him into a quieter corridor. "Are you okay?"

"I'm fine, Zara."

"You don't seem fine."

Tazio realized his chest was still heaving, his eyes wide with fury.

"It's just a game. And we all know Corso was underhanded."

"It's not just a game, Zara," Tazio snapped. "I'm sorry."

"He's under your skin. If you give that to him, he's really won."

"He has an arrow pointed at my back, and I won't tolerate the disrespect. We both know the Guild is measuring us. Considering us for advancement."

"Well, what are you going to do?"

"Something."

"You're scaring me, Tazio."

"Well, you don't know me too well. Maybe it's better to be scared of me. Maybe I'm not who you think I am."

"We all have our shadows, Tazio. But I won't be fooled by yours."

Zara's amber eyes softened with concern, glowing against the rush of the hallway. For a moment, her golden gaze pulled him in, soothing his fury. Tazio watched as she gently placed her hand on his arm. It was kind and fair—and then jarring. As fast as it had come, the warmth fled, touching the hollow in Tazio's heart where the memory of Anya lived. The place that had once been full with hope, but now ached as he saw her walking out of the glade like a phantom. Already, Anya felt unreachable—like a vague song carried away by the wind. Guilt spiked in his heart that he could think of replacing her, and he felt his heart grip shut, the blood drain from his stomach.

"I have to go," Tazio forced out.

"Wait."

Unable to bear the concern on her face, stricken that he didn't know how to explain himself to Zara, but not knowing how to sort his feelings, he stumbled backwards, merging into the main hallway.

Flames blazed above the Aroinn. Aeon fell. Tears rolled down Anya's cheek. The walls began to close. Breath gripping as he pushed his way through the crowd. Seeking a door to the outer world, wanting to scream, to flail, to run forever as he fought to stay together. His vision narrowed, darkness pushing in until he burst through the front door and fell down the front stairs, ignoring the murmurs around him and scrambling to the front gate. More than ever, the statues in the courtyard bore down like ghouls staring at every hidden horror he held inside. His vision tunneled on the gate, ears ringing as tears pushed up. He burst through the gate, spilling into the dizzying streets of lower Auria, running from his pain with each stride.

→

The sun glinted off the morning waves and through the masts of bobbing brigs.

"What am I doing here?" Tazio muttered as a few gulls flew overhead.

The alleys of lower Auria had swallowed him in a blur, seedy sailors and goons burning their souls' waning oil in dark alleys. Vice tempted his spinning mind with escape, and now his soul was drained, his whole body heavy under the weight of empty pleasure.

Just ahead, some sailors unloaded crates from a brig, finding their land legs as they disembarked. Tazio wondered if they'd take him—if he decided to leave the Guild and disappear. His heart beat faster at the idea. *Relief.* Why could he not be like these sailors? Simple and decided. Sail, load, unload. Pillage, drink grog, sleep with women, and move on until death found them. Tazio stood up off the wall and walked toward the sailors unloading crates.

"Pardon me?" he asked the closest man.

"*Seh?*" the gruff, frail man replied. Most of his teeth were missing, his skin like sun-beaten leather. Tazio didn't realize how malnourished he was until he stood before him.

"Is there room for another in the crew?" Tazio asked.

The waves lapped on the docks in the silence, and the man stared back at him long and hard—exhausted, rugged, ready to die.

"You'd be a damned idiot to come aboard," the man said.

"I'm ready to leave this place."

The man rested against a crate, relaxing into what looked like a rare respite.

"Whatever you're running from—it'll find you—stare at you in the patterns on the gangplanks, groan through the creaks in the ropes. Better to face it. Or you'll end up running like us lot. Go back to your life, and don't be a damned ungrateful fool."

Genuine concern shone through the man's rugged outer mask. Tazio's chest knotted up as the man turned on creaky bones, hobbling up the plank with a crate underarm. A stranger's words moved his heart like no familiar man's could. To think that one soul's path would be less burdensome than another's—that one could escape his fate. Tazio's face burned with shame.

What about all the people who died before you? All those you loved? This is not for you alone. But for them.

"Thank you, amico," Tazio said to the sailor, who could not hear him, but did happen to look over one last time before Tazio turned away.

That dreamy veil that comes from a night of sleeplessness accompanied him on his way back to the Guild. The solace of dawn lingered as his footsteps clicked on the cold marble floors along with a few others mulling about under the ever-tended lanterns of the Guild hallways, runners in brown changing shifts to ensure they never went out.

As he wandered through an arched courtyard of exotic plants toward the combat hall, a black cat with white on its chest, nose, and paws watched him. Its ears were long and pointed, with a curled flourish at the tips. It was bigger than any cat he'd seen, truly a specimen. Cats had always got on with him, so he clicked his tongue. The cat flicked its head around, approaching with an air of confidence, a white hourglass on its nose like a mystical mark. It trotted up and rubbed his leg, its purr an unexpected, soothing gift.

"You're a good one, aren't you?" Tazio asked as the cat rolled onto its back for a belly rub. "Sure you weren't a pup in another life?"

The cat looked up as if it understood, and was offended he'd suggest something so demeaning.

Tazio chuckled. "Please, forgive the insult."

The cat sat up, eyeing someone who clicked by in the courtyard.

"You're a survivor, aren't you? Big, proud, sharp. Wouldn't make a bad partner in a fight."

The cat stood up and brushed Tazio, offering a slow blink over the shoulder.

"And you love a compliment. Okay, we'll keep that one on the table for now. But I can tell you're tempted. I've got to go for now, but I'll see you around." Tazio gave it a friendly last pat on the back, and the big cat let out a chortle. "Rare one, you are."

Tazio left the courtyard for the combat hall. The sky above was cloudy as he opened the door, the air moist and cool. Being alone in the arena reminded him of the same intense energy he felt when he performed vaulting acts. Combat was a stage, too. He had seen the *Coliseo* his first day in Auria, and Alesso told him that each semester, two hundred thousand packed into the *Coliseo* in middle Auria to watch fighters from across Novra compete in the Guild Games. Tazio's blood picked up at the thought of it.

He walked to a flat case set on the wall.

It was locked. The weapons inside glistened at him, the clash of metal sounding in his imagination. Then, he heard the actual sound of someone opening the door to the arena.

"Plotting an insurrection?" Leone asked from the door.

"You'll be the first to know, I promise."

"Wouldn't want to be on the wrong side of your scheme, that's for certain." Tazio chuckled. Leone was hard not to like with all his wit and charm. "You're up earlier than a rooster."

"Needed to clear my mind."

"Very sagelike."

Tazio walked into the center of the arena, taking in the windows and balconies overlooking it.

"Interesting they allow others to watch training," Tazio said.

"Adds to the pressure."

"Like the way you made an example of me?"

"Someone had to be the example. Would you prefer I embarrassed Corso instead?"

"Not a bad question."

"My job is to teach the principles of combat. You served an important lesson—even a skilled fighter has to be prepared for cruel disadvantages. You and Corso are a fine match. But you're prideful, and he couldn't care how he wins."

"How is pride an issue?"

"Did you not hesitate to bend the rules?"

"I suppose."

"You're driven by pride, Tazio—that victory has to mean something. It's noble, but combat doesn't care for nobility. And neither does Corso. Your pride is a double-edged blade. The same fire that fuels your fury can burn you to the ground. You may look down on Corso for his lack of pride—but his cold nature gave him the advantage. And when the final blow is dealt, the only principle combat cares for is victory."

Sweat broke out on Tazio's forehead. Leone's eloquence was a living example of the Setian power of persuasion.

"What are you doing here?" Leone asked.

"At the Guild?" asked Tazio.

"No, boy, in this arena at the crack of dawn."

"Do you want my honest answer?"

"I certainly don't want a lie."

"The Guild Games."

"Ah, of course. The Guild Games. The glory all *apprentici* dream of. They're wonderful. And brutal. Two hundred thousand watching the finest fighters in Novra. Big purses, great glory."

"I want to win," Tazio said. Falkone would come later, but for now, a victory would move him up in the Guild.

"Hah! Yes. It's made many an apprentice wild with frenzy."

"Well, that's why I'm here."

"Oh, I know," Leone sat on the edge of a training block.

"Then why'd you ask?"

"It's always nice to test my aptitude for prediction."

"I'm ready to do what it takes."

"And what do you think that is?"

"Training."

"And why should I train you, and give you an advantage over the others?"

"Train them too. Though I don't see any of them standing here at dawn."

"So you're saying that he who's first to act should have the advantage?"

"It seemed that way in class yesterday."

"You learn quickly. At least in a verbal duel."

Leone walked to the weapon case and drew out two wooden swords.

"My job is to show you all your weaknesses so you're less easily exploited. Attack me. Land a blow on my torso." Leone tossed a training sword to Tazio.

Tazio hesitated, thinking of the best approach.

"Attack me!" Leone demanded.

Tazio lunged in, hacking diagonally, and Leone parried him off balance. Tazio attacked again with fast thrusts, and Leone smashed the sword out of Tazio's hand with a few firm counters.

"You're going to need some work," Leone said.

Tazio picked his sword up from the dirt and circled.

Leone wasn't imposing. In fact, he was rather small. But his prediction, fluid movements, and speed were vicious.

Leone dashed forward, his blade a blur, clipping Tazio. Tazio flipped sideways, avoiding all but a nick to the cloak.

"Wow, Neri wasn't kidding about the advantages of being Danui-in," Leone said. "Then you were a vaulter?"

"I was."

"That's something we can use."

Leone lunged again, loosing a barrage. Tazio desperately evaded, handspringing out of the way, then rolling. But Leone pinned him against the wall, his sword point pressed to the hollow beneath Tazio's collarbone.

"Good," Leone said, lowering his sword.

"Not exactly how I'd describe it," Tazio replied, pulling a mirthful chuckle out of Leone.

"Your tendency is to rely on counter-attacking and anticipation. For most others, I'd correct this in the opposite direction as it is almost always to the fighter's advantage to go on the offensive."

"I should just learn offense then."

"Leave the instruction to me. You have a keen ability to manage an attack under pressure. Right now, stronger opponents who know the proper combinations will crush you. But if trained, you can surprise them with evasion and counter-attacking. Of course we will train your offense in the normal school of thought. But we'll also develop your instincts. When we blend the two, you'll have a shrewd style. You can provoke opponents, drawing them into an attack that serves you, rather than just being offensive, or just being reactive."

"Is that it?"

"Hah!"

"And will we learn to use the *talùth* in combat?"

"In time. But fundamentally, I don't teach reliance on it unless for extreme occasions. It's like a strong horse. It can break you if you're not well-versed in how to manage it."

"Can I ask you something?"

"Go on."

"When you bonded with your *talùth*—did you see things?"

"I did." The serious, far-off look on Leone's face gave even more indication than his words.

"When we bonded, Kage had a fit of some kind," Tazio said. "Like she was possessed."

"Fiona informed me. It's not uncommon for darkness inside us to attract darkness. We have to confront our putrid threads. Sometimes we're beset with fearful odds."

"Is that why you avoid the *talùth?*"

Leone grazed his goatee.

"After many trials, I've found it best used sparingly. I've seen many a man twisted by what they thought they could control. Many embrace the... grayer shades of life."

Leone's gaze grew distant, like he was watching the faces of friends who had been swallowed by the pull.

"What a ringing endorsement."

"Don't be too concerned. We all must learn balance. Just know that it promises much, but brings a heaviness I choose to avoid by using my other faculties." Leone twirled his sword around by the hilt in a smooth, repeating pattern. "Like the old-fashioned blade."

"Sensible enough," Tazio said. "Blade me, bleed me, teach me the ways."

"You're even stranger than I am."

"I was raised under canvas and torchlight. Can't blame me."

Leone dashed forward like lightning, a grin slapped on his face. Tazio couldn't help himself from smiling as their swords clashed, sending an echo through the arena. Leone's grin widened as they stood locked. The energy in Tazio's chest lightened. The fight had begun— and Leone was the teacher he needed.

CHAPTER 16

ZARA

An elderly library clerk with soft, gray eyes stood before Zara as she walked up to the stone semicircular front desk. His wiry silver hair tried to make up for a large bald spot.

"Ciao, signore, I'm looking for a book on trade routes and policies in the southeastern kingdoms—as contemporary as possible please," Zara said.

The clerk raised a brow.

Not a good start.

"I'm sorry *ragazza*, we haven't been introduced," he replied.

"I'm Zara."

"A pleasure, Zara. I'm Nicolai. Now, what makes you interested in such a specific topic? Usually first-year apprentices enjoy art, merchandise, history, war—the more enticing reads."

"I've always had a keen interest in political economy. My parents were merchants."

Nicolai seemed to realize she truly *did* want books on such a dry subject. "Indeed, not a common request, but good to see not all apprentices have such shallow taste. Come with me."

Nicolai led Zara through the library, his slippers tapping on the marble floor. They moved past thousands of books on mahogany shelves, most bound in rich leather and metallic leafed writing, awaiting admirers, most destined to sit untouched. Zara was aglow at the trove of information in the Setian Archives, and she made a note to return and dive into a book on the origins of *draeda*, or perhaps the evolution of Setian power and their journey to the new world.

"Don't take too strong an interest in political economy," her mother's voice echoed. *"It could alienate suitors and position your future incorrectly."*

But even her parents fell victim to the charms of her voracious curiosity. Soon, after returning from long journeys, they would relish watching her devour volumes they'd acquired. They weren't powerful merchants, just humble operators in the Setian trade network traveling across Novra—mostly in the Katarian south.

Until they weren't. Cut down during a routine trade like jots on a death ledger. Killed in transit in between Bourgogne and Kataria with no known witnesses, all goods stolen, carriages torched. The only way they identified her parents was from the engraved merchant emblem on their carriages. She wondered what their last words were, or if they were together in the cart when they were cut down like animals. She cut her imagination short as it grew more disturbing, answers she knew she'd never fully find tormenting her.

Thirty-seven days she'd waited in their dune village of Kathib. When she finally received news from an errant traveler, she thanked him, closed the plank door, and sunk into isolation for three days. The ghosts of her parents spoke from the countless trinkets and objects scattered about their home. Unable to tend to a fire, the cold desert lingered with deathly chill inside the thick, mud-plaster walls.

Zara never found the strength to return once she'd walked out. Sometimes she spent a night or two with friends or family, but never found a sense of belonging. Unable to bear the feeling of being a burden on others, she took to the streets, the weight of the world grinding her into a petty criminal. Her bright curiosity dimmed until friends and family became like the lifeless things gathering dust in her old home.

But she got what she secretly wanted. One by one, her distance and dirtiness created the aloneness she believed she craved. Free to drift and stare out at the world like it was a story outside she could remove herself from. Until Neri found her scamming with a sleight of hand gambling scheme. When he dismantled every one of her deceptions, that got her attention.

She realized, lost in thought, that Nicolai was saying something. "Sorry, Nicolai—come again?" She asked, realizing her breath had grown tight.

"This volume. It should cover trade routes," Nicolai said, bowing his head slightly and continuing along after handing her the book.

Zara admired his humble devotion—he seemed to get true pleasure from scouring the shelves.

"And a volume on domestic trade."

"Thank you, Nicolai."

"Will you be able to find your way back?" Nicolai asked, a stroke of concern in his voice.

"Yes, thank you."

I really must focus, Zara thought, worried she'd shown her scars so easily as Nicolai bowed and shuffled away.

Zara held the book like a delicate gift and scurried to an alcove with a window looking over an interior garden. She thumbed through until she found a detailed map of southeastern Novra. Her excitement faltered as her eyes found the plains on the map where her parents had been murdered—a vast, blank space too unimportant to get more than a trade route marking. Enraged, she focused herself back on investigating what she could control, three unbroken hours melting by as she searched for details. Frustration mounted as the information she found described trade routes, but left motivations obvious and surface level. The elementary nature of the books was maddening.

I need to know who did this and why they destroyed the caravan, not why wheat travels from the southern kingdoms to the north in exchange for wool. Even an idiot can figure that out.

She went to find Nicolai at the front reception.

"Nicolai?" Zara called out lightly as she approached the empty desk.

"Momento," Nicolai replied, his voice coming from the side passage behind the desk.

She craned her head to glimpse into the back area. Nicolai closed the iron gate and she nearly came out of her boots.

"Yes, Zara?" Nicolai asked.

"I was hoping to find a volume—" she said, fighting to steady her voice, "with deeper analysis of trade motivations, military implications, and supply ledgers."

148

"I'm afraid our deeper studies on motivational trade economics are restricted to approved researchers."

"And how does one get approval?" Zara asked, putting on an air of innocence.

"I would need approval from your headmaster," Nicolai replied, too principled to crack from her charms.

"Neri, you mean?"

"Yes, Neri."

"Sensible enough. I'll wait until later to dive into that." Zara backed off the desk with a smile, trying not to look disappointed.

Khara. I need answers today. Not in two years after some process of approvals.

She walked back to her alcove to collect her satchel and books.

On the way toward the exit, she hid behind a bookshelf, peering through a small gap in the books to get a better view of the area where Nicolai had emerged. A prestigious-looking Guild member emerged from the back, and he and Nicolai exchanged muted mumbles behind their palms. Eventually Nicolai drew a key from his brown cloak and went to the back area again.

"Hello, little key," Zara whispered to herself as she slid out of the stacks.

Mission failed, she walked at the fastest inconspicuous pace, mulling over how to gain access to the locked area. She toyed with her hair as she envisioned what secrets lay concealed behind that gate. Surely the answers lay within. They practically whispered through the bars like a phantom luring her to closure. The threat that even answers to their deaths wouldn't solve her pain stung her. Their faces had decayed to vague outlines, their voices distant echoes, the hanging mystery of it all leaving her dangling in an endless, murky abyss. She turned the corner into the hallway leading to their dorm and collided with someone. "Oh! *Mi scusi!*"

"Zara?" Tazio said, stepping back. "You look like you've seen death's doorway."

"Oh, I was just deep in some studies. Touchy topics." The excuse sounded lame the second she muttered it. "Why are you covered in sweat?"

She wanted to be disgusted, but the truth was he was a pleasant distraction—blue eyes shining against his flushed face. His dirty-blonde hair was messy, gaze sharp and cunning—yet with a buried softness.

"Is a man not free to sweat?"

"I suppose so. A man's also free to tell me why he's sweaty..."

"Oh, nothing special," he said, tilting his brow playfully. "Just combat training."

"Is there a war I'm not aware of?" Zara asked.

"A few are brewing."

"Well, let me know when the conscription starts."

"You're the first on my list."

"I'm honored, truly."

"The true question is why you're sweating this early in the morning?"

"What?" Zara moved her hand to her forehead, realizing she was, in fact, perspiring. "Just a brisk walk. What are you *actually* training for?"

"No, no, no. Don't change the subject. If you tell me why you're up this early, I'll tell you why I am." Tazio's eyes narrowed.

Is he flirting?

"You go first, and maybe you'll be lucky enough to find out," Zara shot back.

"Stiff bargain."

"Daughter of merchants—it has its benefits."

"I was training with Leone—for the Guild Games."

"Hm, wasn't privy that he gave private instruction."

"Had to wrestle him a bit, but he finally took my poor soul under his wing. Did say he'd accommodate others to keep it fair—you look like you could use some help with your coordination."

"Oh, *khara*. You were just as clumsy."

"Or maybe you've been following me and planned to run into me."

"You wish."

"Maybe I do."

"So are you going to be fair and teach me what Leone teaches you?"

"It all depends how obedient a pupil you are." A flush ran through Zara. "And what were you doing slithering around the halls so early?"

"Nothing particular. Just preparing for all those wars like you."

"Don't play coy. I gave my secrets up—now it's your turn."

Tazio's gaze swallowed Zara like the eye of a storm. The longer she looked, the more she swirled naked before him.

"Secrets are secrets for a reason."

"Sometimes secrets burn less when they're aired."

"Sometimes."

"I was mostly prodding for the fun of it."

Tazio looked ready to leave, and it made Zara flinch toward him.

"Not here," she said, watching the first walls of her heart crumble.

Zara grabbed Tazio's arm and led him to a small reading room, his arm radiating heat beneath her hand. She plopped into a plush maroon chair near the fireplace, heart fluttering as she watched Tazio stoke the logs. Firelight danced in his far-off gaze like it spoke in ever-changing whispers.

"Well, what is it?" Tazio asked, stepping away from the fire. "Now that you've dragged me in here alone for the kill." His face, half-shadowed, stirred Zara.

"I've found something." Zara paused, thinking how much to reveal until the silence grew tight.

"Lose your tongue?"

"I don't know where to start."

He chuckled. "Maybe with what you found?"

"Well, I couldn't sleep."

"I think that's a common theme around here."

"I went to the library. And I discovered there's a restricted section behind the clerk's desk."

"And?" His brow lowered in curiosity.

"I want to get in there."

"Ah, we have a thief on our hands, do we?"

"Not a thief. A borrower," Zara shot back.

"Very gray of you."

"Isn't everything gray?"

"Well—some things are red," Tazio said, voice like bark and smoke.

"And what's red to you?"

A log spit and hissed as Tazio's eyes narrowed.

"Vengeance."

Zara's heart pounded, warning her not to reach too close where vipers may lay in wait. But digging for answers was its own type of venom.

"Vengeance?"

"Justice."

"I see."

But Zara didn't see. She just didn't know how to ask without scaring him. Tazio paused, eyes rounding with sorrow. Zara's heart seized, worrying she'd strangled the moment.

"I don't think you want to know."

"Secrets are secrets," Zara said, echoing back his own words.

"That they are."

Tazio prodded the logs.

"You don't have to say."

"It's all very dark."

Tazio sat, fingers curling around the edge of his armchair, gaze distant again in the flames. He opened his mouth, but froze, and the air grew tight.

"It's okay, Tazio," Zara whispered. "I didn't mean to—"

"No, it's fine—it is."

A glimmer of understanding passed between them when Tazio looked back. Maybe that contact with that pain in her presence was the first step he needed. Zara didn't know for sure. But she did know that she felt safer to tread deeper into her own waters. Something she hadn't felt in a long time.

"What else is red?" Zara asked, breaking the silence creeping through her veins.

"Love."

"Love?"

"Yes. Love."

"I concede. Not all things are gray."

"I'm glad I could please you with my point."

Zara wasn't sure how long they looked at each other as scents of cedar danced between them, but each moment was sweeter than the next.

"I've considered it," Tazio finally said.

"Considered what?"

"Your plan."

"Ah yes, the plan."

Tazio smiled and leaned back, his arms commanding the chair. "Help me understand—you want me to help you break into this library —but I can't know why?"

Zara's chest tightened. "That's right."

"That doesn't seem very conspiratorial."

"I can have Alesso help."

"And you think he'll blindly follow you?"

"I do."

"I thought we had a common understanding."

"You know, maybe you're right. We're diving into waters too dark."

Zara felt bare. She stood and moved toward the door.

"Hold on!" Tazio said. "If you want my help, and you truly can't tell me why, I understand. There are things I'm unable to speak of too."

Darkness stirred between streaks of white and gray in his blue eyes— the kind she wanted to explore, but also the kind that made her neck tighten. Without her admission, she could feel the pieces of her broken past stirring and flowing from her heart to Tazio. Her heart ached, feeling he'd understand the riddles of her past. Maybe not all of it, but some.

She stepped forward and put her hand on his chest, rising to her toes to whisper in his ear, fear screaming that vulnerability would kill her. But Tazio's hand on her back coaxed her, leaving her insides aching to be seen.

"Do you truly want to know?" she whispered.

"Yes, Zara—I do."

CHAPTER 17

TAZIO

Tazio walked through the Guild toward the front entrance. The Guild cat he met earlier trotted beside him like a little panther. Zara, Alesso, and he had debated what to name him and settled on *Mahjul—nameless* in Katarian, Zara's native tongue. Tazio could always tell who not to trust based on how Mahjul kept his distance. But with those he liked, he'd take belly rubs and wrestles and follow along, meowing with his own take on the topic at hand. Given their natural connection, Tazio had practiced *anamea* in secret with Mahjul. Seeing clearly at night and dodging blows with lightning reflexes was brilliant.

Three months had vanished like a summer storm. The skills they'd been learning were intoxicating. Combat, speechcraft, negotiation, thievery, agility, persuasion. One master had even taught them techniques to rapidly assimilate new physical skills through mental exercises. Fifteen extra pounds of muscle from the training and food wasn't something to complain about either. All the others had undergone an equally serious transformation, everyone seemed high on confidence, and their instructors made sure to humble them as often as possible as a result.

And as Tazio suspected, everyone became obsessed with understanding their *talùthae, draeda*, all of it. Despite Leone's warnings, Tazio couldn't help himself from obsessing either, drawing on *draeda* in moments of agility, strength, focus, combat, and even mental persuasion during their exercises. Even Kage tamed whatever she'd encountered early on, and had become brilliant at using her *talùth* to move like a cold shadow.

But Leone was right about the shadow side of it all. Compared to *feantoiil* the Daemonae had taught him, the *talùth* left him even more drained. He found himself constantly having to clear his energy body of murky energy. Each time it required more time, more focus, and he found himself going to the *artifexae* for new reserves like an addict. It made him wonder why their form of *draeda* seemed more polluted.

Tazio moved through the main interchange and opened the giant copper front door, steps echoing off the marble stairs as he smiled at Zara across the courtyard. Their Acquisition Arts exam would soon begin.

"Morning, my Lord," Tazio said, bouncing down the stairs. "How does it feel to be looking at a rich man?"

"You look fine as a noble," Zara said.

"Suppose I'm destined for wealth," Tazio replied, tilting his chin to the sky.

"Look at Alesso."

Alesso plodded awkwardly down the front steps, tugging the waistband of his elaborate, puffy noble's outfit.

"Fean, still figuring out why these merchants like wearing all this shite," said Alesso as he walked up.

"Got some hay in your pants?" said Zara, chuckling.

To execute their exam, they'd been permitted to take from the theater's wardrobe. When Alesso had heard that, he demanded they use the most outrageous outfits possible. No one really put up a fight except Corso, who grunted and urged a more straightforward approach. He was so damned rigid he could be a rock. And the worst part was that his hardness drew Luca and Kage in and cut a line through the class.

And just then, Corso, Luca, and Kage walked out the front door of the main building. Corso's face was pinched and upset, like a boy forced to wear a proper outfit during a celebration when he just wanted to play in the mud.

Tazio and Alesso looked at each other, knowing laughter was on the way before it came bursting out. Even Zara, who normally spared mockery, laughed through a covered hand, trying to maintain some sense of modesty as she looked at how grumpy and out of place Corso and the others looked.

"If you don't shut it, I'll tear this stupid outfit off and fail us all," Luca said, jaw set.

"Sure, I'd love to see that," Alesso said through laughter.

Their laughter took on that rare breed of irrational self-multiplication. They tried stopping, but instead keeled over in laughter, the mere sight of seeing the other laugh provoking more laughter.

"Good morning," said Professor Miani, sliding into the courtyard, eyes flat and empty. "I see Tazio and Alesso are taking the assignment seriously,"

"I'm, we're, we're—" Tazio tried to choke his laughs back.

"We're sorry, Miani," Alesso said.

"Professor Miani," Miani said. "Sometimes I wonder if I've been given ingrates to educate."

"They're just idiots," said Zara. "Please forgive them."

"That's rather obvious," Artu said, finally sucking the wind out of their sails.

Artu Miani was his full name. He had pale, white skin and thin, straight, deep black hair. He hailed from eastern Setia in the old world, and moved silently. Like most at the Guild. At this point it seemed like an unspoken requirement, and it did make sense considering their line of work.

But Artu was on a different level.

In a movement exercise they did one time in a dark room, he'd appear inches from Tazio's face, critiquing him for putting a toe down too loudly. Absurdly impressive to say the least. He also rarely looked anyone in the eye. Most of the time he just walked up on the side of you, like he was taking in a vista as he conversed—even if there was nothing particularly noteworthy in sight. But when he did look at you, it was like there was no soul behind the eyes. Tazio wondered if Artu's yellow eyes helped him see better in the dark, but Artu didn't seem like the kind of guy who would like to be asked about it.

Apparently he'd replaced a professor who, according to him, "retired of necessity." That seemed a little convenient. Maybe Artu just got hungry one day and chopped him up.

"Let's begin, shall we?" Artu said. "As we make our way into town in our groups, please note your approach into the middle quarter. If I or any of my assistants who are already planted, see anything that compromises the Guild, you know the consequences. The examination begins now."

Artu walked away, and the six of them went down a separate road. The task for the exam was to identify a target to lift a purse without detection. If they were caught, they'd endure the consequences.

Probably death. But who doesn't love high stakes?

The main drag was how difficult Corso and the others made practicing. It was like negotiating with a stubborn pig. Nevertheless the group of them slogged through preparation, using instructors and other apprentices as props as they played out theft scenarios, all under Miani's meticulous eye.

Tazio's favorite part of the training was the tradition of pickpocketing and returning other's things in a long game of mischief. Even active Guild members took part when the season began again each year. All guarded their pockets tighter, or used chains to latch their satchels. But that just made for a nice increase in difficulty. Most seemed to love it. A remembrance of being an apprentice, so to speak. Plus, everyone returned their loot after lifting it, so there was no real harm. Only the victory of anonymous token indicating the mark of the thief. Pride was the real prize, and an infamy surrounded the best thieves.

One left a strand of their victim's hair tied to the stolen object. If the hair wasn't long enough, or the victim was bald, he'd leave a lock of their closest friend's instead. No one had caught them yet, and thinking about who it was kept Tazio fascinated. Maybe it was the skinny library clerk's assistant, or maybe it was Kage.

Personally, Tazio used a blood berry with the person's initials carved into it as his mark. If they sat on it, that was their punishment for not keeping tighter watch over their pockets.

The group walked into an alley near a busy city square in the middle district Artu had chosen for the assignment. The bazaar was packed with merchant booths. Hands shook, men cursed, and everyone fought for the best bargain, whether dignified or dirty. It didn't matter, as long as it sold.

Commerce moves the world. At least that's what Setia has proven.

Tazio saw Artu leaning on the wall of the square across the way, looking casual as he drank tea. Steam rose off his small cup, probably the same fragrant Setian *vita* everyone drank. Artu gave the signal, moving a few strands of black hair behind his right ear.

Tazio signaled to the other five that the moment was upon them.

Alesso scanned the crowd for a proper target while the others watched their flanks, and finally signaled for Tazio to come over.

"There. Do you see the man with the purple and pink velvet cap? With the orange tassel—the one dealing with the wool trader." Alesso pointed to a portly man gesticulating in a heated exchange.

"Indeed, he looks good," Tazio agreed.

Tazio and Alesso split from the group and walked into the churning market stalls. Their garb marked them as nobles' apprentices from the northern kingdom of Kalskog. Already as people saw them, Tazio could feel a change in their perception. Gazes diverted. Heads dipped in submission. Peasants parted as he and Alesso walked through the crowd in an unbroken rhythm. It made Tazio feel a little gross to embody the power of nobility. He could only imagine the corruption it would produce over time as the world constantly bent to your presence.

Though the traders didn't waste a moment, immediately dangling luscious deals. He and Alesso righteously declined, holding their gaze unwavering as they played hard to reach. Their performance teacher, Cecilia Bontante, a chipper woman with a mercurial soul, helped them understand the subtle differences in how trained merchant apprentices walked, looked, held their faces, what their inner landscape looked like, the types of emotions and visions they had of themselves. From that, they constructed characters. But rehearsal was one thing, the live act was another. And now that the time had arrived, Tazio was fighting to shake off nerves.

Politically speaking, Setian merchants wanted to eliminate noble influence, especially in Auria. But nobles flung their money around like in the old world, many of them senators, all using their dynastic wealth to buy power and increase tension in Setian city-states.

"He's finished with the wool trader," Alesso whispered as they slinked toward the nobleman.

The target had a bulbous face, a twirled mustache, and a beard doing its best attempt to create a chin line. He fingered his coin purse smoothly like an opia addict getting a hit of joy as he slid the purse into his tunic.

"There—inner pocket," Alesso said, doing his best to maintain an air of disinterest as they closed in. Prying eyes were all around. They couldn't afford to blow their act.

Done with his transaction, the nobleman waddled away through the crowd, looking like he'd fall over from his stiff posture.

"At the next corner," Tazio said, and they diverted along a different path through the maze of stalls.

Clouds of pungent Maladian incense swirled and obscured their sight of the man briefly. They turned the corner, and the man was fifteen paces away, facing their direction.

The nobleman saw their merchant garb and begrudgingly made an obligatory tip of the head to acknowledge their nobility.

They returned the gesture.

"Good morning to you, my Lord," Tazio opened as they came near, knowing their lower rank required they initiate the conversation.

Disappointment lined the noble's face at the interruption.

"Morning," the nobleman replied, his voice uppity.

"Has business fared well for you today?" Tazio asked.

"Surely. Not a day goes by where I can't make a fine deal."

"I am Giorgio Alberto, and this is my cousin Pietro Alberto."

"I am Lord Dimitrius Barbieri," the man said, nose tilting skyward as he rolled out his surname.

Tazio pushed down a quivering laugh. He sensed Alesso in his peripheral vision and knew they'd lose it if they looked at each other. "Our pleasure. We come from Schritte in Kalskog. We're apprenticing under our uncle."

"Very good. Well, enjoy Auria," Dimitrius said, ready to move away.

"Perhaps our areas of commerce overlap?" Alesso suggested.

"Perhaps," Dimitrius said, glancing away like he'd lost his patience.

"Do you trade in wool?" Alesso offered directly, driving to the point.

"Not only do I trade in wool, but I am known as the finest wool trader in Auria," Dimitrius said, interest emerging.

"Well that's wonderful. We actually have a contract seeking wool if you're not opposed to hearing more," Tazio added.

"I could be interested. But I am lacking on time." Dimitrius worked his fluffy collar.

Alesso drew a scroll out, taking his time as he pretended to confirm figures. "We need nine hundred sacks of wool for next spring."

Dimitrius leaned forward off his formerly disinterested heels.

Zara had researched wool figures and told them total exports from Auria ran about five thousand sacks a year. Dimitrius couldn't help his eyebrows flicking up. "Nine hundred you say?"

He's certainly friendlier now that money is flying about.

"That's certainly not marginal," Dimitrius said. "What might you use this amount of wool for?"

"We have our uses," Tazio replied.

"Well, something could possibly be arranged. I'd have to make some aggressive arrangements though," said Dimitrius, leaving the floor open.

"At ten *stellum* a sack?" Alesso asked, so dumbly innocent it was hard to think he was conning anyone.

"Ten *stellum*?" Dimitrius said, his jowls jiggling at the intentionally low offer they crafted.

"Ten."

The silence that followed tested Tazio. He pushed through wanting to add more in order to convince him. Artu had told them to hold silence once the first offer was made—let the other man fill the gap of discomfort.

Dimitrius rubbed his nonexistent chin as he considered the offer.

"We are talking about the same twenty-eight pound sack of coarse wool, yes?" Dimitrius asked.

"That is the common unit of measurement." Tazio threw in a petulant smirk.

"Considering the going price of a sack is two *solis*, which is four times that amount, you can see how I would question your measurement abilities." Dimitrius mirrored the same ugly look Tazio had given him.

"Dimitrius." Tazio intentionally used the most casual title. "We're about to guarantee one-tenth of Auria's yearly wool exports. We cannot go lower than fifteen silvers per sack."

The final offer was well below market price, and Dimitrius snorted in disgust.

"For one gold, ten silvers I can accommodate. No lower," Dimitrius said, boiling with frustration.

"Perhaps the only thing you should accommodate is learning to make a fair bargain," Tazio replied.

Dimitrius' eyes stretched wide, plump cheeks jiggling as he gasped for air like a fish out of water. To insult a noble's fairness, especially when they were unfamiliar, was a harsh affront. Dimitrius took a step toward Tazio, wagging his finger, his musky cologne failing to mask a foul body odor. Tazio turned his nose away just obvious enough for Dimitrius to see.

"Are you jesters in your spare time?" Dimitrius screeched, plump cheeks jiggling. "Making absurd offers. Doling out insults in a foreign market? Tell your Lord to send someone competent next time!"

"Forgive my reaction, my Lord, we're only doing our job," Tazio said, grabbing Dimitrius' hand as he stormed off, catching a glimpse of Corso, Luca, and Zara moving through the crowd.

Dimitrius recoiled, and Tazio seized the moment, stumbling forward into him.

"Marcus, please!" Alesso shouted as Tazio bumped Dimitrius off balance.

In the move, they'd all practiced endlessly, Tazio leaned on Dimitrius, and just then, Zara, Corso, and Luca bumped into Dimitrius from behind, sending the fat man squealing as he tumbled onto the floor with Tazio. Dimitrius rolled off the pile, plump and comedically swift as Zara vanished into the fray.

"Watch where you're going!" Corso shouted at Dimitrius.

Corso stood next to Luca, his feigned frustration painfully unnatural. Plus, he'd broken accent, unintentionally blurring his commoner's accent into his tone. At least his absurdity did the job of distracting all the attention from Zara.

Dimitrius turned to confront who he thought would be a layman, but saw a noble before him. Confusion creased his flustered face. "To you, I'd say the same!"

"It was our fault, my Lord. Please forgive us," Tazio jumped in, diverting attention away from Corso and Luca, who stared speechlessly back at Dimitrius.

"You idiots!" Dimitrius shouted at Alesso and Tazio, remembering the true cause of his chagrin. "Next time you may not be so lucky to find a pleasant and forgiving noble like me!"

Dimitrius shot a final glare at Tazio and Alesso, and shuffled away flustered.

Tazio, feeling hot under the glare of the market, left the scene with Alesso, taking the long way around to reassemble in a side alley with the others. When they arrived, Zara was already there.

"Oh Tazio, you really were so adorable apologizing to that nobleman," Zara said.

"Oh shut it. Did Kage plant the purse back on the target?" Tazio asked.

"Has Artu killed a man?" Zara replied.

"That's a definite yes," Alesso chimed in.

"Where is Corso? He almost blew the whole damned thing," Tazio said.

"Why?" Zara asked.

"He broke accent—almost bent us!" said Alesso.

"Say it to my face," Corso said, appearing from the shadows at the far side of the alley with Luca. His glare swung between Tazio and Alesso, like a predator unbothered by pests.

"You almost fucked us," Tazio slung back.

"It was fine."

"You really are that dumb, aren't you?" said Alesso.

"I'd bet ten silvers Artu will mark you down for that error," Tazio added.

"I'll bet you ten silvers I mark your face down in a couple seconds."

"Take your pissing contest somewhere else," Zara said, tossing a few gold *solis* in her palm.

"Where'd you get those?" Luca asked, wide-eyed.

"While you all were priming plumpy for the kill, I lifted a few *numa* off his competition. Actually... I don't think poor is right—he certainly wasn't hurting for it."

"You'll get us killed!" Luca said.

"When did you become such a flower? I can keep your share if you want," Zara flipped a *solis* toward Alesso, Tazio, then Corso.

"Well, if I'm going to get expelled I should at least be rich," Alesso said, tucking his gold away.

"Gold?" asked Kage as she emerged from a side alley.

"See, even Kage is excited, Luca," Zara said, flicking Kage a gold *solis*. "Shall we?"

They wound their way back to the Guild courtyard to receive their marks on the exam. It was pass or fail, and most passed—so the true measurement was how they would pass. The nature of the criticism was the real measurement. Back at the courtyard, Artu was already waiting for them.

"Any comments?" asked Artu.

Tazio bit his tongue, not bringing up his thoughts on Corso.

"Tazio and Alessandro, you broke character twice. Your first error was five to ten steps from when you entered the square. You moved too quickly, which is not how a noble would. Perhaps you thought your entrance was unseen by your target, and so less important, or perhaps you just hadn't warmed to the act. The other error was your exit. Riding on the relief of the execution of the act coming to a close, you relaxed. While an average eye might not detect the difference, a keen one would recognize your facade. Movements are always watched—especially during an entrance and exit. You can't afford to have that level of error on a consistent basis.

"Corso. Luca. Your character break was so obvious you nearly compromised the entire ploy. I could see the suspicion lined on the face of that fat noble. You're fortunate Tazio intervened. Aside from nearly failing the whole class, you were barely satisfactory."

Tazio didn't dare look over at Corso, ashamed at how good proper justice felt.

"Zara, you were excellent, but you also had the advantage of being in commoner's garb and playing a background part. Though your theft of the purse during the bump, and your pass-off to Kage was excellent—as if you weren't even there."

"Kage, you patrolled and watched for danger so effectively I nearly forgot you existed," Artu said with a rare, misfitting smile. "Truly though, you did what is best for a shadow that supports the main act. You disappeared, but were ready. And when Zara passed the satchel, you planted it flawlessly back as the target left the market. You didn't even employ the use of a hard bump, and the deftness by which you breezed past him and slotted his purse back in his possession was admirable."

"Thank you, professor," Kage replied, their awkwardness endearing.

"You all have passed," Artu said, then abruptly let himself out of the conversation like he did so often, walking to the front door.

"We'll take our ten silvers now," Alesso said to Corso.

"Cork it," Corso said, pushing past him.

"Bump me again," Alesso said.

"And what?"

"I forgot you're not very bright. Do it and hope this bet is better than your last."

Corso looked tempted, but Alesso was a foot taller and it wouldn't be an easy scrap for him.

"See you in combat class," Corso threatened.

"Looking forward to it." Alesso turned to Tazio. "Alright, I'm sorry I played contrarian when you've piped off about him. I now despise him as much as you do."

"Oh? He was starting to grow on me," Tazio said. "Was actually thinking about changing beds to sleep beside him."

"Now I know you're just a liar."

"I'd say we came out on top. Rich with gold *and* a pass!" Tazio said.

"I'd say *I* came out on top. You two got torn to pieces by Artu," Zara said.

"Sometimes we have to make you look good." Alesso threw his arm around Zara as they walked back toward the busy halls of the Guild.

Tazio wanted to throw his arm around Zara too—his feelings for her had been drifting deeper into his heart. As they entered the Guild, the noisy interchange washed over Tazio.

Suddenly he felt alone as Zara and Alesso laughed together beside him, as if in another world.

He saw Zara look over and search him, like she sensed his distance.

"I'll see you at dinner," Tazio said, taking his arm off of Alesso's shoulder.

"Don't want to gamble your gold away to me over some *rischio*?" Alesso asked.

"Losing could only put me in a worse place."

"What's gotten you?" Zara asked.

"You can just admit you're afraid to lose your money," said Alesso.

"That's something I'm not afraid of," Tazio said, trying to be light.

"Something really has you, doesn't it?" Alesso said.

"It's nothing."

"We'll see you at dinner though, yeah?"

"I haven't lost my stomach."

"Good. See you then."

As Tazio turned away, he caught a glimmer of worry in Zara's eye.

Maybe she's worried about me for the same reason I am.

As their laughter faded, a pit opened in his stomach.

I can't allow myself to care. Not again. Only an imbecile accepts an invitation to be gutted repeatedly.

He quickened his steps, the shadows of loss biting at his heels, trying to shake away the voices, the cold threat he'd lose them leaching his veins.

And if they're hurt because you abandon them?

He clenched his jaw. *That* he could not bear. Pulling his cowl up, he blurred through the crowd, clinging to two words in the storm of his mind like a sailor to his mast.

Not.

Again.

CHAPTER 18
ZARA

THE THREE MOONS hung behind scattered clouds, casting a soft hue on the damp stone of the Guild exterior. Zara descended from the rooftop on a rope, the padded touches of her feet nearly silent. Light vapors of breath wrapped their way around the edge of her hood and merged into the sky. Tazio was braced on the roof, holding the line and keeping his eyes peeled for danger.

Zara straddled a window and slid a shim into the window frame, testing the tension of the inner latch as quietly as possible, her face stiff in concentration. She fiddled it out of its home, suspending it so it wouldn't make noise. A long breath she'd been holding poured out.

Like a spider contorting itself around prey, she moved to the other side of the window, feeling the rope tense and creak. She drew a vial and poured oil down the edge of the hinges before carefully cracking it open, listening for noise inside, ready to flee. Only the hum of silence and the faintest thread of sleeping breath greeted her.

She squeezed through the tight window, dropping in, the slightest click coming off the stone floor. Ready to strike, she checked the corners. But only a pool of moonlight lay solemnly in wait, its beams painting the floor.

Two wooden beds, each with a sleeping man, rested at the far side of the room. Nicolai was the first man, sleeping on his back, chest rising and falling as his jowls lay slack. Even though he was asleep, imaginations crept into Zara's mind that he was faking, one eye tracking her every move. She'd feigned sleep before.

It could all end that quickly.

Patrizio, another clerk she knew, though not as well as Nicolai, slept coiled on his side, entirely covered by his thick fur blanket.

She searched the trunks at the foot of each bed first, hoping to find what she came for, but shook her head in frustration as rummaging came up empty. Weighing her options, she decided, as much as she didn't want to, that she could work the task more easily on Nicolai, given his blanket rested partially off him.

Working up the courage to hover over him, she lifted Nicolai's blanket and saw the simple, loose cord-belt he wore around his brown robe. She moved her hand toward a leather loop that hung off it, tugging at it carefully. The weight of an object hung at the end, and as she pulled at it, Nicolai shifted.

She froze, shadow spilling across his face, ready to bolt if his eyelids flipped open. But he settled back into sleep. A pang of guilt and the settling of the bloodrush made her dizzy.

The moral quandary will have to wait.

She shook her head, reaching for a stiletto to cut the loop on the belt, arm stiff as she inched toward it.

"I'm sorry, Nicolai," she mouthed silently, grabbing the key and scuttling toward the window, louder than she wished.

Through the window. Three tugs on the rope and up she went, the gaze of the three moons judging her. When she reached the top, Tazio helped her over.

"It went well?" he asked.

"Well enough."

"You don't sound pleased."

"It's fine. Let's get to Alesso and be done with this."

Zara jogged away.

It wasn't fine. She hated needing them. Compromising her secrecy and opening herself to exploit.

Her stomach pinched.

Friendships meant loss.

Deal with it. Get your answers, then deal with it.

She could feel her heart squeeze at the coldness of her resolve. But getting what she needed required sacrifice. And her parents came first. Tazio and Alesso would understand. And if they didn't—well, they would. That was all she could hope for.

→

ALESSO

A heavy deadbolt thunked into place. The sound of it bounced off the library shelves. Alesso emerged from the deep stacks where he had been hiding, double-checking that no one remained behind after the door locked.

He'd tricked the clerks, evading them as they combed through the stacks earlier. Now he'd have to wait for a few hours as Zara and Tazio pulled off their portion of the plan.

Feeling it was safe, he walked through the empty library, his boots bringing back hollow echoes. The torches had been snuffed, and pale moonlight lit the room through ornate panels of stained glass lining the interior courtyard walls. The moons wavered through the glass, gliding across each window as he walked by. He stopped at one depicting a mounted soldier holding a sword over a foe. The image reminded him of his brother, Cassius.

Gifted in riding, Cassius had left to join a mercenary cavalry when he'd come of age, and Alesso remembered watching him ride away on a chestnut-colored stallion given to him by the conscription officer.

Cassius promised to send word back on his journeys, to visit Alesso and his two elder brothers. But when Alesso saw the distance in Cassius' eyes the day he left, his heart twinged at knowing it was the last time he'd see him. But that was what countryside boys did—farmed or fled to something greater.

After Cassius left, Alesso and his brothers would craft stories of how Cassius was fighting valiantly in battle or was promoted to head of his unit. But as months piled up, their heroic imaginations of his journeys stopped and darker wonderings took their place. Alesso's gut turned out to be right. They never heard from him after that day, but he did live on like a ghost on the farm. A few years prior, they'd lost their parents to the spotted plague. That was hard. But losing Cassius started a rapid slide into sorrow.

His brothers raised each other after that. Famine swept through the southern plains of Bourgogne when Alesso was eleven. So Alesso and Dominic could survive, Lucian, the eldest of the three, calmly assured them they could eat his portions. Until, one day, Alesso found him dead from exhaustion in a barren field—yet another victim of the three-year famine.

The first night after Lucian died, Alesso and Dominic cried through the night. When they woke in the morning, they didn't speak. Where the presence of three felt like a small family, the loneliness of two made absences glaring. Around every corner, Alesso expected his brothers to appear, but only found empty reminders of what was missing. Some mornings later, he found Dominic with his wrists opened beside the meager fire they'd built to fight the biting winter. He cradled Dom's head in his lap, heavy tears rolling off his cheek. The next day, two lanky farmers with sallow skin and dark bags watched as he dug a makeshift grave on the farm. Thinking back now, Alesso wondered why the farmers didn't offer a word. Or help. *Anything*.

When spring arrived, Alesso was bone thin, the drought of brotherhood draining any benefits he received from the surplus of food left in their absence. When Dom was with him, his humor would distract from their barren life—a face on a potato or a bird crapping on him. But without Dom, all that remained was a pit of loneliness growing deeper with each passing week.

In the early spring, he holed up indoors, leaving only to gather firewood or whatever roots and berries he could, gaunt weakness spurring a primal drive to survive. Eventually he went to the door of a newly settled family. Finding no reply, he let himself in and found Beatrice, the mother, with dead, half-shut eyes set on a smoldering fire, her newborn rotting in her arms.

He buried them too.

Having passed out under the pall of exhaustion, he awoke at dawn with his shovel in hand and peeled himself out of the crude grave, collapsing again in a trough on the next plot.

A gentle steer roused him awake some time later, its broad, gentle face hovering in front of him. It reminded him of Cassius' parting gift—

a whittled bull. Tears came forth. Though Lucian and Dominic, and his parents before them all rushed into him like winds of spring, breathing in a burst of strength. Enough for him to roll off the ground onto all fours and rise. To walk from the pit.

The steer walked with him too. His only friend. At least before it meandered off to feed on a prime patch of grass.

At the next farmhouse, Alesso dragged himself up the porch steps and fell with his cheek against the heavy wooden door. He knocked three uneven times and prayed an answer would come. The door swung open and he collapsed like a felled tree into the arms of someone. He looked up and saw an old man with thin gray hair and beard and warm eyes, Alesso's weakness being the only introduction he could muster. The man carried him to a bed and laid him down.

He didn't have the strength to protest the shame of it.

With a place by the fire to cut the spring chill, the old man fed him broth and porridge between fever fits. He shuddered and groaned through nightmares as the farmer quietly watched from his fur-covered chair, warm light and shadows from the fire flickering on his round, worn, gentle face. A picture of who Alesso would be in decades to come.

After two weeks, Alesso began to renew. He'd wake and stare at the fire, too tired to speak, occasionally glancing at the old man to acknowledge him before reentering his own sadness.

When Alesso finally stepped out of his cot, he fell from weakness. The old man tried to help, but Alesso refused the help, choosing to hang his head and collapse onto the crude wooden planks. Deep down, despite the shame, he craved help.

When the man helped him up this time, Alesso clutched to him, struggling between his desire to die and live, to cry and be strong, to run and stay, crawling back under the covers for another night.

Light broke through the farmhouse's shuttered windows the next day, and Alesso felt release, confident he could stand on his own. The man opened his eyes drowsily at the creak of Alesso's feet on the floor.

"I'm sorry for the burden," Alesso said, hearing his voice as his own for the first time in days.

"You're not a burden." His voice was deep and kind. "I lost my family to the spots, and I haven't had a soul beside me for five years."

"What's your name?"

"Loredano."

"I'm Alessandro," he said, unable to mutter 'Alesso,' the name his brothers actually used.

It was the longest conversation Alesso could muster that day, each word like lifting a boulder from the depths of his soul.

He appreciated that Loredano didn't press.

Over the next few weeks, Loredano gave him small tasks around the farm. Peeling potatoes, grooming the skinny animals. When summer arrived, Loredano taught him to farm, cook, ride horseback, and work wood. All the essential duties.

Sadness began to melt into bittersweetness. The sun brought him in the day and walked him out, the winds washed away his thoughts, the cool water slaked his lonely drought drop-by-drop. The balm of labor working its regenerative powers, stimulating passing joys.

Two summers passed, and as Alesso grew in stature, Loredano grew weak. So Alesso repaid him, settling him to sleep each night, feeding him, taking care of him as Loredano had done for him.

Until, one night, as Loredano sat in bed for supper, he said, "My time is coming." He stared into the fire like he'd been working up the strength to say it.

"Don't speak like that," Alesso replied. "You'll be good by autumn."

"Do you remember the first thing you said to me?"

"I don't."

"'I'm sorry for the burden,' you said."

"Well, it's the damned truth."

"At the time, I didn't tell you, but I want to tell you now."

"Don't get sappy on me."

"Alesso," he said weakly. "You're the greatest gift I've had in this life."

The words hit Alesso deep in the stomach.

Loredano looked frail sitting weakly against the crude pillows. "You've made the end rich with joy."

"Please don't talk like it's the end, I can't take it."

"I have a gift for you. Your whittled bull. You know you're like a bull?" Loredano's eyes looked long and weak. "But you're also like a bear. Able to endure the harsh winter of life and come out stronger."

Loredano reached beside his bed to a table, handing Alesso a whittled bear from the drawer.

"Thank you, Loredano." The sight of the beautifully carved bear stirred sorrow and love and tension in Alesso. And watching Loredano drift back to sleep brought forth tears.

Over the next three days, they spent their days as if the conversation never happened, the old man whittling as he did, sharing stories of his family, Alesso thinking maybe Dano had turned a corner. They spoke of increasing the next harvest and perhaps even trading again. The rains had become more favorable in past seasons.

But Loredano passed in his sleep. Three nights after their conversation.

All Alesso could do when he saw him limp was stand next to him. Feel tears force their way through shut eyes, haunted by his undeniable deathly stillness. Thoughts of grief and loneliness closing in like a storm wall as he ran to the fields to scream and pound the earth.

Through the brisk spring night, Alesso dug a hole and the steer found him again. It slept beside him, stirring every once in a while at the hoot of an owl or a lick of wind. Somehow Alesso found the strength to comfort it back to sleep each time.

When the grave was done in the early light, Alesso went back inside and spoke to Loredano through choked tears. A look of peace rested on Loredano's face, coloring Alesso's sorrow with some relief.

"Thank you, Dano. For saving me. For bringing me back to the living. For everything I don't even know yet. Even if life is a hell hole."

He wrapped Loredano in his favorite fur blankets and emerged from the humble farmhouse into the cool morning. The heavy walk through the field. Laying him to rest. Climbing out of the hole and looking to the sky to say a prayer.

Not knowing what to pray, he just said, "Thank you." Then he filled it, each mound of dirt covering the past.

The months that followed held a shade of sorrow softer than the shock of his other losses. Like a soft wind that never left, Loredano remained with him. In the trees and flowers. In the sun glinting off the morning dew. Speaking to him as he worked the fields in somber focus for the next year.

And as he walked back to the farmhouse with a hoe one summer evening, a smooth dark voice sailed through the air, appearing like an apparition in the tranquil place. "Fine harvest."

Alesso turned slowly, too hardened to care about caution.

"Working alone?" the man continued.

"I manage."

"I can see that," he said, taking in the farm. His green velvet cape with gold trim was too fine for the country, his long, wavy, black hair too clean. But it was the shadows beneath his brow that made Alesso grip his splintered hoe tighter.

"I've come with an offer. I've been told you've lost all that's dear to you."

"And who told you that—a little bird?"

"I've been known to speak with crows."

"Well tell your crows to fly off."

"I can offer you a purpose."

"I have a purpose." Alesso took a step toward him.

"If you'd prefer to farm alone until the end of your days, I can understand that."

"Get off my farm," Alesso said, turning to walk away.

"What of your brothers?"

Alesso stopped, brow lowering as rage trembled up from his feet.

"What did you say?"

"I can offer you brotherhood."

The urge to drive the hoe into the man's head flashed through Alesso. But the man continued, unmoved by the heat radiating off Alesso.

"Loredano wasn't as simple as you think. He wrote to me—his last report was of 'a boy who'd lost all his brothers and turned into a young man with resilience beyond any I've known.'"

"You don't know anything about me. Or my brothers."

"Not much, except that he said I should consider you."

"Consider me for what?"

"Now you're asking the right questions."

"My brother already joined a mercenary force. I'm not interested in abandoning my duties."

"No, no, not more meat for the cavalry. Power, my boy. Prestige."

"It reeks."

"Have you heard of the Setian Merchants' Guild?"

"Who are you?"

"Neri."

"*Neri?*"

"Yes, *Neri.*"

"That's not a real name."

"Of course it is. It's mine."

Alesso certainly hadn't heard such a name, and he laughed. Neri didn't seem pleased.

"Good to see you've regained your humor," Neri said.

"Look, *Neri*—I can't leave my animals and this farm. I have my duties."

"Plenty would kill for this. Consider it a gift. From Loredano. From me. From the Merchants' Guild. But keep acting like a stubborn cow and you'll squander it."

The wind kicked up dust on the simple dirt trade route. Alesso didn't know what omen that was, but it definitely felt like one that demanded he move. Or die a worn farmer.

"You've been through much," Neri said, his shadow stretching long in the waning light. "But if you don't come with me then, the offer will not stand."

"No need for slippery merchant's tactics."

Neri chuckled. "Good. Think on it. I'll return in the morning."

Neri rode away to wherever the hell he was staying. There wasn't an inn for miles, and strangers certainly weren't taking him in. That night, Alesso stared into the roof planks, mind running as he wrestled with the decision. The promise of a new life. The fear of what this man's promises really meant. Some restless hours later, he got out of bed to tend the fire, Loredano's favorite chair calling to him. Loredano was there as he whittled wood, his thoughts curling away into the shavings until the fire eased him to sleep.

When the cock crowed, he walked onto the porch. The same planks he'd collapsed on years ago. Mist hung in the valley as Neri emerged from obscurity.

"You're up early," Alesso called.

"We have a long journey ahead."

"'We?'"

"I know you're no fool."

"My animals. I need to give them to the farm just there." Alesso pointed down the road.

"Fair enough."

When he tended to them one last time, Alesso stood especially long with the steer, whispering goodbye as it gazed at him with its innocent eyes. When he pried himself away, Alesso's heart sagged. He was certain it knew it was losing a friend, but he forced himself to walk to the man called *Neri*—knowing it was his best escape from the fog of loneliness that had settled on his life.

He walked to the gray, spotted stallion Neri provided, fighting away the surging sadness of leaving the familiar. The stallion's spots reminded him of the plague that killed his family. He patted its neck. "Hopefully your spots will be a blessing," he muttered as he mounted the stallion.

Neri clicked his tongue and began up the path to the east as Alesso paused in his saddle, taking in the farm a final time. Chirping birds curled over the fields. A deer raised its head at a cracking branch near the brook. Soft clouds of pink and gold glowed on the horizon as the last whispers of morning mist snaked their way through the valley. He saw himself crumble into Loredano's arms on the porch. Their joyful labor together in the fields. The lonely grave where Loredano now rested.

Caws pulled Alesso from his trance, scattering other birds from the forest edge as crows swarmed the valley. At first he gripped his reins in protest of the invasion. But Loredano taught him crows were harbingers of change, their darkness showing death to the old, life in new horizons. His loved ones were not in the place. They were with Alesso now. In his heart. Lost, but never forgotten.

Then, through breaths of acceptance, great blades of light shined through mist onto the fields, tears thrust their way out, acceptance swirling inside him. Unable to dwell any longer, Alesso clenched his jaw and reared his stallion, spurring it forward. The beast heaved forward, hooves pounding the past away, countryside disappearing in the wind, the path ahead winding and gray.

CHAPTER 19

TAZIO

Tazio knocked three times on the library door using the code they'd determined. Two firm knocks returned.

Alesso cracked open the door and let him and Zara in.

The hinges of the lantern housing squeaked as Tazio lit a lantern they'd stolen from town during a weekend jaunt. He hovered near Zara as she went behind the clerk's desk and slid the key she'd stolen from Nicolai into the gate. She gripped the wrought-iron bars, tugged the gate open, and a low creak grated through the library. Tazio watched her slide into the shadows of the back stacks. Alesso gave him a nod, and he followed Zara in as Alesso watched for danger.

The restricted stacks were tighter and more spare, about ten rows deep. But there were still easily over five thousand volumes.

"What the hell is this?" Zara asked, squinting at the labels.

"What?"

"The organizational codes are in a different language than the rest of the stacks."

"They're in ancient Setian. This stack is biographies and journals."

They sifted through the shelves until they found the section they needed, and Tazio saw Zara's eyes light up as her hand paused on the work she was looking for. Her wonder was everpresent, even during stress.

"Come on, grab it," Tazio said.

Zara tugged the book free, breath catching as she fumbled it. A slap echoed through the stacks, and the book's title glared in the lantern light — *Work of Shadows.*

"A little jumpy?" Tazio whispered in Zara's ear as she stood up from retrieving it.

"*Khara,*" she hissed, flinching then shoving Tazio—somewhere between playful and mad.

As she rearranged the books, her hands shook. Stress slithered into Tazio's mind as Zara tried to obscure the ominous gap in the shelf. Clerks combed these stacks meticulously—it was only a matter of time before the administration noticed a restricted copy missing.

"One more," Zara whispered, and they moved to the political section.

"What's that one?" Tazio asked as she drew out the next book.

"No time," Zara whispered back before hurrying out.

"We done here?" Alesso asked as they slinked out.

"Done," Tazio replied.

"This place haunts me even in daylight."

Tazio put the key on the clerk's desk. It would already be obvious the key had been stolen, so replanting it on Nicolai wasn't worth the risk.

"You okay?" Tazio asked Alesso, who looked like he'd come out of a nightmare.

"Yeah, fine. Just too much time to think of all the fun ways Neri will cut our balls off."

"Let's go!" Zara hissed, waiting near the door. She cracked it, checked her corners, and slipped into the hall.

"Suppose that's our cue," Tazio said, and they disappeared with her, riding the wind of the heist.

→

"'*Draeda* flows freely in all living beings and throughout the cosmos'," Tazio read from *Work of Shadows.* "'It is most valuable when captured in a *talùth*, a practice dating to the origins of its discovery by Set, the first *draedic* practitioner.'"

"Captured?" Zara asked.

The word hung in the air.

"Let him read," Alesso said.

"'Animals contain higher levels of *draeda* as related to their level of intelligence. Though regardless of potency, each living soul carries a distinct qualitative energy that produces power related to its capacities. Human souls contain the highest *draedic* reserves, and similar to animals, higher intelligence leads to higher reserves. *Draedic* practitioners have the highest noted levels. When a soul is captured, it can be drawn upon later by someone versed in this power.'"

Tazio looked at Alesso and Zara, who sat with him in the firelit reading room.

"'...to an unpracticed user, drawing on a powerful animal or human soul within a *talùth* can be overwhelming. In the case of drawing from a human soul, the practitioner also suffers from an intrusion from the mind and life force captured within it. It is not possible to fully combat this, but the practitioner can manage energetic contact with souls captured inside a *talùth* through progressive levels of training to prevent the loss of self.'"

"Wait—enough." Alesso said, whispering tight and close. "This is blood *magae*. Soul capture? I'm done."

"Quiet. Sit down. There's no done, and you know it," Zara added.

Tazio found his place on the parchment again, "'...manufacture, distribution, and market control of *talùthae* produce most of the Guild's commerce. By releasing *talùthae* with minor potencies in common circulation, a dependency on *draeda* can be nurtured, leading to an increase in demand.'"

The book felt putrid in Tazio's hands. He dropped it on the table, mind spinning. Zara took a deep breath and sat back in her chair and Alesso rubbed his brow in a rare show of tension.

It explained how the merchant in the alley that had attacked Tazio had a *talùth*, and how the Guild was so wealthy and powerful—it traded all kinds of things, but this is where the real *numa* was made. What *Work of Shadows* didn't mention was if they knew *feantoiil* or *anamea* like the Daemonae. Tazio's earlier suspicions that they practiced an entirely different branch of *draedic* power were confirmed though.

"So they're trading in human souls?" Zara asked aloud like she was seeing if she could fully digest it.

"Well, they're clearly not trading in wool," Tazio said. "And now we're deep in it with them."

"We never should have stolen this book," Zara said.

"I'm ready to start selling *talùthae*," Alesso said.

"Be serious for one moment of your life," Zara said.

"Well what's the point? What are we supposed to do with this?" Alesso said, pointing to the book. "You want to break down Neri's door and dismantle the Guild?"

"Too much peril if we confront Neri," Tazio interjected.

"No, better to know what's going on than be an idiot in the dark." Alesso pointed to the other book Zara held. "Do I even ask what that one is about?"

"Trade politics and motivations," Zara replied.

"Seems like casual reading after *Work of Shadows*. What's the point of it?"

"It's for me."

"Well, pardon me."

"You're going to keep it for yourself?" Tazio asked.

"Yes."

"I tore the skin off my palms holding that rope, and Alesso almost shit his pants in that damned library. We both could be killed for this, and we can't know what it's for?" Tazio asked, looking to Alesso for support.

"It does feel like we're in this together," Alesso agreed.

Zara looked pinned to her chair, her eyes darting between them. Tazio had never seen her this flustered.

"I trusted you, Tazio. I asked you to help me but not need to know why—and you said you understood. Do promises fade so quickly?" Zara said. The words stung Tazio's heart.

"I mean this seems a bit different, does it not?" Tazio asked.

"Just trust me. You don't need to know what this is."

"Don't think it's about need," Alesso said.

"I'm not interested in discussing it anymore," Zara said, moving to the exit.

"Zara, we didn't—" Tazio went after her, but the door slammed in his face.

He burst into the hallway, catching a glimpse of Zara already turning the next corner. Regret plucked at him, and he stopped his fist inches from the stained glass in the door. Breathing to calm down, he went back into the reading room. Alesso sat there with his elbows on his knees, head hung low. He looked up with pitiful eyes, as if drifting in a sea of doubt.

"Fean, I'm sorry, Alesso. I didn't know she'd react like that."

"It was both of us." Alesso sounded drained.

He reached for *Work of Shadows* and flipped through it as Tazio sat to think about how to repair the rift. The harsh truth, that time was the only cure, settled in, and he pushed the problem aside.

"Alesso, there's something we can do."

"About Zara?"

"No. That'll have to wait. To find out more about the *talùthae* trade."

"Oh, I'm sure this'll be light."

"Come on, you know you're gonna like it."

"*Cazzo*." Alesso shifted off his knees, a bit of light returning to him. "I'm a glutton for punishment—give it to me."

CHAPTER 20

ALESSO

AFTER A SOMEWHAT GRUELING FIRST SEMESTER, Alesso wished he could let himself relax into the jubilee of the year-end winter festival all around him. Performances took over every square and alley, commerce intensified, and classes of all types mingled in the streets. Children munched on hot biscuits and many an adult loosened on mulled wine under a ceremonious dusting of snow. But they had a job to do first.

"Thank you, good sire." Alesso took his meat pie from the beefy dealer who gave him a warm look.

On a stage in the main square, the lead man of a juggling group lit three torches, the flames drawing oohs from the packed crowd. The juggler incorporated more and more torches until seven twirled through the air. His stage partner, a beautiful woman with long red hair, brought the count up to fourteen as they tossed them to each other in a feat of juggling mastery. The crowd held back no pleasure, mugs tipping and chants breaking out.

Alesso walked through the crowd and found Tazio posted at the back, taking in the scene between bites of steaming apple pie.

"You're an apple pie fiend," Alesso said.

"What does that make you?"

"Meat-man."

"I'm a fiend for both."

"Never a truer word has been spoken. Ready to go?"

"Verily."

They downed the last of their pies, and Alesso wiped the flakes from his beard.

"You really are an animal," Tazio said.

"That's *animale* in Auria."

Tazio took a steady look at him. They shook hands and put their hoods up, splitting away from the square toward the bustling markets a few blocks away. Alesso scanned the faces of merchants and peasants as he and Tazio walked through the festive markets where traders sold celebratory dresses, toys, jewelry, and gifts of all kinds.

Alesso peered from beneath his hood to where the market split into side exchanges, an area Neri had warned them was strictly prohibited—" where unsavory types brooded in the swamp looking for victims of trade."

Alesso saw Tazio enter the alley of a side exchange to the right, and cut toward the alley to the left. At its edge, light broke through a canopy of tattered fabrics hanging over it. Hacking coughs and gruff chats dotted the eerie gloom. The smell of piss and rot assaulted his nostrils as he entered, his boots pressing through layers of muck, blood rolling through cobblestones from fresh butcher cuts.

"Good for virility," a Katarian medicine dealer purred, clinking a vial with a strange fetus inside.

Alesso choked back his disgust and slid deeper into the alley.

As the booths grew smaller and more dilapidated, the vendors grew more ragged. He began to wonder at what point he'd take a knife in the side, half-heartedly joking to himself about it, but growing uncomfortable.

"Wutchya lookin' fer, mate?" a man with a round, disfigured face said with a twisted toothless grin.

"I've come with an offer," Alesso replied.

"Only selling, ragazzo." The man's eyes were wide and demented.

Alesso took in the booth from beneath his hood. A haggard door stood behind the man, and the man had no obvious wares for sale.

Alesso's gut dropped as he realized the man wasn't selling goods.

The man was selling people.

The man cracked a hoarse laugh as Alesso stepped back, doing his best to show he wasn't concerned, but suddenly realizing how out of place he was in the alley. He looked down at his own outfit. He looked like a noble in a group of commoners, his cloak and boots clean in comparison to their rags. People were watching, heads cocked his way, and none looked like they wanted a friendly trade.

Alesso trudged deeper as a grim tension grew.

Stay on task and get out.

He continued searching for the right person to talk to, taking in the broken faces of those who made their life in the dregs. Eventually, a gray haired woman caught his eye. She sat huddled by a small fire in her booth of elixirs, smoke drifting through the patchwork canopy. Her face had an unnatural air of approachability, and Alesso was relieved to find someone relatively normal.

"Afternoon, *domina*," Alesso said, ducking into her cramped booth.

The woman turned and Alesso caught himself recoiling. The left side of her face was melted and burned, her eye gray with blindness. He tried to recover and not offend her.

"Keep gawking and you might go stiff," she wheezed, her slack face sagging.

"I'm sorry, my lady."

"My lady! Hah! Haven't heard that one in a while!"

He regretted stepping into her booth, running through his options and settling into the bleak fact she might be the most normal option around.

"I've come with an offer." Alesso cut through her witchy laughs.

"Have you now? Maybe an ointment for my face?"

She cackled wildly to herself again.

"Afraid not, Miss," Alesso said, feeling sympathetic. "But I can offer you something else."

Cupping his hand to shield from onlookers, he flashed a gold *solis* into his palm. The woman's eyes opened wide, a glimmer of innocence shining through. He flicked his hand and the *solis* vanished. She looked up at him and her scarred face haunted him. Tazio taught him the illusion, and it was already paying dividends.

"You're a bold one. What're we talkin' about, lad?" Her crazed tone was more balanced now.

Alesso crouched beside her and drew in close. "Do you know where I can find the Tenebri Emporium?"

She grabbed him by the sleeve and yanked him even closer.

"Stitch your lips," she hissed.

"*Calmati.* Any information about where I can find the dark market, and I'll pay. Two silvers for a location, one gold for a name."

"I'll lose my head," she replied, drawing a finger across her neck.

Alesso showed five silvers to her in the tight space between their chests. She stared down at them, head shaking atop her thin neck as she licked her lips. Her hand shook as it moved toward the stack in his palm, greed getting the best of her.

Alesso closed his fist.

"Where is it?" Alesso asked softly.

"You're a devil, you are."

"A devil in need of the truth."

She leaned in, whispering in his ear, and Alesso did his best not to flinch away from her damp, rotten breath.

"Thank you," Alesso said, pulling away with relief.

Alesso opened his palm, and the *numa* dropped into her hand with a clink. He backed away, his heart aching from her hardship. Maybe she was an innkeeper or a maid before she was burned. But now she was just another hopeless soul living in the filth, riding the edge of insanity.

He made another copper appear in his palm. "For something you'll enjoy."

The woman looked like she'd cry from the kindness. "Thank you, ragazzo. Be careful."

"I'll be fine." Alesso turned from the poor woman.

A red door.

He walked deeper into the alley in search of it.

I'll bring Tazio later. For now, let's see if she was worth the coin— could've bought a few ciders and a meat pie or two with that bribe.

Vendors thinned as the alley grew darker, and Alesso became acutely aware of the sounds of his footsteps tapping off stones and puddles. A one-legged butcher twitched and sniffed at him before returning to hack on a rancid cow's leg. Alesso walked past, seeing a small dead-end alley with no one in it—catching a glimpse of a red door at the end on the left. His legs felt stiffened, like they knew not to lead him there. He checked around and no one was with him, forcing himself into the dank alley. No lanterns lit the way, and clouds darkened the approach. With each step, the red door seemed to beckon him forward. A rat scurried by his feet and Alesso flinched. On the door, nothing obvious marked it but cracks and faded crimson paint.

He raised his fist to knock, arm as tight as wood.

I should have brought Tazio.

As he turned to leave, a shadow blurred in his periphery. Something blunt smashed into the side of his head. Vision flickering as he hit the cobblestones, he raised his arms to defend himself, glimpsing the vendor with the disfigured face looming over him.

"I've come with an offer," the man mocked. And with freakish eyes, he brought his wooden club down, time slowing as Alesso wondered how this would be his end. Here, in this alley, looking into the gaze of darkness, was not how he imagined it. But as he peered into the soul of this man, Alesso felt pity—murdering people in cold alleys, probably for a few *numa*. Maybe he never had a family. Like Dom, and Lucian, and Cassius, and Loredano—who coasted through his heart, soothing the doom. His blood slowed in acceptance, trusting he would see them soon, unafraid and painless as the club turned everything dark.

→

TAZIO

Back in the square where he and Alesso had met, Tazio watched the same jugglers move into their second act.

A few minutes bled into twenty, and still, no sign of Alesso.

"E cazzo, Alesso," Tazio muttered, his breath pluming in the chill air.

He stood off the wall, uneasy, and walked toward the alley Alesso had gone down. The sun was low, bleeding into the gloomy transition to darkness.

Tazio stepped into the mouth of the alley.

Only a few straggling vendors and drooling opium addicts remained. Crows and vultures had already descended. They tussled and cawed over the remains of the meat stalls. Tazio walked up to a man with hair that looked like it'd been cooked by a torch.

"*Perdono*, have you seen a lad about my height in a similar cloak?"

"Get lost," the man replied, gravel in his voice.

"Friendly lot around here," Tazio muttered, moving deeper into the haunting alley. Where the one he'd gone down earlier made him on edge, this corridor made his skin stand taut. His boots tapped on the wet stone. Practically no one remained in their stalls except a few stragglers in the alley.

"*Perdono*—" he asked one more vendor carrying a basket of tattered clothing. The man eyed him with suspicion, then hurried away. A rat darted beneath Tazio's feet, sending a jolt up his legs.

"What have I done?" Tazio muttered to himself as he picked up his pace, eager to find Alesso and get out of the putrid place. "I dragged him into this. And he's gone."

Tazio hurried under the arch of a side street as panic rose. Now, only drips of water from melting snow remained, every denizen evacuated to their dark hovels. His neck was tight, belly sick at what could have happened to his best friend. The idea of finding out where black-market dealers were and how they dealt *talùthae* was thrilling beforehand. But now it felt like the stupidest gamble he could have made.

"You imbecile. Do something. Do something about it."

An insane man he hadn't seen beside some stalls stirred from a shallow sleep, laughing at Tazio like the alley had summoned him, its cruel jaws seeking a fresh victim.

"Quiet!" Tazio shouted, but the man only laughed louder, then spit thick phlegm on his boots.

"Quiet! Quiet! Quiet! That's what they all say!" the man sputtered, arms flailing nonsensically as he cackled.

Tazio turned and stumbled back to the main alley. He looked left and right, the corridor like an empty, haunting tunnel to nowhere. He knocked on shutters and doors, but no one answered.

"Alesso!" he shouted, but his screams were swallowed by the darkness.

He ran toward the festival, blurring back through the alley, the cold night numbing his face, burning his lungs. As wide as the rift felt to cross, he needed to tell Zara. She had a way of finding clues. As he reached the edge of the square, he saw her standing in the crowd with a few others watching the final act. He bumped his way through the crowd, grabbing Zara by the shoulder.

"I... Zara... it's—we have to talk," Tazio said, catching his breath. Zara flinched away, the pain of his last betrayal still lingering in her attitude. "Zara, please. This is serious."

"What is it?" she asked, face slightly opening.

"Alesso—"

"What happened to him?" Her face matched his concern.

"It's Alesso."

"You said that. What happened?" Zara took him by the shoulders.

"He's gone, Zara—he's gone."

"What do you mean, *gone*?"

"I don't know where he is. I don't know where he is. And it's my fault." Tazio trembled, the dam of sorrow he'd held back beginning to crack. He looked away in shame, but Zara grabbed him, taking him in her arms. The sea of people around them watched the performance on stage, unaware of the pit of doom opening in his chest.

"You have to tell me more so I can help," Zara said as Tazio gathered himself.

"After you left the other day, we decided to take things into our own hands. To find the Tenebri Emporium. Bribe a few people for information on the *talùthae* market."

"Why?"

With Alesso now missing, the simple word felt like a stinging indictment.

"We thought... well, I thought it could give us leverage over the Guild in case we found something out. Perhaps we could use it."

"For what?"

Tazio wanted to tell her the real reason. That he was worried the Guild was running a dark operation. That Neri knew he was Daemonae and would use his power somehow. That he needed power over them if it came to it.

"For anything! The Guild is clearly sinister, Zara."

"Fean, Tazio—how did you lose him?" Zara's brow creased with concern.

"We decided it would draw less attention to go separately into different alleys. But he never came back. I went to find him. But it was just a bunch of drooling opies cackling like madmen. Fucking cazzo, what've I done?"

"It's okay."

"It's not!"

"Think, Tazio." She put her hands on Tazio's cheeks, pulling his gaze into hers. Calmness in the midst of the stress.

Focus, you fuck. You fucked this up, now solve it.

"What will you do to find him?"

"Tomorrow. We'll return. And we'll find who did this."

⭢

Tazio had spent the whole night wrestling with fears of what had happened to Alesso. And now, as he and Zara walked into the alley, its denizens glared at them like figures in a feverish dream.

"That man on the left," Zara said. "As we passed the tincture man—he eyed us sideways."

Tazio walked up to the booth where the man was selling half-rotten fruits and vegetables.

The man sat slackly against a wall and didn't move an inch at their approach.

"How much for a bushel of carrots?" Tazio asked.

"One silver," he replied as he looked them up and down.

"That's a steep bargain for some rotten carrots."

"Hard times. You buying or not?" the man replied.

Zara nudged Tazio in the back.

"We'll take them," Tazio said.

"Leave the *numa* and piss off."

"One other thing. Yesterday," Tazio held his coin back, "did you see a lad close to my height? Bigger build with a long beard?"

The man's nose twitched like he smelled something fishy.

"*Vaffanculo.*"

"We can pay," Zara interjected.

The man stood up. "You don't leave and you'll pay with something else."

"Just the carrots, then," Tazio said, stepping closer to the baskets.

"Unless you've miraculously remembered something." Tazio closed the gap in an instant, pressing a dagger against the pit of the man's stomach.

"Ragazzo, best not to play games in the wrong place," Tazio said, gradually increasing the pressure of the point, working it through the man's ragged clothing until it touched flesh. The man flinched but didn't fold, so he pressed further, until the point pricked through skin.

"Stop," Zara said.

But Tazio pressed deeper, growing nauseous as the man began to whimper.

"*Basta!* Wait," the man finally gave in.

Tazio released the pressure but kept the dagger on him.

"There's a basement door in the alley to the left—at the end. It's red. He could be there." The man's eyes searched left and right.

"What's in there?"

"They'll kill me—I cannot say."

"No, you have it wrong—*I'll* kill you," Tazio hissed, some vicious part of him taking over as he twisted the dagger again into the new wound.

"Wait, wait! Just knock, and tell them you're there to gamble. To play some *rischio*. That'll get you in. They love good coin."

Tazio held the dagger, testing the man's resolve for a few moments. "Let's go," he uttered to Zara, pulling off and hurrying toward the alley. A rush of relief spread over him at not having to gut the man.

"Tazio, what were you doing? When we talked about asking questions, I didn't think you'd be torturing people."

Tazio stopped, the criticism stinging.

"You think I wanted to? Alesso is in danger. If you want to go back, *go*. I won't force you."

Zara looked frustrated at not having a rebuttal.

"I'm sorry for pulling you into this," Tazio admitted, "but I won't stop until I find him."

"Let's go."

Tazio turned around the corner down the center of the alley, his fit of anger providing tempestuous confidence, rats scurrying in his wake. Zara was right—if he had to, he would have gutted the man then and there.

Tazio saw the red door and walked up to it, putting his ear against the ragged wood and hearing the muted rumble of commotion. He took a step back, looked at Zara for confirmation, and rapped on the door. The door opened and a wall of a man stepped into the frame. He was bald and scarred, pores like craters, and the stench of ale and fish drifted off him.

"What do you want?" the big man grumbled in a dialect Tazio didn't recognize.

"We're here to gamble," Tazio replied.

"*Seh*?"

Tazio flashed his purse.

Unconvinced, the man's face didn't flinch. "How you find here?"

Tazio's heart skipped a beat. As he scrambled for a good answer, the man caught a gold *solis* Zara tossed to him.

"We love to gamble," said Zara.

"*Seh*," the man uttered, holding the gold *solis* up to his eye. "You have more?"

"Yes, plenty," said Tazio.

"You come then," the man said, stepping inside.

As Tazio walked by, the man grabbed him by the lapel, pinning him to the wall and frisking him—finding all four stilettos, even on the ankles and thighs. Then he frisked Zara.

"No *stiletto*s," the man said, shoving them toward the interior.

The entry chamber was a windowless room lit by square lanterns. The sound of cheering reverberated from a brick stairway that descended on the opposite side. Tazio hurried down, gut tightening as he saw a seething crowd backed up to the bottom of the steps. They pumped their fists, entranced. As Tazio got to the penultimate step, he peered over the rumbling crowd. In the center, two shirtless brutes slugged each other, gamblers screamed their wagers, and ringmasters collected *numa*. Clouds of *opia* filled the air, and sweat soaked everyone in the packed pit.

The thud of the heavy fist of one fighter meeting the cheekbone of the other drew raucous reactions. The bigger of the two was built like a bull, and the other was close in size. But the stark realization he was destined to lose showed in his wavering steps. A moment's hesitation cost him, and a leaden fist to the teeth drove him to the floor. Tazio recoiled as the brute kicked the limp man beyond reason, and the crowd cheered in delight.

The ringmasters dragged the unconscious mess of a man out of the crowd by the arms, leaving a trail of blood behind. A buzz circulated as they pulled the next fighter out of the crowd and threw him into the ring. Tazio's heart dropped as the next fighter stumbled into the ring— friendly face, broad shoulders, and thick beard unmistakable. Tazio's ears rang as the crowd yelped, their cheers a deafening mockery of the horror dragging his gut down.

Alesso.

CHAPTER 21

TAZIO

"ALESSO!" Tazio shouted over the crowd, voice swallowed by the chaotic din, panic rising in his chest as a ringmaster slapped Alesso on the cheek to spur him on. A few onlookers shot Tazio ugly looks for his outburst.

"Tazio, quiet," Zara hissed.

"Quiet? He's about to be killed in there."

Zara stood on her toes, and her face sank in terror as she spotted him shirtless, eyes bloodshot and wild.

"We have to get him out of there," Zara agreed, her face pale.

"Stay close."

Tazio merged into the throng, the grinding masses jostling him, each bump fraying his nerves as he forced his way through. One man shoved him hard, and he fell in a tangled mess against some others. Yells erupted and Tazio scrambled away quickly, dragging Zara with him to escape the quarreling mob—luckily most of them were drunk and disoriented.

As they pushed closer to the ring, gaps closed, shoulders walled him out until he had to forcefully pry people apart. But no one was budging this close to the spectacle, and a mangy fellow blocked Tazio out. Tazio saw the ringmaster call for final bets, then shove Alesso and the other fighter into the center—another beast of man a hand taller than Alesso, and even brawnier.

"Alesso!" Tazio shouted, the jeering crowd consuming his plea.

"We can't get through this way!" Tazio shouted to Zara.

The ringmaster lifted his arm and threw it down to start the fight. As if under a spell, Alesso lunged to strike, but the big man caught him in the jaw, clobbering him sideways to the floor.

"Alesso!" Zara shouted.

Alesso got up, blood spilling from his mouth, evil burning in his eyes. The other man reared back and laughed, clearly enjoying his odds. Alesso dashed forward and threw a hook. The big man blocked, and as he went to counterpunch, Alesso thrust a kick into his knee, crunching it grotesquely backwards, and the crowd pulled breath through their teeth at the vicious efficiency of it. The big man screamed and folded unnaturally over, unable to support his weight, staring at his other mangled knee, bravado reduced in an instant to sheer submission.

Alesso slinked around the helpless man, then spat on his face before driving a brutal heel into his head. The man snapped sideways toward the floor and Tazio averted his eyes, stomach turning over at the sight of it. He struggled to accept that Alesso could be so senseless, but there he was—roaring in victory as the ringmaster raised his arm and escorted him out. The other poor bastard was dragged out too.

"When does the winning lad fight again?" Tazio asked a scrawny man nursing a lip of opia.

"Tomorrow, ragazzo. Next round." The man looked excited by it.

"I feel sick, Tazio," Zara whispered, voice faint.

"I know. Come this way." He led them to the back and around the outside of the ring, the image of Alesso spitting and bludgeoning the man making his gut turn.

On the far side of the pit, a set of stairs led upward like a mirror of the entry stairwell. Tazio moved toward it as the crowd roared behind them for the next fight. Using the commotion, they slinked up the stairs. At the top, Tazio peered over and saw two guards sitting on a stool in front of a doorway about twenty paces away.

"Follow the act," he mouthed without a noise, and put his arm around Zara's hip, laughing and nuzzling her as he dragged her toward them.

"You're not supposed to be here," one guard said, rising off the stool.

"Sorry, *ragazzo*... I thoughtthis wastheexit," Tazio slurred.

193

"Come onn, yuu dog," Zara added, rubbing Tazio's chest and stomach, making it seem like they were two drunks looking for a place to work one out. Despite it being fake, Tazio couldn't help being aroused by her touch.

As Tazio hoped, the guards came closer to deal with them.

Tazio stepped forward, kneed one in the jewels, and elbowed his face against the stone wall. Zara sprang into action and kneed the other in the balls too, reducing him to a groaning pile before putting him out cold.

"Fean, Tazio," Zara said.

"Don't look at me like that. You ended that poor bastard just like I did."

"It's different—doing that in real life, instead of class."

"I know." Tazio wondered if she'd mistrust him for the things he'd lead them into that night. "Let's go."

Tazio cracked the door the guards had been guarding and they slipped through, finding themselves in an old indoor fish market. Dilapidated wooden stalls lined the space. In one, the fighter from two rounds ago was bleeding out unattended. Tazio wanted to check on him, but there was no time.

At the end of the hallway, Alesso was being escorted into another stall by two men. Tazio checked for an empty stall, and they ducked in. As they stood pinned against a wall, Zara pressed closer.

Tazio looked down at her, and she glanced up at him, her amber eyes nearly aglow in the mixed shadows. The sudden urge to protect her came over him.

"I can take them both," Tazio whispered.

"Don't be a hero. I'll take one."

"Perfetto."

Tazio picked up a wooden board off the ground and handed it to Zara. He climbed silently to the top of the stall through a hole in the old market stand's roof. As the guards walked past, Tazio dropped, jamming his heel into one man's neck, driving him to the floor, then turned to help Zara. She jammed the board into the other man's neck, sending him into spasms, and finished him with the heel of her leather boot before Tazio could blink.

"Fean, Zara. You're right, it is different doing it in real life."

"I feel less sick than before. Is that bad?"

"Cazzo. Wish we had time to break that down, but we don't."

They hurried to the booth where the guards had placed Alesso, and Tazio raised the corner of a threadbare sheet draped over the entrance.

Alesso lay on a cot, sweat beading his face and chest, his breathing irregular. Vials were strewn across a wooden bench beside the bed.

"*Khara*," Zara said, crouching by him and feeling his face with the back of her hand.

"Alesso," Tazio whispered, gently shaking him.

Alesso's lids cracked open. Milky eyes stared out.

Tazio felt Alesso didn't recognize him. Hate boiled up toward the people who did it. And hate toward himself for involving Alesso.

"Alesso, we're taking you out of here," Tazio said, then turned to Zara, "I'm going to walk him out. Can you see if there's another way out?"

"Allora," she said, and went out.

Tazio hoisted Alesso up and stumbled out with him. After a few steps, Zara emerged from the shadows.

"Everything on this side of the building is locked shut. We'll have to go back the way we came."

"Fean, no way."

"No, it's the only way."

Tazio scanned for a way out while Alesso groaned in delirium.

"I've checked it all. We need to cloak him," Zara insisted.

"What?"

"We'll disguise him as you. I'll support him, and you go without the cloak."

"That's insane. How are you going to hold him up?"

"It's our only option."

Tazio rubbed his brow and looked toward the brawling pit.

"I think it's better if you go without cloak," Tazio suggested, "I'll walk with him. You'll draw attention since you're a girl, and that will be good."

"Fine."

"Hurry."

Zara took her cloak off and wrapped Alesso. Tazio couldn't help but notice the grace in her touch. Even on the knife-edge of violent potential, she still managed to bring peace.

"Are you ready?" Zara asked.

"Yeah," said Tazio, holding Alesso's head up—but it fell and swung limp. "Cazzo." Tazio tapped his face, and Alesso's eyes sprang to life briefly before he fell under again.

Tazio pried his arm up the sleeve of Alesso's cloak and grabbed his hair to control his head, Alesso's neck tightening just enough in response.

"This will have to do. He's deep in it," Tazio said.

Zara led, checking corners as they clambered toward the fighting pit. Echoes bounced through the throat of the stairway as Tazio wrangled Alesso past the unconscious guards and down the stairs.

The intense spectacle hit Tazio like a wall. Zara wound through the crowd as she merged into the chamber of heat and pressure. Adrenaline sharpened Tazio's focus as the gyrating crowd bobbed around him, fear creeping in that at any moment they'd be discovered, their lives cut short.

I could distract the crowd for Zara to escape if something goes wrong.

They were halfway through now.

The crowd roared, a trance of sickos, faces stretched with bloodlust as two more men beat each other to a pulp. The fighters grappled on the floor, both nearly unconscious as one bit the other's cheek open, then savagely choked him out with a sloppy spurt of energy.

Following the frenzied cheers, the energy from the crowd began to wane as the focus shifted away from the main spectacle. Side conversations kicked up, bets for the next round were collected, pisses were taken along the walls. The change in focus made Tazio tense.

"Watch it," a rangy fellow with a hawkish nose said as Tazio accidentally bumped him.

"*Perdono.*"

"*Perdono?*" the man mocked, looking for trouble.

Tazio ignored him and kept walking, but could feel the man's glare on his back.

"What's with your friend?"

Tazio ignored him again.

"Ey! I'm talking to you!"

Tazio kept walking, braced for the worst.

"Ey! *Vattelo a pigliare in culo!*"

Heads turned toward the clamor.

"I've got this," Zara whispered to Tazio.

Tazio shot her a look, trying to dissuade her, but she turned around and walked to the nuisance of a man.

"You look like you could cool off a bit." Zara stroked the man's hawkish face and neck like a trained alley whore. Steadily she won him by his lower impulses, and he took her by the waist.

Rage flew through Tazio.

If you stop to help Zara, you'll blow Alesso's cover.

"You're a fine pussy, aren't you," the man said to Zara, his face curled with desire.

"Let's go get you sorted," Zara tugged him by the hand toward the exit, but he tugged her toward a corner room where a trickle of men and women were going in and out for lewd release.

The temptation to intervene stretched through his muscles.

"No, no," Zara purred, "I'm no den slop, but I'll work you better than you can imagine back in the brothel."

The man's eyebrows hit the ceiling and his head cocked sideways.

Zara grabbed his ass and led him to the front entrance.

"Next time, you're dead," said the ingrate, shoving Tazio as he and Zara walked past.

Rage streamed through Tazio's veins at the provocation, and he wrestled Alesso up the stairs toward the main entry in haste. Alesso felt like a dead weight, feet rolling awkwardly over the steps like a limp doll as Tazio strained to hold him upright.

"I have to use my *talùth*," Tazio muttered, Leone's warnings of the risks of dependency echoing in his mind.

As his eyes closed, the strand of *draeda* connected to the *anima pontem* on his chest, the thread widening as he manipulated it. Power opened in him like a raging river. His muscles screamed, and he breathed through the inky colors swelling in his vision as sounds grew rich and abstract. Blood pressed into his face, veins bulging as he lifted Alesso off the ground, hoisting him up the stairs and propping him against the wall at the top.

"Ey," said the huge guard at the main entrance.

"My friend had a bit too much—you know," Tazio said through raspy breaths, the man's face morphing before his eyes.

"Out." The guard cracked the door and pointed outside before settling back onto his stool to pack a new lip of opia.

Tazio dragged Alesso off the wall around his shoulder and shielded his face the best he could. As he went past the guard, the outside air nipping his face, the guard's meaty arm thrust out, blocking the way.

"Who that?"

"My friend. He came earlier," Tazio said.

The guard's eyes narrowed as he considered Tazio's lie, and he stood up off his stool. "Your friend just walk out with other man."

"Hm," Tazio said, cracking his most relaxed smile.

The big man shoved Tazio hard against the nearest wall, and Alesso crumbled to the floor, hood falling off his face. Alert flew into the guard's eyes.

"No gamble! I'm no fucking idiota!"

He threw a huge fist, but Tazio ducked it, and the wall spit stone from the impact. The man plowed into Tazio, barrel chest suffocating him against the wall.

Body blows rattled Tazio's ribs and kidneys, and an uppercut snapped his head into the wall, leaving his ears ringing. But having taken enough blows in his training, he gathered his focus and drove a stiff palm into the man's solar plexus. The man grunted, stumbling back and leaving a small opening for Tazio to dive forward. The brute turned and charged as Tazio rolled backward and sprang into a twist. As he hit the floor near the door, his foot slipped, sending shock through his system. Clawing his way backwards, he scrambled toward the alley, inches from a better fighting position as the man dove and crushed him into the cobblestones. Rough stone cut Tazio's head as he writhed on his back to find guard. The man pinned him with a forearm, despite his best efforts to grapple and strike. Punches came down like boulders until Tazio felt his nose pop inward. The world began to blur as he coughed blood. Between punches, ugly rage painted the man's face as punches sent Tazio closer to darkness.

The punches stopped, and the man began to choke him, leaving Tazio gasping. Not even *draeda* could help now, as Tazio's vision began to narrow, chest grabbing for air. Muscles stopped responding, power draining from every fiber.

Fight!

But there was nothing left to fight with. So he released, and as he did, a vision of Anya flashed into his mind—her ice-blue eyes on the peak of *Stùc Naom*. Desperately he reached for her in *Etria*, pulling from every particle of his body for a connection. A feeling that started as a spark expanded from a point in his heart, first faint, then explosive like lightning unfurling from the calm. Cobblestones around him burst from the force, the brute atop him yelped in pain, releasing Tazio. With newfound energy, Tazio's fingers clawed into the man's hamstring, blood gushing as he pierced through flesh and tore muscle from bone. A chilling scream filled the alley as the man fell over writhing. Catching his breath, Tazio rose, hovering over the man with menace.

"*Miserere mei!*" the man begged, horror in his eyes.

"Mercy?" Rage burned in Tazio's throat. "After you enslave my friend in this sick place?"

"Please, no kill me," he wept.

"The people that run this place," Tazio said, disgust rising in his throat. "They'll burn."

Closer to the entrance, Tazio heard a scuffle. Turning, he saw Zara drive a kick into the side of the horny man's head. A squeal pitched out of him and he fell unconscious.

"Tazio!" he heard Zara shout as she ran toward them.

Beside Tazio, the man whimpered and crawled away, disabled leg bleeding profusely as muscle hung from bone. He'd be dead within minutes and there was nothing Tazio could do.

"*Fean*, Tazio."

"Alesso," Tazio muttered back, walking back into the foyer.

"Yes, Alesso."

Finding Alesso in a stupor, they pulled him up and hastened away, the dark alley seeming to rage at losing them from its clutches. Tazio's whole body was numb as snow drifted down. When they stumbled into an inn just inside the middle quarter, the simple innkeeper understood their need from their bludgeoned state, asking only the necessary questions.

He and Zara left Alesso to rest in a firelit room. In a second room,

Tazio collapsed onto a bed, hoping he would drift into oblivion, unable to understand the events life had just imposed upon them. But his throbbing face tortured him awake, forcing him to deal with his pain. His regret. His conscience.

Tazio heard the door shut and opened his eyes to Zara letting herself in. Her eyes were calm, but ravaged.

"We must find out what poison they've used on Alesso," Tazio muttered.

"First we have to set your nose," Zara said, kneeling beside the bed.

Tazio moved her hand away. "He could die."

"If you don't do this now, the bleeding won't stop."

"You know how?"

"My mother trained me."

"*Fean*. Then do it."

"Hold still."

She put her fingers on either side of his nose.

"Tell me when you're ready."

"I'm—"

She snapped the ridge into place before Tazio could assent.

"*Cazzo!*" Tazio griped.

"You'll be fine."

"*Fean*, I pity the other bastards you helped."

"Oh shut up. Clearly you feel good enough to spout off a poor joke."

"At least I can breathe without hacking out a mouthful of blood."

"I'll take that as thanks. Since you're too proud to say it."

"Thank you, Zara," Tazio said, her closeness apparent now the pain had lessened. She seemed to notice too, moving the hair from her face and shifting backwards, the room growing quiet.

"They said Alesso would be fighting tomorrow," Zara said. "So whatever they had him on wasn't lethal."

"That's promising."

"I'm going to find some ointment for your face." Zara moved to the door.

"Zara, wait." Tazio's words stopped her. "I'm sorry."

"Please, not now."

"I'm sorry for bringing you into this. For bringing Alesso into this.

I'm so sorry, Zara. Please forgive me." Tazio choked back tears, a rush of painful guilt rising.

Zara walked back to him and knelt again. Her touch was kind as she brushed hair off his face.

"You're a fool sometimes, but your heart is good. And I'm glad we're alive."

"Don't go."

"I'm not leaving Auria. Don't be so damned dramatic," she said, smiling as she walked out.

Without Zara there to distract Tazio, pain made its pestering appearance again. Tazio felt an urge to be in the cold and walked outside. In the inn's small interior garden, he saw a barrel full of rainwater sitting in the corner.

Fean, that will be good.

He groaned as he submerged his entire head, groaning underwater as the frigid water numbed the pain. He pulled out of the water, eyelids heavy, head hung low as the water poured into the barrel, its rhythmic waterfalls a gentle distraction.

Is this what I swore I'd become? A violent bastard?

Shut up. That's exactly the reason this is worth it. For them. For the Daemonae.

Where is Anya? And the others. Left to the wilderness.

Tazio missed her. Plain and simple. But the endless distance had turned her into a distant memory he was having a harder time holding onto with each passing day. It scared him that she already felt gone. He looked up to the sky. The clouds had broken up and puffed along in front of two of the sister moons in a morose procession.

From hence to thence, where do the clouds drift? Where do I drift from here?

Drenched, he stumbled through the wooden hallways back to the room.

When he opened the door, Zara was on the bed. He walked past her and sat on the bed facing away, looking through the small shuttered window.

The day hung over like a dark fog.

Disturbing images of Alesso fighting flashed through his mind.

Alesso will be forever scarred. Because of me.

"Tazio," he heard Zara say from the other side of the bed in a whisper.

"Yes?"

"Are you well?"

"I'm fine."

"You don't seem fine."

"We'll need an explanation. For Neri—about our wretched state."

"Yes." Her response tapered off into the crackling hearth. "What if we admit the truth?"

"We can't."

"Sometimes it's the wisest thing to do."

"They'll ask why we were there in the first place. And I won't give up on finding out how the *talùth* trade operates. How the Guild is tied to all this—especially after what we just went through."

"I'm not sure it's worth it anymore, Tazio. We all nearly died, and I nearly had to service a man."

Tazio turned to the fire, watching flames flicker through the channels in the logs, feeling them coax the truth out of him. "My parents, Zara... right before my eyes... I watched them, Zara. I watched them be slaughtered. Dragged them out of a moat of bodies and burned them on a pyre I built with my own two hands. I watched them burn. And when I did, I made a promise. A promise I'd do anything to avenge them." Tazio looked at Zara. "I helped you get those books because you said you needed the information in them. Well I need information too. I need to know how the Guild's network is run to get what I need."

Zara shifted on the bed, lips parted like she wanted to ask, but muted by the tense silence. Tazio wanted to tell her more. To tell her how worried he was that the Guild knew his power from the Daemonae, that they would use him and interfere with his revenge. That he was afraid of the power swirling inside him and felt trapped—like an animal in some scheme he thought he could manipulate to his own advantage.

"It's all too complicated, Zara," Tazio said, breaking the silence. "I don't know why you're at the Guild, but not even what we experienced will stop me. I won't ask you for help again if that's what you want. I never want to put you in danger. I just had no one to turn to and Alesso—"

"You don't have to explain. I'm just afraid like you are."

She looked down at her lap and rubbed her hands. Something morose lingered beneath the surface of her countenance.

"My parents were killed too. That's why I was hunting for the books —to find out how and who," Zara admitted. "Not in front of me. But still killed. They were traveling merchants. One day they never came home. For thirty-seven days. When I finally got word, no one knew why, or who, or anything." Zara looked at Tazio. "I know it's sick to say, but I almost envy that you shared the final moments with your parents. That's why I'm searching. For anything that will help complete the story. For anything that will help me understand. I don't know if it's revenge I want, but it's the void that drives me mad. It hangs over me like they're asking to be found—like they're speaking to me."

Tears rolled down Zara's cheeks.

Tazio's heart swelled to comfort her. He shifted, hugging her, tears falling from his eyes, too.

"Of course I want to help you," Zara said after a minute, pulling away, "I just can't lose sight of my own purpose."

"I understand. I want to help you too."

Tazio wished he could promise her more. To find the information she sought. To avenge the people who did this to her parents—to her.

Zara looked at him and the room stilled again. The space between their hearts grew warm. Zara took a cloth from a table beside the bed and leaned to wipe blood rolling down Tazio's cheek. She steadied herself with a hand on his thigh, her fingers warm. Amber light flickered on her rich skin as she lingered, her touch sending warmth through him. The urge to bring her close raced through Tazio, and he reached around her, lifting her legs over his as she cradled into his chest, time disappearing as she breathed into him. His hands moved to the nape of her neck, and she breathed release as he kissed her cheek, following the trail of her desire, heart swelling as their lips locked and unlocked. Zara leaned back, her golden gaze sending waves of comfort through him. The cold wind howled outside, the shadows in their hearts danced away, and the last candle begged to be snuffed. Beneath the thick fur covers, the touch of her skin sent shudders through Tazio as he settled behind her, hand exploring her valleys and curves. Just this moment. Surviving. Fear stripped naked and turned to heat. Heat in the dark of night.

CHAPTER 22

TAZIO

THE RISING sun filtered through the inn window, dancing on Tazio's eyelids. Zara slept peacefully in his arms, and his heart ached for the moment to last forever, swearing it would make him content. But deep down, he knew life wasn't all comfort. And his face hurt. The cold barrel in the garden called to him.

Tazio gently shifted Zara off, letting her settle back to sleep. In the dawn light, the humble garden hummed as the morning fog burned away. In a weaver spider's web that hung on an awning, a firefly struggled for its life.

Like the three of us the night before.

Tazio opened his heart to it through *Etria*. It let him gently pluck it out, shaking the webs from his wings in his palm, staring up at him through metallic eyes before taking off. For a brief moment, through *anamea*, he saw the world in glowing light—just as the firefly did.

He plunged his head into the barrel again, letting the cold shock him awake and work its numbing wonders. When he came back to the room, Zara was lying on her side, awake. Firelight traced the quiet curves of her body.

"You and the barrel have a bond, don't you?" she purred with the coarseness that follows a long night.

"She's a cold lover."

"That she is."

Zara paused, eyes lingering.

"What is it?" Tazio asked.

"What if we lose this?"

"Don't think about it."

"Our friendship."

"I know. Don't fret. I'll be there for you, no matter how it all works out."

Tazio hoped it was true. The future tended mostly to be a liar. And right now, Tazio could barely think straight with Zara before him—a beauty with a golden gaze a thousand spans deep.

Zara leaned forward, eyes fixed on Tazio, and slid her hand onto Tazio's member, other hand pulling him down by the shoulder. Their flame roared again as uncertainty about what they would become burned away. Ecstasy shot through Tazio as he disappeared into her, and she moaned her assent.

Rising. Holding. Peaking. Returning to the burden of reality—of Neri waiting, of Falkone—all of it rushing back, the escapade flitting away.

"I'll take the fall," Tazio whispered.

"So quickly in thought." Zara put her hand on Tazio's cheek.

Problems faded with her lying on him. "We'll say I got drunk and got into a fight," Tazio continued. "That someone said something cross to me, and I reacted poorly. They teamed up, and the mismatch left me like this. Alesso, on the other hand—we'll say he drank too much. Recovering from not handling himself so well."

"We can't even be certain he'll recover soon enough for that to make sense."

"Aside from telling them outright, I think it's our best chance." The sobering reality of the situation finally doused their spark. "We should check on him," Tazio said.

"Yes, you're right."

Zara slid off him, her lithe curves setting his blood racing as she walked toward the fire. She looked over her shoulder, her softer side beckoning. Tazio stood, alert, and pressed into her from behind, fire roaring as she gasped. In the swirl of heat, fear surged from the outposts of Tazio's mind, pulling him away, urging him to seal the cracks in his heart. Love would distract him from his purpose. Love would abandon him. He demanded the procession of thoughts to cease.

"Tazio," she whispered, sorrow in her eyes.

Tazio picked her up. Once inside, he never wanted to leave, gazing into her eyes, their pain a bridge. Gripped by a future just beyond their ecstasy, every pulse deeper, but knowing—shadows waited.

—

"Don't take me for an imbecile, Tazio!" Neri shouted, brow driven down.

He tore his gaze away and paced in front of the floor-to-ceiling bookshelves behind his desk. The plush carpet and chairs in the office were so luxurious they almost brought Tazio comfort.

"Neri, it's the truth," Tazio feigned conviction, hoping Zara wouldn't cave and let out the truth.

"You think I believe that Alesso is drunk? And that your face was bludgeoned in a brawl at the local alehouse?"

"It's the truth." Tazio's words felt weak as he uttered them.

"This is your last chance to tell the truth," a livid tightness stretched across Neri's face. "Silence?"

"It's the truth," said Tazio, committing to the ruse.

"Do you think I run this Guild without knowing the whereabouts of my apprentices?"

Tazio's heart beat in his ears, head light from holding the line.

Maybe someone had seen them. Someone in the pit must have been from the Guild.

"It seems you'd have broad purview," Zara said, voice mostly steady.

"Broad purview indeed. Tell me, how were the fights? How about the bedding at the inn? Plush to your liking?"

Neri knew that much, but maybe not why they were there.

"I'm sorry, Neri. Please don't blame Zara or Alesso. It was my idea," Tazio replied.

"What was your idea?"

Caution screamed.

"We wanted to see what the dark markets were like."

"You were told not to go there," Neri seethed, jabbing a finger toward the markets.

"I know. We wandered around, and Alesso went off to look for some goods to buy. He didn't return and I went looking for him. When I couldn't find him, I came back with Zara the next day. I was ashamed of the mistake—that's why I tried covering it up."

Neri turned to the bookshelf and lifted a decorative dagger from its stand, then balanced the tip on his finger.

"To the trained expert, this balances with stability. But a simple miscue—and it falls." Neri shifted his finger, and the dagger flipped and lodged into his desk. Tazio's knee twitched at the thud. "When we warn you to stay clear of somewhere, it's for your protection. Next time, you might not be so lucky. Don't take your talent for the right to do whatever you find pleasing."

Neri's finger had opened from the dagger's point, and he licked it clean before pulling the dagger free from the table.

"You're all restricted to Guild grounds. Report to Leone at the beginning of each day for service duty. You'll work a minimum of four hours a day, or as needed. Is that understood? Or do I need to carve it into you," Neri said, miming a slash midair.

"Understood," Tazio and Zara echoed.

Tazio exhaled. If that was all Neri knew, it went better than expected, even with the punishment. The motivation of gathering knowledge about the *draeda* market was the most incriminating part. There must have been someone in the fighting pit or the marketplace that relayed their whereabouts to Neri, which suggested the Guild *was* tied to the Tenebri Emporium.

"Next time, I can't promise a lenient punishment," Neri added. "Your behavior is grounds for execution. I'm not the only one assessing your behavior. I can only protect my *apprentici* for so long. Now get out."

"Thank you, Neri," Tazio said.

Zara left without a word, and Tazio ran after her. "I'm sorry. I don't know how he found out," Tazio said. A wall seemed to stand between them.

"That could have been the end."

"We'll be fine."

207

Zara stopped. A strange hardness lay in her eyes.

"Tazio, this is all too overwhelming."

"What do you mean?"

"All of it. What happened at the market, what happened last night, this morning, all of it."

Before he could get a word in, Zara pulled away, and his gut cinched tight. With each passing step, a hollow, heartsore strain gripped his chest —the same pain as when he'd been severed from Anya in pursuit of Falkone.

Anya. And now Zara. Like sand slipping through my fingers. Maybe I'm not supposed to know love. Everyone I love, crushed before me. No matter how hard I fight.

For a heartbeat, he considered running after her—asking what had changed, what he'd done wrong. But she never looked back, each passing step making his heart hurt more—until she finally drew her hood and disappeared into the crowd.

Tazio pulled up his hood too, shielding himself from the bustling hallway, falling into the pit growing in his chest. A new sorrow to be carried alone. A blossom of love ripped from the soil. Perhaps he should loathe her for abandoning him. Opening up to her so soon was a grave mistake. Hatred burned in his hands for opening his heart like a fool. Aimless, like a leaf in a tempest, he tumbled through the crowd.

Love is a distraction. I'm here for fury. For vengeance.

CHAPTER 23

TAZIO

Tazio pressed another Setian Rosebush seed into the soil. After weeding most of the exterior of the Guild, Zara, Alesso, and he were tasked with replanting the gardens for their misbehavior. Zara was only paces away, but a vast distance lay between them, and the world seemed gray despite the shining spring. Disembodied for several weeks. Despite Tazio's best attempts to stop himself, he'd eventually talked with Zara about why she'd distanced herself from him. It proved worthless, the gap only growing wider. With it, the torment of losing her.

His appetite had shrank, his fervor for life suffocated. Losing her gnawed at his chest, the warmth of her touch lingering, his heart craving it, mind screaming at him to distance himself. He wished he'd never have to see Zara again, but he also wished he could see her every moment, his world swinging like a pendulum between pain and hope.

But at least Alesso's recovery was one remaining joy. In the weeks following his rescue, Tazio fought to be present with Alesso, lashing himself to snap out of his malaise and focus on his friend. Alesso's *talùth* had, in fact, been cracked. Neri also informed them that a practitioner could coerce someone to agree to a side channel into their *anima pontem*, using it to gain access to the *talùth* and force the user to draw on *draeda*. The attacker was like a puppeteer controlling a marionette energetically.

In Alesso's case, the dark marketeers had combined two types of drugs to make his submission easier—opia and *diabium*. *Diabium* left its user mentally relaxed and open to suggestions. Luckily, it wore off over time and the Guild had accelerant remedies.

It also explained the possessed behavior Alesso showed inside the ring. The image of Alesso cracking the other man's knee backward still jolted into Tazio's mind, but at least he could trust it wasn't truly Alesso.

Though the experience did seem to linger darkly on Alesso. He joked less, his retorts coming a beat later than usual. The way he'd drop back into himself, as if from a distant place. Tazio hoped it was the substances clearing from his system, and not memories permanently etched, ready to torment Alesso like Tazio's did to himself—but watching Alesso force jokes hinted at pain behind his mask of cheeriness.

Tazio tried taking on the role of the comic to cheer him up. But it just didn't feel as funny without Alesso driving the jest. Thankfully, as the weeks went on, natural humor did find its way back into Alesso, like the first flowers in spring—at first scattered and waking from slumber, then in full and glorious bloom.

When Tazio told Alesso what had happened with Zara, a flicker of hurt showed through his nonchalance. "You two are obviously close," Alesso had said.

Tazio had known Alesso liked Zara from the beginning. Any man with two eyes would want her—and that, oddly, made him feel better. In the end, it would be up to her—that the power of beauty.

Lately, what made interactions with Zara maddening was the volatile ecstasy. The way she'd slide into his bed, her breasts pressing against him. Her whispering persuasion to forget the past and enjoy slipping back into each other. The touch of her silk skin banished all reason, the present obliterating all worry and doubt, only for the bliss to fall short of its promise, leaving Tazio empty as she slipped away and kept her distance in the hallways.

At times, he wished he never had fallen for her. The hints of hope, the tease that perhaps time could alchemize their loss of love back into a bond again. But all he could do was place the hope on the same shelf of other losses he didn't know how to feel or understand, and wait in patient confusion for some resolution.

After five weeks of struggle, Tazio decided that Zara was more important than just a lover to have, the power of their friendship outweighing his desire for love. Of course he wished they'd be more, but he couldn't fight the truth that he needed her as a friend regardless of his passions—the heart, after all, could change on a whim, so could it even be trusted? And what *was* certain, were the trials his gut sensed just beyond the horizon. The Guild was harrowing, the training difficult, and given what he'd discovered in the dark market, Tazio feared the dangers would only grow more complicated. All of it was sufficient to focus on purpose, and to allow her to focus on hers. And as his head grew clearer, it also became obvious why she'd retreated that day after Neri sentenced them.

My need to forward my purpose threatened hers.

As much as she'd wanted to help, he'd exposed her—emotionally, physically, strategically. She could have been expelled or sentenced to death for betraying the Guild, and with either, the possibility of discovering the answers she needed about her parents would have been obliterated.

"That's enough for the morning," Leone said from across the garden, dropping his shovel where he'd replanted a crop of annual flowers.

"About time," Alesso griped.

"I'll make sure to have some extra work for you next time."

"Why does that not surprise me?"

"Sometimes I prefer the obvious. Tazio, we're off to train," Leone said.

"Don't let Leone bully you out there." Alesso winked as he walked away with Zara.

"Not possible," Tazio joked back.

Tazio put the gardening implements back in a small shed, catching himself thinking of Zara, hoping Alesso was bringing joy to her since he couldn't. Leone held the door and they walked into the Guild.

"Something between you two?" Leone asked.

"Not sure what you're talking about."

"Don't play coy with me. You can save that for Zara," Leone flashed a charming, askew grin. "You've been walking around like a lovestruck fool lately. I figured I'd let the wind take it away, but we've already seen a month of spring and I've lost my patience."

Tazio chuckled. "We took a liking to each other. Or so I thought." The tiles moved past rhythmically on the floor as he moved through his thoughts. "I suppose looking back, it'd been there the whole time, our—I don't know what to call it, but it hardly lasted. Even if I thought it was real."

"Love?" The word made Tazio flush when it came from Leone's mouth. "Perhaps lust? A little dalliance?"

"Aren't we supposed to be talking fighting, not love?"

"Come now, they're practically the same! Everyone knows that."

"Cazzo, you're a genius."

"Aren't I? Don't worry, your wit will appear soon enough." Leone laughed to himself.

Now that Tazio had bared his heart to Leone, he expected greater wisdom. Instead, Leone just sauntered next to him with his crooked little gait and eternally contented smirk.

"It's not entirely funny," Tazio said.

"Soon it will be. If only you could see the way you wore the trials of it like a tortured soul, you'd soon cast it off!"

"How can you be so unfazed by life? It runs right through you like it's not even happening!"

"I understand."

"There! There it is again." Tazio stopped walking. "Do you ever react to *anything?*"

"Is that what you truly want to know?"

"I don't know! You're so damned balanced you're not even mortal!"

A few people in the hallways spread wider than normal around Tazio.

"Keep it together," Leone said, walking forward.

"Where are you going?"

"To train."

Tazio caught up.

"Why are you frustrated by it?" Leone asked.

"I just don't understand how you stay so calm."

"Not by that, by Zara."

"Oh, well. I don't know what I want with her anymore, and it's driving me a bit mad."

"I think you do know what you want," Leone said, "You're just frustrated you can't have it."

"Well, of course I want to be with her. But I've damaged it beyond repair and now friendship is more important." Suddenly his conclusion about being friends seemed terrible. He wanted her deep down, and the ugliness of indecision was grating on his self-esteem.

"That seems wise."

"It's not freeing me from the feelings. I want them gone."

"Ah, the shadows of love. That's why I avoid it," he said, winking.

"Very helpful. You're probably right, better to train than think."

"Add it to the tally of things I'm right about."

"Oh, fean."

"This is good! Now you can hack your rage out on me!" Leone crouched in an intentionally amateurish stance with a silly smile on his face.

No doubt Leone was Tazio's favorite mentor. But Tazio also loathed the idea of becoming so immovable like Leone demanded. He believed rage and fire were some of his finest attributes. They were his power. If he dulled all impulses he feared he'd be like a weak monk.

They walked the final passage to the training hall and Leone pushed open the slab door to the open-air arena. The pink cherry blossoms had burst to life in the past week and their scent perked him up.

"Come now, let's breathe," Leone said.

Tazio sat beside Leone on the cool dirt and drew a long breath through his nose. They ran through deeper breathing exercises, the rudimentary piece of Leone's method. When they first began training, the loops and rhythms of it would drive Tazio mad. But after several months, his mind craved serenity.

Leone called it *transcendentia*. It was similar to how the Daemonae accessed *daemonia*, but Leone's method seemed much more reliant on breath and focus to find a heightened sense in a more practical way. The training anchored Tazio's practice, allowing him to also replenish his natural supply of *draeda* and keep the harsh drain of the *talùth* at bay.

But it was hard to fight the reliance on the *talùth*. Every time he used it, it took a little longer to get balanced emotionally and to replenish himself. The side effects were much more harsh than the drain he experienced using *draeda* without a *talùth*. He found himself going to Guild *artifexae* for *draeda* replenishments far more often.

Tazio moved through his breathing exercises, sitting with his legs crossed on the floor. Anxiety ebbed and flowed until his focus sharpened and his vision felt lucid. He didn't know if that happened to others but he suspected his attunement to *daemonia* enhanced the exercises a bit.

He opened his eyes and the world seemed to breathe around him, sun sparkling on the clouds and trees.

Leone tossed him a training sword, and they ran through warm-up duels now written into memory.

"Can you tell me the state of war?" Tazio asked between the clatter of the wood swords.

"Hah! Which war? They're as widespread as famine."

"Come now, the only important war."

"Yes, yes. Falkone has taken every major kingdom south of Bourgogne and the Aroinn Forest."

Leone transitioned to the *vespae* stance. Tazio adjusted.

"With what losses?"

"Inconsequential. Petty lords can't handle a force of two hundred thousand. Falkone was wise to swallow Bourgogne first and build his force early out of the Eistal Passage."

The thought of Falkone's army spilling out of the Eistal Passage and swarming into Bourgogne to kill his clan pulled Tazio away. A hard blow from Leone's wooden training sword cracked him on the forearm.

"*Focus.*" Leone paused. "I know it hurts to remember the fall of Bourgogne, but a foe who knows this, uses this. Use your soft gaze."

Soft gaze—breathing, opening the mind's eye into space outside the body, slowing things down, preventing narrow vision.

"Will they move on Auria?" Tazio countered with an unusual combination.

Leone parried. "It would be bold—but bold seems Falkone's spirit. Riding on a string of victories, many in the Guild think he'll be tempted by the biggest prize of all."

"You think he'd attack Auria?"

"It's certainly up for consideration."

"Would Auria attack Thorace first?"

"If it came to it."

"And the Guild?"

Leone stopped sparring. "My, you're full of questions today."

"Have to empty a full mind, am I right?" Tazio winked.

"I thought love was on your mind."

"Someone wise once told me they're one and the same."

"Do introduce me to them. They sound like a fine specimen."

"Come now, don't dodge the question."

"Well, the Guild and Auria's political interests are intertwined. But the Guild's strongest interest is in maintaining stable trade. Money is our main lever, and without trade, influence begins to slacken." Leone put his finger where his dick should be and let it drop lazily. "That said, without Auria under our control, we cannot operate."

"Then war must happen."

"War seems like a simple solution, but often it produces more problems than it solves. Compromise and subtle maneuvers, while exhausting, tend to produce better results."

"Like, what, control the political levers even after an invasion?"

"Go deeper."

Tazio thought for a moment. "Threaten to bring trade to a standstill, stunting the invaders and all of Novra... give up overt control of the city, but work in the way of shadows."

"Indeed!" Leone reignited his attack, surprising Tazio. He flurried and jabbed with blazing joy painted on his face, relishing the way Tazio ducked and parried.

Tazio pinned Leone's sword in the dirt.

"Bravo!" Leone exclaimed. "As you see, sometimes we're forced to let the solution rise out of the pressure of chaos."

Visions of Falkone raping and pillaging his way unchecked through Novra stirred in Tazio. He grew furious that none of the lords who claimed to have power had stopped him or even left a dent in his forces. And the idea of Auria caving to Falkone to maintain economic power disgusted him.

"Come now," Leone growled, exposing an overly ambitious combination Tazio launched. "Enough. That's enough for today." Leone stepped away, looking disappointed. "Did you not come to me because you wanted to win the games?"

"Yes."

"Well, I can't guide a broken rudder in a thrashing stream!"

"If you knew what I've been going through, you'd understand how minuscule the games seem in comparison," Tazio said.

"The time for emotionalism has passed. You have to conquer your weakness."

"Enough with the platitudes."

"Platitudes?"

"Yes! Platitudes! You stand there with that silly smile stuck on your face all the time, free of cares. Then you tell me to move past my emotions?"

"I don't mean to offend."

"Then what do you mean to do?"

"To teach. Your emotions are not *you*, Tazio. They're temporary storms. If you succumb to them, you will always be their slave."

"Condescension at its finest."

"Tazio—"

"No. I'm tired of it. Of you. Of your equanimity. Your endless lessons. It's exhausting." The bright twinkle normally cresting Leone's eye wavered. "I'm sorry. I didn't mean it."

Leone sighed, eyes cast to the dirt as he walked over to rack his sword.

"I think I've taught you what I can for now," Leone muttered.

"What do you mean?"

"I've spent decades polishing my worst impulses to bring balance to others, but I'm not perfect either. I was once shattered like you were, and rebuilt myself like you're doing. But don't mistake my tranquility for weakness. I've found it requires far more strength to be unmoved. I understand your rage at the world, Tazio. But I'm afraid my voice has become just another enemy to feed your darker impulses."

Leone donned his cloak and walked out of the arena, his cloak snapping as he went.

"Where are you going?" Tazio asked, shocked to see him leave.

But the sad words did nothing to stop Leone.

He just drifted away, leaving Tazio alone with his rage.

Tazio hurled his sword against the wall.

It clattered to the ground, its echoes making the pit feel stunningly empty.

Cherry blossoms swirled through the arena on a gust.

"I don't need them," Tazio whispered, eyes fixed on the dirt. "Or Zara. Or Neri. Or anyone."

The trusting boy inside winced at the bitterness poisoning his heart. But Tazio smashed innocence down, whirling his cloak in an angry arc, storming out of the training hall, delicate pink blossoms drifting to the floor in the wake of his fury.

CHAPTER 24

TAZIO

THE CHEERS of two hundred thousand rumbled the giant wooden doors behind Neri. Torchlight flickered along the stone tunnel walls. Alesso jumped up and down in anticipation. Zara stared straight ahead, ready. Kage looked pleasantly sinister, Corso calm and deadly, and Luca was more jittery than usual. The Guild had stripped them of their *talùthae* for the tournament, and Tazio decided he would not use any Daemonian power either. This fight would be pure and raw.

The other fourteen fighters standing in line with them were rugged mercenaries who had entered through a rigorous qualification tournament—three Aurians and eleven foreigners from across Novra. Mean, focused energy radiated off all of them. For them, winning would bring the kind of prestige that would get them hired into the finest private entourage, and the coin that came with it.

Neri gave both lines of fighters a sly grin, then pushed open the doors.

As they all moved forward, Tazio's eyes adjusted from the dark, the scale of the *Coliseo* staggering as they stepped into the open air. Roaring fans packed rafters that stretched into the sky. Diverse flags from far regions and nearby Aurian districts snapped in the air, colors flapping in the churning sky. In the pit, drummers pounded wardrums and dancers in long silks swung on beams and ropes along the edges. And as if called forth by anticipation, the scattered clouds churned black and gray as four huge horns blared across the stadium. Tazio and the others arranged in the middle and the crowd fell to attention.

"Welcome to the 156th Guild Games!" Neri boomed, his voice amplified shockingly well by the design of the *Coliseo* and the aid of a ram's horn mounted on a longstaff. "The road to compete in the Guild Games is fraught with rigor, and the toil of discipline! There are few greater honors. *Per favore*, give our fighters a grand welcome!" The crowd roared. "We will now begin!"

Neri turned from the crowd to them.

"You know your foes. Grab your rapiers and find your first fighting ring."

Tazio walked with the others to the table where the rapiers were laid out. He tested the blade, swinging and twirling it. It was like an extension of his arm. An exact replica of the one he trained with endlessly. He dragged the blade against his leather armor—not razor-sharp, but lethal if used right.

In the first round, the objective was to land a blow on the chest or back, and be the first to two points. Everyone fought at the same time for the first round, and he had drawn Kage.

A favorable draw.

She was good. But underpowered. Liable to temper despite a cool shell.

Drumbeats grew quicker as they all lined up in their fighting rings.

Tazio saw Kage sink into the balls of her feet, calm and focused.

The grain of the red clay under Tazio's feet was compact with a touch of give—perfect grip for a fight.

All the fighters settled, the air tight as they breathed and jittered, ready for their cue, adrenaline spiking.

The first horn blared, quicker than Tazio expected. Kage seemed thrown off too, and Tazio took advantage of it, springing forward.

Kage dodged, slippery. She'd wanted him to take the offensive. He backed off and let her attack, seeing what she was made of. She stopped, and a twitch of disdain darted across her face.

She didn't like that.

Kage dove in again, attempting to prove herself.

Tazio batted away her thrusts, making sure to appear like they didn't impact him in the least.

Like a stew, she began to boil as the fight dragged on. Slowly she fell apart, and before Tazio knew it, he'd landed two blows and the first round was done.

Kage turned away, blushing. Though Leone had beaten "win at all costs" into Tazio's head, he still felt sorry for beating her with mental warfare.

"You fought well," Tazio muttered as they walked back over the tent where the fighters retired between rounds.

"You fought better."

"Afraid so."

"Now you have to win the whole thing. At least that way I won't look like a complete pig's ass."

"Well now that I have you in my troupe..."

"Don't go too far. Just win."

The hint of a smile struggled to find its way into her eyes.

She was a curious creature. Definitely battered. And she seemed to respond to that through intense loyalty. In this case, to the strong arm of Corso.

Tazio sat and Kage hovered near the back of the tent, muttering every once in a while to herself.

The first round came to an end.

Corso, Alesso, Zara all made it through. The other remaining fighters were mercenaries. Back in the tent, most everyone was beaten and bloodied. One brute nursed a large gash.

In the second round, fights would be one at a time.

An attendant pulled Zara and a huge bearded fighter from Bourgogne out of the tent. They walked to the center of the arena and squared up, the crowd cheering them on.

A horn blew again, and at the first drop, Zara disrupted the burly man with staccato parries. Looking to put the nuisance to an end quickly, the man tried taking the fight to the floor through brute force.

Fool.

He left an opening, and Zara used the assault to slide around him and jolt his arm out of socket. The man roared as she slashed his back for the first point. The stadium erupted—cider splashed from mugs, faces stretched in glee as the crowd lost itself in the foolery of large gatherings.

For the rest of the fight, the man was a gimp, and Zara cleaned him up with adroit movements, pestering him on his disabled side like a cruel mantis. When it was all over, the big man walked back sullen, and Zara walked back the image of lethal composure. She looked at Tazio, giving him a subtle nod.

A fighter from Kataria who moved like a skittish bug gave Alesso a scare in the second round. Took him to the floor and split his cheek with a sharp elbow. Blood poured over the dirt and the pool grew as Alesso struggled to fight from the bottom. Their swords came loose and the Katarian tried battering Alesso down with punches and grapple holds.

But the Katarian was impatient.

Alesso found a gap to flip him off and scrambled to grab the closest sword off the dirt. The other man grabbed at Alesso's ankle, tripping him, but Alesso stretched and got the rapier he needed. He turned, grappling the skittish man with a cheeky leghold and finished him like a scorpion sticking its prey.

Corso lined up and made easy work of an Aurian named Emero. To finish the round, he parried the sword from Emero's clutch, seizing the advantage, and knocking him unconscious with a rapier's hilt to the helmet. The Aurian went blank and was forced to withdraw. The attendants could barely remove the dented helmet.

"Tazio! Omkenyo!" an attendant shouted from the tent's edge.

Tazio stood. The Nebian fighter looked toward him, his black orblike eyes mesmerizing, even from a distance.

They walked to the pit, the vast stadium once again lifting Tazio's blood.

They squared off.

Gems were woven into Omkenyo's skin, shining like brilliant signals of his power.

Neri murmured something in the background.

Time was a blur as Tazio waited, staring down the Nebian, who looked calm and unmoved.

The horn blared.

Tazio went on the attack, but Omkenyo consumed his attacks. Like fighting a shadow. Half of Tazio's attacks just caught wind and he nearly fell off balance several times. After hacking with little avail, Tazio blinked, and Omkenyo was suddenly behind him, as if he'd closed the gap without moving, his rapier sliding across his back, slow and insulting.

Khara, that's one point.

Tazio tried hiding his frustration as they lined up for the second point. The jewels in Omkenyo's face glowed like his life force pumped them brighter. Tazio wasn't aware whether they could channel *draeda*, but it seemed suspicious.

Tazio looked to Neri, as if to confirm his suspicions, but Neri just put his hand out to indicate the next point would start.

I'll have to bait the shifty bastard.

Neri's arm dropped and Tazio dashed toward Omkenyo on the offensive. Omkenyo was utterly relaxed. Cocky. Like he was ready to absorb anything Tazio flailed at him.

Tazio pulled away, refusing to play into his little game.

Omkenyo smiled, his teeth black like polished stones. Tazio had never seen a Nebian smile before, and it was unnerving to say the least.

"Come now, Nebian," Tazio said in Omkenyo's tongue, having learned some phrases in preparation for fighting most types. "I've heard of the glory of your people. Do you all fight so afraid?"

The jewels on Omkenyo's face glowed red. "You haven't earned the right to speak in our tongue," he replied in Setian.

"I could say the same."

"Enough foreplay," Neri said, and the horn blared again.

They circled. Omkenyo was like a horse ready to kick.

Oh, the glories of a little prodding.

Tazio jabbed and pestered mockingly, giving the nonchalance back in droves.

Omkenyo was twitching on his toes now, hungry to attack. Despite the veil of confidence, Tazio sensed he was probably used to people over-committing in frustration.

Tazio lunged forward, feigning a strong offensive, and Omkenyo jumped on the counter-offensive.

Tazio slipped the counter, side-kicked him in the leg, and drove his sword into his ribs.

Omkenyo yelled in clatters and hisses, the outburst making Tazio's neck hairs stand up as he moved into position for the next point. After a few steps, he looked over his shoulder and chuckled, seeing if he could get under Omkenyo's skin. Tazio respected the man, but he'd need every advantage he could get. He was one of the best Nebian fighters, blessed by their emperor to come and fight.

Omkenyo grew more frustrated at the web of attacks and feints Tazio spun around him during the next point, flipping and dodging, moving between offense and counterattacks like Leone taught him until Omkenyo lost his patience and lunged in recklessly. Tazio side-flipped, evaded the hack, and dove forward, slashing him clean across the back. Omkenyo screamed, hurling his sword across the pit.

The crowd roared over Tazio's acrobatic display. Arms spread wide to join the shaking stands, Tazio reveled in it.

"You fight well!" Omkenyo shouted, pulling him away. "But dirty." Then he smiled out of respect.

"You too. Not easy to manipulate a master of the art."

Omkenyo bowed his head, leading with one eyebrow, cool and collected again. They shook amid the remaining cheers, the crowd enjoying their gentlemanly respect. They walked back to the tent, where the three other remaining fighters rested on the front row of chairs.

"You slid by in that one," Alesso said.

"That's saying a lot coming from you," Tazio said.

"You'd better hope you don't face me next. I won't be as graceful as the Nebian."

"You're as graceful as a swan."

He wanted to say something to Zara, but she didn't look his way.

Neri walked up. "The draws are Alesso and Corso, Zara and Tazio. Alesso and Corso, you will begin."

"Caught a break," Alesso jabbed Tazio before walking to the ring.

Corso walked ahead of him without a care.

With the others gone, the silence grew uncomfortable between Zara and him.

"I guess fighting each other is one way to settle it all," Zara said as they watched Corso and Alesso line up.

"Not much to settle, is there?"

Zara looked at him, layers of mixed emotion in her eyes.

"Good point, we both know where it all stands."

"That we do."

In the ring, Neri gave his speech to the crowd, and dropped his arm at the sound of the horn.

Corso and Alesso started like two bulls vying for dominance. Their points to reach 1-1 were more bludgeon than blade, but the crowd didn't mind the reprise from elegance. At 1-1, Alesso misparried a blow and Corso cracked him in the cheek with his hilt, and before Alesso could respond, Corso was on him, and that was it. Tazio was also relieved he wouldn't have to fight his own best friend.

Assuming I don't have to take down my other best friend. Or whatever she is now.

Alesso walked under the tent, dazed and upset.

"You alright?" Tazio asked.

"Yeah, losing to Corso really makes me feel alright."

Corso heard the comment and offered only a side eye, wasting no more attention than necessary.

"At least I won't have to beat you in the final," Tazio said.

"There's always a bright side."

"Who said *you'll* face Corso in the final?" Zara asked.

"I suppose we'll find out soon enough." Tazio smiled.

"Try not to kill each other. Don't want to have to befriend Corso as a replacement," Alesso said.

"Do I really rank that low in quality?" Zara asked.

"So you *do* think you'll be the one to fall?" Tazio said.

"Tazio, Zara—to the ring," Neri said from outside the tent.

"Not sure who to root for here!" Alesso said.

"Her. She'll need it," Tazio said, winking.

"Maybe I will kill you out there," Zara replied.

The crowd was a blur of noise and movement as they walked in. Tazio could barely hear himself think as the very scenario Tazio prayed to avoid unfolded.

"Nothing personal," Zara said as she faced him.

"Nothing personal."

As was customary, they touched swords.

"Ready?" Neri asked.

"Ready," they both replied.

Neri put his arms into the air and the crowd urged him to start the duel.

Tazio's heart beat into his head, his ears ringing, vision tightening on the girl he'd loved. Her beauty was still arresting—amber eyes like torches through the slit of her helmet. Memories of her touch. Her softness. Of the secrets they shared and knew. All rattled around.

The horn blared and Neri threw down his arm. "Begin!"

Zara wasted no time, diving in like a cat in a wild combination of spins and kicks.

The fond memories flew out of Tazio's mind under the barrage.

Tazio parried and threw in a back handspring to free himself from the worst of it. Prior fighters couldn't cope with her ethereal approach, and few in the Guild could, but Leone had taught him to dance to the cues of chaos.

Zara's eyes burned like a forge as she pulled back and looked for her next opportunity. A twinge of hesitation—remembering how close they'd been—dropped into Tazio's mind. At that moment, Zara dashed to his side and slashed away. Tazio's parries fell a touch late, and she scored the first point, catching his shoulder.

Focus! This isn't the time for compassion.

In the second exchange, Tazio mixed up his approach—some attack, some defense. Unpredictable. Attack when they expect defense, defend when they expect an attack. From it he gained a point.

If there was fire in her eyes before, now there was pain. It had been easy to attack him, but she seemed hurt by enduring his fury toward her.

It did not hurt only her.

Tazio turned away, unable to bear looking at her.

Deep into his mind he went. To find the cold. The numb place that would let him win against her.

Win it here. Be done with it.

He charged straight at her chest, abandoning his fluid approach, each strike fueled by the darkness in his veins. His speed shocked even himself as he spun, hacked, and finally beat the sword free from Zara's grip, and it clattered into the clay.

Nothing personal.

She said it, not him.

Zara froze, staring at him. The honorable thing would be to surrender—but she didn't. She dove for her sword and Tazio sprang on her, carving a line into the back of her leather armor before she could swing around with her sword.

Zara froze when Tazio stepped off her, head hung as she stood and walked toward the fighter's tent.

"I'm sorry, Zara!" Tazio shouted as the crowd cheered.

She whirled around. "There's nothing to be sorry for! You won! It's what you wanted! Look, they love you!" Her voice trembled under the weight of a forced smile, eyes narrow.

Tazio sheathed his sword and walked to the tent, the cheers an ill backdrop to the pain swelling in his heart from eliminating Zara. As Tazio approached the tent, Alesso looked thoroughly confused at how to celebrate Tazio while consoling Zara. She wasn't having much of it though, and retired to the rear to take her armor off.

"Congratulations, but it's not over yet." Alesso said to Tazio.

"It has to be finished."

"If you don't beat him, I'll beat you after."

"Nothing like a good threat to get the blood flowing."

A full procession of horns played a triumphant tune to mark the final round, and drums beat as Tazio and Corso walked out from the tent. The revelry infuriated him—a reminder he'd traded love and friendship for hollow glory.

"Welcome to the final round!" Neri boomed to the crowd through his horn as the crowd hurriedly exchanged final bets. "Only two remain. And only one can be the victor!"

Neri milked the rapture, then turned to him and Corso.

"Fight well. First to three. Don't embarrass the Guild, or a victory won't feel like one later."

They nodded.

The crowd thundered like the storm brewing overhead. When he met Corso's eyes, his heart beat like a rabbit's. Long, deep breaths mixing with the rush concocted some primordial feeling as time slowed and his mind cleared of noise. The weight of the blade settled him, it being his closest companion in recent months. He still hadn't forgiven Leone for walking out on him. Nevertheless, he felt Leone with him as he trained alone each morning—hacking dummies, sparring imaginary fighters until he was no longer guiding the sword, but it was guiding him. And now he felt him there as Corso stood still, cut in ice as he settled into a fighting stance.

"Blades together," Neri said, looking at each of them.

Edges locked.

Corso pressed hard. The first subtle challenge for dominance. Tazio pressed harder, then let off, smiling as Corso twitched off balance before pressing again to help stabilize him.

Their blades sheared away.

Tazio opened his soft gaze, pushing out against the tightening rush as Neri raised his arm in the edge of his vision. His body flickered with anticipation.

Neri signaled the start.

The ethereal backdrop caused by waiting in such intense focus snapped into clarity.

Tazio flew at Corso, unleashing.

Corso's blade rang as he battered him away with impressive fortitude.

Tazio threw more, but Corso didn't budge.

Tazio withdrew and Corso took the invite, spinning in with a side swipe followed by a diagonal slash.

Tazio handled it, and on the second parry, caught Corso's sword by the hilt with his own, pinning it into the dirt. He rolled over Corso's shoulder and hacked him down from behind, scoring the first point.

Tazio roared with the crowd as they celebrated the bait and switch.

Corso didn't seem impacted in the least.

Have to respect the lad's immovability.

At the next cue, Corso surged at Tazio, using his direct pressure to push Tazio to the outside. He kept the pressure, making Tazio dance around the unrelenting push.

Corso dashed forward.

Tazio expected a sword blow, but Corso dove at his legs, then jumped up and hacked him down for a point.

"Learned that move from your mother," Corso taunted as Tazio stood and brushed the clay free from his eyes.

"Makes sense your finest move came from my lineage," Tazio retorted, hiding his deep rage, knowing that was what Corso wanted.

The next point started, and Tazio gave the center, this time containing Corso, lunging here and there, cutting and pestering him like horse flies. Then, Tazio changed his pattern and jumped in a flip, feigning an overhead blow. At the last moment, Tazio pulled his sword in and rotated again, deflecting Corso's parry as he landed behind him. Corso turned, a moment behind as Tazio jammed his sword into Corso's gut, blowing the breath out of him.

Corso spilled over into the clay and the crowd roared. Tazio felt sorry, and offered a hand to Corso.

"Fuck off, southerner." Corso shoved Tazio's hand away, drawing jeers from the crowd.

From then on, the points were grueling and precise, scored only by the smallest of margins—a well-thought out combination, a last ditch defense. A miscue here, an error there. Finally, the score sat 3-2 in Tazio's favor. One more to end it. Or, if Corso leveled they'd go to a final round.

"He's quite the teacher, ey?" Corso muttered as they squared off. "Good guy, Leone. Walked out on you though? You're unteachable is what he said," Corso twirled his sword by the pommel.

"Blades," Neri interjected, alternating his gaze between them.

Tazio tried to tame the fire raging in him that wanted to cut Corso's head off.

Don't lose your head. He wants that.

"Leone taught me how to beat Alesso too. That was nice—beating his face in earlier," Corso carried on. "Strong like an ox, but not the brightest."

Tazio's blood burned, the desire to end Corso pounding through him.

Neri gave the cue.

Tazio charged, gambling Corso wouldn't expect directness despite the taunts, hoping to throw him off balance and open his defense. Tazio hacked at him in a fury, the crowd cheering at the clamor of steel.

But Corso parried it all and threw a knee into Tazio's hip as he blazed by during an attack. Tazio felt off-balance, and before he could recover he saw Corso bring his sword down on him near the neck, slashing into the opening between his armor and helmet.

Tazio gasped as the blade split flesh, shock searing through him as steel cut nerves. He crumpled to the ground, each breath a lance of pain, the murmur of the crowd adding shame to the agony. Tazio put his hand to his neck. Blood gushed out of the deep gash. Already he felt dazed, but he rose to his feet, a guttural groan spilling out by reflex. White spots dotted his vision as he stood shaky and out of order.

"Come on!" Tazio shouted, rubbing his eyes, accidentally grating sand into them.

"Pathetic," Corso grunted.

"Can you proceed?" Neri asked, putting a hand on Tazio's shoulder.

Tazio struggled to get a word out, "Yes." He shuffled over to his place, light needling his eyes, nerves weak and gross as the world tilted woozily.

"Blades," Neri said.

Corso wasted no time when they started, barreling Tazio over with a simple shove. Tazio careened to the floor, coordination absent from the duel. In an attempt to stay in the fight, he rolled around on the floor to get up, but felt pitiful.

"Come on, Corso!" Tazio shouted.

The crowd was eerily silent, and his shouts bounced around the *Coliseo*. Hushed whispers trickled through the stands as he stuck his sword in the dirt to pry himself up. Barely standing, he saw Corso, his sword hanging loosely by his side.

"It's done," Corso said.

"Fuck you." Tazio tried tackling him, but stumbled like a lame man.

Corso took a step to the side and kicked him over.

Tazio fell on his face, tasting bitter dirt. Blood poured down the left side of his body as he pushed through shallow breaths to stay conscious.

It can't end like this.

Tazio struggled to his hands and knees.

"It's done, Tazio. You lost," said Corso.

Tazio lunged at Corso's legs, grappling them.

"Get the fuck off me!" Corso shouted, kicking him away.

From his back, Tazio saw the mass of spectators watching on with pitiful faces. Clouds drifted above the stands like a dream. Spasms gripped his stomach as blood pooled in his throat like the shame he drowned. Through coughs and sputters, his vision spun—then faded.

I've failed, Anya.

Nothing came back through *Etria*.

His eyelids moved with delayed reaction as the sun flickered on them. Amid his own unintelligible groans, he let his eyes fall closed, a wall against the sting of loss.

There she is.

He could feel her—Anya. The one who truly loved him. Telling him he did not fail. That he could not fail. That the Daemonae needed him.

That there was still work to be done.

→

The infirmary spilled into view as Tazio slid back into consciousness, one eye at a time. His whole body groaned, stiff with aches, and the wound on his neck hissed.

A matronly nurse in linen glided by, placid and efficient.

"*Perdono.* How long have I been out?" Tazio asked.

"Three days. You took fever from your wound."

Tazio remembered drifting in and out, but it had felt like a night's sleep, not three. Graduation for second year apprentices would be today. Hopefully with that happening, his humiliation at the Games would be a foregone topic. Then, after graduation, all the first year apprentices would be off to summer apprenticeships.

"Fean, apprenticeships," Tazio muttered.

Neri had relegated Zara, Alesso, and him to staying at the Guild for the summer as further punishment. Surely there was a lot sly Neri could teach them, but Tazio envied those who got off campus assignments with merchants, combat specialists, merchandisers, thespians, politicians. The fact Alesso and Zara would be there that summer helped, but they all seemed sore about it, and Tazio felt responsible for their plight.

"Have there been any visitors?" Tazio asked as the nurse attended to his neck wound.

"Yes, Alesso, Zara, and your professors."

"And Signore Leone?"

"Yes."

"Am I permitted to leave?"

"If you can walk, I'll permit it."

Tazio swung himself up and rolled his neck lightly.

Tight, but passable.

He stood and walked a few steps, feeling far more uneasy than he showed.

"Steps seem sure enough," the nurse said.

"Seem is the key word." Tazio winked and the nurse seemed tickled.

"Well maybe I should hold you here then!"

"No, no, just like to keep you on your toes."

"I've seen many lads and ladies come through here from the Games with worse. Some wished they hadn't competed at all from the injuries they took."

"I can sympathize."

"Ciao, ragazzo."

"Grazie, ciao ciao."

Tazio staggered out. How low he'd fallen—now even nurses pitied him.

He chuckled at the absurdity of his self-pity.

The hallways were unusually quiet.

Most were probably in town enjoying themselves before the graduation ceremony. On the way back to the dormitory, he heard a click on the stone.

Someone was following him.

No—something.

Tazio whirled around.

Mahjul playfully pounced out from behind a column, attacking his legs.

"Sweet Mahjul," Tazio smiled. "Come, let's go now."

Mahjul gave up his kill and trotted beside Tazio back to the dormitory. Seeing Mahjul reminded him how he still hadn't told Zara or Alesso how he'd bonded with Mahjul during their heist, or that he ever could. All the secrets were beginning to rot him, especially after the dark market blunder.

Tazio changed out of his patient's linens. The weight of his familiar black cloak hanging off his shoulders brought instant comfort. There was something special about a heavy cloak—like carrying a traveling home.

The door to the dorm room creaked open behind him.

"Tazio?" he heard Zara ask.

"Hello, Zara."

"Oh, don't act so glum."

"I didn't intend to hurt you, Zara. Ever."

"It's okay, Tazio, that can wait," Zara said softly, eyes glancing over Tazio's wound. She stepped forward and hugged him, though tentatively, like she wasn't sure whether to hold on or pull away. Distance, unspoken questions, lack of resolve all lingered in it. "Tell me how you are," she said as she pulled away.

Mahjul let out a little growl from the next bunk over, probably jealous of the attention.

"Hello, Mahjul," Zara said, picking him up. Mahjul was so huge slung over her shoulder, Tazio couldn't help but chuckle. Tazio could swear Mahjul still thought he was a kitten at times despite his menacing size.

"He really gives it up easily, doesn't he?" Tazio asked.

"He can pretend he's a tough one. But we all know he's soft in the guts." She put Mahjul down and he retired to groom himself, satisfied. "Are you okay?"

"As good as they come," Tazio said, doing a little jig but clearly encumbered.

"Let me see," Zara said, pulling back the cloth around his neck.

"The wound is deep. You should have stayed in the infirmary."

"Thank you, mother."

"Well no doubt your attitude is alive and well."

Tazio chuckled and sat down to put on his boots. They fit like a glove and he realized just how precise they fit after being out of them for a few days.

"You did well in the Games," Zara said.

"Well isn't the word I'd use."

"*Well*, you certainly handled me well."

"Well enough."

The door swung open, hinges banging as Alesso barged in. "I heard a bastard named Tazio is alive?"

"We were just talking about how well Tazio did," Zara said.

"Don't be delusional. That loss to Corso looked almost as terrible as his face does daily."

"At least someone around here is honest," Tazio said, smiling and hugging Alesso.

"Oh, shut up," Zara said.

"The Guild is awfully empty, is it not?" Tazio said.

"Everyone is either in revelry or gone to summer study."

"Not looking forward to a hot summer under Neri's searing eye," Alesso said.

"We're lucky it's not worse," Zara said.

"It'll be great. We'll learn of the dark smears of the Guild by scrubbing toilets," Alesso said, and they all laughed.

"You're truly loose," Tazio said.

"We shouldn't have gotten caught!" Zara said.

"Good point. Still should've done it—just shouldnt've got caught!" Alesso said.

"Anyone hungry?" Tazio asked, happy to be in good company.

"Why complain, you've only fasted for three days," Zara said.

"I'm a pauper."

"I'll never fight a meal," Alesso said.

"The damned truth that is."

The three of them walked out, Mahjul behind. Tazio felt light being back with Alesso. But a few corners later, the weight of the loss at the Games hung over him again. Something lurked deeper. He twitched as he remembered Corso bludgeoning him to the dirt. And the cell at Bourgogne, the tumbling cart, the rage rising as he watched Aeon fall to Falkone. Tazio's back grew sweaty, face draining of blood as the stupidity of his pursuits gripped him. The Games had been an utter distraction.

Falkone ravages the world while I chase laurels.

The weight of the time he'd wasted slammed into his shoulders.

"All good, *amico?*" Alesso asked.

"Yes, I'll be fine," Tazio replied. Alesso's eyes narrowed in concern. "I just need to speak to Neri."

⇀

Tazio stood alone in the hallway outside Neri's office, knowing it was easier to corner Neri in his office, where there weren't endless demands on him from others.

Desperation demands audacity.

"Neri," Tazio said as Neri gusted around the corner.

"Tazio. Oh, you're up and about! A welcome surprise," Neri made for the door.

"Can we talk about something?" Tazio asked, blocking the door.

"I spoke too soon. Perhaps it's *not* good to see you up and about. What do you want?"

"I need a reassignment."

Neri's face tightened.

"For the summer," Tazio finished.

"You never cease to amaze. No. Move aside."

"If you think I'm an utter fool after hearing me out, I'll leave."

"Cazzo. I really am a glutton for curiosity. Speak."

"If I stay here for the summer, I'll languish. We both know that. I need to progress—and it won't happen here."

Neri waited, as if there was more coming. "Well, that wasn't nearly as entertaining as I'd hoped." Neri moved for the door latch.

"Neri, please," Tazio said, stepping in front of him.

Distaste crept into Neri's smile.

Careful.

"I'm not going to be the best I can for the Guild by sitting here all summer."

Neri locked onto him.

"I lost to Corso because of my rage, my pride, my weakness. He sent me over the edge. I need to learn control. Even when I know it's coming, they throw me."

Neri's eyes narrowed. "That lashing from Corso worked wonders. Better than any teacher I could have employed."

As much as it ached, Tazio fought the urge to wrestle with the topic.

"I was waiting for you to wise up in your old age," Neri continued. "I have an apprenticeship in mind—in case you were ever humble enough to submit to your pride."

"You wanted me to come to you?"

"My design is to develop, not destroy."

"Thank you, Neri," Tazio said, truly wanting to hug the bastard.

"Thank me with your actions."

"Where will you send me?"

"Somewhere... necessary."

PART III

CHAPTER 25

TAZIO

STIFF PLANKS RATTLED against Tazio's head from the side of the cart. As they hit a bump, a grim Guild associate named Eddardo bounced on the cart's bench, muttering to the donkeys who pulled them on their final day's journey to Kataria. The coastal trade route had dipped and curved atop pine-covered cliffs towering over the Rabbian Ocean. The landscape finally turned arid, palms and olive trees now took precedence. Neri had assigned Eddardo to accompany him, and the quiet man spoke mostly in grunts. Tazio didn't mind having time to think. Last thing he wanted was an overly chatty companion for a two-week journey.

The journey south had been pleasant, and made Tazio realize how much the tight, damp alleys of Auria had worn him—the endless horizon, the sea wash, and the jostling cart all worked together in a kind of curative rhythm, reminding him how much he craved open expanses.

Saying goodbye to Zara and Alesso had been raw. When he broke the news that he'd been reassigned, Zara acted like she understood, but Tazio could smell the burnt undertones. Alesso took the news with classic joviality, but even he seemed gutted. Tazio quickly followed with the news they'd be reassigned too, and that banished their frowns.

Zara was sent to study under Fiamma Vesta, a powerful Aurian Senator. Alesso had been assigned to study trade and supply under Marcus Alfini, a powerful Senator and merchant master. Tazio was overjoyed for the both of them, and only left anxious to know his own assignment. Probably to punish him with some casual stress, Neri withheld details, promising him it was necessary to leave them unknown. All Tazio knew was that it was in Kataria, at an address his driver would know, and that he'd meet his mentor there.

"The rest is in your mentor's hands. Just don't make a fool of yourself," Neri told him.

Helpful.

A falcon soared above, catching Tazio's eye. The bird reminded him of a debate he, Alesso, and Zara had one evening. Were falcons or crows the most cunning bird? Alesso argued falcons were natural killers, and that was enough.

"Plus, who wouldn't want to fly that fast?" Alesso had said.

He loved how simple and jovial Alesso could be. It was always refreshing as an escape from his own constantly scheming thoughts. If Alesso was that clear on the inside, he was a lucky man.

He couldn't be. Or maybe he was. Bravo.

Zara had argued that crows had to work together for brilliance and territorial dominance. More of an argument for intelligence being supreme. All too appropriate a reflection of how cunning she was.

That Alesso and Zara were respectively assigned to mentors who were each like the bird they preferred made him smile.

Amusing how life matches us up to what we need. Like a song behind the scenes, telling our tale.

Tazio saw the merit in both, but birds of prey spoke to him.

His father told him they were messengers from *Etria*, and the experience with the *iolair* only confirmed his love for their elegance and freedom. It wasn't their fault they were chosen to kill, and they did it well. There was also a certain kind of cunning it took to wait in the air, observe from a mile, and choose the precise moment to strike. Not to mention that anyone who's seen a falcon fight off crows also knows the steel it takes to deal with a murder of crows.

"Nearly there," Eddardo grumbled from his seat ahead.

"Are you nearly here?" Tazio said.

Eddardo didn't say anything, instead cracking the reins.

The donkeys on the end stubbornly took it but didn't accelerate in any tangible way. Eddardo's shoulders twitched as he tried to shake off his frustration. Tazio couldn't help but see the comedy in how Eddardo and the donkeys had been fighting each other the whole damned trip.

As they crested the last hill, the kingdom of Kataria spread across the horizon. The walled city sprawled more than fifteen miles across, the whitewashed sandstone shimmering through heat waves. The infamous golden spires, where criminals were left to bake, scraped the sky. It sat in a flat basin of only small desert trees and bushes, and the barren desert south of the city stretched into a white blur like a never-ending ocean of sand. Only legendary Katarian *abnawaa*—desert jackals—had ever been known to navigate it and live. Aside from them, lunatics, suicidals, and exiles went there to perish. What lay within it few knew. What was beyond it, fewer still. But if anyone did, it was the *abnawaa*.

Hot sand stung Tazio as they came off the steep side of the cracked basin and made their way across the long plain leading up to the city walls. Neri had told him to learn the workings of the geopolitical and cultural landscape. That it was essential to navigating the intricacies of a region. To blending in. Tazio had read a book on Kataria before the journey, and learned that its father kingdom, Malad, sat off the southern coast of Aontir in the old world. The nation was politically neutral, known for its strong sense of national identity and religion. Malad was a mix of thick jungle and desert, and encapsulated hundreds of cultures under one ruler. Over thousands of years, Malad realized resources from Setia and other nations were far more important than destabilizing itself with warmongering. Kataria tended to follow the father nation's policy in Novra.

They pulled into the growing trickle of travelers passing the outer wall. Katarian guards in bronze armor with cream leather and white tunics eyed their cart. Rich oranges and greens lined their outfits, and their helmets were adorned with decadent wavy filigree. The eyes of the soldiers were dark, calm, and menacing. If not for the thin veil over his face, Tazio would have stood out like a white ox in a herd. Most Katarians had dark-hued skin, from deep midnight to sand and amber, like Zara's.

They passed the outer wall checkpoint and made their way into the heart of the city. Where Auria felt fast and aggressive from the rush of everyone looking to scrape some coin, Kataria felt as if those in the same street knew each other. Kids ran about, and Tazio got the sense many people raised them. Neri warned that Katarians were suspicious of outsiders, and their cart certainly drew looks, especially as they descended into a more unsavory part of the city near the port.

Now it felt more like the lower quarter of Auria. Men wore suspicion, and gaits looked tighter and more aware. Nevertheless, the threat mostly felt suppressed, like the ugly parts happened behind closed doors and the rest was reserved for the sailors and merchants who mixed here. The threat provoked a nice mix of fear and excitement though, Tazio had to admit.

Eddardo turned a corner and pulled to a stop on a shadowed street one block off the port.

"Off here. Knock on that door. Pleasure," Eddardo said glumly.

Tazio didn't get the sense Eddardo felt any pleasure from having transported him. Tazio would probably be bitter about the job too.

No judgment here.

"Grazie, Eddardo. Pleasure, indeed," Tazio said, giving a little bow.

He considered giving Eddardo some silver for his troubles, but figured it would just be insulting. The Guild paid well. So he shook his hand.

Eddardo whipped the donkeys and off he clattered into the dusty streets.

Tazio looked down to the slip of paper with Neri's directions on it. It described a modest three-story whitewashed building, which, in truth, stood in front of him. It had some simple blue shutters, nice geometric carvings along the roofline and balconies. By no means was it spectacular.

"What the hell has Neri sent me to?" Tazio muttered.

The whole thing was feeling like some sort of cruel joke.

I've made the case for it though, haven't I?

The house did have the marking of the three-headed snake on the gold doorknob. He knocked. A short minute went by, and still no answer came.

Tazio looked around and saw a small, cunning middle-aged man in a loose olive tunic walk up. He had thick, wavy eyebrows, a pointy chin, and a dark goatee and mustache. It all gave him the look of the finest Aurian painters—those reserved for frescoes and portraits in esteemed placements.

"Looking for someone?" The man's eyes were sly.

"Yes, I'm looking for Jacomo Boatto," Tazio said.

"Well, I'm not sure he's looking for you."

Tazio smiled at the glib comment.

"Don't be surprised," the man said.

"Well, it's just—"

"I'm the man you're looking for. It's just that I'm not looking for any man. I'm looking for afternoon tea."

"Neri didn't tell you I was coming?"

"Neri tells me many things."

"It was more of an advance notice. About my assignment."

"Well, I do take notices from Neri, but I don't always take notice."

"Very well. He said you were aware I was coming for a summer apprenticeship."

"I'm aware."

"Well, no, I mean that you're prepared to receive me."

"I rarely prepare for such things."

"Signore Boatto, I've traveled from Auria to apprentice under you. My name is Tazio—"

"Ahhhh, a tranquil journey—the way the hills roll along the sea. Very soothing, yes?"

"Yes, very beautiful," said Tazio, growing impatient.

"Did you learn anything?"

"What?"

"On the journey?"

"There's much time to think. I often learn something great from a peaceful journey. Well, even on the rough ones too."

Tazio thought for a moment, and Jacomo stood there smiling, looking quite expectant. It made Tazio feel pressure to cough something good up. "Well, I learned that while all roles in the Guild pay well, it does not pay to be placed in any role in the Guild."

"Very nicely put! I pity the poor bastard who transported you too! Best to remember that when you're thinking of misbehaving or getting lazy. Everyone thinks they'll end up as a master merchant, but few master much more than a couple donkeys!"

"He hadn't even managed that!" Tazio added.

They both laughed that time. Feeling he'd cracked the shell, Tazio started in again, "So you are aware of my apprenticeship with you, then?"

"Yes, I already said I was aware."

"Are we going to talk in circles until sunset?"

"Circles are symbolic of many things—a fascinating shape."

"I'm perhaps bordering on rudeness, but I'm supposed to study under you, and you seem entirely evasive of it."

"That's because you won't be studying under me. I've too much to do this summer."

"That can't be possible. I've just traveled from Auria for two weeks."

"Do enjoy your time here! Beautiful people, wonderful cuisine."

Jacomo shuffled past Tazio and worked the key into the door.

"Signore Boatto—"

The door closed in Tazio's face.

He stood confounded, acutely aware of the sweat rolling down his ribs from his armpits. Being in a foreign land changed quickly from fascination to skin-crawling frustration.

"What the hell!" Tazio hissed after a few seconds of disbelief.

A shutter cracked above him on the second floor.

"Please, don't linger and make an embarrassment of me in the street there. I've got to maintain a good standing with my neighbors, see," Jacomo chirped from the window above.

"Wait! Are you actually not going to take me in?"

"What more do I need to say to make it clear? Go to the local market and find transport back to Auria. Truly a charm meeting you!"

The window snapped shut.

"Jacomo!" Tazio's voice bounced off the walls into the evening as he stood there stupidly on the stoop. The embarrassment of shouting unreturned grew on him as a few locals gave him sidelong looks.

Jacomo's pleasantly rude, or kindly dismissive, or *whatever it was*—it was infuriating. The man brushed him off like a stray hair.

"I'm going to ride back to Auria and wring Neri's neck. Cazzo, maybe I can still find Eddardo."

He ran in the direction Eddardo had taken.

Jacomo had seemed dead serious. At this point, Tazio was ready to pay half a load of gold just to endure a few more mindless grunts from Eddardo for transport. But after a half mile, he hit a bazaar, and there were so many stalls, he knew there was no chance of finding him.

Exhausted, Tazio put his pack down to rest. The bustle of the colorful bazaar grabbed his attention. Where the average Katarian market seemed calm, this place was pure chaos. Deals were struck between shouts and erratic arm waves, people beyond brash.

One rich looking man wearing a beautiful white and gold robe held a proud posture as a squabbling merchant yelled at him. Some details went south, yelling and a few dramatic exits and reentries ensued. The charade eased the anxiety of Tazio's nightmarish ordeal, and he eased his way into the patchwork of tents. Even though he had his cowl and mask on, he got the sense they knew he was a foreigner. No one else carried a full pack, and others seemed to move quickly to their point of interest and collect what they needed.

One vendor had an entire wardrobe of the most intricate multicolored stitchwork he'd seen, another a spread of Katarian sweets that looked like they were made of thick cream and honey.

"Do you know where I can find a transport cart?" Tazio asked the first merchant he could collar in broken Katarian.

The man frowned, then shouted wildly at him. Clearly the Katarian Tazio had learned was not great, so he outlined the crude shape of a drawn cart with his hands, hoping for the best. The man's face contorted in deeper confusion before he turned to shout at more fluent prospects.

"Excellent start," Tazio muttered.

After working his way through three more merchants, and growing increasingly frustrated, Tazio saw a fat fellow with round cheeks, a simple cap with five small tassels, and a long black beard waving at him.

"You from north?" the friendly man asked in broken Setian.

"Yes, I'm looking to return there. Do you know about transport?"

"Yes, yes. Cart?"

"Yes, exactly!"

"Yes, I show you. Come."

The man wrapped his arm around Tazio, guiding him along. "What bring you to Kataria?"

"A friend."

"Ah, friends good."

"Debatable."

"Ahhh, friend make you mad?"

"It's rather complicated."

"Complicated?"

The man paused and pulled his arm off of Tazio.

"Yes, complicated."

The fat man's eyes flicked upward just before someone crashed onto Tazio's shoulders, slamming him into the dirt. A man in a black tunic stepped off Tazio, then stole his pack before sprinting off with his partner.

"Hey!" Tazio shouted, scrambling to his knees, heart pounding. But already, they had slipped away into the shadows of another alley. Too exhausted to maintain his rage, he slumped back in the dirt, exhaling in frustration.

Overhead, two desert doves flapped by. The hum of cicadas cut through the evening as he lay under the lonely purples and oranges of the setting sky, a sense of surrender settling over the moment. So much yearning had driven him like a mad horse since he'd been at the Guild—no, since his parents had died.

Is this how the bottom of the pit feels?

Minutes drifted by in a woozy release until, first in bursts, then uncontrollably, he laughed. Until his stomach hurt. Until the ludicrousness of the whole situation jolted away much of his long-held seriousness.

A mother with two children walked by. One child smiled before the wary mother took her under her wing and away from the lunatic in the dirt.

Tazio stood and brushed off the dust. His shadow stretched long ahead of him in the street like a reminder of reality. He did feel less burdened, but he needed a place to sleep. After trying a few inns, none took him despite his best attempts to barter. There were no barns or haystacks in the cursed clay city, so he wandered outside the walls.

Under the blazing starry sky, a fire kicked up light against rock croppings in the distance. With hands up to signal his harmlessness, he approached three strangers hunched by a fire, gaining a place in the circle. That was all they seemed able to offer.

None of them showed any sign of knowing one another. Tazio was grateful to have found his anonymous tribe for the night. Faceless, nameless strangers fighting the sharp chill of aloneness, drifting together in the flames, the stars watching from above. Alone, they were together, fighting their frigid future, bonding through lowliness.

Tazio leaned his head against a stone wall behind him, which was now warm from the fire and closed his eyes, satisfied in solace. Sinking deep into the stillness, he felt Anya reach out to him.

"Tazio?" Anya whispered, her voice swirling in his mind.

"Anya?"

"I'm afraid, Tazio."

"What's the matter?"

"Something is coming."

"What do you mean?"

"Find your courage, Tazio."

Her voice, though distant, crossed a chasm, urgency impelling it.

"Anya?"

The connection disappeared like sand falling through his fingers, leaving only the dust of memory. His eyes shot open, heart pounding. The other men flinched, looking at him like he was insane. The lonely desert beckoned to him, and he stumbled away from the circle into the cold night, fear running wild in his veins as he wondered if Anya was in trouble—if she'd been trying to reach him earlier—if Falkone had found the last of the Daemonae. Her message rang like a repeating chorus through Tazio as he tripped and groped in the sand.

"Find your courage, Tazio. Find your courage."

→

Tazio knocked on Jacomo's front door again as the midday sun cooked the streets.

"Yyyeeees?" Jacomo piped from somewhere inside.

"Perhaps we could have some tea?" Tazio asked through the door.

When no answer came, he pressed his ear to the door, and it swung open, sending Tazio stumbling to the floor.

"Well, hello!"

"Hello, Jacomo. Excuse my entrance," Tazio said.

"Did you say tea?" Jacomo smiled down at him.

"I did."

"Who told you the way to my heart?" Jacomo took him by the arm and lifted him up.

"Nothing like the desert night to clear the mind. Let's say it came from the ether."

"Ah, riding the divine winds for answers, are we?"

"'Twas the only transport I could afford!"

"Very well, then let's have some tea."

Jacomo closed the front door and led them down a long corridor.

"It's remarkably cool in here," Tazio said as they opened into an inner courtyard. Despite the heat, the previous night's chill still persisted in Tazio's bones.

"It's the *bâdgir*—a wind-catcher." He flicked an eyebrow toward the roof. "It catches prevailing winds and funnels them across pools of water beneath the house to cool the hot breath of Kataria. Chambers on the opposite side draw the air through the building."

"Fascinating."

The square tower whistled as it brought wind through its spined portals as they sat down in the shaded courtyard.

A beautiful woman with a long dark braid down her back entered with a tray of tea implements. She was gentle, her presence like the cool, steady breeze in the courtyard.

Seems a suitable balance to Jacomo's edge.

"Thank you, *tesoro*." Jacomo took the tray from her. She gently touched his hand and their eyes kissed. "Tazio, this is Atalia, the water to my desert."

"Of course, *tesoro*," Atalia said, her eyes radiant with purity. Even though she'd probably heard the compliment a thousand times before, she shimmered like it still hadn't lost its luster, then exited like a graceful wind.

"Well, Tazio, you managed to weasel your way into my courtyard," Jacomo said, pouring the tea with playful ease. "Tell the truth, did Neri tip you to my tea proclivity? Or did you just know that everyone loves tea after lunch in Kataria?"

Tazio had read about the southern obsession with tea, and he flushed red at being sniffed out. "I did my reading."

"A scholarly victory. I can drink to that!"

"I'm sorry to pester you again. You're likely wondering why I'm back?"

"I thought just for tea, no?"

"I think we both know I don't love tea as much as you."

Jacomo smiled. "Still fishing for an apprenticeship."

"As you asked, I went to market to secure a return journey last night. But I was robbed. I'm rather desperate and running out of options, as much as I hate to admit it."

"An inconvenient robbery does spoil a trip, doesn't it?"

"I won't grovel. If you aren't willing, I will find a way home, with or without your help."

"Resourceful at the least. That's worth something."

"You won't be disappointed with me. I'm more driven to succeed than you can imagine."

Jacomo tilted his eyebrow.

"There's a problem though. You haven't even sipped the tea. How can I trust a man who doesn't drink tea?"

Tazio took a sip.

The floral flavors shifted from musky to bright, finishing with a spice that gently warmed his chest. He was about to comment on it when he saw a silver *stellum* sitting at the bottom of the cup, glinting through the fuchsia tea.

"There's a silver in here," Tazio said as he looked up.

"Use that *stellum* to send this to Neri," Jacomo said, pulling a letter from an inner pocket. "It's a note informing him you've passed your first test."

"Hah! Cazzo, that was sly."

"It's good to see you can appreciate a con."

A day ago, Tazio was screaming at Jacomo like a damned idiot. His stomach sank imagining what would have happened if he'd made it to Auria successfully. He was thankful he'd been waylaid by the robber. If he ever saw that pudgy merchant again, he'd give him a kiss on the cheek and buy him a new tassel for his colorful cap.

"Let me show you to your mighty quarters," Jacomo said, springing up from his seat, spry still for a man just past middle age.

Jacomo led him up a set of tight spiral stairs and opened a small door to a room sitting in the corner tower. Its ceiling was high, probably to keep it cool. Two small windows cut into the thick stone walls over-looked plains that blended slowly from bush to dunes far in the distance. A low cot sat on one wall and twin candles, a quill and inkpot, three volumes, and a cloth sack rested on a simple desk made of palm wood.

"Mighty indeed." Tazio said, taking in the tiny room.

Jacomo laughed. "Some of your lucky friends might be lodging with elites, but you have the honor of a Katarian tower nook!"

"I'm not worried. Compared to last night's lodging, this is like a royal chamber."

"Indeed. And from the look of it, you could use a wash. I'll have Atalia draw water."

"You're relentless."

"Keeps you young in this world."

"Could I ask for a change of clothes? I hate to ask but—my pack."

"Ah, of course. Though, do you remember the fellow you dealt with in the bazaar?"

"Not sure what you're talking about."

"The plump fellow with the tassel. The one who walked you into an alley somewhere and robbed you."

Tazio smiled and rubbed his face. "I know where this is going."

"His name is Mustaefa. Tell him 'the ship has sailed,' and he'll give your satchel back. Hate to set you up like that, but I can't have you on one pair of undergarments for your entire apprenticeship."

Jacomo flitted out the door and Tazio could hear him chuckling about his ruse.

Well, studying under Jacomo certainly won't be dull.

CHAPTER 26

TAZIO

TAZIO SCRUBBED the tile floor in quiet defiance. Two months in and he was worn thin. He thought he'd come to learn, not to endlessly clean and polish and fold garments, with practice in juggling, satire, music, and oration mixed in at Jacomo's whim. Zara and Alesso were probably dining with power brokers and learning espionage. Thus far, picking out short rice nibs from Jacomo's supply had been Tazio's favorite torturous task.

"They throw off the mouthfeel," Jacomo had said.

The peculiarity of it drove Tazio mad. He found himself cursing and muttering to himself by candlelight in the dark pantry as he sorted through the gargantuan, dusty rice sacks. Jacomo would occasionally poke in, once telling him the light was turning Tazio altogether ghoulish in the dark before bounding off laughing. Occasionally, Tazio would get relief by running letters to Jacomo's network of merchants and other alley cats.

Nevertheless, Tazio slogged dutifully through the tasks, doing his best to learn from the mind-numbing work without losing his cool, sensing it was a test of character. Either his sanity or the tasks would have to break soon, though.

"There's a tile here in the common area that you missed," Jacomo said from the other room. "Taaazzio?"

"Yes?" Tazio jerked up in frustration, wiping away water that flung on him from his rag.

"Come, come, I'll show you."

Tazio walked into the large, tiled common area full of colorful seats and cushions and Katarian rugs. "Jacomo?" Tazio asked with a low, restrained voice.

"Yes?" Jacomo asked, seated, reading a treatise.

"I was thinking," Tazio said, doing his damnedest to stay humble.

"Well, spit it out," Jacomo replied, eyeing him over his parchment.

"Is there something more challenging I can take on?"

Jacomo lowered his parchment, and after a long pause, "I was beginning to wonder how many more floors you'd scrub before you asked!"

"What?"

"What a relief. You've outlasted all the other poor fools I put through it. Pity the fool is an understatement! I've been wanting to give you something better for weeks now. Do you really think I despise short rice grains to such a degree?"

Tazio dropped his rag into the wooden bucket he was carrying, wanting to throw the whole thing across the room.

"Fean, Jacomo, I'm tired of the jokes."

"Come now, what's life without some play!"

Not wanting to forfeit the months of toil he'd invested, Tazio stood still, sensing he was inches from being free of near slavery.

"I suppose a bit of fun never hurts," Tazio said, but rage and frustration churned inside.

"Wonderful. You've been practicing your juggling act, yes?"

"I've known how to juggle since I was four."

"Of course you have. There's a jester's motley in the closet there. Have you seen it?"

"Yes."

"Good. Then your next assignment begins!"

→

Though the outfit was hot, it wasn't inappropriate to walk the streets of any city in Novra in a motley. Low fools made their name all across the world to earn clout and a place in court. Even in the old world, since the first epoch, performers had been worshiped for their wit and influence in the old cities in Aontir.

Jacomo told him they shouldn't be seen together, so Tazio trailed behind. As he rounded the next corner, the crescent-shaped port stretched out in front of him. Bells clanged and sailors unloaded hauls from all edges of the world. The sight of a port always provoked intense wondering in Tazio. Of where these rusty sailors had come from and where they went next. Of the raging seas they crossed to make a few more *numa*.

"Psst. Fool," he heard someone whisper.

Tazio looked to his right and saw Jacomo nestled away beneath a doorway. He beamed at Tazio like a kid playing a trick. Sometimes Tazio felt Jacomo was twenty years younger. Other times he felt Jacomo was a thousand years old.

"You're clearly enjoying the act already," Tazio said.

"Do we know each other?" Jacomo poked him in the ribs, then pointed across the port. "That sailor's lodge—you'll perform there."

"Found the dirtiest place in Kataria, did you?"

"Only the finest for you!"

Jacomo jaunted across the port toward the bar. As Tazio trailed behind, sailors eyed Tazio in his loud outfit, hissing taunts. The bar was barely standing, like it'd been patched one too many times. Tazio walked up the stairs onto the raised porch that looked like it had been made of driftwood. As he swung open the squealing door, a filthy-looking man sized him up, the lodge raucous in the background with chatter.

"Oy, look! A fool! Over there!" one man shouted.

The same man scrambled over and grabbed Tazio, shoving him toward the stage where a gorgeous lyre player was being catcalled at the end of her performance. She didn't seem to mind, giving a caress of the arm here, a kiss on the forehead there. *Numa* followed plentifully.

That's a performer who knows how to pull free a few more silvers.

"We've got a fool 'ere!" another random sailor shouted.

A chorus of jeers pushed Tazio on stage along with the shoves of the man who'd grabbed him originally. The crowd was the most culturally mixed he'd seen in Kataria, the only common identity seemed to be that they were rough enough to enter. From onstage, Tazio saw Jacomo sitting with a pint of ale. He raised a mug, and winked.

"Pardon, miss, could you play a jolly song to back me?" Tazio asked the lyrist as she collected her things from onstage.

"It'll take some coin, honey," she said with a sultry look.

"How about half my earnings?" Tazio suggested.

"Better be good." She picked her lyre up, sat down, and sparkled a colorful tune.

Tazio pulled out his juggling balls, and started into a sequence he'd known since he was a boy. With only three bags in the air, the boos came quickly.

"Come on, fool!" one man crowed.

Tazio pulled out two more, raising it to five.

"You think five is a show?" another goon shouted.

Tazio went up to seven, spun and changed the shapes and arcs of the bags and caught one, then two on his feet, juggling like a contorted tree. Finally, a few men banged their mugs in raucous appreciation, and the rush of delighting the audience lit a rush in Tazio. He sank deeper into the act.

Eight, then nine bags.

But now that he'd tasted victory, he wanted the full conquest.

He worked his way slowly over to the edge of the stage, juggling all the while. On the closest table to the stage, he snuffed a candle with his foot in front of the goggling eyes of some lanky sailors. They banged their mugs and shoved each other in excitement as he worked off a slipper with the other foot and picked up the candelabra with his toes. One leaned in close to the candle, testing Tazio's poise, but Tazio kept his balance and the pub walls shook in appreciation of his audacity.

Tazio flung the candelabra up into the juggling circle and got a few rotations in motion. The asymmetry was a real challenge, and he smiled, pleased with how things were going. Then, from the front table, he saw a mug headed straight toward his face. He ducked it, but it threw his rhythm.

Down went the bags.

A mess plate clanged hard off his head.

The crowd erupted into laughter.

"Hey! Fuck you! You want a different kind of act?" Tazio broke out of the performance and brandished the candelabra with venom.

"Shut up, you fucking fool!" a wide man shouted from the front.

"Well come shut me up then, piggy!" Tazio boasted.

The chunky man fumed and charged.

Tazio slipped a big hook and came around the side of his overcommitted move, delivering an ugly blow to the ear with the candelabra and sending the man ringing.

The place erupted in chaos. A horde of sailors mobbed the stage, and Tazio fought off as many as he could, splitting eyebrows, kicking groins. Eventually they overran him. After clobbering him good, they doused him with ale and sent him flying out the door by the drawers.

Cheers followed Tazio out, and he hit the wood porch fuming. He shot up to go back in and fight, but the door guard stepped in front of him, his sweaty chest inches from Tazio's face. Tazio weighed the risk, then a second man stepped in, stacking the odds.

"Find another lodge, fool. We ain't got time for shit shows," the big man said, then unleashed a thick knot of phlegm onto his face.

A dark shadow came over Tazio as he wiped the hot snot from his cheek. He flung it to the floor as the men turned around to go inside, laughing all the way. Rage drew him to them like a siren's song.

Pulling, pulling, he crept behind them, ready to strike. Right in the neck. First one, then the next. Simple, quick, dead. These fucking bastards.

"Tazio."

Tazio whipped around and saw Jacomo standing in the street.

Tazio heard the other men turn around at the sound of Jacomo calling his name.

"I told you to piss off," the big man said, shoving him from behind.

Tazio rolled off the porch to break the fall, at least getting pleasure from seeing the panic sitting in the bottom of the man's eyes. A twisted laugh came out.

The big man knew he was inches from being taken blind if Tazio's approach hadn't been blown.

"I'll find you soon, big man." Tazio lunged toward the man, who flinched backwards. "Pathetic."

Tazio turned to find Jacomo, who was already walking down the docks next to the seawall.

"Quite the show," said Jacomo as Tazio caught up. "I'm not sure if the juggling or the fight was more entertaining. What's your take?"

"My take is it was destined to fail."

"*In bocca al lupo*, Tazio."

"What's that supposed to mean?"

"Fortune comes from the jaws of the wolf."

"You call that fortune?"

"The point, my lad, is that we are made by our trials. Forged by our hardships. That is when we are in the jaws of the wolf, *that* is when we are tested, and when we choose to rise."

"I do like that. But look, I've nearly lost my fingerprints from scrubbing, then your first choice is to toss me in there like chum?"

"You're here to learn, yes?" Jacomo said. Tazio held his tongue, preferring not to be wrapped around a post by another questioning streak. "Tell me, what did you come here for?"

"To improve."

"Wrong."

"Oh, yes, I forgot! To clean—I'm looking to be a servant!"

Jacomo's eyes narrowed.

"Polishing," Tazio admitted, hating he was bending to the exercise.

"And?" Jacomo asked as they walked down the planks of the port.

"I'm here because I need polishing." Resistance writhed in Tazio's chest. "And pride."

"Do go on."

"Give me the tasks I want, and it'd inflate me further. Keep me in a lowly way and break me. It's so obvious it could be in a monk's handbook."

"Obvious it may be. But your own pride had to be held up to you, and *you* had to be the one to deal with its ugliness. Tell me, wise one, do you think learning is an easy task?"

"I think learning should be fast, direct, and useful."

"That's where you're wrong. Do you think by some dialogue I could convince you to surrender your pride? Or what if I gave you a book about your faults and the solutions to them—do you think that would be more direct and useful?"

"Well, since you have a perfect answer, please continue."

"I could have told you your faults as a theory, but you'd probably have fought me or consumed the advice like a Katarian sweet morsel. Your pride would entrench you in resistance at hearing your errors or your intellectual stimulation would peak and fade, and you'd be none the wiser. But now, you've grappled with your soul, and the most intimate and accurate teachers are the enemies within. Your experience has wrested the answers from the depths. And you'll remember them because you fought your pride, me, and the shadows."

Tazio digested the thick ideas.

"Tell me," Jacomo continued, "when did you know I was working you into the ground for the sake of it?"

"After a week, it seemed rather obvious."

"And you waited two months to surface it?"

Now that Jacomo mentioned it, it did seem a little ridiculous he didn't bring it up earlier.

"I thought you'd see that I'd endured enough, earned my right," Tazio said.

"Yes, but why resist asking?"

Thoughts fired off as Tazio searched for the answer.

"Because I hate being imposed on."

"Why?"

"No one likes to submit!"

"No, there's a deeper reason."

"I don't know. I'm sick of this exercise!"

"You do know."

"Because no one can control me!" Tazio snapped. "Is that what you want to hear?"

Jacomo grabbed Tazio by the collar and threw him against the rock seawall they walked beside. "I am not your enemy. Your enemy is that you think you are wise beyond what you know. Tell me—is everyone a fool but you?" Jacomo hovered close to his ear. "Neri for telling you not to go to the market? Or Leone trying to mold you only for you to defy his training?"

"They told you?"

"Wake up, Tazio. You're part of something bigger. But if you don't trust others, you'll be fed to the dogs," Jacomo pulled away, and for the first time Tazio was afraid of the man. A deep, suppressed rage Jacomo had probably contained for only the right circumstances sat in his eyes. Decades of careful control bore down on Tazio.

"It's not true. I trust my friends," Tazio replied.

"You trust *no one*. I can smell it on you like a dog. You believe you're the only one to chart your way. But was it not you that led Alesso into darkness? And Zara with you to rescue him?"

Jacomo's incisive jabs drained the will to fight out of Tazio.

The hot, wet evening felt suddenly heavy as he melted into the wall.

"But why this charade?" Tazio asked, pulling off his motley cap and holding it out.

"Because you're weak when provoked. You build your foes higher than they actually are. *E cazzo*, what some random sailors think of you —but they owned you the second you reacted. Think of Corso in the Guild Games. He didn't beat you with skill, Tazio. He beat you with provocation."

"You were there?"

"Yes. It was like child's play."

"You heard what he said?"

"It doesn't matter what he said. In that moment he owned you. A perfect example of your slavery to your foes. It was devastating to watch. There was no reason you should've lost, aside from that weak point in your mind."

Jacomo was right—he thought he was high and mighty and powerful, and Corso gutted him with a single stupid statement.

Jacomo sighed. Golden dusk poured on his face, casting shadows across it. Tazio wondered where the jovial man he had come to know had disappeared to. Behind all the jest and mirth, Jacomo was profound and formidable.

"I am not your enemy, Tazio. I was once as dark and warped as you. Most of us at the Guild were—many still are. But we're wedded by our pain. It's why we rout each other's darkness. Do you understand?"

Tazio looked out to sea. Past the masts and sails. Thick clouds were turning to purple, the fading sun tracing solemn light along their edges.

"There is a lesson in today, I assure you," Jacomo continued. "Think on these things. Don't return too late."

Tazio didn't respond.

At some point, Jacomo drifted away, leaving Tazio to sit with the lesson. It hurt to be wrong, and Tazio's stomach burned, churning over the truth of it. Suddenly his pride seemed ugly and worthless, like a supposed friend stripped of his disguise, his merits a mask of deception.

All the times pride had betrayed him came flooding back—moments he'd fallen victim to proving himself that cost him trust, respect, and victory. The same promise pride made, it broke.

Exhausted by the punishing realization, he closed his eyes. The squawk of southern gulls echoed in the distance. The lapping of waves on brigs and docks. The heavy sea air. And like in the alley where he'd been robbed the first night, he drifted on the licks of the wind, flying away from his problems on the planks of the docks. Escaping into the freedom of disembodiment. Wondering if he could ever trust. Wondering why he couldn't. Wishing he could.

CHAPTER 27

ZARA

"PLEASE HAND me the file on the Katarian developments, Zara," Fiamma said, walking a half step ahead of Zara as usual. Her long red hair was pinned in a gold geometric clip and poured down her back valiantly. Fiamma's fiery intelligence seemed like a blatant expression of her name, which meant *flame*. She was impressive, even intimidating. Zara gained great pleasure in seeing the hardened male Senators get twisted by her wit.

"Seh, Fiamma." Zara shuffled through the treatises in the runner's satchel she carried as they walked to Fiamma's booth in the Setian Senate chamber.

Senators and assistants were all filtering into the tremendous semi-circular chamber for the weekly session. The auditorium always awed Zara—glistening marble, sweeping stained glass depicting Aurian history, and interlocking arches that climbed the half-dome like a geometric tree shading the speaker's platform. A wall divided the Senate chamber from private meeting rooms and other offices behind the facade.

"This Katarian situation needs handling," Fiamma said, mostly to herself, as if strengthening her belief before public discourse.

"Anything else I can do for you?"

"No, Zara, thank you." Fiamma's narrow-set eyes and peaked eyebrows flashed with focus as she turned to speak to an aide.

Normally Zara loved seeing the Senate meetings live, but this time something more important beckoned. So she bowed and made her exit, winding back into the halls.

Where the Guild building's architecture held a traditional prestige about it, the Senate constantly funded projects that renovated and introduced a dazzling display of experimental craftsmanship—swirling columns, inverted-pyramid rooms, interlocking arches—feats once thought impossible and still confounding to other nations. She wondered if *draeda* was at work somehow, but hadn't found an answer yet.

At first, Zara had been uneasy and eager to impress Fiamma, resorting to listening in a state of clammed withdrawal. But as the summer went by, she realized that Fiamma was fond of her—perhaps because she sensed a similar drive to gather and wield information, or because there were so few women in power. Zara didn't dare ask her about it, feeling it would be naive. It simply hung between them as an unspoken understanding of each other's essence.

After a few turns, Zara reached the office where she and Fiamma worked. She went in, closed the door, and placed a small door block she'd acquired at market, sliding it under the main door.

She entered Fiamma's private office.

As she opened the door, a view of the Rabbian Ocean poured over her. The lavish office was awash in warm tones—cream walls, blood-red and black carpets, and a rich oak desk gleaming with polish in front of floor-to-ceiling bookshelves. Warm notes of Aurian cedar filled the air, drifting off a burning incense stick on the desk. All the senators' offices were arranged on the cliffs overlooking the ocean, and they'd recently installed huge glass windows, clearer than any Zara knew. Just a few years prior, Setian craftsmen had learned to purify melted sand by adding an esoteric compound that made glass both transparent and strong. She hadn't yet discovered the formula, but it was on her list of curiosities.

Focus. You can dream later.

Zara pulled a lock-picking set she'd secured from Duarte, the slippery merchant who'd also sold her the door block. She had to really work him over for the pick set, paying a hefty price to assuage his fears of being gutted for selling to the wrong buyer.

Zara went to work on the lock of the private drawer in Fiamma's desk.

A sound from the hallway made her jump.

She stared at the door like a child caught stealing sweets, but nothing came as her heart thudded.

She went back to getting the job done as quickly as possible. She smiled at the fact that, to get what she desired, she was now committing her second capital offense in six months. Though the lock was proving to be more complex than even the toughest ones she'd practiced on.

"*Khara*," she cursed under her breath, hands shaking from the anticipation. "Calm down." She let out a tense breath, holding the pins she'd clicked into place thus far, working the hook with the tension rod, taking one pin at a time until the lock tugged.

"*Buono*," she said, gently turning the lock. "This is better than sex. Well, some sex."

She thought of how Tazio made her roar with fire, but also why she couldn't love him. Her mission was more important, and love would bludgeon her off course. She squashed the voice of desire, feeling her heart wither as it did each time she smothered the impulse.

The polished oak drawer glided open. Parchment folders, neatly labeled by topic, sat inside—files yet another Setian invention. One was marked "Trade and Commerce." Carried away by the excitement, she dumped it on the desk and started devouring its contents.

"Too high level. Not relevant. Fean, where is it?" she muttered.

The door blew open.

"What are you doing?" Fiamma shouted, fire in her eyes.

"Fiamma! I'm sorry—"

Fiamma slammed the door shut.

"I could have you killed for this." Fiamma moved like a sandstorm to the desk, collecting the strewn files on the desk with rage sparking off her. "Trade disruptions?" She looked at the file Zara had lifted, eyes wide in disbelief.

"Yes."

"This is what you steal? Something so trivial—after all the trust we've built?" Fiamma inspected the drawer further, but found it reasonably undisturbed before slamming it shut. "I'd expect that if you were to take such a tremendous risk, you would at least acquire something more valuable."

"It is valuable to me."

"That's not the point!"

"I'm sorry, Fiamma."

"And why is this file valuable to you?"

"I can't tell."

"You *will* tell, Zara—or things will sour very quickly."

Fiamma looked ready to ignite, and Zara's chest tightened, palms breaking out in sweat. "My parents—they were killed by trade disruptions south of Bourgogne. They were merchants for the outlying Setian networks."

"That is your justification for stealing from a Senator? From your mentor?"

Zara nodded.

"You baffle me. You didn't think to simply ask if I knew anything about what happened to your parents?"

The question tore into Zara, and she burned from stupidity.

"I didn't."

Zara's eyes fell, and she wished she could drain away into the pools of marble on the floor. She could be killed for it. And more than that, she would lose Fiamma, the one person who saw her for who she was, and valued it.

"Where were your parents killed?" Fiamma asked.

Zara looked up. "On the Plana Via. About one hundred miles north of Kataria."

Fiamma looked down her sharp nose, her intensity bearing down. Zara looked away, unable to handle her gaze.

"I'll look into this," Fiamma said.

"Into their death?"

"Yes." Fiamma was calm now, as if the storm had passed.

Is that it? Am I free? Don't say something stupid now and provoke her.

"Thank you, Fiamma. Thank you so much."

"Don't ingratiate yourself. I prefer you when you're bold," Fiamma said, a faint smile tugging at her lips before disappearing. "Perhaps I'm a fool for seeing too much of myself in your brazen idiocy. But don't mistake my forgiveness for indulgence—evolve or fall."

Fiamma turned away.

Cazzo, she really does care for me. She's embarrassed at her compromise.

"How did you know I was in here?" Zara asked.

"Sheer intuition," Fiamma said, flashing an impish look at Zara. "There is a *maginnico* I had crafted by the *artifexae*. It uses a *draeda* link to my *talùth* to alert me when the office has been compromised. It's hidden within the lock."

"I truly am a fool, aren't I?"

"Yes. But it's good I know your past. It will manipulate you from the shadows if you never bring it to light."

"Forgive me, Fiamma. I won't let you down again."

"You don't have a choice."

While the words weren't explicit, Zara knew she was a debtor in Fiamma's ledger, whether Fiamma loved her or not.

Stealing from a Senator is punishable by death, and the debt you owe her is life and loyalty.

"Now," Fiamma said, "I believe it's time you learn how to gather information in a more persuasive manner."

→

"*Mi dispiace*, Fiamma!" screamed the sniveling man strung on ropes in the damp dungeon beneath the Senate.

Zara's *talùth* pulsed as Fiamma bent his will, siphoning answers from his mind. She'd already cracked his *talùth* by physical proximity and specialized commands, and now, as she burrowed into the recesses of his inner world, she alternated between wordless concentration and vocal coaxing to ease him into submission. Zara always imagined interrogators being louder and more physical, but on the outside, Fiamma, at least, was calm, almost comforting.

Through the bond between their three *talùthae*, Zara could feel Fiamma tearing apart the threads of his energy body that were woven into his *talùth*, combing his thoughts and feelings. The process reminded her of when Alesso had been cracked into submission in the Tenebri Emporium, and Zara fought to shake the tension creeping into every muscle from witnessing a man's soul laid bare like a frayed rope.

"Silas, is it unreasonable to let me in on why you turned? Perhaps it's easier for everyone now that you're here," Fiamma's tone was soothing and low. She played both friend and tormentor, and the poor man was swimming in confusion.

"It was Falkone! I had no choice! It was Falkone! He paid us, all of us," Silas groaned as sweat dripped down his whole body.

"I understand, Silas. It sounds like it was hard to resist," said Fiamma. When she spoke calmly, he was like a broken child desperate to be free of pain, and answers would spill out. It was the first time her passion for studying under Fiamma turned to nauseous regret.

"Yes, it was. So much *numa*. They told us to turn on the Guild because it would be destroyed very soon. As well as Auria."

"Destroyed?"

"Yes. And that it would be better to join them. It all made so much sense. And they were threatening us! To kill us!"

"I understand, Silas. It seems like a trying situation to be in."

Zara saw images from Silas' mind appearing like vague dreams in her mind's eye as Fiamma eased thoughts into his mind, bringing forth images she could comb through. It was terrifying to see her break the privacy of the man's mind. But a twinge of pleasure went through her too, and it worried her.

"And what did they want from you all?" Fiamma asked.

"To disrupt the Guild's supply chain in the wider networks of Novra."

"It sounds like there's more to this," Fiamma's tone deflected downward, like a fine courtesan coaxing a man—another technique she employed to build a false sense of safety.

"They wanted us to disrupt the extended network trade routes—so they could reestablish them under Thoracian banners."

"We have received no reports of Thoracian attacks."

"Mercenaries."

"And which mercenaries were used along the Plana Via?"

"The Chetan."

"Thank you, Silas." Fiamma exited the intrusion into his mind.

She gave Zara a look to confirm her work was done.

"Will I be released now?" The hope in Silas' eyes was almost unbearable.

"Soon, Silas," Fiamma said, turning to leave.

Silas slumped over and shuddered on the ropes, his long brown hair dripping with sweat.

Zara followed behind Fiamma.

This debt to Fiamma is one I'd best rid myself of—and rapidly.

"There is your answer, Zara," Fiamma said as they walked up a tight spiral staircase out of the bowels of the Senate.

"Then Falkone was working with the Chetan. His reach has stretched even beyond the Luxen Mountains west of Bourgogne," Zara reasoned.

"Yes. His reach has grown immeasurably."

Zara fell silent. For five years she'd sought the answer to who killed her parents—and now it hung in her mind like a tattered cobweb drifting in the wind.

Is that it?

She waited for the answer to satisfy her—to drive her into rage or release a torrent of resolve. But the pursuit had been a cruel master, demanding the relentless, stupid task of finding out meaningless details about how her parents were killed.

For what?

How stupid to shrink her world to a single obsession. Running from Tazio. Shelling up like a scared child. Risking her place at the Guild. That might explain why Fiamma had been so forgiving—it truly was a childish pursuit.

She glanced at Fiamma, groping for guidance, but finding the Senator's profile etched with quiet steel.

"If the Chetan support Falkone, who is left to aid our fight against the Thoracians?" Zara asked, trying to hide her sense of doom.

"Setia, Thorace, and Kalskog fought a vicious battle for the northern strongholds above Auria after the first passages from the old world. Those wars lasted about fifteen years. Auria, through a critical alliance with Kalskog, pushed Thorace inland and over the Vestian hills and beyond the Aroinn mountains. Eventually Thorace settled into the cold mountain area called Norgane where they built Kaltung, their mountain stronghold. They knew it was wise to control the Eistal Passage that leads to the plains and forests north of Bourgogne—Landstat, as they call it. There are other Kalskog strongholds in the northeast.

And Thoracian constituents who oppose Falkone. Once again, this war will hinge on the north."

"Then Falkone will conquer the north next?"

"Yes. But first, he must conquer Auria."

"Are we doomed?"

"Doom is a choice. If we don't maneuver correctly, Auria could fall, yes."

Zara had expected Fiamma to reassure her, and when she didn't, it only made the future seem more bleak. "It sounds like we could soon all be strung up like Silas."

Fiamma gave her a look that said it all, and just kept walking along the hallways of the Senate. Zara could see the endless toil Fiamma had poured into fighting for Auria's survival worn on the lines of her profile. Especially the uphill fight against the conservative contingency in the Senate who believed Auria could weather any attack. Too proud to believe anyone could crush Auria. That all of Novra could be ruled by Falkone.

This is what Fiamma spared you for. A war threatens to consume us all. This is what can fill that void inside you. The search for an answer to your parents' death was only an outpost in my education. But my design is for something greater.

Zara's heart, despite the surging fear, felt lighter. She trod along beside her focused mentor, basking in her mentor's radiance. The fear that Zara had felt just minutes before flooded down the spiral stairs behind her.

Fiamma needed her.

The Guild needed her.

And she was ready to give her life now. Not out of debt—but in service.

For Auria.

For Novra.

CHAPTER 28

TAZIO

"It's important you act like you've been here before," Jacomo said as Tazio walked beside him up the Katarian palace steps.

"Not a care in the world."

"Precisely."

They approached massive gold double doors that led into the rugged palace. Raised engravings wove in abstract patterns. Depictions of sandscapes and desert scenes rested elegantly on the walls. The palace was made of thick sandstone, one of the few buildings not whitewashed with plaster.

"There's enough gold in that door to feed a kingdom," Tazio said.

"You're impressed—and already failing," Jacomo murmured, then turned his attention to speak with a palace attendant.

Tazio stood to the side. All manner of merchants and nobles filed into the palace, everyone dressed like it was their final celebration. Jacomo had stressed the importance of learning to mix with these types. Of navigating their unwritten etiquette. Learning the subtleties of demeanor. Tazio suppressed a grin—proximity to power players boded well for his future at the Guild.

"And so we go," Jacomo said, leading them in.

Chatter poured over Tazio as they entered the massive royal chamber. Glasses clinked, people guffawed, chandeliers sparkled. Boyish excitement ran through him.

"Contain yourself," said Jacomo, letting out a chuckle at Tazio's wonder.

"Yes, sorry."

The chamber was pentagonal, reflecting the Katarians' belief in the five forces of life—power, order, unity, sanctity, and love. Massive carved sandstone columns formed an inner pentagon, dividing the chamber into a main center area and an outer procession. The room had an easy, concentric flow. Well over a thousand people mingled about, with most of the festivities in the center. Couples stole away in the shadows on the outside, servers darted to and fro, and an arrangement of musicians on a raised platform in the center filled the air with a scintillating tune.

"May I?" Tazio gestured toward a table with an exotic assortment of foods.

"Try not to eat it all in one pass. And don't involve yourself in any conversation that would reveal more than we discussed."

"Noted."

"Find me soon." Jacomo slid away.

Tazio's mouth watered as he walked toward the table of cured meats, cheeses, figs, apricots, sweetcakes, nuts, and foods he didn't even know the name of.

"Masa alward, what would you like, young Lord?" a prim manservant asked with just the right touch of propriety.

Tazio felt himself inflate a bit at the stupid title.

"Your choice, I suppose," Tazio said.

The servant hesitated with his serving utensil and looked down at the twenty-foot table he and other servers picked from.

A tall noble in a white and blue cape lined with ornate jewels cocked an eyebrow at Tazio.

"A joke, of course," Tazio said, addressing the noble with a nod.

First mistake—never defer to a servant.

"I'll have some of your finest kebab, a stiff cheese, and some apricots."

"I'm afraid all we have is *khafta*." Tazio flushed with embarrassment at the second mistake of misnaming the food. "Of course—*khafta*."

The social errors Tazio committed were sapping his appetite, and the servant looked flustered and ready for Tazio to be on his way.

Tazio turned back to the rush of the party and waded through the grandeur. Women stood like goddesses in decadent golden-scaled or silk dresses, ornate headdresses, hair gleaming. As he merged through a gap in the crowd, he saw a beauty with sumptuous cream skin and thick, golden hair speaking to a handsome Katarian. Her toned lines stood in the opening of her backless dress. Entranced, Tazio traced her up and down, until, as if by intuition, she lowered her shoulder and slanted her gaze toward him, pausing, then sending a coy smile with a hint of danger.

Warmth ran through Tazio.

She brushed her fingers over the man's shoulder, whispering to him before drifting away, eyes catching Tazio's before she vanished into the party. Tazio followed her invitation until he found her beneath the branches of some palm planters on the outside of a sandstone column. Leaves cast private shadows over her pristine face. And while her beauty had captured him at a distance, up close it was ravishing. Demure lines laced with siren intrigue made her beauty dangerous. Strong, dark brows framed almond-shaped eyes—a deep green that churned his blood.

Tazio didn't know what to say—their eyes had spoken enough with that intangible energy that supersedes words. Her gloved fingers turned up as he took her hand, sending a wave through him.

"Do you always stare like a brute?" she asked.

"Only when I'm captured."

"Is that right?"

Tazio leaned in beside her ear. "Do you always lead men into dark corners?"

She cooed, quiet and seductive. Then put her hand on his chest, and leaned in close to his neck. "Only when I've captured them."

Tazio was shocked at how they'd come together like two colliding waves, raw urges driving them. Thrill screamed through him as the pull to kiss her gripped him. He leaned in slowly to her lips, then lingered, feeling her chest rising and falling.

Tazio's blood rushed.

Tazio pulled her close, each inch a chasm crossed, until their lips pressed, and she moaned, pressing into him, fire raging in Tazio, lust charging past the gates of reason.

Fear spread through Tazio and he broke away.

"What?" she whispered, pulling at the cowl of his cloak.

"We'll be seen."

"I don't care."

"I don't even know your name."

"I don't care."

"Neither do I," Tazio said, chuckling at her insolence.

"It's Electra."

"Electra..."

"Yes."

"Tazio."

"Tazio..."

She hugged Tazio, hands exploring his back as she kissed his neck. Jacomo's warning about endangering his future at the Guild echoed in his head.

"Don't go," she said.

"I want to stay. I do. But I have to go. Can we meet again?"

"Come now."

"I can't. Can I send for you?"

"Fine. Send for my aide Lena at the palace. I'll be here for the next few days."

"I'll send for you," Tazio said, checking if anyone was watching before giving her one final kiss.

As he walked away, the world was luminescent. Chandeliers twinkled brighter, the music coasted effortlessly, and all was aglow. If he looked back, he wouldn't be able to pull himself away again, but he hoped he hadn't uprooted the seed by leaving. Unfortunately, there were other priorities.

Near the next giant sandstone column, he saw Jacomo standing with judgment carved into his brow.

"Come with me now."

"Jacomo—"

Jacomo walked quickly into a side hallway off the main auditorium. "Spare me. You may be trained in stealth, but I'm a master. Do you know she's a princess?"

"That explains 'send for me at the palace.'"

"You will do no such thing, you imbecile," Jacomo's finger tapped on his temple sharply. "Are you blind to the significance?"

"Who is she?"

"It doesn't matter!" Jacomo hissed.

"It does."

"She is *not* for you. This is the end of the discussion. I should have you castrated. Didn't realize the Guild has employed such a feral dog."

"Then at least let me know," Tazio said, not in the mood for a laugh.

"Electra Herrscher, daughter of Falkone Herrscher. Are you that blind? Banishment is death, Tazio."

"Daughter of Falkone Herrscher?"

Tazio's heart dropped.

"Yes, you fool. Now snap out of it. We must get back to the party, not spend time managing your recklessness."

"Then I won't be banished? Why?"

Jacomo grabbed his arm.

"Get off me," Tazio growled, jerking free of Jacomo's grip. "It's time you stop treating me like a child in your game."

"You don't even see the board, boy. Keep pushing and learn the meaning of defiance."

"Then Neri told you everything. Just leave me."

Jacomo pulled a dagger and held it against Tazio's neck. "You're lucky I don't end you right now."

"Do it."

"You're a fool in love, Tazio." Jacomo hovered inches from Tazio's eyes, brow cinched. "I'm not sure why I intend to spare you—perhaps your blind recklessness reminds me of myself." Jacomo lowered the dagger. "I own you now. Be glad I'm a kind teacher. When you're done licking your wounds, find me—this is no ordinary eve."

Tazio pushed off the wall as Jacomo disappeared down the hallway toward the party.

"Falkone's daughter. Of course," Tazio muttered.

He wished he could hate Electra for being related to Falkone, but his heart was ensnared. Logic marched in rank and file, screaming of barriers. He was a commoner, she was a princess. He fought the Thoracians, she slaughtered his people. But she'd seared her mark. Her touch. Her piercing eyes drawing a sword and cutting a veil to transport him somewhere the heart alone ruled. Tazio rubbed his brow to pull himself back to reality, hurrying back to the frenzy of the ball. It felt dull amidst the rug ripped out from under his hopeful spark of love.

He searched for Jacomo—but a different familiar face stood out. Tazio's pulse spiked. Across the room, in the opposite hallway beyond the arches, a royal guard escorted the strident Sieg Herrscher. Groomed to lead the Thoracian kingdom, his cockiness was more pungent than a rotting corpse. Heads turned and murmurs flitted around the room at his mere presence. Nothing attracted the eyes of powerful people more than *more* powerful people, all ready to suckle the teat of power.

Sickening.

The memory of Sieg sparing him near the drawbridge at Bourgogne flashed into his mind, along with the thought he should have some gratitude for the man for sparing him. It felt perverted considering what the Thoracians had done to Novra. At the end of the day, Sieg was the next Falkone—the next conqueror and killer and rapist adorned in prestige but corrupt throughout.

Tazio looked for Jacomo, then back to Sieg. As he looked back to Sieg, not wanting to miss a beat, he saw him.

Falkone—wearing the same brutal armor he'd worn at the slaughter at Coille Solais, with a gray dress cape hanging from it, and an onyx crown adorned with rubies sitting on his head like an ode to bloodshed. Like the unyielding presence of a storm cloud, he moved slowly, eyes relaxed, never in a rush. Even from a distance, Tazio could see why his magnetic power made people bend the knee to his brute force. Hate burned in Tazio's chest like a ball of fire as he took in his face free of a helmet for the first time—harsh, with a scar across a blocky nose that met a hard, strong brow that hung over brown eyes that were nearly black. His hair was black and gray, thick, and to the shoulders, and he wore a gritty beard. The decision to obey Jacomo or get closer to Falkone split Tazio in two, but Falkone's presence gripped his guts, and he broke away to watch Falkone more closely.

Tazio blended into the crowd, keeping his profile toward Falkone in case he would be recognized, stealing glances as he wound through the endless shining tunics and dresses. Sieg laughed and talked and the other soldiers laughed at every quip. The dynamic of constantly placating royals was pathetic. Even Falkone seemed to share Tazio's distaste for the petty men trailing him.

Falkone trudged steadily around the outer procession toward a door on the side opposite of the entrance. From that door emerged Maratan, the dashing King of Kataria. His strong investments in domestic affairs, water, food supply, and relative independence from wars made him a well-loved ruler. Most turned a blind eye to his endless harem of women, and his obsession with supplying his guard likewise. Not to mention the widespread genocide of the Namanian people, a minority culture known for resisting Katarian authority. Tazio wasn't surprised that some percentage of the population tired of conforming to an oppressive government and an obsession with cultural uniformity and order.

Maratan spread his arms and smiled at Falkone.

Tazio strained to read their lips. After moving through their pleasantries, the two rulers sauntered away through the door where Maratan had entered. Tazio looked back to Jacomo, and saw him pull away from a conversation with a man he hadn't seen before, and move toward the front entrance. Jacomo's head was on a swivel, probably looking for him. Taking the cue, Tazio bumped through the crowd to beat Jacomo there, and walked up to the same servant who had served him earlier.

"I'll have some more khafta, please," Tazio said as he came up to the table and suppressed his shortened breath.

"Excellent choice, my Lord," the servant said.

Jacomo walked up. "Tazio, we need to be on our way now. Much to do tomorrow."

"Of course. Khafta for another time," Tazio nodded to the manservant, who smiled back like Tazio was the only one who had truly cared about him that night.

Tazio followed Jacomo out the front into the cool, dry night, leaving behind Electra, Falkone and Sieg, and an assortment of emotions more varied than the food spread.

"Did you see Falkone?" Tazio asked.

"Am I blind?

"A bit edgy, are we?"

"Affairs need tending."

"Anything I can help with?"

"It's beyond your domain."

"How far?"

272

"From here to Auria."

"That's far. Is it about Falkone and Maratan?"

"Stop pushing into dark waters."

"We both know anyone in that ball would have to be blind not to see that was a threatening move—prancing in and slinking away together like they did. It's a clear move toward an alliance."

As they turned the next corner, horns blared through the streets. Jacomo's head tugged toward the sound.

"Hurry," Jacomo said, fear swirling in his eyes.

Jacomo broke into a run and Tazio followed. Mothers shooed their smallest children inside, but all others filtered into the street to confirm the horn was blaring as it did. The streets grew tense as Tazio blurred by buildings to get home. Jacomo threw the front door open.

Atalia was standing in the courtyard.

"*Tesoro*, we must go," Jacomo said.

"What is happening?" Atalia asked.

"It will have to wait. For now, we must escape to some other place. Go gather your things and hide your face."

"Yes, my love."

"Tazio, there is a set of armor in the closet. And a shortsword," Jacomo said. "Those horns and drums are sounded only in the event of military escalations. We're going to find out the meaning of all this. I will lead and you will protect Atalia beside me."

Tazio nodded, pulse quickening as he strapped on the armor. He gripped the kilij shortsword. It reframed his focus. Quick, one-edged, and curved. Five minutes ago he was like a lovestruck adolescent, but touching the sword's hilt shot clarity through his veins.

Atalia reappeared in the courtyard in a black cloak covering her face.

"Onward," Jacomo said, wearing elegant light armor.

They blew out of the house. Already, a mob brandishing weapons filled the streets. Red sand kicked up in swirls, adding to commotion as they blended into the crowd. Bated breath and dark hues hung on the faces in the mob as they chanted in response to the horns resounding through the city. Two blocks from the palace square, the crowd was raucous. The three of them squeezed along a wall to a corner overlooking the main square. Tazio could feel Atalia holding the edge of his armor like a child grasping at its father.

On the huge procession of stairs they'd just descended from the gala, King Maratan and Falkone stood in front of the captain of the city guard and his men, who were gagged and on their knees. A full battalion of Thoracian Morders and Maladian Muraqib kingsguard loomed over the gagged men. The party seemed to have simply trickled outside, as the other royals from the gala watched from an adjacent balcony, chatting and laughing at the cruel display.

Muraqib meant 'Watcher'. When Tazio had first seen a Muraqib, Jacomo told him there were only twenty Muraqib appointed at a given time. Five were required to stay within twenty paces of the King of Kataria, and while most of their training and powers were held in strict secrecy, they were known for having a startling ability to appear and disappear in unexplainable ways. Tazio suspected they used some sort of *draeda* to move the way they did, but hadn't seen how yet.

Morders, the Thoracian highguard, stood like statues of menace. Known for utter brutality, one in five thousand soldiers advanced to their rank. Chosen from childhood by combat ritual, where thousands were pitted against each other to death, at twelve, they were required to bring back the head of an enemy. During the process, either they killed the target, were killed by them, or were killed if they returned empty-handed. For every fifty sent out, one would return. Tazio had seen a few Thoracian boys wandering city streets as a boy, and the look in their eye was enough to scare even the most rugged man. Even now, Tazio caught himself standing in awe at their hard stares, at the stories of their ability to dispatch thirty men without thinking about it, a hundred if they did think. And though Morders weren't permitted to wed, they certainly indulged in the spoils of war. Concubines were even known to seek impregnation from Morders for the prestige of the bloodline, and many lords didn't mind a strong bastard.

His awe cut short as each Muraqib raised a Kudu ram's horn and a trembling resonance blew through the courtyard. Maratan stepped forward under the cleared air for the crowd, who waited with reverence.

"Beloved people of Kataria!" Maratan roared, his words rippling through the courtyard. He pointed a sword at the captain of the city guard. "This traitor and his men plotted insurrection to replace me with an Aurian puppet!"

The crowd roared, spit flying, crude weapons thrusting in the air.

The message was clear regardless of Tazio's rudimentary grasp of Katarian.

Blood.

Retribution.

Maratan thrust his shortsword skyward, provoking the crowd's bloodlust. Then, amid a crazed cacophony of support, so loud it rang Tazio's ears, Maratan drove his blade through the city guard captain's back and out his stomach.

Blood spewed and the captain writhed on the blade as Maratan twisted and kicked him off the skewer. The captain, hands tied and still alive, spasmed as he took stairs to the face. A mob at the bottom hacked him into a pulp far beyond death, his body thrashed about as the remaining city guard had their throats gashed open by Morders.

King Maratan pointed his shamsir blade in the air, its soaked metal dripping gruesomely as the Muraqib blew their horns again.

"We could not capture all the snakes!" Maratan continued. "There are still many guards who have hidden rather than face justice! Find the rats! And for those who know him, find Jacomo Boatto! The Aurian who has sewn these threads of treason! We march on them! And we march on the birthplace of this plot—Auria!"

Jacomo turned around, face pale, the look giving Tazio chills.

The crowd, like a massive ship reversing course, turned and surged toward the northern wall—toward Auria. Faces twisted with blood-lust, teeth bared, eyes wild. The air reeked of sweat and fury as the three of them surrendered to the current of the mob like a branch in a writhing river. Tazio gripped onto Atalia's arm with urgent force, protecting her from being swept away. Gripped by urgency, Tazio shoved forward through the mob, using the advantage they had at being closer to the rear of the crowd. The mob grew thinner, and Tazio pushed through a gap onto a side street, sprinting toward Jacomo's home.

"Both of you, grab only what's necessary. We leave immediately for the port," Jacomo implored as they reached home and opened the door.

Tazio sprinted to his room and threw his belongings into a cloth bag.

The view out the western window caught his eye—a desert jackal ran through the flats under moonlight from one tree to another. Nature

—completely unaware of the churning city, hauntingly opposed to the politics of man.

The peaceful repose haunted Tazio.

He tore away from the view and ran downstairs.

Back in the main courtyard, Jacomo poured oil on fine rugs, trailed it into his study, and lit his study ablaze.

"Out the back," Jacomo said, as he came back into the courtyard.

They went through the kitchen and Jacomo loosened the grate of an exterior window and leapt out.

"Atalia, come," Jacomo said.

Tazio heard banging from the front door reverberate through the house.

"Hurry," Jacomo said, ferreting them toward the port as flames consumed the home, thick smoke already spewing into the sky as they moved out of the alley into the main thoroughfare.

"Auriaaa!" the mob droned.

The density of the crowd had multiplied dramatically. Citizens who had been avoiding danger inside before now joined the churning mob, and city guards who'd been discovered were being surrounded and dismembered at intersections in random frenzies. Fortunately the increasing chaos provided cover to move more discreetly.

They diverted off the main road, using side alleys to snake the short distance to the port, bobbing lanterns coming into view on the decks at the end of an alley. Freedom stirred in his chest as they broke into the port and onto the docks.

Jacomo sprinted toward a small brig, and at the sight of them coming, sailors aboard sprang into action, unfurling sails and calling commands.

They ran up the gangway, and over the lip. The ship drifted off the dock, and Tazio, still catching his breath, leaned against the rail.

"Thank you, Tazio," Atalia whispered to him, then looked over at Jacomo who was talking to a man resting in the shadows of the ajar door that led into the captain's quarters.

The man's crimson hood was drawn, and beneath it, the pits of his sunken face drank the moonlight. Hearing what he needed to hear from Jacomo, the man faded back into the obscured quarters as the sails popped tight under a favorable wind.

They glided along the water, narrowly avoiding the clutches of the rumbling frenzy of Kataria. Torchlight bounced out of the streets of Kataria, glowing in the night sky beside fiery chants of vengeance. Vengeance—a familiar foe Tazio knew so well. One he knew could quickly burn out of control. Tazio gripped the ship's rail as they lapped over waves toward Auria, a looming pit opening in his stomach. Another home that could soon be in ashes. But also, another home he could fight to save.

CHAPTER 29

TAZIO

ON THE WAY back to the Guild from the port, Auria felt dead. Markets were sparse, merchants bartered half-heartedly, and joy seemed to have fled to other lands. Auria had always been gray and blue, but gray now seemed the primary hue, especially as the weight of the Katarian affair clung to Tazio like a shadow. As he walked down the final cobbled alley, the Guild building felt suddenly small after a summer away. He turned through the gate into the courtyard and saw Zara and Alesso standing on the steps.

"Alesso! Zara!" Tazio said, familiar faces sending a burst of bliss through him.

"You look different," Zara said, hugging him briefly before stepping back to study him. "Older, maybe."

Tazio smiled faintly, unsure how to respond to her appraising gaze.

"You do, too. Well, not older. Just more refined."

"Well, Fiamma has been running me through a sieve, so I hope I'm at least a little more refined."

"A sieve, ey?"

"Cazzo. She truly is brilliant. Tough though."

"Tough is the only suitable option for you."

Zara looked at him slant.

"I hope I look older," Alesso said, grabbing him by the shoulder with a smile.

"You'll always look like a big baby to me, no matter how rough you grow that beard."

"Forever virile. That's the way I like it."

"I hate to break up the brotherly love, but Neri's asked for us. It sounded urgent," Zara said.

"Then word traveled to Auria," Tazio said.

"We heard the south is in a shitstorm," Alesso said.

"That explains the sullen faces. Looks like the news beat our journey."

"Rumor travels faster than the wind," Zara said.

"I'm not sure what I'm allowed to say yet. It's best to wait until we meet with Neri," Tazio added.

"Well, let's get on with it. The wait is making me sick," Alesso said.

They walked briskly toward Neri's office.

Jacomo had hoped to deliver word of the failed operation in Kataria to Auria himself, but safety, not expedience, had dictated sailing the rough seas home. It looked like word had traveled faster by some other whisper. Only time would tell now how quickly Thorace would be upon Auria. Over the journey, Jacomo opened up more about his work. He made it clear that he operated a network of informants and contacts in Kataria and other southern lands. Either Jacomo finally trusted him or wartime had necessitated lowering the usual confidence barrier.

They turned the final corner and reached Neri's office. Every time Tazio stood in this spot, it felt like a sword was waiting to come down on his neck. Alesso knocked on the door and raised his eyebrows— probably feeling similar and trying to lighten the load.

The door cracked open.

"My three favorite apprentices," Neri said. "Tazio, you made it safely."

"Concern for my well-being?"

"It was more a statement of fact."

Neri led them in, and as they took their seats, Corso, Kage, and Luca walked in behind them.

"Nothing better to do than follow us around?" Alesso chided.

"Quiet," Neri said, clipping the tension before it could go anywhere. "Everyone take a seat. As I'm sure you've all heard, Falkone and Maratan have finalized an alliance, and they're pushing against Auria. This city hasn't faced a siege at this scale for over seventy years. Falkone is more ambitious than we expected, and we aren't positioned to fight man-for-man."

Tazio shifted in his seat as Neri paused.

"As you know, we rely on trade. Unfortunately, the chaos of the new realm has proven suitable for Falkone to seize power. But we knew we needed a way to fight it. With proximity. With jesters. For thousands of years, there has been a type of advisor few know of that operates in the shadows—the *Jestaera*."

"A *Jestaera?*" Zara asked.

"A fool who wields a *talùth*—who can advise from the depths of *Etria*. Kings and nobles value them as their best councilmembers, military strategists, mystics—some *Jestaera* are even military commanders themselves. With this position comes money, stability, access to the court."

"Is that what Jacomo is?" Tazio asked.

"That is a question for him."

"So you've been using this position for leverage?" Kage asked.

"Only recently."

"Seems like they'd suspect it," Tazio said.

"There is a sworn code that *Jestaera* must serve only one paying patron at a time."

"And this code has never been betrayed?" Zara asked.

"*Jestaera* prefer to keep their heads. There are also ways to monitor them through *draedic* bonding. Not to mention the small detail that any party found corrupting the role for gain is subject to unilateral destruction."

"Sounds like a brilliant bet for Auria," Luca said.

"Thank you for that vote of confidence, Luca. If I needed an advisor, I'd hire one."

Tazio couldn't help chuckling with Alesso and Kage.

"We'll be crushed by Falkone if we do nothing. Auria stands to fall, and I intend to navigate that by being as close to Falkone as possible."

"Then one of us is going to serve him?" Kage asked.

"Serve—or manipulate," Neri said. "We intended to tell you about the role you'd play to prepare you for year two of your studies, but the invasion has accelerated our needs. We'll do our best to accommodate the extreme responsibilities you now face in serving the Guild."

"I don't need accommodation," Corso said.

"I appreciate the audacity."

"When do we find out about our responsibilities?" Luca asked.

"Tonight, when you're initiated into the *Sacraorda*."

"The *Sacraorda*?" Alesso asked flippantly.

"Yes, Alesso, it's not an afternoon street show," said Neri. "You all will serve under a special attaché. You're all a bit unpolished, so I'd advise you to treat your admittance into the *Sacraorda* with tact."

"Tact it is," Alesso said.

"Meet in the courtyard in your dress cloak at midnight. Don't be late."

→

The *Sacraorda* meeting took place in a small brick chamber through an unmarked black door in the middle district. Only Tazio's class and four elder members sat in the candlelit room. Guild tapestries with the three-headed snake hung on the wall, and a circle of stiff, ornate wooden throne chairs sat along the edges of the spare room. They all wore hoods, and that seemed rather ridiculous considering they'd all met and knew each other's identities. This wasn't every member of the *Sacraorda*. According to Neri, a few more were scattered across Novra.

Neri and Marcus Alfini, the Senator Alesso had studied under, had been debating Neri's scheme for about ten minutes, and tempers flared.

"I have my doubts," Marcus said stiffly from beneath his hood. "We're practically giving Falkone the victory if we compromise. The plan *already* approved in the Senate to flank the Thoracians is reasonable."

Marcus was a renowned *artifex*. Jacomo told Tazio that practically every trade ledger passed his desk in some form, and Neri despised him. As for Marcus' *draedic* interests, they went far beyond creation of devices into distribution and exchange, weaving webs wherever he could.

"The information we've gathered estimates that the Thoracian forces, even if reduced in size by a flank, could still overwhelm Auria,"

Neri stated. "Their siege would almost certainly be successful, and we would only provoke their rage."

"That's not certain."

"Nothing is *certain*, but we must trust our sources. Thorace has swallowed three major and four minor fiefdoms in the last three years. They're the largest land force seen in the history of Novra. Not to mention they have a Katarian naval fleet one day away poised to block sea access. Our port saved us in prior sieges, but without it, we'll be crushed from both sides."

"I'm familiar with Aurian military history."

Neri hissed beneath his hood.

"I have to agree with Neri," Fiamma said.

Fiamma made Tazio uneasy.

Every sentence she spoke seemed lined with an ulterior motive. Perhaps double-mindedness was essential for the kind of maneuvering she did in the Senate, but being stabbed from the front seemed better than constantly worrying where someone stood. Why Zara trusted her so much worried Tazio.

"Falkone is routinely slaughtering or converting Guild members across Novra," Marcus growled. "Thorace is our oldest enemy, and Falkone seeks to destroy our way of life. And you suggest we bend over for him like a common street whore? We should do everything we can to make our flank successful. At least we'll be left with options."

"The flank is hopeless!" Neri exclaimed. "Falkone will crush Auria no matter how many men we throw at his flank. And you say options? We'll have no negotiation leverage if we pester him with this absurd flank."

"We have a chance to destroy a huge portion of his forces! The north, seeing our strength, can be persuaded to come to our support."

"That's not a risk we can wager on," Neri said. "If the flank fails to make a large dent in his force, and the north abandons us, we will be left with nothing, and negotiations will be worthless. We must act *now*. Strike a deal while we can maneuver."

"You act like losing is inevitable! Does this not sound like blasphemy to anyone else?"

"He is power hungry and irrational!" Neri snapped.

"Neri—lose your temper at me again and you'll find out just how irrational I can be."

"Marcus," Fiamma interjected, her voice a cooling balm. "We need Falkone's favor. Don't be brazen."

Marcus scoffed. "So we undermine the Aurian Senate?"

"No. We avoid throwing lives away on a doomed flank. To a simplistic nationalist, it might seem like treachery, but I intend to preserve Auria—and the Guild—by whatever means necessary."

"Have you not considered that if we undermine the flank, the powers within Auria will be the Guild's enemy too?" Marcus asked. "You think they'll sit with their thumbs in their ass and accept they've been gutted by us?"

"Assuming you're capable of keeping your people obedient, I'm sure the rest of us can hide what is necessary."

"Your plan is made of straw."

"For a simple-minded brute like you."

"And where will this leaked information about the flank come from?"

"A fearful soldier afraid to die could expose the flank," Fiamma suggested.

"It's believable enough," Neri added. "We have enough people in the right place to support this."

"What would you propose?" Jacomo asked Marcus, sounding neutral.

"I propose to support the flank, endure the siege, and call on Setia and the north to reinforce us immediately. We can buy the time."

"Tens of thousands will die if we wait. Perhaps more," Jacomo said. "It will take months to get reinforcements from the old world, and there is no guarantee from the north."

"But we can sleep at night, knowing we fought to preserve Auria," Marcus replied.

"The weight of our conscience is no measure for proper action," Neri said.

Consideration hung over the room.

The only council member who hadn't spoken was Redan Vitante, the man Tazio and Jacomo had sailed back with from Kataria.

Tazio kept wondering if Redan would weigh in. If Fiamma made him uneasy, Redan twisted his insides. Tazio had never seen his eyes, and for the entirety of the trip from Kataria had caught only a few glimpses of Redan's gaunt, leathery face. When he shook hands with him, just once, the bones in the man's hands were bulging and warped, like he was living on borrowed life from the disturbing things he'd done.

"So which of these poor apprentices will you send then?" Marcus asked.

"Luca," said Neri.

"Luca, are you prepared to do this?" Marcus asked.

"I'm ready for anything," Luca replied.

"Are you prepared to go to Falkone's war camp outside the walls and ingratiate yourself to him?" Neri asked.

Why in Novra are they sending Luca? To choose him is idiocy. By most measurements, he's the least effective.

"You will tell him of the details of the flank which we discussed earlier, and earn your way into the court. Their suspicions will be heightened, but the information you will provide them will be ripe. Thoracians are practical—known to embrace traitors who can prove useful."

"I'd like to go," Tazio interjected.

The air turned thick.

"You're not in a position to volunteer," Neri said.

"I'm prepared to go."

"We've already settled this decision."

"Please—"

"Enough!" Neri burst off his seat.

Tazio gripped the edges of his chair, restraining himself from arguing again.

"Let him speak," Redan said, his raspy voice full of subdued authority. The three words put Neri back into his chair.

"Go on." Redan pointed his bony hand at Tazio.

"I mean no disrespect to Luca," Tazio began, steadying his voice. "But for the sake of Auria, I am impelled. I can achieve your mission without fail. I have the skill, the resolve, and I'm not afraid of the task. Where doubt could steal the victory, my conviction is stalwart."

"We cannot send you," Neri cut in, voice heavy with finality. "Your emotions are too entangled. When the object of our desire stands before us, even the finest among us falter. An entire nation cannot go off your word."

The comment hit Tazio like a blow to the stomach. Tazio searched for some other argument, mouth cracked. But the frustrating realization he had lost his hold on the room choked the words out of him. Stunned, he felt himself sit, boiling beneath his hood, eyes burning, stomach tight, toes gripping the leather of his boots, an explosion stopped only by a desire to prove he wasn't subject to the exact impulses Neri described.

"There will be other ways to help, Tazio."

The concession only stung.

"I look forward to the task," Luca said.

Despite being veiled by his hood, Tazio saw Luca turn to him. He could only imagine the sadistic smirk on his face.

"Thank you, Luca. We have two proposed courses of action," Neri said. "Of the elected members, all in favor of proceeding with the plan and sending Luca?"

Neri, Fiamma, Redan, and Jacomo voted "Seh." The majority ruled.

"It is settled," Neri said. "Luca goes to Falkone tomorrow when the cock crows."

"Thank you, Neri."

"Thank me when you've succeeded."

Luca bowed his head.

"Now, we must finish the initiation for you six. This involves bonding our *talùthae* together in a *pontis communis*. Just like the *anima pontem* that connects you to your *talùth*, practitioners can be bonded to each other through a common link."

"Sounds personal," Kage said.

"Yes, it will give us an intuition as to the location and movement of others, and the ability to draw from common *draeda* reserves when needed. The *pontis communis* connects us."

What will this do to the traeda cumanta bond I share with the Daemonae?

"Are there drawbacks?" Zara asked.

"Once we're connected, we're liable to each other's *draedic* usage and fluctuations. So it's important none of us act like a parasite."

285

"Can someone be a part of more than one of these pools at the same time?" Tazio asked.

"If you form a bond with a *pontis communis*, it is the only one you can bond with."

The answer didn't satisfy Tazio's underlying worry. Perhaps because it used a different form of *draeda,* and because the pools were different, they could coexist.

"To start, we will join hands and you will open your *anima pontem.* As I originate a thread—allow it to move through you. Close your eyes. When you hear me invoke an incantation, repeat it, accept it, and it will be done. Let us begin."

They all took each other's hands, elder members included. Alesso and Kage were next to Tazio. After a year of fighting, sparring, and stealing, holding their hands felt deeply intimate. Alesso's were large and tough, Kage's cold and bony.

"Repeat after us," Neri began.

"*Pons ex animo...*" he and the other elders said.

"*Pons ex animo...*" the six *apprentici* echoed.

"*...viam meam aperio ad pontem communem aedificandum.*"

"*...viam meam aperio ad pontem communem aedificandum.*"

"*Accipio hanc draedicam unitatem.*"

"*Accipio hanc draedicam unitatem.*"

As the final incantation echoed, the others manifested into view, their bodies glowing in threads of energy. Coming out from Neri, a sinuous thread of *draeda* slithered into Alesso, who struggled and groaned until the thread shot out of him into Tazio's left hand and up his arm. Alien and invasive, it darted for his heart, coiling around it, hissing as it constricted, wriggling for a way in. Tazio clenched against the intrusion, chest tight as he felt the connection to the Daemonae resisting it.

"Allow it in!" Neri boomed.

The words cracked his resolve, and the thread pierced a hole in his heart, shooting through and emerging out the other side. His *talùth* vibrated and hissed as it flowed through and burst out of his veins toward Kage, who writhed in response. Tazio's chest heaved as he watched it pass through the others. Each time it completed its work on someone, their energy signature burst into Tazio, palpable and rich.

The thread completed its circuit back to Neri, slithering out of his *talùth*, though still connected to it, and coiled into a ball of energy in the center of the circle. Neri muttered another incantation and Tazio felt his heart open, a thread coming out of it to join the ball at the center along with everyone else's. Yellow and orange, the energy was like a pile of vipers lighting the faces of all in the room, transfixed in awe at the orb.

"Factum est," Neri murmured. "It is done. Welcome to the *Sacraorda*."

The thread with the Daemonae snapped free, tearing out of his veins like a whip cracking. Panic gripped his chest as he reached out for Anya—but only a hollow silence hung over.

Anya?

Fear swelled, a suffocating storm rising over the horizon of his mind. The last buds of hope in the garden of his soul trembled under despair, the last roots of his connection in *Etria* with the Daemonae raked free of the soil of his heart.

Factum est—the deed was done.

CHAPTER 30

ALESSO

ALESSO FOLLOWED Marcus down the same alley he'd searched for the dark market with Tazio just a few months prior. Marcus insisted they wear neutral black cloaks rather than the normal lavish blue and gold Marcus so loved, and the abnormality of that request wasn't helping the tightening feeling in Alesso's chest.

"I didn't want it to come to this, but it has to be done," Marcus growled. "Something sinister is going on."

After the tense *Sacraorda* meeting that night, Marcus had received a dispatch that pissed him off royally.

"What is it?"

"You look pale. I know you've had quite the experience in the place we're about to go—but it's good to confront fear."

Alesso breathed deep as they passed the same half-burnt woman he'd spoken to his first time through. She looked at him like she'd seen a familiar ghost. They rounded a corner and Alesso saw the same blood red door at the end of the alley.

"I may have to break trade conduct here. Put on your hood. We're to remain anonymous," Marcus said. His square face and nose that'd been broken and repaired several times made him seem even more serious in the moment.

Marcus pounded on the door that had swallowed Alesso a few months prior.

A brick wall of a man opened the door. Tazio told him he'd fought this guy to get them out, and that he'd torn the hamstring straight from the bone.

Marcus flashed his talùth, then a ring, which was different from his normal Senatorial ring.

The man let them pass.

Wouldn't mind giving him a good knee to the leg as a friendly hello.

They approached the pit, which Alesso hazily recalled.

It was quiet and empty this time, with the exception of five men sitting at a lone table by candlelight. They were shooting a game of dice —probably rischio.

Yes, it was rischio.

The sight of the game loosened him up.

Wish I could scrape the bastards in a few quick games.

The lanky ringleader sat with his legs perched on the table, chewing a stick of opia.

Nice way to stay hooked without totally slopping out.

Alesso recognized him, and it was darkly comical to be encountering all the characters he'd met in a haze that Tazio and Zara told him about.

Marcus flashed his talùth and ring again to the ringleader, and the man sat up out of his lethargy, eyeing them suspiciously.

"Seh, this way," he croaked, giving an ugly sniff as he slurped some opia in his lip.

He led them to the back corner of the chamber where he pulled a thick rug off the floor, revealing a hatch to an underground stairwell. He unlocked it, smiling unhinged as he did his best to sneak a look under their hoods for who they might be.

"Bet the nick," Alesso suggested.

"You're loose in the head," The ringmaster said, peering back at the game of rischio. "The nick won't hit."

Alesso turned his face to let light reveal it, flashing a knowing smile. "Wouldn't want you to lose a good bet," Alesso said.

The man's face stretched in horror.

"I'll see you later," Alesso said, chuckling as he trotted down the stairs.

Poor bastard looked like he's pissed his pants.

The hatch door closed above them and Marcus shoved Alesso against the wall.

"Do you know the meaning of anonymous? He'll have to be killed for your little joke now." Marcus' stern look imparted the grave nature of the situation.

Marcus let off him and started down the long tunneled stairway.

The sound of faint muttering trickled up. At the bottom, two sinister Guild *Sicariae* stood at the door decked in black armor and cowls. They each had five throwing blades in leather straps, and their *talùthae* brandished openly with glowing threat.

The Guild's top dog killers.

Not the type you'd want to fuck with on any given day.

The *Sicariae* opened the doors.

Marcus wasted no time, weaving in and out of the rock halls, the catacombs like a beehive carved into orange stone. A few hundred hooded merchants talked in nooks and curves, hushed and surreptitious, the amorphous chamber creating a garbled, indistinguishable cacophony of whispers. Everyone was hunched over tables nailed to the catacomb walls, their hoods drawn, hands cupping their conversations as they obscured their negotiations.

The Catacomb Forum.

Marcus had told him this was where the bulk of *draedic* contracts were negotiated. Alesso was gushing with questions about the details of the exchanges, but this wasn't the time to be inquisitive. These didn't seem like the kinds of characters you wanted knowing your voice, your name—or anything about you for that matter.

They navigated deeper into the tunnels. Marcus knew exactly where he was going. He walked up, no questions asked, to a Guild member wearing navy and gold, and clobbered him. The man's *talùth* had been glowing and hissing in the middle of a draeda incantation to finalize the contract. The blow sent the man limp against the rock wall.

The other man in a dark gray cloak he'd been dealing with grabbed the contract and sprinted away.

Marcus charged after him, cutting to the right through a different part of the maze, busting through a few other groups to come out in front of the runner. He jumped on his back and brought him to the floor. Hushed whispers turned to murmurs as people gathered around and drew weapons.

"If any of you are interested in saving Auria, you will stand down," Marcus said to the offended onlookers, his voice modulated intentionally, "Or you can die by my sword."

The words held the mob at bay.

They're more interested in closing their contracts and bedding the next whore. But if the Sicariae catch wind of the commotion in here, blood will spill.

Marcus hoisted his victim by the collar.

"You don't know who you're playing wiff!" the man cursed, as he thrashed about.

"I should have cut you in half months ago, Traeger," Marcus said, throwing the man down and yanking his hood off.

Traeger's thinning blonde hair, gaunt cheeks, and sunken eyes made him look worn beyond his age.

"But you didn't," Traeger said, "because you Setians are so in love with coin, it makes you weak."

As Marcus pulled out his *cinquedea*, Traeger snuck a stiletto from his sleeve. Alesso unsheathed his sword, lunging forward and skewering Traeger's arm to the floor.

"No!" Marcus shouted.

"He was going to kill you!" demanded Alesso.

Traeger moaned and stared at his arm, blood draining all over the sandstone as Marcus snatched the *draedic* contract. "Traeger, I can save your life. Just tell me who you're making this deal with."

Marcus held the contract in front of Traeger's eyes.

"Fuck you. Fuck the Guild. Fuck Auria," Traeger laughed, bewildered.

"This is your last chance." Traeger spat in his face. "That's how it'll be then." Marcus drove his *cinquedea* into Traeger's stomach, twisting for emphasis, ripping his dagger free, dumping Traeger against the wall, and stripping the man's *talùth*.

Alesso stared at Traeger's convulsing body, stomach turning. Death was familiar, but the cruel finality of Marcus' twist brought a hollow ache to his chest.

"Come," Marcus said from ahead, his bulky frame parting the onlookers.

"Coming," Alesso replied.

They ascended the stairs from the catacombs and banged on the latch. As the ringmaster opened it, Marcus plunged his *cinquedea* into him too, then kicking him off the blade like an animal. The other gamblers, hearing their compatriot scream, bolted up.

"Your choice," Marcus growled, flashing his *cinquedea*, blood dripping down it as he walked past.

Not a soul budged.

Marcus turned to him when they made it out to the alley. "Make no mistake, Alessandro. I just broke one hundred and fifty years of Setian trade law in Novra by killing in the catacombs. I promise that you will not be held accountable for my actions if we're found out."

"I'm sorry for stabbing him, Marcus," Alesso said.

"No, you acted correctly—I simply didn't want his death on your conscience. I should have been more careful. My suspicions were confirmed, but I wish we could have dug for more about Thoracian motivations. That, unfortunately, isn't outlined in the contract—only the details of the exchange."

"Who was he?"

"A Thoracian Dradier. Representing their draedic interests here over the last year. Under Setian law, he was entitled to trade with anyone willing to make a deal. Most Guild members did not dare touch him. Until now."

"Someone on the inside was trying to cut a deal?"

"It looks that way."

"Why don't we question the Guild member he negotiated with?"

"He was likely a front man, and I'd rather not risk revealing our identities."

"Is that why you changed your voice when speaking to the mob?"

"Yes."

"Auria is rather threatened now, isn't it? Far worse than I thought." Alesso's stomach felt heavy.

Marcus stayed quiet. When he finally stopped walking and looked at Alesso in the damp alley of the dark markets, his eyes were solemn. The man who could command rooms with a single glare, who could withstand waves of chaos like the Aurian bluffs, now riddled with doubt.

"I've done all I can to stop it. But almost surely, Auria will fall. Now it's only a matter of which pieces can be saved."

CHAPTER 31

TAZIO

Tazio slipped from shadow to shadow, stalking along the rooftops next to the Gran Parete. The dark was brighter thanks to the *anamaeic* bond with Mahjul—better vision just one of the benefits.

Mahjul's head and front paws draped lazily over the lip of his satchel. Though short on quips, the big cat responded to the subtle shifts in Tazio's blood, understanding the weight of the mission. With passage in and out of the city gates utterly restricted, the only way out was over—though the guards were likely more worried about people entering the city than leaving it.

Tazio hopped onto the final roof section that sat just across from the Gran Parete's interior wall. He stopped, pulled out a rope with a cross-claw at the end and hurled it some thirty feet up to the parapet wall, targeting the section closest to the guard tower. Hopefully there would be less attention there.

The hook clanged faintly as it caught hold, its sound muted by the wax he'd dipped it in—offering a hope of evasion, but no guarantee. He tugged on the rope—it at least, was tight and secure.

"Here we go," Tazio muttered to Mahjul, who trilled in response.

Tazio ascended.

Five feet from the top, he felt someone jerking at the rope near the top.

Fean.

A guard looked over the edge and saw them, eyes wide. Mahjul hissed, sleek body tightening as the guard hacked at the rope, looking to plunge them to their deaths.

Tapping the power of the *anamaeic* bond with Mahjul, Tazio gripped the rope and hurled himself up. Covering the five vertical feet, he grabbed the guard around the neck and crunched his face downward into the top of the parapet wall. Mahjul sprang out of his satchel onto the wall, and Tazio quickly climbed over the unconscious guard, ready to fight any others guarding this section. About thirty paces off, another guard crept toward them with a torch. Mahjul stalked near the shadowed wall, then pounced on the man, fangs sinking into his neck. Tazio sprinted through the shadows, springing off the wall onto the remaining man, dropping him with the butt of his dagger.

"Far too much strain, isn't it?" Tazio asked Mahjul, who seemed displeased by all the effort.

Tazio loosed the claw-hook and cast it over the other exterior wall. About five hundred meters away, Thoracian campfires cast a threatening glow from behind battlement walls.

"Down we go, Mahjul."

Mahjul let out a guttural growl and hopped on his back, thankfully still a willing participant. Tazio put on gloves and they slid until Tazio's feet touched soil. Under the pall of night, Tazio crossed the pastoral fields toward the Thoracian camp. All the farmers had sought shelter inside Auria, and the empty barns and homes made Tazio feel terribly alone. It reminded him how the bond with the *Sacraorda* had severed his connection to the Daemonae. Only now did he realize the connection he'd held to them, no matter how subtle.

He shoved away the thought he'd never see Anya again.

Electra will be in the war camp. I'll have to bet on the fact she'll hold her tongue for at least the opening act of this bloody dare. Neri will be fuming when he finds out what I've done.

But he's left me with no choice.

Sending Luca. What a pitiful choice.

Despite the raging justifications, Tazio still felt conflicted about fealty to his mentor and the Guild.

Mostly across the fields, Tazio crouched in a siege ditch. The wooden rampart wall was practically complete, but soldiers worked through the night on final touches.

"Wait for me outside this wall, Mahjul. Stay safe for now."

Mahjul stared back with earnest affection as Tazio gave him one last scratch on the cheek.

Tazio bounded toward the wall.

The speed and power he got from Mahjul was wicked. His feet felt like lightning as he approached. He leapt up most of the fifteen-foot wall, grabbing hold of a gap between the wood poles. As he hung on the outside, he heard a guard on the ramparts above. And smelled him. There were some things he wished he hadn't gained from the bond with Mahjul.

Before the man could squeak, Tazio vaulted over and ripped a dagger across the man's throat, laying his body down silently, eyeing two more men conversing ahead. Sneaking up, he drove a dagger through the back of one's neck, then the other. Before the gurgles stopped, he leapt into the camp, the night air brushing his face as he descended like a harbinger of doom. His feet kissed the soil, black cloak a blur as he ghosted through tents like a whisper. Now deep in the concentric ring of Thoracian tents, he saw the main command tent standing ahead, guards buzzing about it.

Stealth won't do here.

It'll have to be bloody or cunning—or both.

Smoke drifted out of the center portal of the large tent, catching his eye.

Of course.

Waiting for the right moment, Tazio bolted straight toward the command tent entrance.

"Hey!" a soldier shouted, raising alarm.

Five guards brandished halberd lances.

Tazio cut to the left, and they scrambled, taking off after him as he changed directions on a button. He ran around the spear of the soldier on the end, jumped, and planted his foot on the man's shoulder. He sprang off him onto another man's head, then another, then jumped onto a wooden support beam rising to the center of the large tent. Balancing gingerly, he scrambled up and dove through the tent's smoke vent. Heart raging with bloodrush, he crashed onto the firepit in the middle of the war tent. Logs splintered and ash spewed as Thoracians inside burst from their seats and guards poured in from outside.

"Wait!" Tazio shouted, jumping up from the fire and brushing off embers. He rolled to the side and threw his daggers away. "I have information that will save your army!"

The guards charged, ignoring his appeal. He dove through slashes and hacks, dodging in a blur of feints and flips. He could practically feel Mahjul purring in appreciation of his agility from a mile away. He stunned one guard with a blow to the face, flipped off the chest of another, grabbed the saber of another, and wrapped it around the neck of a fourth before dragging him into a corner.

"I mean no harm! I can save your army! Hear me!" Tazio demanded.

"Cease!" one of the Thoracian commanders shouted.

The flustered guards stopped their flurry.

"Commander, he came from nowhere," one guard moaned, filling the silence.

"I don't want to hear your shit," said a man he recognized—Sieg. "You—drop our man and your weapon or die."

"Easy enough." Tazio released the soldier slowly and threw the blade he'd commandeered across the room. He held his arms wide to appear unthreatening, blood settled enough to see that Sieg and a few other officers were assembled around a battle map of Auria.

And Falkone. The man I've burned for for five long years.

"Check him for weapons," Sieg said.

The head soldier came close and roughly searched Tazio. "I'll fucking kill you," the lead man whispered. When he came to Tazio's neck, he found his *talùth,* ripped it off, and kicked Tazio to the floor.

"Charming amulet." Sieg picked Tazio's *talùth* off the table where the sentry had tossed it. "Xiomar, what do you think?"

Sieg gave the amulet to an intelligent-looking officer with a narrow face and a cropped red beard. Sieg walked to Tazio and lifted him off the ground by the collar. He was about Tazio's height, with a thicker build and breath that reeked of dried meat and figs.

"How did you get into our camp?" Xiomar asked, dropping the *talùth* on the table.

"I can't reveal all the tricks of my trade, can I?" Tazio responded.

"You do realize you're a dead man?" Sieg said, hovering uncomfortably close.

"I think you'll find I'm better off alive."

"Is that right?"

"If you'll give me a moment to explain, you'll see I'm not speaking merely from my ass, but to save yours."

"Why don't I just have your ass broken instead?"

"Because you're curious what I have to say, aren't you?"

Sieg looked like he was ready to pop, and Tazio did his best to hide his utter delight at it, knowing he'd levered the bastard. Though Tazio was in a physically weak position, no reasonable commander would forego valuable intelligence, especially in front of his fellow generals.

"Perhaps we could hear him out," Xiomar offered, treading lightly.

Sieg shoved Tazio to the floor. "Make it good—or that little smile will be stuck on your face and thrown to the dogs."

The room was hot under the glaring gaze of the war council. This would have to be the best performance of Tazio's life. But it was a stage after all. And the stage breathed confidence into Tazio. As it always had.

Tazio stepped forward and gained his legs.

Electra was seated on the far right, face calm, but colored as if she'd stomached some rotten stew. Tazio looked away, holding calm, not daring to risk drawing the others' attention to her.

I have to trust she'll spare me for a few moments. She too will be wildly curious, and I can count on one moment to weave my web.

Falkone sat shadowed off the center of the table, a looming presence like a wolf ready to rip its prey to shreds. No matter how tempting his neck was, it wasn't the time.

Very unfortunate.

"Get on with it!" one of the other gruff officers shouted, waving a meaty arm, animal pelts rustling around his neck. He was a bulky man, and despite being older, had an aged strength that was in some sense more intimidating than youth.

"Pardon me, what is your name, good Lord?" Tazio said, maintaining a jolly facade as he bent a knee.

"Lord Drannen, silly fool. Falkone's blunt hammer!"

"A pleasure, Lord Drannen. You're probably wondering why I've stumbled my way into your camp."

"That would be an understatement," Xiomar said. "Are you Aurian?"

"Quick to the questions. I do live within Auria. But I am not necessarily Aurian."

"Then what are you?" Xiomar continued.

"I am a *Jestaera*."

Tazio expected this would make an impact considering Neri's entire plan hinged on it, and they took pause.

This is good. I may have more leverage than I suspected.

Xiomar looked carefully at his *talùth*, as if to confirm what Tazio said, and leaned over to whisper into Falkone's ear. Falkone's jaw tightened as he assessed Tazio like a butcher inspecting a carcass.

Eventually, Xiomar started again, "Then you've come to betray Auria?"

"Betray is an ugly word."

"Your actions are rather ugly, are they not?"

"I understand. It seems I'm standing here before you as a traitor. A *wretch*. A damned fool ready to throw his own nation to the wolves. But I posit I'd be a fool not to come to your side. With the information I have, I can turn the tide of the war in your favor and make a potentially losing position into a winning one. One that will serve me and you. The world is a game of constantly shifting pieces, and in this case, I'd prefer to bend the odds in our favor."

"And why should we not just take your information and be done with you?" Xiomar said.

"The information I have can only be verified if I'm alive to guide you."

"We're familiar with how to conquer a city," Sieg said. "We don't need your worthless information. Or we can torture it out of you."

A manic cackle burst out of Tazio—all the pent-up desire mixing with the fear he now stood in. But he leaned into the insanity, committing to the act to instill fear into the Thoracians. "If you think I haven't been trained to endure torture, you know very little about the way of the *Jestaera*."

"Tell us, then," Drannen said.

"Setia. Auria. The Guild. They're not castles or nations like the others you've pissed on. They're a plague. You can crush one boil, but it will reappear again. So go ahead, dispose of me. But you'll lose my knowledge of how to maneuver against Auria and the Guild from the inside."

"Were you a member of the Guild?"

"No. But I dealt with them on many occasions in my work for dark merchants. I know their channels and means quite well. You'll wage a slow, grinding war against endless shadows, never knowing when you'll take a dagger in the back. Or, you can use me to move among them and grow your power."

"I've had enough of this diatribe. We know the workings of the Guild. And of Auria. We've fought them for thousands of years," Sieg said.

"And still you've never won."

Embers burned in Sieg's eyes.

"One more thing before I divulge the information you desire," Tazio continued after some silence.

"This fool is relentless. I'm beginning to like his petulance!" Drannen chuckled.

"I want to serve Thorace," Tazio admitted with a touch of subservience.

"This is absurd!" Sieg said, standing in protest.

"Sit down," Falkone growled.

Sieg sat like a recalcitrant boy.

Falkone leaned forward, the candlelight turning his brown eyes amber beneath his hard brow. His black and gray hair spilled down from his onyx crown, framing his rugged beard, a countenance the image of power.

"Divulge, or lose your head." Falkone's voice was like a rusty sword drawn from a scabbard.

Tazio's blood pounded against his temples.

"Thank you, Lord Falkone." Tazio wanted to vomit saying the words, but made them sound believable. "Two days ago, before your army had encamped here outside the Gran Parete, the bulk of the Setian army moved north of the Vestian Pass. They're hidden in the forest, and they're aware of your position. Their plan is to flank you as morning breaks."

"We've searched those forests, and there's not a soul," Xiomar explained.

"The Vestian Gorge is a special hidden feature known only by a few Aurian figures prior to this day. Without knowing the area, even the finest scouts in your army would miss it. The bends and crannies of the landscape are a tactical feature used only in case of an attack deemed capable of leading to defeat."

After a few stiff moments, Xiomar whispered something in Falkone's ear, who stared grimly at Tazio.

Promising. They're taken aback. But now they need a push.

"The caves hold twenty thousand or more men," Tazio added.

"Twenty thousand?" The subtlest hint of worry lined Xiomar's tone.

"Yes, and you won't be able to find the exits in time on your own. And if you attempt to reposition to defend your flank without my precise understanding of waypoints and timing, Aurian scouts on the Gran Parete will see your shifting men, abandon the attack, and you'll face the same stiff odds of the siege you're attempting." The lies made Tazio uneasy, but he had to increase the perceived threat from Auria to encourage action. "Even with the port blockade, I doubt you'll succeed. There is already rumor of the north coming to stop you. If I hadn't told you of this flank, you'd surely lose half your forces, perhaps more. Then if the north comes, you could face catastrophe."

Falkone looked angry. He clearly hated being put in a corner, and Tazio savored seeing the rage line his brow.

But now he had to win Falkone over.

One thing Jacomo insisted on during training was that you can't persuade a man by crushing his will. They will only despise you and bite back like a dog on guard. The wisdom echoed through Tazio's mind, balancing his actions.

"Lord Falkone, if I may—please bear in mind, I only want to verify this information with your men so I can demonstrate my value to you. From what I know of Thoracian culture, value is placed on doing whatever is necessary to win. In this case, I thought it best to win by serving you. This could have been a grave miscalculation on my part. My fate is in your hands, but I hope you'll take my forwardness not as disrespect, but as a gesture of my confidence and respect." Tazio took a small step back, bowed, and put himself on the scales of fate.

There was nothing left to say or do, the decision now teetering in the hands of Falkone and his advisors—the same men who'd trampled the guts of those he loved twice—now on the verge of slaughtering Auria. He might win this persuasion, but it would feel like a blow against his desire to put their heads on a pike. Every part of his body raged to unleash his fury upon them.

Do it now.

Draeda bubbled in his veins, begging him to rip them to pieces with *feantoiil.*

No! Think of Auria. Of Alesso. Of Zara. Of Electra...

She sat in the corner of his eye. Tazio ached to speak to her, to comfort her, to know what she thought of this madness—if she'd accept him.

Wait—wait with brutal patience to kill these rats on your terms. Save those you love. It's possible. Intricate, but possible.

Leone's wisdom steadied him amid the inferno in his heart. Breathing deep into his heels like Leone had taught him, he held fast as Falkone leaned forward from the shadows, his gaze a storm of steel and ash. "You have mettle, fool," Falkone growled, voice like rust and gravel. "But mettle is not proof. Tomorrow, we'll play your little game, and we'll see if your balls match your word. If not—I look forward to feeding them to the dogs."

CHAPTER 32

ZARA

Break of dawn. Where we meet for top matters.
R.L.

Z<small>ARA</small> <small>READ</small> the note delivered by falcon just minutes ago as she wound her way through the Gardens of Mercatorum off the backside of the Senate building. The sun was burning away sea fog that hung over the trimmed hedges, floral displays, ponds, and sculptures. Oranges and yellows glowed through the vapor, giving the morning a damp ebullience. But serenity was not enough to stop war.

L and R—the second letter from either side of 'Alessandro,' but reversed. When Alesso, Tazio, and she had formed the code for sending sensitive communiques, Alesso insisted that using his full name more effectively obscured his identity. Zara found it comical how serious he was about it—like a boy scheming at playtime. It was endearing, even charming.

With resources focused on more suspicious or powerful actors as war threatened to cut Auria in two, it wasn't likely the three of them were top targets. Nevertheless, Zara scurried tensely to the rendezvous point. She went under the long pergola covered in Setian amber grapes and crossed the bridge over the reflection pools and into the open-air rotunda. The parties held here for the elite during summer evenings were forever seared into her memory. Its spiral columns and elaborate insets in the dome allowed the sun and moons to perfectly rest in the portals built into the massive dome at varying changes in the seasons. As she stepped out the far side, sadness swept over her.

This may be the last peaceful moment these gardens see for decades.

She followed a path into the hedged garden maze. It rose gradually uphill until it met a set of stairs leading to the fortified sea wall. She wound through, the solution memorized, and ascended the stairs. Statues of the first five Senators and merchants of Setia stood on the Novra side of the gated archway that led through the seawall. Their backs were to Setia and the ocean, representing no turning back, their gaze steady over the maze, representative of overcoming the complexities Auria must navigate in the new world.

She knew it was just her imagination, but right then their stone faces looked particularly rigid in light of the odds.

She opened the gate in the archway. Alesso stood facing the sea in the grass-covered garden. Its modest row of trimmed hedges flanked the edges for privacy from outlooks along the curving seawall, but the forward view looked over the rough ocean. Private meetings or solitary meditations were frequent here, and the gate latch sounded a small chime to alert of any entrance.

"Alesso."

"Zara."

Zara hugged him. His bearlike frame soothed her.

"Why do I feel like five years have passed since last night's meeting?" Zara asked.

"Only five?"

"Well at least the stress hasn't stripped you of your humor."

"It's all I have left."

"Don't say such things. What's going on? I don't think you sent a coded falcon to tell a few jokes."

"Unfortunately not." The weight of whatever Alesso was bearing shaded his normal sunniness.

He turned to the ocean where rays of light were breaking through thin spots in the drifting clouds.

"Marcus and I went to the Catacombs after the meeting last night. He insisted," Alesso said.

"You saw the Catacombs?" Zara had been wanting to see them, but it was so furtive. Few were granted access.

"Yes, but that's not the point."

"Well?"

"For months, Marcus tracked a Thoracian peddling *draedic* contracts in Auria. No one dared touch the offers—until Marcus got information that someone had bitten. Last night, we caught them in the act."

Heavy wind buffeted the plateau.

"What happened?" Zara asked.

"He felt it was enough to justify taking action."

"And?"

"Marcus cornered him," Alesso said, eyes far off, consumed by the waves. "And I stabbed him..."

"Alesso..." Zara said, touching his arm, which felt frozen in the past.

"...when he attacked Marcus," Alesso muttered. "Then Marcus killed him. We found a Guild member was working a deal with him. The incantation was nearly complete when we saw him."

"Did you find out who it was?"

"No, Marcus preferred we try and obscure our identities. Even changed his rings to gain access."

"Cazzo."

"It's good we stopped the deal. We don't know if Falkone knows the deal caved yet."

"What was outlined in the contract?"

"Providing *talùthae*. Lots of them. And something called *draedum*."

"*Draedum?*"

"Marcus said there has been a breakthrough in turning weapons into *draedic* items."

"That's not possible."

"It is now. When you kill, these weapons allow anyone, including practitioners, to replenish reserves using the victim's soul."

"It's forbidden."

"It's happening."

"Novra will fall into chaos with these in circulation."

"We never would have known unless we acted. And whoever was making the deal in the Guild must have been stockpiling *talùthae* to provide Falkone. A long-term scheme, no doubt."

"What was the Guild dealer going to get in return?"

"An assload of coin. But our guess is, sensing impending doom, whoever the Aurian was, they were looking to save their ass."

"And to be in Falkone's good graces."

"Yes."

Zara's mind was spinning thinking of who in the Guild, or Auria, might do such a thing.

"Have you told Tazio?" Zara asked.

"No." Turbulence swam in his eyes as he turned away.

"Tell me." Zara's heart pattered and her breath quickened like the answer already coursed through her as Alesso delayed. "Alesso?"

"Tazio left last night."

The wind cut in.

"To Falkone's camp. Before Luca could."

"No." Zara's legs felt loose.

"He's gone, Zara."

"Stop it. This is not a joke." But Zara knew it was the truth. Her words felt empty and childish, like she was grasping onto false hope, trying to convince herself of some other story. "Tazio doesn't know about the deal. We have to send a falcon." She stumbled backward and bumped into the seawall, fighting against a wave of nausea as she fumbled to find the gate and leave.

"I have to send for Tazio," she mumbled.

"It's too late!" Alesso interjected, stopping her in place. "The message will be intercepted. Then we'll be really fucked. We must maintain our information advantage—you know that better than anyone."

"I'm spinning, Alesso." Zara leaned against the wall, breath accelerating.

"Zara!" Alesso shouted, catching her as her knees gave out.

She struggled to stay conscious as he steadied her against the wall.

"Zara," Alesso said, voice far off as vision began to tunnel. "Breathe, Zara, *breathe.*"

The world spun around Alesso as he peered down with compassion, a glow around him. Guiding her through slow breaths. Face like a sun in the clouded world of her fears, his arms strong beneath her.

"Alesso, have we failed?"

"Not yet. But we've got to be like steel. For Tazio—and for Auria."

Zara's breath steadied as his words cut through her panic, grounding her.

"You're okay," Alesso said. "Can you stand?"

"I'd rather not."

"I'm not surprised you fainted. I lost my mind when I found out Tazio had left. It's terrible to drop the entire weight on you at once."

"You're definitely a bastard for that."

"Ok, you've definitely recovered from whatever fit that was. No more help from me," Alesso joked through the squinted smile Zara had come to love.

Love?

She blushed at the thought, brushing it away to consider later.

"Thank you, Alesso," Zara said as Alesso helped her up.

Zara brushed the grass and dirt off her red cloak. Her mind spun again. But this time for solutions, grit sharpening into resolve.

"Now, we need to figure out what in Novra we're to do next."

→

Zara entered one of the Guild's fifth-floor common rooms that had been converted into a war room. Clerks shuffled to and fro around the huge rectangular table, normally able to seat about thirty, now covered with maps and papers—and whatever else Neri was contriving from his seat at the center—so absorbed in conversation with Luca he didn't even see Zara enter.

Luca was wearing a *Jestaera's* motley, and preparing to make his exit to Falkone's camp. The motley was green and silver, regal, more refined than a low fool's motley. The traditional motley's cap was replaced by a small pointed cap and a striped velvet hood. Overall it was menacingly beautiful.

"Neri," Zara said as she approached the table.

"Zara," Neri replied.

"May we talk in private?" Zara asked.

"I'm rather busy as you can see," Neri replied.

Neither he nor Luca looked pleased at Zara's interruption.

"I wouldn't interrupt if it was trivial," Zara said.

"Then speak."

"The conversation may be better suited in privacy."

"Well I think I'd rather hear it here. I trust everyone here." Neri gestured broadly to everyone mulling about.

"Tazio has gone to Falkone's camp."

The news hit Neri like he'd heard the death of his mother, color draining from his face. Silence suffocated the room as a few clerks who overheard stopped what they were doing, unable to hide their shock. Neri slowly stood from his chair and wandered to the far side of the room. Standing still, he stared at the wall, the silence gripping Zara's chest, no one daring to move. Then, he paced back and forth, muttering like a man possessed until he walked over to the table, tension radiating off his shoulders. He put his hands down on the end of the table and took a few deep breaths, and Zara breathed a sigh of relief. Then, he exploded—thrashing papers into the air like dry leaves in a storm, tearing books off the shelves, hurling vases across the room, aides narrowly ducking them. Then, with a maniacal scream, he drew his sword, charged the war table and drove the blade deep into it, splinters spewing as the blade quivered in place.

"Now then, you stay there!" Neri exclaimed to the sword.

Zara's spine stiffened. She hadn't thought the outburst possible, and apparently, given the stunned looks on the aide's faces, no one else did either.

Neri sat down and pushed his long black hair off his face, a deep exhale pouring out of him. "What are you all looking at?"

The room whirled back into motion as if the outburst never happened. Luca looked clearly uncomfortable, and very unnatural in the regal motley.

"*Bastardo*, Tazio. I should have known," Neri muttered. "Thank you for bringing me this information, Zara. This will change things."

Zara's throat tightened. "Allow me to apprentice under you," she blurted out.

Neri paused, then chuckled, his laughter growing into a sharp, mocking fit. "*Cazzo*, you're full of surprises today! Where is this sudden fit of ambition coming from? Has Fiamma already cast you aside?"

"You're asking *me* about sudden fits?" Zara snapped back, looking at the mess Neri made.

Neri cocked his head in surprise. "Sharp. Unfortunately for you, I don't need another assistant."

Zara squared her shoulders. "Fiamma trained me, you know that. War is here, and I can manage information more effectively than anyone here."

"Perhaps." Neri leaned in with a crooked look. "But that's not the real reason you want to help, is it?"

"I'm not sure what you're implying."

"We're at war. And you're in love with *Tazio*."

Zara blushed.

Luca snickered.

A few people gave sideways glances.

Zara hesitated.

Stay balanced. He's baiting you.

"Tazio has lost his balance," Zara said. "His actions are on the verge of compromising Auria and the Guild. And as much as I care for him, he's betrayed us. I'm one of the only people in this world who knows him so well. Perhaps I can help you lever him back into a position of advantage for the Guild. I don't think he is interested in undermining the Guild. He's simply driven by revenge."

Neri leaned back in his chair and put a hand to his cheek, thinking. The silence lingered, and Zara knew he was testing her—so she stood there staring back at him, committed to her argument.

Yes, she cared for Tazio, but she was more interested in being close to the well of valuable information. Fiamma was a summer study. But Neri was the prize.

"If it came to it, could you send a *Sicarius* to end him? Or kill him with your own blade?" Neri asked.

"If it came to it." The words hurt as she uttered them.

Zara truly didn't know if she could do what Neri asked, but knew she had to maintain the illusion for now.

"Very well. I'll try you out. But if I sense any weakness—" Neri drew his finger across his own throat, "it's over."

"You're going to appoint her that easily?" Luca interjected.

"Don't act jealous, Luca, it's unbecoming. And either dance for us or take off that outfit. If I wanted another fool in my presence, I'd hire one."

"Are you kidding me? What will I do now?" Luca shot up from his chair, tugging off his motley cap.

"Does it seem like I'm kidding!" Neri boomed. "We're at war! There will be plenty to do, and you will do what you're told! Frankly, Zara may have saved your guts—Falkone is a brute, and Tazio is probably already on a pike for all we know!"

"Did you expect I'd die?" Luca asked, face turning pale.

"Don't act so surprised. If you didn't know that going in, you're dumber than I thought. This news of Tazio taking over, as much as I hate being undermined—we'll just have to figure out how to use this. Pietro! Contact Fiamma. We need updates on the flank." Neri turned to Zara. "The fate of Auria will be determined in the next hours. Listen and do as you're told. Luca—go find Corso and Kage. Corso will explain how you can support him."

Zara watched as the wheels turned in Neri's head, intrigue burning gray in his eyes as he paced, giving orders, pulling the levers of his machine for a new course. And just like that, he was fighting to be back on top. Zara had stepped into a complex game. And Neri was one of the masters.

Luca shot her a glance as he left, embers in his eyes. She'd crushed his push for glory and humiliated him. Now he was demoted to supporting Corso. Which reminded her—what in Novra was Corso doing amid all this?

Maybe that mention of Corso was a rare slip by Neri. I'll have to find out what his role is.

"Zara! Deliver this message to Fiamma," Neri said from across the room, calling her over and handing her a letter with his *Sacraorda* emblem on it—three vipers coiled around a *talùth* with an 'N' in the center of the stone, all in black wax.

"Yes, Neri," she said, bowing then hurrying toward the Senate.

She'd be uttering those words a thousand times in the coming months. Bending the knee to Neri was the bitter potion she'd willingly drink, masking her distaste with every sip. Her heart pattered as she rubbed the cream envelope between her fingers, the first of many messages she'd piece together. Soon—soon her subservience would pay its returns. Soon she would shape the world—not with swords, or *numa*, or *draeda*.

No. *Information is my power.*

CHAPTER 33

TAZIO

IT BEGAN to sink in for Tazio—that he was riding beside Sieg through the damp forests of Vestia to betray Auria—like watching a nightmare he could not stop. For years, he'd been searching for these Thoracian bastards, and now he bowed to them.

"How much longer?" Sieg's voice cut through the misty wooded silence.

Tazio walked his horse closer to Sieg and lifted a finger to his lips. He'd already warned them of the need for quiet, but the petulant prince clearly didn't give a tinker's cuss what he recommended.

"We're close," Tazio whispered. "From here on, speak only of necessity."

Sieg gave him a stiff look, but didn't explicitly disagree, so Tazio took it as confirmation and took the lead again. He could tell it pained Sieg to submit to following, and suppressed a small smile wanting to find its way on his face.

Deeper into the forest, they rode along the southwestern side of the snaking Vestian River, its shifting bankings ideal for cover. The river originated in the Aroinn Mountains far to the northwest, and Tazio couldn't help but think of Anya and the Daemonae as he looked down into its churning waters.

Tazio had studied this area outside Auria as a part of his curriculum on geography and military strategy, so he knew it well—at least from maps. After a few more bends, through the edge of the treeline, Tazio saw the infamous Snake's Tongue Falls. In the distance, its two huge columns poured hundreds of feet into the gorge. The hills on either side crawled toward the three moons watching down from above.

The maze of the Vestian Gorge caverns they sought was inside the hill on the opposite side of the river. When the Setians had first discovered the natural hollows a few years after settling, they'd steadily carved them deeper into the hills and built access into both sides of the hill. Tazio knew the eastern side over the top of the mountain was more heavily guarded, serving as the operational depot for soldiers and supplies. The southwestern side where they approached from would have scouts, but very few, so as to keep their positions hidden.

But inside, battalions would be preparing for combat.

After another fifty or so paces, Tazio stopped his horse and dismounted. "That rock outcropping with the boulder in front of it is one of the entrances," Tazio muttered to Sieg. "There's an entrance to the caverns beside the falls which bypasses the main entry. Men will be watching, so we must be prepared to fight when we go through the waterfall."

"They'll handle any guards," Xiomar nodded his head toward the three lurking Morders who stood with their bows poised.

"Vektane will lead from here," Sieg said, flicking his head in the direction of the lead Morder. The man had a mean crow's face.

"With pleasure. Don't catch an arrow." Tazio winked at Vektane, who frowned at the presence of any kind of humor in such a situation.

By Etria, the poor bastard should lighten up.

Vektane snuck forward and checked the gorge area where the falls poured over. Seeing nothing, he gave the signal for them to come forward.

"That cliff face is where we descend." Tazio pointed to a small cliff on the same face where the waterfall spilled over.

Sieg signaled Vektane to go forward, and they all worked their way down and across a series of small ledges to get close to the raging falls. Vektane hugged the wall with his back, notched his bow tight, and peered under the wall of water. The moment he saw an opening, he let the bowstring snap free. He sprinted after it, disappearing under the falls like a prowling demon.

The rest of them followed quickly behind, ready to fight. Tazio ran under the wall of water into the cave hidden behind the falls. Vektane had already dispatched a unit of five Aurian soldiers, arrows sticking out of three, and throwing axes lodged in the faces of the others. Vektane wrenched his axes out, ready for whatever was next.

"The man's efficient," Tazio muttered.

"Did you forget we're Thoracian?" Sieg replied.

"Is this good enough evidence of Aurian presence?"

"I need to see the army."

"Always good to take unnecessary risks. Know that from here, I don't know every turn to follow, but there will be thousands at some point or another."

"Then we'll have to be extra careful, won't we?" Sieg shoved Tazio aside.

Sieg walked forward, axe drawn, peering into the entrance the dead men had been guarding. He cleared the first corner, looked back and waved everyone in. They crept in, hugging the walls. It was near pitch black until, in the distance, they all saw bobbing torchlight casting shapes on the walls.

Sieg pulled back around the previous corner.

Vektane and the other Morders were already positioned in a nook. As the patrolmen rounded the corner, the Morders chopped them down, catching their corpses, weapons, and torches before a noise could be made.

Without delay, Vektane advanced into the next hallway, turning through a series of bends until he stopped.

Tazio and the others pressed up behind him.

They all saw it.

Twenty thousand armored Aurian troops churning into marching formation in the massive chamber. The clink of shuffling armor echoed around it like an ominous war song. Massive red rock columns carved of the natural stone held up the features in a brilliant display of architecture.

Sieg turned and looked at Tazio, and the stark realization Tazio was not lying sat in his eyes.

He thought I was lying? What an ass. Only with the evidence slapped in his face does he wise up.

"Vektane, you and your men put on the armor of the guards you dispatched, and wait near the exit. We'll clear the dead bodies over the falls. They can't know we found this entrance."

The Morders snapped into action, stripping the men, ready to sacrifice themselves without question.

"Gerran, you speak Setian," Sieg said to another Morder. "You will communicate with the Aurians as their army moves out. The success of this deception depends on you blending in—make yourself utterly normal as the Aurian army moves by. Once the army is moving, you will likely go unnoticed."

With that, Sieg ran toward the exit.

Xiomar followed, and Tazio scrambled behind, bumping into the rugged walls as he found his way through the dark into the waterfall cave where they'd entered.

They rolled the five Aurians that had been killed over the falls and ran to their horses.

Mounted, they galloped toward the Thoracian war camp, slamming through limbs, jumping fallen trees, hooves pounding dirt until they flew into the war camp two miles later.

"Prepare for battle!" Sieg shouted as he galloped into camp in a frenzy.

"Battle ready!" Xiomar shouted.

"You! Stay by my side or lose your head," Sieg yelled at Tazio, whirling around on his horse, a near mirror image of the day he'd saved his life at Bourgogne.

Sieg galloped through camp ahead of Tazio. Thoracian soldiers awaiting the scenario sprang into action with shocking efficiency, lining in strict formations seemingly out of nowhere, increasing the speed of the doom Tazio had helped set into motion against Auria. Cruel, efficient killing machines. Horror crept into his gut—there was a stark difference between planning a betrayal and seeing it unfold before his eyes. All hope he'd sequestered that Auria would somehow survive strained under the weight of guilt.

I'm a traitor. Thousands will die from my actions. Innocent Aurians.

It wasn't just you—Neri planned this. You simply executed the plan. Luca would have done the same.

He rolled his neck around to try and ease the tension, but nothing could quiet the swirling voices in Tazio's head. His head spun as the air clamored with metallic bloodlust, battalions crunching toward the northeastern side of the camp to prepare for their push on the Vestian gorge.

Tazio followed in a numb daze as Sieg led them to Falkone and his entourage, who conversed on horseback.

"Sieg, we are to march immediately to close on the Aurian positions," Falkone said. "The *Jestaera* has earned his life for now. On the way, gather the rest of the Aurian positions from him."

"Yes, father," Sieg said, then turned to Tazio. "Come now, we're off to spill some blood." He unsheathed a second sword from his horse and tossed it to Tazio. "How better to test your loyalty than with the blood of your own?"

The blade in Tazio's hand felt like a freak appendage. He gripped the sword until his hand hurt, wanting to kill Sieg on the spot, knowing that with it, he would have to kill his own people.

Knowing he'd passed the point of return.

Knowing he'd never be the same after he spilled Aurian blood.

Knowing the only other choice was to die.

→

In under two hours, fifteen thousand of the finest Thoracian troops moved across the valley and into the hills near the Vestian caverns. The numbers were kept low so the movements could be quick, and a favorable, thick sea fog hid the move.

Tazio stood beside Sieg.

Sieg's personal battalion stood around like ravenous dogs waiting to rip the faces off the Aurians. It made Tazio sick. He eyed the Snake's Tongue through the trees, its waters hissing death. His mind was numb from the hours of staring for ambushes in the haze of early morning, but finally, after a few hours of tense waiting, the sunrise was warming the hanging fog off the dawn forest, and the impending carnage sharpened his mind.

Tazio still hadn't had a chance to speak to Electra directly. So far she hadn't outed him, and was currently leading her battalion of archers and tactical swordsmen to the south. Once inside the forest she would ascend over the mountain to the eastern entrance of the caverns.

The rest of the battalions moved to gain an uphill overwatch on the different exits from the caverns.

Another battalion lurked in the foothills of the pass to pincer the Aurian forces that would soon flee the descending push, and the remaining battalions had spread about the camp—to maintain the illusion that Thorace was unaware of the flank.

About thirty paces out, a scout in a suit of foliage and brush emerged from a cropping of bushes and slid up to Sieg.

"Lord Sieg, they're moving out of the falls," the scout said, eyes white against his mud-covered face. "Out above the gorge on the western side. Vektane and the others have not been foiled."

"How many Aurians march?"

"Some seven thousand."

Sieg nodded and the scout hurried to a forward position.

Sieg lifted his cutlass and motioned the army forward. Tazio followed suit as blades scraped out of their sheaths in the quiet woods. The Thoracian longsword he held was brutal and spare. Tazio could already feel Aurian flesh opening on the end of it.

They watched the column of Aurians coming out of the falls dwindle to a trickle and the battalion lurched into motion down the mountainside and into the river just upstream of the falls. Cold water pressed through Tazio's boots and pants, chilling him awake. Everyone was aware that the Aurians were just an arrow's shot away.

They exited the river and stationed behind trees, their feet muffled by the sound of rushing water as they curled around the Aurian flank. Sieg motioned them forward again, and they picked up the pace, a silent horde ready to unleash. Tazio saw the Aurian rear line, and the Thoracians fanned out, using the cover of a small ridge. Tazio's heart raced as he watched the Aurian forces walking downhill cluelessly along the gorge's edge as the bulk of the Thoracian force was now concealed, a lurking death wish with generational vengeance in their breath. Sieg motioned to notch bows. Tazio notched his own, his arms trembling as he took aim.

I can't.

You must. They'll be watching. You'll be strung up.

Every archer found a target.

Then Sieg uttered his command, and with it, Tazio's destiny was set, and the ingenious Aurian plan that could only be spoiled by a traitor was torn apart.

"Loose."

Tazio released his arrow, its arc lost among the hissing swarm of five thousand arrows blurring through the woods. The man he'd targeted took his arrow to the neck, then another, and stumbled into the gorge. A chorus of Aurian death groans haunted the forest.

"Charge!" Sieg roared, and the army pushed forward from the rear and side under the support of more lobbed volleys.

Aurians dropped in shocking volume.

Tazio sprinted with the charging mass of men, the momentum of the high ground from the rear closing the gap rapidly as the side flank swung around and slammed the deeper part of the line. The Morders made it in first, cutting down numbers fast. Aurian lines caved. Men spilled into the gorge by the handfuls while others scattered into the forest, attempting an escape from the hellish cliffside.

Tazio plunged into the Aurian line behind the Morders, stabbing and hacking in a horrified frenzy, knowing he had to prove his loyalty without hesitation.

The sword jammed through armor like butter.

Blood splattered Tazio with hot shame.

Aurians ran from the messy slaughter and were closed down.

Sieg flashed beside Tazio like a man out of his mind.

Harvesting souls.

Face fixed with grit, but not with the craze that accompanied many men in battle. Like it was a normal day to cut down twenty thousand, to suck the wind from the sails of an enemy one life at a time.

Aurian horns blared from the front, and the remaining Aurians sprinted along the thin path skirting the gorge, retreating desperately away from the Thoracian push. A large group of them escaped and fanned out in the forest, dodging arrows and cavalry.

The force of the surprise attack was more brutal than Tazio could have imagined. He stopped, knowing he'd done his part, unable to kill anymore. He looked over the gorge. Thousands bobbed down the river. The forest floor was littered too. Utter shock seemed frozen on Aurian faces, as if none of them could believe their fate—or the fate of their nation.

Tears pushed into Tazio's eyes.

What have I done? What have I done!

Downhill he heard screams and knew the retreating Aurian force had been pincered where the forest bled into the valley. Thoracian cheers rang through the woods. Men rode their horses across piles of bodies, looting without delay and tending to the few wounded Thoracians. Tazio wandered in anguish among his murdered people.

Are they my people? Do I even have a people? Am I not just a wandering bastard? A curse to those I know and love?

He staggered through the carnage, sword heavy in his hand. A young Aurian soldier sputtered nearby, reaching out. "*Per favore,*" he groaned. "Mercy."

Tazio's fingers twitched on his blade's handle, and he raised the sword, heart pained, and drove the blade into the man's heart to free him. The man slumped, the last glimmers of light disappearing from his eyes.

Look at him.

Paint this nightmare in your soul so you must bear it day and night and never forget the things you've done.

Look at him!

"Look at all of them," Tazio groaned, dark and quiet as he eyed the gaggle of corpses as far as he could see.

He gripped his blade, joints about to explode before he hacked a nearby tree—until he couldn't breathe, couldn't think, until tendons threatened to tear, until he hurled his sword and beat his knuckles to pulp against bark.

"*Jestaera.*" Xiomar's voice cut Tazio's fury short.

Tazio's neck tightened. He turned, breathing hard, seeing Xiomar sitting mounted, extra horse in hand.

"Yes, Xiomar?" Tazio asked, masking his embarrassment.

"Best not to cripple your hands—they're important for war," Xiomar replied.

"Fair," Tazio said, straightening up, blood dripping from his knuckles into the soil.

"You don't have to hide your guilt. If you showed no remorse for

319

killing your own kind I would have serious doubts about you. Many *Jestaera* have switched sides before and endured the burden of betrayal for gain. Now your soul can only hope that Auria submits rather than face the blade again."

Tazio's jaw tightened at Xiomar's words. The cold logic echoed the same reasoning he'd used to persuade the Thoracian commanders to unleash this carnage. Guilt burned in his chest, but he couldn't shake the grim gratitude that the same rationale had spared his life.

"Life is a cruel ruse, is it not?" Tazio muttered.

Branches creaked overhead as Xiomar searched for response. "I can't say I haven't thought the same."

Tazio tilted a brow in response, conflicted by finding the man reasonable.

"We must return to camp," Xiomar said, holding out the reins of the other horse.

Out of the forest and into the valley they went until an officer intercepted them.

"Lord, only the highest Aurian officers are left alive as requested."

"Thank you."

Centuries of Thoracian rage uncorked mercilessly against their ancient enemies. Thorace knew that Aurians would never bend the knee and join forces anyhow, so they were useless alive.

They rode up to Sieg who waited ahead, armor drenched in blood. "Falkone will be pleased," Sieg said, wiping his sword clean with a cloth.

"This will undoubtedly turn the tide," Xiomar said with measured pride.

"I had my doubts, jester. But the advantage of your information is difficult to deny." Sieg pointed his sword out to the valley strewn with bodies. "One misstep and I'll add you to the pile. For now though, come. Feast with us! If you can stomach betrayal."

Sieg clicked his heels and trotted off and they merged with the rest of the army near the camp. Tazio saw Electra at the front of her battalion. Even covered in blood and grime, she was magnetic.

"Hello sister, I trust you managed your little task," Sieg said as they rode up to her.

"Yes, like you manage your little manhood—with a strong grip," Electra replied.

Sieg laughed, but Tazio sensed it took Sieg down a notch.

"Well let's not delay, I've worked up a nice appetite from all this slaughter!"

Sieg led the Thoracian army back to camp through the Vestian valley that overlooked the Gran Parete in the distance. Bells rang across Auria. Surely by now the Aurians knew that something terrible had happened.

The victory lifted everyone's gait except Tazio, who rode under a dark burden. He put on a face of carelessness, doing his best to stuff the pain deep inside. Electra looked displeased too.

Curious.

The army gathered in the camp to celebrate, and Tazio saw Electra talking with her officers. Her face shone from under her harsh helmet, blood dotting her golden skin in a rare display of beauty amidst horror. As Tazio hoped, she found his eye after finishing her conversation.

She walked over and called out, "Jester! I have some words for you from Lord Falkone. Come."

Sieg gave a cursory glance but didn't protest, too interested by the goblet of ale he'd just received.

Electra led Tazio away from Sieg and the others deep into the maze of tents. Some turns later, in the rear of the camp, far from the main commotion, Electra pulled Tazio into a tent by the wrist.

"What the hell are you doing here?" she demanded.

"I can explain."

"You have two minutes before I cut you down and tell my father why."

Despite the threat, Tazio could sense the same cruel desire he had for her twisted in her eyes too. The inextricable link that preserved him. For now.

"When you met me in Kataria, I was studying under a *Jestaera*." Tazio held back the specifics, hoping she wouldn't press. "You heard my reasons for coming here. When I saw the Thoracian army had allied in Kataria, and word of the flank made its way to me, I knew it was time to choose a side. Do you think I didn't know you'd be here? If I'm being frank, it was just further motivation to come."

Electra studied him, searching. It hurt having to hold back the full truth from her, and he felt filthy lying to the one he longed for.

"You've betrayed your own nation to serve my father."

"It's unconscionable, surely. No matter how it's cut."

Electra's gaze faltered, a flicker of doubt crossing her face before she took off her helmet. Blond hair fell in waves of beauty, vixen eyes cutting through him, lighting a fire. She took his face gently in her hands, whispering in his ear. "I'll never know the burden you'll carry for having done that. But I understand you, Tazio. Something about me knows something in you. It beats for you."

"I've muddied my soul, Electra." Tazio felt the welling pain he'd shoved deep down rise up in a rush. "Why do you permit me to live?"

"Men have done worse, Tazio—and my banner is not pristine. Not to mention, when you're the daughter of Falkone, things are always more complicated than they seem," Electra said, eyes tightening before she looked down.

Curiosity slithered through Tazio's insides at her veiled dissent toward Falkone, but Tazio knew better than to press—at least for now. He wrapped his arms around her, kissing her, feeling her battle hardness fall away as their bond shot through him.

"Do you always capture men like this?" Tazio said.

"Only when they've captured me."

"We have to go. They'll discover us," Tazio said.

"I don't care," she said.

"Like you always don't."

Electra gasped as Tazio kissed her neck, taking her hair at the nape. A dagger rested on her hip, and he unsheathed it, leaning back and suspending it before her eyes with a playful smile, candlelight dancing off it as a knowing smile curled across her face. Slowly, Tazio slid the blade under a strap on her armor, cutting it free. Piece-by-piece they stripped away the layers that separated them until she lay before him, bare and gleaming in sweat, blood, and longing. Pain and fury swirled in her eyes, a mirror of his own torment.

Electra reached out, pulling him close. Her skin was smooth, breath warm against his neck, whimpers defying the blood-soaked world outside. Tazio crossed into her, their bodies rising like the storming waves of the Rabbian Ocean, flying like the gales, bursting through the dark clouds together in shimmering splendor. But just as golden bliss poured over Tazio, a shadow crept in. He could feel her next to him, but her soul was foreign. A hollow pang twisted in his chest.

What have I done?

Sweat prickled his skin back. How had he exposed himself so recklessly to the daughter of his enemy? To someone he barely knew? And the same enemy he'd served at the price of twenty thousand Aurian souls. He closed his eyes, heart beginning to race, fighting to keep his chest from heaving as the hands of twenty thousand Aurian souls pulled at him from the turbulent sea of guilt. Through the clouds, he fell—the dark, churning waters consuming him, pale Aurian faces all around him, clawing him deeper to the depths, wide-eyed and horrific.

"Tazio?" Electra whispered, snapping him free of the horrid vision.

"Electra," Tazio whispered back, taking her hand to make sure it was real.

"Are you here with me?" Electra said, stroking his hair.

"Yes, Electra. I'm here."

"You're burning up."

"It's nothing," Tazio said, unable to expose the churning currents roaring through him—unsure if he could trust her—or himself.

Electra shifted, resting her cheek on Tazio's chest. Her blond hair spilled over him like threads of fate leading back to Falkone. Tazio composed himself, drawing slow, quiet breaths. There was no time for worries of intimacy. Falkone would soon decide the destiny of Auria— of all those he loved.

If he does choose to destroy Auria, I will intervene. In death or glory, I will stand against his cruelty. For those I love. I'm here—right near Falkone—his shadow my cover, his blood my trail.

323

CHAPTER 34

ALESSO

"Let me through," Alesso demanded to two Aurian Senate guards dressed in puffy, ridiculous outfits. They stood at the choke-point into the Senate auditorium where an emergency meeting was underway.

Alesso flashed his *Sacraorda* ring, coiled vipers emblazoned on it, but the guards offered no indication that they knew its significance.

"I will kill you both. The information I have will determine the fate of Auria."

The guards unsheathed their *cinquedeas*.

Alesso drew his too, ready to thrash.

"Alesso!" Zara ran up from the end of the hallway with some parchment. "Everyone calm down."

The guards recognized Zara and backed down.

"Why are you here?" Zara asked.

"I received a message. We've got to deliver it to the Senate."

"What kind of message?"

"I'll explain, but Neri must know now before a vote is taken."

"He's with me," Zara said to the guards.

Zara led them into the hall, and Alesso took in the vast chamber—stained glass windows, towering arches, and polished marble. The hall was raucous as Senators debated siege versus surrender. Side conversations were short and fast, like every word was worth a *solis*. A heavy tension rested on most faces.

They reached Fiamma's booth against the back wall.

Neri stood there speaking to an aide.

"Alesso? What are you doing here?" Neri asked.

Alesso leaned close to obscure the message, "I have a message from Tazio."

"How did he send it?"

"You might not believe it."

"Try me."

"Mahjul brought it to me."

"Mahjul? Who in Novra is *Mahjul?*"

"The big cat at the Guild."

"The black and white creature?" Neri looked dumbfounded.

"Yes. I know it's absurd. But the little beast ran up to me with a scroll tied around his neck. When I opened it, it was in Tazio's pen, and with a code only he and I know."

Alesso made sure not to implicate Zara in the detail about the code.

"This situation is becoming increasingly ridiculous." Neri massaged his brow.

"Before Tazio left, he insisted that if he sent a message, this would mean he had convinced Falkone that a path of compromise was more valid than utter destruction."

"Oh, wonderful. Shall I announce to these bickering Senators that we've received an urgent message by *cat courier?*"

Neri was wild-eyed and stressed. Alesso grappled with how to temper Neri's frustration.

"Does it matter how the message got here?" Zara interjected.

"When a cat has delivered it, I'd venture to think so!" Neri said acerbically. "We cannot afford to reveal that Tazio sent the message. Or that he's with the Thoracians. At this point, he can't be trusted, but he must be used."

"Tazio wouldn't betray Auria," Zara said.

"Being on the winning side is a potent intoxicant."

"What Tazio did stepping in for Luca was wrong, but he wouldn't betray the Guild," Alesso added.

"We'll find out soon enough." Neri walked to Fiamma, who was intensely engaged with a few of her aides.

"Do you think Tazio is trustworthy?" Zara asked Alesso.

"Mad as a cat, he is. But I'd trust him with my life," Alesso said. The worry in Zara's eyes didn't fade, and he wished he could reassure her somehow.

Fiamma blazed over in a fury.

"Alesso, if what you say is true, we must vehemently urge for surrender and negotiation. Many still support the siege despite this horrific loss. But if I were to try and deliver this new information, it could be seen as mere manipulation—I've been fighting publicly for more nuanced approaches for too long. For the message to hold weight, it must come from you."

Alesso hesitated. Imagining speaking in front of the hundreds in the auditorium made his hands immediately sweat.

Fiamma bore down on him with intensity, and Alesso realized he had no other choice.

The fate of Auria rested on it.

"I suppose, yes, I can speak," he said, like his voice came from some other place.

"Try to sound a little more convinced," Neri sighed.

"Yes, yes, I'll speak!"

"Good. Remember, as Neri suggests, we must obscure Tazio as the source. Nencia," Fiamma called to her aide, "bring this message to the speaker. This must be introduced for consideration."

Fiamma handed Nencia a chit for the Senate speaker, and the girl scurried away like an obedient mouse. With each little stride, the knot in Alesso's guts tightened until his mouth ran dry—in moments, he'd soon address every powerful figure in Auria.

"Zara, I'm going to lose my breakfast."

"You'll be fine. I'm here with you," Zara held his arm and looked into his eyes.

This isn't what I do. Cazzo.

A loud chime sailed through the air as the speaker called the meeting to order. He was a portly fellow who looked like he spent just as much time speaking as eating.

"An urgent piece of information has been introduced by Fiamma Vesta by way of Alessandro Capucci, apprentice at the Setian Merchants' Guild. Before we take a final vote, Fiamma insists we hear from *Apprenticius* Capucci."

Fiamma turned to Alesso. "The floor is yours."

Alesso stepped forward to the railing at the front of the box, legs shaky. The room grew so quiet in anticipation of his words he could hear parchment shuffling in the auditorium. Flushed with embarrassment, he wiped his palms on his cloak and cleared his throat. The immaculate acoustics carried it effortlessly, and a few mocking chuckles came back.

Zara handed him a glass of water. He took a sip—then choked, coughing it out in a fit.

"This is going charmingly," Neri said from behind as the hall erupted in laughter.

But the laughter made Alesso comfortable. He was used to being the clown.

"Well, now that I'm through the hard part," Alesso said, drawing more chuckles from the auditorium. "If you're unaware our flank was compromised, you may want to hire new aides."

A few bitter laughs and murmurs rippled through the hall.

"And while we've been betrayed, I'm here today as I've received information from an informant inside the Thoracian camp."

"Who sent it?" someone shouted from across the auditorium.

"Bastardo!" others shouted, their voices echoing as chaos rippled through the chamber.

Alesso faltered, words trapped in his throat as the room surged in anger.

Neri burst from his seat. "Enough!" he boomed. "Most of you know this was a battle we were destined to lose. Yes, someone undermined us, but we must play the cards we're dealt, or perish otherwise."

The rage settled into uneasy murmurs.

"Go on, Alesso," Neri muttered before sitting.

Alesso straightened, gripping the rail to center himself in the tense silence. "I wish I could tell you who the informant is, but revealing them would destroy our advantage."

"Tell us of this brilliant gem you hold!" someone shouted.

Alesso stumbled, thinking of how to put it without exposing Tazio. Words flooded out as a void opened in his mind. He turned to his side and hoped Zara would step in, but she just nodded encouragement. Alesso swallowed, grasping for words.

"The information. Well, his reason for sending it. For divulging the flank."

"Spit it out!" someone interjected.

"Defeat was inevitable. He told me that the Katarian fleet and the Thoracians were too great a force for Auria to overcome. And that, while brutal to imagine, losing twenty thousand soldiers today was better than enduring a hopeless siege that would leave Auria in shambles."

Hisses and clicks rattled through the auditorium.

The disrespect struck a hot chord in Alesso.

"Better than losing hundreds of thousands! Is it not?" Alesso roared over the snakes. "This informant is more brave than those of you who hide behind the Gran Parete, ready to let your people starve and die." Silence fell like a shroud over the hall. "The note said that Falkone has considered compromise rather than destruction of Auria. There is a chance to undermine Falkone with intrigue rather than force. To step willingly into his jaws—*in bocca al lupo*—kill from within the mouth of the wolf. If Auria doesn't surrender, Falkone has guaranteed he will eradicate Auria to the last soul. So you decide. Decide whether your pride is worth the lives of all that live within these walls."

Alesso stepped back from the bar, pulse thumping.

Fiamma stepped solemnly forward. "We must commit fully to this surrender. I know there is a constituency that believes we still have a chance at enduring this siege, of warring against Thorace. But I entreat you all to take this information, and vote with reason, rather than vengeance."

Hushed chatter rolled through the hall.

"Alesso, that was incredible," Zara whispered, coming close.

"I was only mimicking you." Alesso's voice was still shaky.

"The floor is open," the speaker proclaimed.

Marcus stood up in his booth on the opposite side of the chamber. He cut a noble figure in his navy and gold Guild cloak.

"Surrender is a word many of us despise, *especially* when referring to Thorace," Marcus began, voice resolute. "My father, and his father before him, and countless before them, have stood against the cruelty of Thorace. My conscience will never allow me to endorse it. So even if the vote today is for surrender, I will keep the embers of fury stoked—ready to oppose any who would undermine Auria—within or without. Whether it takes one day or a millennium, Auria will rise, and we will find a way to regain our home, our lives, and our glory."

Half the chamber applauded passionately as dread poured over Alesso. From across the room, Marcus fastened his eyes on Neri, who returned in like, each sending poison-filled glares.

Lines were being drawn more firmly, and now Alesso didn't know which side he was supposed to be on. The idea of choosing between Marcus or Neri made his stomach turn. It would be a choice all would have to make. If Auria wasn't wary, infighting could soon prove the most difficult foe.

The applause subsided. No more comments were made. The vote began.

Low, nervous murmuring permeated the chamber as Senators cast their votes, faced etched with burden. Alesso's stomach churned as he watched the procession of votes cast and counted by the Speaker. Beside him, Zara squeezed his arm in silent reassurance, though her brow looked tight and set as she eyed the podium. The chamber quieted as the Senators settled in their seats. Alesso wiped away a bead of sweat making its way down his temple, every rustle of parchment, every whisper sending echoes off the dome in the oppressive stillness.

Finally, the speaker rose, his face like stone, "By a count of 182 in favor of surrender to 151 opposed, the vote has passed."

Chatter spilled across the auditorium. Marcus, stiff-jawed, stood and exited the hall, his contingency of dissenters flooding out behind him, drawing measured looks from the remaining Senators. Though Neri and Fiamma, probably expecting such a display, shook hands in privacy, a tight acknowledgement of success chiseled into their eyes.

Now Auria dangled on Thorace's promise of compromise. If Thorace was lying, Alesso's head would be the first on a pike—and not by the Thoracians. Zara, Neri, and Fiamma would come next.

On the bright side...

Alesso's throat grew tight. For the first time since his brothers passed, he couldn't see a bright side. Only a labyrinth of looming turns, each holding one punishing consequence after the next.

There must be hope.

If I can't see it, then Tazio must. Because if he doesn't—we're doomed.

CHAPTER 35

TAZIO

"ARE YOU PREPARED TO FACE HIM?" Electra asked as she fastened her armor.

Tazio already missed the warmth of her body against his.

"Falkone won't be the worst thing I'll face."

Tazio knew it was a lie.

"Then you do not know him."

If only she knew.

"Why have you spared me?" Tazio asked, helping her re-tie the leather he'd cut during their passion.

"Not everything is as it seems."

"Almost never is." Tazio kissed Electra's neck.

"I had you thinking I'd cut your balls off, didn't I?" She smiled mischievously over her shoulder and bit his lip on the next kiss.

"I won't confirm such a suspicion."

"We have to go." Electra kissed him once more and put on her helmet.

They walked out into the war camp toward the edge of camp. Food once rationed for months now lay strewn across tables. Aurian cattle were butchered and roasted, ale barrels were tapped and flowing. Drunk Thoracians gave Tazio sideways looks now that decorum had dissolved into filth.

"Just ignore them," Electra said. "They won't touch you."

"Wish they'd try."

"You'd be wise not to spread that sentiment."

Tazio felt sick over the message he'd sent through Mahjul to Alesso —a deliberate misdirect. He truly had no idea if Falkone would surrender or not, but the job had to be done. If not, the result would be the same anyhow—war. So he had to bet on a better outcome.

As they exited the battlements, Tazio saw Falkone sitting on horseback with his entourage on a high hill overlooking the valleys rolling toward the Gran Parete. They walked up the hill toward five Morder sentries, including Vektane, whose stony mood was unmoved by victory. Tazio stepped past them, eyes fixed on Falkone. Every time Tazio saw him, the same fire burned in his blood.

The scum is just twenty paces from me.

Xiomar, Drannen, and the rest of Falkone's officers sat with him.

"A sight to behold, isn't it?" Falkone said, holding his arm out to the field where Thoracian units burned fallen Aurians.

"A great victory, my Lord," Tazio forced out.

"Where is Sieg?" Falkone asked Electra.

"You know he likes a celebration," Electra responded, a bit of sting in her voice.

"He's certainly earned it."

"As we all have together," Electra replied.

"Jealousy is unbefitting for a Herrscher," Falkone said, dismissing her.

Then Falkone favors Sieg over Electra.

"Fool, your word is worth something after all," Falkone continued. "This time at least."

"As I promised, my Lord," Tazio bowed, allowing the disgust on his face to spill out only when his face was to the floor.

"We'll keep you under close watch, but do enjoy your share of the victory."

"Thank you, my Lord."

"Tell me, fool, what was it like? Cutting down your own people in the interest of Thorace?"

"As pleasant as one could imagine." Tazio smiled.

331

Falkone let out a hearty laugh, enjoying his sick question.

"If your sword is still bloody I can have one of the remaining Aurian captains clean it if you'd like."

"No, no, it's not bloody anymore. But it could be soon, if you'd like." Tazio smiled again.

Falkone's good mood dimmed as he considered whether Tazio had shot a threat over or not.

"You're a wild heart, you are," Falkone said.

"I assure you, it's all in jest." Tazio bowed.

He and Electra began walking back toward camp.

Tazio stopped and turned around.

"May I ask something, my Lord?"

"What is it?"

"The battle of Bourgogne, were you there?"

"Yes, it was a wonderful day."

"Yes, yes... a very nice victory." Putrid sarcasm dotted his tone. "Do you remember the first charge?"

"What are you getting at, fool?" Falkone bridled at the disrespect.

"You sent your men through the camps at the gate, didn't you? Through the Danuiin Raichiin."

"Yes, we flattened them."

"Flattened." A twisted laugh ripped out of Tazio.

"Tazio!" Electra pleaded, sharp and pregnant with warning.

The Morders shifted behind Tazio as he cackled, and Falkone's officers sat straighter in their saddles. Rage burned hot and uncontrollable, like the furnace of a thousand burning fields.

"You should be careful who you flatten, Falkone Herrscher," Tazio seethed.

"Watch your tongue!" Drannen said, unsheathing his sword with Xiomar and the others.

Fury radiated off Tazio like a gale force wind.

"You killed my *family*. My *clan*. Their blood spilled by your petulant men. Sprayed across the fields of Bourgogne for your sick conquest!" Tazio roared.

"Enough Tazio!" Electra shouted, but more desperate to stop him than demanding.

Tazio could feel the Morders sprinting up from behind him through the thuds of his heart, the tightness in his breath, the shimmering heat in his stare directed at Falkone, who stared back at him with recognition of a true foe.

Aeon's voice echoed through Tazio's mind.

"Anam Teine. You will always have àite lùtha. That home. That familiar place you go to draw the power of daemonia."

His mother's kindness.

His father's joy.

Anya's light.

Daere's touch.

The feeling of family that had once been and was no more.

Time slowed as he closed his eyes.

As he found *daemonia*.

Letting it rush through him until it nearly tore his veins out.

He opened his eyes.

Colors bled.

The world moved in waves.

Things seemed like a liquid coursing around him. Slower. Richer. Calmer. But still imbued with fire and power.

Tazio snapped around, sensing the Morders had closed the gap.

Vektane was there, crow's face intent on death, sword in motion.

Tazio flipped, wrapping his legs around Vektane's neck and breaking it with a wretched crank, the man's last words merely a grunt as they hit the ground. Tazio took Vektane's arming sword, and the other Morders hesitated.

"Little hesitant, are we?" Tazio mocked. His voice sounded different. Like an echo.

"Kill him!" Xiomar shouted.

Tazio sank into focus, springing to the right side of the formation they'd formed in front of him. He jumped and slashed, baiting the Morder on the edge into a counterattack.

The Morder hacked at Tazio's legs while he was still midair.

At the last second, Tazio pulled his sword in, rolled and kicked the man in the head. The Morder's head shot sideways, and Tazio came down the full force on the man's throat, leaving him gasping. Tazio hacked at the next Morder, who parried. Another closed in, the others circling. Tazio found an opening, tapping *draeda* for vigor and batting the man's sword arm across his body, pulling a dagger from his chest strap and ripping it across his neck.

The last two charged and Tazio rolled and sprang up, catching one off balance and cutting his arm off. The final Morder tackled Tazio to the floor. They tumbled downhill, and Tazio kicked the man off him and rolled into a backflip, landing upright.

"Hello, Morder," Tazio said, and drove his sword into the man's eye.

Falkone and his officers watched from the hill with cold contempt, their swords and eyes glowing with *draeda*.

Then it's possible to make draedic weapons...

"You look surprised, fool," Falkone said, a wind stirring about them. "Do you think we conquer the world without a few secrets of our own? And your secret—the last of the Daemonae. It will be good to rid the world of your kind."

A tortured, guttural roar tore out of Tazio, his veins feeling like they'd explode.

"Move aside!" Falkone said, pushing through aside the officers stepping in front of him. "I knew something lurked beneath the surface in you. I'm sorry we had to slaughter the rest of you in the Aroinn—couldn't have rats biting our heels."

"Come see how a rat bites!" Tazio laughed.

"A feud from the beginning of time! The Thoracians and Daemonae battled in the forests of Aontir eons ago." Falkone's gaze tilted down. "We're the same, Tazio. Power runs in our blood. It's undeniable. Two arms of the same body. Did you know the Setians were born from a eunuch—a rapist? He was spared for his crimes, but perhaps he should have been quartered. Instead, he spied on Father and Mother when they went into the forest to discover Etria. Over those three days of fasting and listening following the first dreams. And the eunuch watched. He stole the power. Found a way to capture it—and sell it. And now, Setia plagues the world with its *draedic* commerce."

Tazio stood locked in place, Falkone's words tugging at his gut like he'd known these truths in some primordial place.

"We're not enemies, Tazio! You are just on the wrong side of destiny. And for vengeance? Vengeance is a fool's game!" The wind howled louder. Tazio was frozen, paralyzed by Falkone's words. "Then what? More blood on your hands as we burn Auria to the floor? First you betray them, then you destroy them? The world is cruel, jester. Your vengeance won't change what has happened, but you can change your course forward."

Falkone's words slithered into Tazio's mind like oil as he dismounted and took a few steps toward Tazio—unwavering, unafraid, eyes black like a soulless void, his dark stallion whinnying as blood tension stretched through the air.

"I understand your pain, Tazio," Falkone said, his voice low and coarse with coercion. "Power runs through us. But it torments us. *Bends* us. It needs a way to be free. To come out of us."

Falkone loomed over him ten paces off, his iron power brute and intimidating, rippling with *draedic* charge.

Kill him, Tazio. Do something. Move.

"*Jestaera* have served kings for thousands of years—and the Daemonae are the greatest among them."

"I'll never join you," Tazio forced out as doubt bent his will, making his stomach turn.

"Not me, Tazio. You will unite with your own destiny. I am the gate-keeper. I know you feel it. The force inside you burgeoning to escape—to find your greater purpose. *Your power.* That's what you and I need—the power to change the world in our image." He lifted his gauntleted hand as if reshaping the world from clay, eyes in the distant ether. "If you join me, you will be the greatest *Jestaera*. Even more than *Jestaera*. Last of the Daemonae. Last of the *Jestaera*. The greatest beside the conqueror of Novra. And if you don't, you will never be satisfied, always remembering this moment as the path you didn't take but should have."

Falkone looked away from his vision and locked onto Tazio, his pitch black eyes swallowing Tazio, the world behind Falkone dropping away into darkness, leaving only the two of them. The wind grew sharper, cutting across the hilltop as the same tree from Tazio's vision when he united with his *talùth* branched out from the floor behind Falkone.

"Get out of my mind!" Tazio roared.

He felt helpless like a cruel echo of Bourgogne, and Coille Solais.

"We've been pulled together by forces far greater than you can understand, Tazio," Falkone murmured. "Our destiny is greatness. I rule, and you unleash your force on the world beside me. We've been searching for each other, *Jestaera*. Let me guide you to become what you're meant to be."

Power seeped out of Tazio. The tree in the center sagged and bent as Tazio's will waned. Just a few steps away now, Falkone's boots pounded in Tazio's mind like boulders hitting dirt.

"If I had known what you were, I would not have killed your family. But it has brought us here. It connected us. The spark that lit the fire brought our fury together."

The sword in Tazio's hand felt like a thousand pounds as he tried to raise his sword against Falkone, his muscles screaming like he'd been cutting logs for a week straight. Panic surged through Tazio as Falkone reached for the sword, his gauntlet brutal and nearing.

Run, fight, do anything!

But Tazio was paralyzed, staring into the beastly tyranny in Falkone's eyes as the conqueror put his hand on the blade. Falkone put his arm around Tazio's head and brought him close, the embrace against cold against his pewter armor as he pried the blade free of Tazio's weakened grip. A voice screamed inside Tazio to fight. To kill. But weakness slithered through his muscles like venom, the temptation to surrender like a song in the void, his limbs quivering under inevitability.

"Forgive me, Tazio. For killing your family. The Daemonae. Can you forgive me?" Falkone pleaded.

Tazio wanted to forgive Falkone, to let the heat of revenge free, to let the veil of darkness lift, to allow the tree coming to spring back to life crept in like a black flower bursting from the soil.

"You can forgive me," Falkone whispered. "Free me. Free yourself. It's too late to go back. Look at the thousands of Setians dead by your hand. You think they'll welcome you back after this?

"With power, you will never lose another you love. You will be the master of your destiny. You will be in control. Is that not what you want?"

Falkone's voice echoed all around—firm but subtle, like a vise closing. In the dark place they were in, Tazio felt tiny in his arms, like a famished boy. The skinny prisoner he'd once been in Bourgogne. He grew cloudy and confused, the agony of fighting Falkone's grasp overwhelming, head feeling like it would explode if he chose anything else but what Falkone suggested.

Scream. Break free!

But the darkness closed in—until Tazio's will shrank to a pinpoint.

"Together," Falkone whispered. "Together we'll burn the world to ash—and rule what rises from it."

CHAPTER 36
ANYA

THE HOWLING blizzard stung Anya's face. Her fur-lined hood offered little protection as she trudged through deep snowpack with firewood. Using *Etria*, she reached for the presence of the others sheltered inside the cave—but instead, Tazio pierced the veil of her mind with a visceral appeal.

A flurry of red and yellow threads lashed through *Etria* as a wave of Tazio's fear surged into her. The floor of her heart dropped as a thread snapped loose from the *traeda cumanta*. Tazio's solemn gaze at the glade flashed through her mind—their first kiss in the pool, and their last at the glade. Emptiness hollowed in her heart.

Anya dropped the firewood, scrambling desperately as the wind threatened to blow her over. Panic coursed through her, every step growing more frantic until she saw the ice wall a few paces off that led to the cave opening. She slammed against it, her hands freezing from stumbling like a mess through the snow. Following the wall, she reached the opening and fell onto the cave floor as snow blasted in behind her.

"Mother!" Anya shouted as she hit the ground, gasping for breath.

"I know, Anya." Daere was already beside her, giving a hand to lift her up.

"Tell me he's not dead," Anya said, peering with wretched hope into her mother's eyes.

"We can't know for certain. There are other reasons to sever the *traeda cumanta* than death."

"Just tell me he's not dead!"

"I cannot know, my *leana*."

"Don't call me a child. Tell me the truth." Anya said.

"Anya, there's nothing I can offer you but hope."

Anya collapsed into her mother's arms. The weeping could not be stopped. She pressed into her mother's furs, wanting all of it to end—the running, the searching for the Daemonae Atram.

And now, Tazio.

Weakness she'd hidden for years rushed up in a torrent of sobs.

"Anya," Daere whispered, "my *leana*... I trust it was a severance rather than a death." Heavy tears welled in Daere's eyes, though she refused to let them fall.

"Why did we ever let him leave?" Anya cried.

"He chose his way."

"We could have stopped him. We should have."

"It's not our place."

"I don't care!"

The others huddled by the fire glanced over.

"Enough, Anya." Daere stood, letting Anya fend for herself.

"What are we even doing in this forsaken place? Searching every crevice of the Mora Mountains for the *Atram*? Who we haven't seen in over a hundred years? It's pointless!"

"Watch your tongue."

"No, mother. We've followed your plan long enough. It's time for a new path. Before we freeze or starve in this wretched place. Not even Roane knows where we are—and he's our finest tracker!"

"You supported this move north."

"Well I no longer support it. It's cursed, this plan. We all know it."

"We must find the *Atram*. It will give us new life."

"No, mother. The path is closed. Every step we take, *Etria* places walls before us."

"Perseverance is needed." Hints of doubt cracked through.

"Perseverance? Or willing it? Forcing it."

Daere went quiet.

"If Tazio is alive, he needs my help," Anya said. "I cannot stay here anymore."

Daere studied Anya silently.

The cave felt lonely and cold.

The others sat huddled around the fire like souls with no home. The feeling of it made Anya want to scratch her skin away.

"Hiding. Running. The last of the Daemonae resigned to this?" Anya asked, sorrow and rage mixing in her heart.

"If that's what you want, I cannot stop you. Like I couldn't have stopped Tazio."

"But you do not want me to go, do you?"

"I cannot say I agree with you."

Anya looked at the others. Their faces were worn from the grueling months amid the desolate peaks. "And the others?"

Daere looked over as if she'd forgotten about them in the midst of their tussle. "What do you all want?"

Roane rose from beside the fire. "We trust you'll make the right decision, Daere. But if I may speak more plainly, I've begun to wonder if our search has become more about avoiding death than finding the Atram. Though Anya's wisdom is sharp, it may be what we need right now."

"Have I been blind, Roane?" Daere asked.

"We are often blind before we see. And in these times, with this destruction, we're all a bit lost, are we not?"

"In more ways than one," Anya agreed, sensing Roane was supporting her point.

"I've lacked courage," Daere admitted. "I too have felt a trembling in the back of my mind for many months. I could feel Tazio drifting too—in danger, in pain, our own path going nowhere through these frigid peaks."

"I felt it too, mother. We've all been wrestling with our intuition," Anya said.

"We all have," Roane admitted.

"Aye," a few others added.

"Have I been the last to change my heart when I should have been first?" Daere asked.

"Leading brings a heavy toll. There is no shame." Roane said, full of care.

"Enough pity then. It sickens me." Daere turned to Anya. "What do you suggest?"

"We need to fight back, mother."

"Anya—"

"I know—there are only a handful of us."

"It would be suicide."

"I know, mother. We'll need an army."

Daere straightened at the proposition.

Anya continued, "We fled Falkone, but I don't think any of us is under the assumption that he won't hunt us down and grind us to pulp eventually. Tazio was right. We must find a way to stop him."

Bronwyn, one of Daere's oldest friends, stood to speak. The fire flickered off her open countenance. "There are no armies left in the south or east. But the west is open."

Anya was glad someone else had reached the same conclusion and was supporting it.

"In the west, over the Reota pass, live the Chetan and the Shēdo," Roane added.

"What makes you believe they will ally with us?" Daere asked. "No affairs in the east have brought them out of isolation."

"When Falkone completely conquers the east and moves north, which he will do, they know he will soon look west," Anya said. "And if they don't know this, we can open their eyes to it."

Daere looked toward the cave's exit, where the storm spat snow and ice like a beast daring her to act. The snow howled, battering the world with frozen shards. Daere stepped closer to it, her silhouette cut against the punishing white, the storm seeming to roar louder. Hands clasped behind her back, Daere stood in consideration, her stillness louder than the screaming wind. When Daere turned around, the fire that normally burned so full in her was alive again—a furnace inspiring retribution in Anya.

"Thank you all for killing the doubt inside me," Daere said. "Please accept my apology for delaying this long. For forcing us in this way."

The humility of it only made Anya love her more. All bowed their heads in acceptance.

"The time has come for us to rise."

Faces that had been gaunt moments before now gleamed with defiance, eyes crisp, the risks of facing total annihilation scattered to the wind as they set their shoulders back.

"West we go," Daere said, branching their destiny permanently.

Now Anya's voice found its way out.

"Yes, mother. West."

CHAPTER 37
CORSO

THE OCEAN BOBBED through Corso's legs.

He stood aboard a whaling frigate off the coast of Nyttjem.

Home.

Not a place he thought he'd be anytime soon. He'd escaped Nyttjem, and the only reason he'd ever come back here was the one Neri had sent him here for. The familiarity of the scene grated on Corso, drawing old memories out he didn't want to encounter.

He pulled up a trolling line that hung off the frigate of Ulfane Frae, King of Nyttjem. Frae had ruled the island kingdom for fifty ugly years. Nyttjem was technically part of Kalskog, three hundred miles north of Auria, but Frae had done his damndest to isolate and put a vise on anyone who came too close. Luckily for Frae, the island was rugged and only accessible by sea and up sheer cliffs lining most of the island.

Swinefucker.

"Set sails!" the pilot called from the quarterdeck.

The words dug up memories of Corso's father.

He tried pushing them away.

But the undulating waters, the lapping white-peaked waves, the gulls—they all coaxed the chambers of his mind.

"Aye, Pa," he heard himself reply, remembering being a boy.

The sea rocked the modest fishing trolley as he'd worked the line of the sails beside his father. Frigid water spilled over the brim onto his

343

thick fishing sweater. The fishing that year hadn't been fruitful, the winter cold. His father's hopes after emigrating to the coast dampened. And a shortage of work in the pastoral center of Nyttjem had driven their family away.

The gales and billowing clouds of Nyttjem had ushered Corso into the world. His parents named him after the new course they'd set in life. A symbol of new beginnings, they'd told him.

They had a daughter after him—Helga. And his mum lost a third in labor that tipped her into insanity.

Corso would hear his father urging in hushed tones, "Revna, look at the family left in front of you. You have *us*."

"Yes..." she'd trail off.

But Corso could tell she never meant it. Just sitting there in her rocking chair at the fireplace. Staring. Knitting mutely in some distant realm.

Occasionally she'd return to life when Corso would hug her or bring a gift he'd found while fishing with his father. But eventually, nothing enlivened her.

"Mamma gone," little Helga had babbled when he and his father returned from the boat one day.

After three days of searching, his father came through the front door with rain pounding the muddy streets behind him.

"Did you find mother?" Corso asked.

The answer sat silently in his father's eyes. Perhaps saying the words out loud was too much to bear.

His father was a quiet, calm man. Corso always remembered him wearing pain on his immovable face. But this pain brought a dark emptiness to his eyes. A solemnity on his wind-lashed face that never left. And just like his mum stared into the flames of the fire, his father stared into the breaking waves as they fished. They fished for seasons. Days blurred into each other in a trance of waves until, one day, his father broke out of a trance in a rushed tone.

"Draw sails. Quickly," he'd said.

Corso followed his father's eyeline.

A bleak two-masted brigantine sailed up on the starboard side.

Corso tugged at the rigging on the small sail as his pop manned the long oars, rowing vigorously through the rough waters to put distance between them and the brig bearing the royal mark of Nyttjem on its sails.

Their efforts were wasted.

The brig soon coasted up and loomed beside their small ship.

"Good lot today?" a skinny sailor called from the rail.

"Afraid we didn't catch much," Sven responded.

But Corso knew the cages were full.

"Your Lord King is on board. Spare a few loads of crab for his Highness, and we'll be on our way."

"We'll starve," Sven growled.

"Oh! Well, forgive us for the trouble," the man said with a wicked smile. "Let me go check with the king!"

The skinny man backed away from the rail.

Sven picked up the paddles again and rowed vigorously.

A pit opened in Corso's stomach. It was rare for his father to act frantic.

Corso looked back at the ship as he manned the lines.

The skinny man reappeared at the rail and raised a longbow.

Corso's hands went slack.

Frozen—he saw the arrow notched, string pulled back, sailing through the air until it plunged into his father's back. Wet, wheezing gasps poured out of him, blood spurting from his mouth, trembling as he crumbled onto the planks.

"Father!" Corso stumbled over and brought him into his lap.

Why did I not warn him? Dive and push him out of the way? You idiot!

"Give them what they want—" Sven eked out, hard face soft from the pain.

"Father," Corso said, struggling to hold him up as warm blood gushed freely.

"Corso. I've not been a good father." Tears of regret poured out.

"It's not true, pop."

"Forgive me. Please forgive me," his father sputtered between strained breaths.

"What do I do?"

"Helga..."

"Please!"

His father's eyes turned blank.

"Father!"

Corso shook his father's face, praying, hoping, begging for life to snap back into him. But with each passing second, the lifeless body was more frightening. The man who was once his father, now just an empty vessel. Corso turned and saw three haggard sailors with contorted grins pulling up in a dinghy that had launched from the main brig. They boarded, chuckling at Corso. They took the cages and one cut a hole in the small sail, winking at Corso as he did.

"Don't cry, boy, only girls cry on the sea," one croaked.

Corso blinked a few times, watching the brig sail off like it was a dream as the churning waves rocked him into a trance. The weight of his father turned his arms numb, but Corso refused to let go as the winter sun dipped behind the sea's edge, fighting with the night, numb and defiant until delirium finally submitted him to slumber.

Violent waves awoke him as his head snapped against the deck, alerting him to the churning swells. The moon was full, the water dire and alive. Black waves roared, calling for him, demanding he surrender. Death's proposal began to sound attractive—to rest and dream inside the sweet finality of darkness.

The boat thrashed over the crest of a wave and slammed into the trough, throwing him off balance. He clutched the edges instinctually and saw his father, with no one to hold him, wrap over the edge and plunge into the water.

"No! Pop!" Corso shouted.

But already he was gone over the peak of the next wave.

What about Helga?

He let out a wrenching scream at the wind and waves, wanting to plunge in, to drown his wave of sorrow before it could swell anymore. But Helga needed him.

"Fean!" he shouted. It was the first time he'd cursed, and it felt right.

He took the oars and rowed and roared and strove against the tides, palms tearing, back straining until he collapsed in a fever.

Sun awoke him, sprinkling his eyelids.

A loose crab pinched his leg.

Bells rang.

Port bells.

He pried himself up on shaking arms. Blood dripped down his fore-arms. Whispers and looks abounded in the docks. A sympathetic group of fishermen guided his boat in and lifted him out. Corso cried as one slung him over his shoulder.

"It'll be okay, lad," the man said as he carried him home.

But Corso knew it wouldn't be.

The men dropped Corso at home, leaving as Corso hugged Helga and collapsed onto the cot in the corner. When he awoke, Helga stood beside his bed, plump face gripped with worry.

"Where is papa?"

"He's gone to be with mum."

"When is he coming back?"

"It'll be just the two of us. Don't worry, I'll take care of you now."

"But I miss papa." Little sobs that came out of her pierced Corso's heart, and he hugged her again.

"I know, Helga. Me too."

Responsibility soon beat reality into him. He fished the winter alone. The catch was thin and his body was thinner. When Helga caught frail fever, he ran into the street under a cold sleet when her wheezing stopped. His cries echoed through the poverty-stricken port streets, and fell on helpless ears.

Unable to afford a burial, he released her out to sea on his next haul. With stones around her ankles, he watched her angelic face sink to the bottom of the abyss along with his own heart, the water fluttering her eyes open, haunting him.

That was where Neri found him. He sailed up and called from the edge of his brig.

"I saw you there as we sailed into Nyttjem," Neri had said.

"Keep sailing," Corso said without looking at him.

"A little young to be sending souls into the sea?"

Corso turned to him and stood up with hate in his eyes.

"I mean no harm," Neri put his arms out. "I come with an offer."

"I'm not interested."

"They all say that before joining."

Corso sat and took up the oars.

"You're suited for the Setian Merchants' Guild."

Corso paused. "The Merchants' Guild?"

"You see, everyone grows interested. But remember, not everyone is invited."

"Stop," said Corso.

"Stop what exactly?"

"I'll go."

"Well, you're an easy sell." Neri smiled.

"There's nothing for me here. Just tell me one thing. Why did you choose me?"

"You said it yourself. You have nothing. Well, not nothing. You have *pain*. And with that pain, you have callous grit. With this, you can achieve nearly anything with the right training."

The waves rocked beneath Corso.

This man is right.

"Fine," Corso said, putting the conversation to rest. He couldn't stand a drawn-out point. He almost regretted asking the question when the answer was already obvious. But he needed to hear it from the man's mouth.

"Good," Neri said.

Corso did not visit home.

He did not collect his things.

He did not turn to look back to Nyttjem or his past. If Neri hadn't found him, his wrists would have been drained free soon enough.

He abandoned his little boat to the sea and climbed the rope aboard Neri's brig.

After Neri showed him his quarters, he walked onto the deck. A storm was rolling in from the north, its ominous cloud wall pushing forward. Thunder and lightning rumbled. He could feel his heart beating above its normal slow thud. It didn't matter if this man Neri was lying. Far away from Nyttjem was all that mattered. Far away from this cursed place.

"*Set sails!*" the first mate echoed, and Corso's memories stopped, the bobbing waves tilting him back into the present.

"Aye," Corso replied.

"Oy, you."

Corso ignored the name but felt the pinch in his back knowing the man was singling him out.

"Oy!" the first mate shoved him off the line. "Take off your helmet. Do it now."

Corso slipped his helmet off slowly, looking down as he opened the anima pontem to draw draeda from his talùth.

"You're not Bjornson..."

"Standing in for him today."

"I don't know you—" the mate said.

Corso jammed the point of his helmet into the man's face, cracking his jaw and wrenching the sword from his grip. The other sailors charged and he cut the first man's throat before taking the next one's head. The rest he turned to a mess of guts and blood, dodging halberds and shortswords, throwing men into each other, and kicking a few overboard in their armor to give Helga some company in the depths. The last man fell, groaning as Corso pulled his sword out. With fifteen soldiers mopped, ten more sailors clung to the rigging above like flies in a web.

"Don't shit your pants," Corso said to them, walking toward the captain's quarter. "I need my crew alive."

"Aye," one brave man shouted back. One jumped into the ocean to try the five-mile swim to shore.

Frozen in thirty strokes, if that.

Corso walked toward the captain's cabin. He wished he'd felt more of a spike from the battle—maybe some sympathy? But instead, it felt like chopping logs. He wondered if others felt as dull behind the blade as he kicked in the door to the captain's quarters.

Five kingsguard stood in front of him in heavy armor.

Clunky choice.

"Who the hell sent you?" Ulfane Frae shouted, face slack and sagging.

"Your son," Corso grunted.

"What?"

"Clearly you two have some issues," Corso said, lodging his shortsword into a beam and drawing two throwing knives.

"Kill him!" Ulfane shouted as he drew a shortsword.

Corso's two knives found their marks in the eye slits of two men's helmets, and they fell over limp. The other three charged—two with sword and shield, the other with hand axes.

Corso loosed more knives to induce parrying. Using their flinched blocks, he charged and kicked the legs out of the shielded man on the left. The man crashed into the others in a pile, and Corso drove his sword into the shielded man's side, feeling his lungs collapse around the blade.

"Kill him, dammit!" Ulfane shouted like a pestering hound, increasingly desperate as the guards, encumbered by their silly armor, struggled to stand up.

Corso picked up the dead man's shield. The axe-bearing man was up and charging him. Corso threw the shield at his face. The man hacked it away, but was left blind for an instant. An instant that Corso used to crouch down and cut his feet off at the ankles. The man wailed for his mother on the floor as blood poured out of him.

The third man, on his feet now, charged with a shield.

Surprised he still has it in him.

Reading the charge, Corso absorbed the battering shield and slammed backwards against a wooden beam. He rolled off, using the small space near his shoulder before the man could skewer him around the shield. The swordsman stumbled as Corso slipped out, punched his shortsword into the man's neck, and kicked him off the blade.

"Is your entire army this incompetent?" Corso asked as he wiped his blade on the fallen soldier's Nyttjem uniform.

The king stared at him like a trapped animal, his loose, ugly face jiggling as he twitched in disbelief.

"Wait. Wait!" he begged as Corso walked closer. "I can pay—whatever you want. Or women. I have plenty!"

"I don't want your money. Or your women."

"Tell me why!"

"Why what?" Corso stopped on the other side of his desk. He was growing impatient with the man.

"Why are you here to kill me?"

"The Guild finds you a thorn in its side."

"*The Guild?* Then it was Neri who betrayed me!"

"No. You betrayed the Guild."

"Never!"

"In your next life as a pig, you won't be capable of abandoning Auria's request for aid. But you'll make a tasty loin."

"Fucking fuck you! No!"

"Also, your son Frone finds you intolerable."

"My son? Fuck my son. His lust for expansion will destroy Nyttjem."

"You destroyed Nyttjem through your isolation."

"Don't lecture me on how to protect Nyttjem. You're just a meaningless puppet in someone else's plan. Neri is going to chew you up and shit you out when you least expect it!" Ulfane laughed a gross, chortling laugh.

Corso's head pounded with rage.

"You're pathetic!"

"Ah! So you do have some soul in there. You demented boy."

"Fuck you. The other kingdoms of Kalskog agree you're a worthless dog too. Thorace is conquering Novra, and the north is next. The Guild can't save Novra with an isolationist bitch in the north."

"Don't make me endure any more of your bullshit. Go ahead and kill me, you animal."

The king's acceptance of death leeched the thrill from Corso's vengeance, leaving him sober and hesitant.

I feel like a fucking child. End the pig now.

"Your men. On one of your whaling hunts. They killed my father. Put an arrow through his chest so you could eat our crab."

"We would never do such a thing."

Corso's veins went cold—like snow so frigid it burned.

Corso pulled out an arrowhead, eyeing its cruel edge one last time, remembering the day he'd broken it off the arrow that killed his father.

He tossed it, and it thudded heavily on the table—letting it speak for the years of pain he'd endured.

Ulfane stared at it, frowning as he realized there was nothing he could offer. Desperate, Ulfane let out a curdling scream and jumped over the desk at Corso in a frantic flurry.

Corso widened the *anima pontem* and *draeda* ripped through him.

Ulfane screamed as Corso slid to the side of the king's overcommitted attack, skewering Ulfane through armor and sternum. The king wriggled on his blade and Corso hoisted him to the closest wall, pinning him into it with his blade.

Ulfane blubbered and jerked around.

Corso breathed deep, hoarse breaths.

An ugly smile spread across Ulfane's face, and he laughed through spurts of blood.

"Tell Neri, and my pathetic son—I'll find them in the depths," Ulfane said.

Corso wanted to rip the man's arms off and feed him to the gulls. Skin him alive and open him up. As he came into contact with the root of the twisted violence that had been festering inside him, Corso shuddered.

"Shut up!" Corso shouted, disgusted at the sight of the blubbering bloody king pinned to the wall like an animal.

Ulfane laughed deliriously.

"Enough!" Corso slashed Ulfane's throat open and put an end to the demented show. Blood poured out of Ulfane's neck, spreading over the king's ankles onto the floor to meet the edges of Corso's boots.

Corso gazed into the pool of blood, seeing the vague outlines of his own face in it. Dark pits sat where his eyes should be—like looking at a dead man. Shame at his own brutality bubbled up, and he thrashed his foot across the pool of blood, clenching his fists until the cords of his arms felt they'd snap. He roared in the face of the lifeless king hanging from the wall. All the pain he'd stored. All the years he'd waited for this vengeance making his lungs burn in anguish. The king's limp response only disturbed Corso more. He wanted him alive again. Killing him had cracked him open, and the emotion was worse than the kill.

"Please!" he shouted out the window, but the ocean just murmured endless dark waves back to him.

He slid down the wall and let his head fall back against the planks, trembling as he fought the tide of sadness pushing up from his stomach into his eyes, unable to stop the tears, the drops warm and foreign.

"Get up you bastard!" he screamed at himself, wiping them free, embarrassed by his softness.

He picked up his shortsword and sheathed it, then tore the king off the wall, dragging him by the hair to the main deck. The sailors were still perched above like scared cats. Corso jammed Ulfane's body against the rail as the boat rocked under the churning sky, and yanked Ulfane's head toward the men.

"This is your king?"

Corso drew his sword and hacked at Ulfane's neck until his head came free. The king's corpse slumped sideways onto the deck and Corso kicked the bloody stump.

"This proud king here is the man you bowed to?"

Corso threw Ulfane's head to the middle of the deck—fear ensured obedience. The sailors did their best to hide their disgust as Corso heaved Ulfane's body onto his shoulder, the man's blood dripping freely over him—the same blood that had taken his own blood. The king's body plunged into the sea, waves swallowing it. Soon, he'd be chum. It was only appropriate the crabs had their way with him.

Corso turned back to his crew. Two familiar words bubbled to the surface from deep in his gut, like a current swirling in the cold sea.

"Set sails."

The men hurried into motion, and Corso turned to the sea, already wanting solace from his new crew. The darkening sky hung heavy. The last of the brave gulls made their way landward, and white caps rose and fell in their endless, chaotic pattern—a pattern like the fabric of his soul.

"Forgive me, Father," he whispered, feeling his pa in the storm. "Forgive me for what I've done—and will have to do."

CHAPTER 38

TAZIO

"Together we will change the world." Falkone's wicked invitation permeated Tazio's mind like a fog as he hung like a doll in the conqueror's arms, the dark realm around them like the belly of darkness. "Will you join me, Tazio?"

"What did you say?" Tazio croaked, eyes as heavy boulders as looked up at Falkone.

"Will you join me?" Falkone repeated.

"My name. How did you know my name?"

"What do you mean? You told me."

"No."

"Don't be a fool," Falkone insisted, his eyes making the world spin.

"No," Tazio said, shutting his eyes in protest. From every corner of his being, he searched for whatever hint of light he could to press out Falkone's poison. Thought by thought, feeling by feeling.

"Tazio!" he heard Falkone shout, as if from another room.

Tazio plunged deeper, flying out of his mind into the greater spheres of *Etria*.

"You cannot run, boy!" Tazio felt Falkone's hands close around his throat. "Die, *Anam Teine*, last of the cursed Daemonae!"

Pushing through a fiery layer at the edge of some boundary in his soul, Tazio broke into a weightless place. He drifted—free of the body, free of the drain, but still, the muted sensation of Falkone gripping the life out of his throat lingered in the background like a distant memory. In the dark, starry sky of his mind, a faint star twinkled. From a point, it began to expand, the night sky rumbling as it came closer from a million miles away, like an arrow shot through the cosmos. The light grew, swallowing the horizon as it blared closer, every fiber of his being seeming to melt free of limits as it blasted past, radiating through his body, the force of it throwing his energy body back in surrender, pulling blissful screams from him as *draeda* coursed through him.

His eyes snapped open.

Falkone was drenched in sweat. He stared at Tazio, trembling.

"You know the power that has found me," Tazio said.

Falkone gripped harder, but Tazio drove his thumbs into the underside of one of Falkone's wrists, feeling the skin break as he wriggled into the tendons and muscles of Falkone's forearm. Screaming, Falkone let go, and Tazio fell from his clutches. As he splashed into the waters of the dark realm, the place exploded into a shower of light.

When the light settled, they were on the hilltop overlooking Auria. Tazio scrambled from the grass as Falkone remained kneeling, holding his maimed arm, malice in his eyes. The other officers dismounted and ran to his aid.

"Get away from me!" Falkone shouted, waving them away. "I can handle this petulant bastard."

Tazio picked up the sword Falkone had taken from him and twirled it. "Your tricks are bewitching, I'll admit. But I never told you my name."

"Don't pretend you know my methods." Falkone, his brutal armor grinding into place as he stood .

"You were controlling my mind. But the soul is beyond your corrupt power."

"Give me my longsword," Falkone said to Xiomar, who retrieved a longsword. A *talùth* was set into the handle, and along the blade, markings glowed like the sun might breathe.

"Enough!" Electra shouted from the side.

Tazio wanted to look at her, but feared his resolve to kill Falkone would fade if he did.

"It really is pathetic you have to lull your enemies to sleep," Tazio continued, driving the wedge deeper. "And to use weapons like that? I would expect more from *the great Falkone.*"

Blood gushed from Falkone's wrist as he stepped forward, his face dropping into calm as he raised his longsword. All previous pain he'd shown disappeared like the end of a long winter. Behind him, shafts of sunlight broke through the morning fog, striking the rolling hills.

It's just for vengeance to be served under the light of Etria.

Tazio stepped forward. A wave of energy poured across the front of his body as he adopted the dragonfly's stance Leone had taught him.

"The dragonfly is strong in its speed, wise in its landings, and always seeks where it should land next."

Tazio could nearly see Leone's charming eyes as he remembered the lesson.

"Must it come to this?" Falkone muttered.

"I won't be your dog."

Tazio saw a flicker of pain in his eyes—Falkone truly believed they would conquer the world together. The thought that Tazio had somehow gained his respect, or that he was far more powerful than he believed—all of it came rushing through him.

"So it is," Falkone said.

The wind swept Falkone's onyx hair across his eyes. Xiomar and Drannen stood rigid, swords planted in obedience, tension carved into their brows.

They fear for him...

Tazio looked at Electra.

She took her helmet off. Tears rolled off her cheek, trailing into the wind beside her golden hair.

She cries for me...

"My daughter has never loved before," Falkone said. Tazio looked back at Falkone. "Don't look so surprised."

"Tazio, please." Electra pleaded. "He'll destroy you."

Tazio drew a long, deep breath, trying to calm his racing heart.

"It will be okay, Electra," Tazio said, eyes locked on Falkone, who now swung his longsword in a circle, its hum a deadly chant.

Tazio opened his heart to *Etria*, allowing *draeda* to flow freely through him, feeling the presence of the Daemonae with him. The presence of his parents. Of all those who had died before him. Of all the pain that had driven him relentlessly to this moment.

The world seemed to slow as Falkone walked toward him, circling to the left.

Tazio circled the other way, Falkone just feet in front him, and as weak as he ever would be. But stiffness and fear stood like a wall before him, racking him tension.

"Attack me, then!" Falkone shouted, swinging his sword.

Tazio snapped out fear, parrying and and lunging at Falkone. Electra's screams joined the clash of steel as Falkone parried, and Tazio dodged.

"Seize without delay." He could hear Leone whisper.

Tazio plunged into a forward roll beneath the hilt of Falkone's sword, slashing at his thigh. The blade sliced through armor and caught flesh, but only enough to breed shock in Falkone.

Tazio sprang back before Falkone could recover, circling again, pestering with quick movements, twisting Falkone up in his heavy armor.

Now there only raw focus burning from the slit of Falkone's helmet.

"Unpredictability and speed. That is your power." Leone's voice echoed.

Tazio feinted and prodded—like a cat playing with prey as Falkone tried to keep him at bay with broad swipes.

Then, Falkone paused, lowered his sword, and muttered something indistinct. Tazio opened the channel inside him, letting *draeda* roar through him. He darted toward Falkone, blade poised for the kill, world turning on its axis as Falkone stood defenseless. Then, the world turned red. Tazio crushed into an invisible barrier, ribs cracking as his vision spun—suspended mid-stride in blood-curdling agony, his back bent in impossible tension.

"Stop pestering me, you fool," Falkone said, walking up beside Tazio's suspended body.

"Father, please!" Electra shouted again.

"Quiet, Electra!" Falkone snapped. "You have forsaken yourself."

Electra drew her sword and charged Falkone.

"Stop!" Falkone roared.

Tazio reached into the depths of what was possible, pulling *draeda* from deep in his guts. Sensing the twisting rebellion, Falkone snapped back to him. But it was too late. Too late to stop what he had created—a poor fool turned into a weapon of vengeance.

Lightning tore down, cracking open the earth.

Wind howled over the rumbles, swirling into a rising column.

"What is this!" Falkone screamed.

Tazio broke free of his suspension, rising with energy as Falkone grasped at him.

"You, Falkone!" Tazio shouted, voice booming through the cascade, all the rage he'd buried making his voice hoarse. "*You* have forsaken yourself!"

"Look at your power! Together we can be unstoppable!" Falkone shouted, pushing forward against the gale force of energy, face lined with grit.

Tazio coaxed the wind and dove, gripping his sword, ready to drive it into Falkone's skull. But as he drew closer, Tazio saw a glimmer of softness behind his hardened gaze. Not a conqueror. Not a king. But the boy inside him—innocence set in an iron face. And in that moment, Tazio's heart ached, knowing they were inextricably connected. But still, he could not stop the deathblow, feeling it enter between Falkone's eyes, blood, and bone, and brain exploding free. Tazio's knees slammed Falkone's chest down, the impact cracking a fissure in the earth and turning the conqueror's torso into a bloody ruin. Falkone's head lay in two pieces, each eye staring back lifeless at him from its own half-face, brains scattered about.

It was you, Tazio! Your soul demanded this path of vengeance. But Falkone is you. You are Falkone. Light and shadow, driven by darkness, brought to light. Now you wear the burden of revenge.

Disgust rose from Tazio's insides. He stumbled over, vomiting into the deep fissure as lightning crackled off his body, before falling into the mud.

"Retreat!" Drannen demanded to the other officers, mounting his horse and galloping away.

The clouds drifted above.

This is it then? The blood I've sought just an empty promise.

"Tazio," Electra said, stepping into view.

"Electra," Tazio said, ashamed to be in her presence. "Forgive me."

Downhill in camp, the army was sobered out of its revelry and began assembling into battle formation. Tazio hung his head, staring into the mud.

Electra will abandon me. She must.

Tazio heard Electra blow a bone whistle toward the encampment. Footsteps tapped along the mud as she approached.

"Don't come closer, Electra," Tazio said, standing up in front of her mutilated father.

"I need to see," Electra said as she pushed past him, her gaze blank and far off.

"Please, Electra. Don't."

"I need to see!" she screamed, her plea piercing the valley.

Electra pushed past Tazio and knelt beside her father, her face tightening in sorrow as she touched Falkone's cheek, her confused agony a dark mirror for Tazio holding his own parents in the moat at Bourgogne.

"I'm sorry, Father," Electra muttered. The words sounded final. She looked over at Tazio, her emerald gaze coming back from a far off place.

"Electra." Tazio kneeled beside her.

A few reluctant tears rolled out of her eyes. Afraid she'd pull away, Tazio reached out slowly toward her hand, relief pouring through him as she reached back and took his hand. Somehow, Electra remained.

"I'm a wretch." Tazio whispered.

"No."

"Then what am I?"

"You are *Jestaera*—the greatest Novra will see."

The words scared Tazio, shooting him back into the otherworldly experience he'd just had with Falkone.

"I don't know what I am, Electra."

"It had to be done."

"What did?"

Electra looked back at her father. Tazio half-expected Falkone to listen from beyond the grave. If anyone could, it would be him.

"My father was a near unstoppable evil. If you hadn't killed him, all of Novra would have fallen."

"I'm not sure I understand," Tazio said.

Electra peered into Tazio, present and penetrating. "Did I not tell you things are not as they seem?" From the camp, horns and drums beat as the Thoracian battalions arranged themselves and began to face the hill. "I know I've made you afraid. I loved my father. But I also despised him." Electra looked toward the camp. "He needed to be dethroned."

A tight knot formed in Tazio's stomach. He didn't know if it was from Electra's explanation or from seeing the army crunching into action. Her explanation made sense, and she was the only ally he had—and she was intoxicating. The swirl was overwhelming.

"Those battalions assembled outside the ramparts are mine," Electra said.

She pointed to several battalions retreating out of the ramparts into the fields that led toward Auria. It made up about one third the Thoracian force. They moved in haste away toward the woods in the north. A small detachment of cavalry split off and galloped toward the base of the hill where he and Electra stood.

Tazio stood. "You've commanded this?"

Electra looked toward the remaining forces led by Sieg, Drannen, and Xiomar. Just inside the ramparts, at about five hundred paces, the massive army faced the hilltop.

"They're deciding whether to charge and slaughter us," Electra mused.

"Us."

"Yes, us. They know where I stand now."

Tazio wished he felt fear staring at the sea of metal men, but rage burned instead. Somehow, more rage. A relentless master driving his blood.

"I'm cursed, Electra. This vengeance has only made me darker. Emptier. Like a hole that must be filled with more blood."

Sieg rode his black stallion back and forth at the front of the force like a restless beast, calling commands.

"It is *power*, Tazio. Use it." Her eyes burned like ember, arousing Tazio as much as it scared him. "They're not attacking immediately because they saw what you did. No one has seen anything like it. Only legends of the ancient Daemonae describe such things."

Sieg reared his horse, raising his sword and pointing it at Tazio.

"And so the ugly story rhymes," Tazio muttered.

Electra's cavalry guard, about twenty men, rode up the backside of the hill behind them.

"Princess Electra," the lead officer, a square of a man, grunted. "Haste is favorable."

"Thank you, Agimar."

Another scout rode up holding the reins of two spare horses.

"Then the jester is coming?" Agimar peered out from his brutal visor. Even through it, Tazio could feel him measuring Tazio with a touch of fear.

"He is *Jestaera*. You will address him as such," Electra said.

"Very well. *Jestaera*. I advise we go now," Agimar urged, working his reins restlessly as he stared toward Sieg's army.

The rest of Electra's forces were now running across the valley toward the woods in the northeast.

"This is not the moment for this fight," Tazio muttered.

He and Electra mounted their horses, and the entourage tore toward the retreating force, columns of light striking the verdant pastures through scattered clouds.

"The caverns?" Tazio shouted through the wind, their horses nearly grazing.

"It's a fine choice, is it not!"

Tazio dug into his stirrups and checked over his shoulder. There, on the hill, Sieg stood alone—watching his sister, his father's murderer, and a third of the Thoracian army disappear across the valley. The same valley he'd just had his most decisive victory in. Even Tazio felt the sting of pity for the bastard.

Electra peeled to the left and reared her horse at the edge of the woods. Tazio and the other officers pulled up beside her, trees rustling behind them under the breeze.

As the rest of the force continued into the woods, Electra looked across the valley at Sieg. A lone prince on a hill. No—a king now. Tazio had never seen him so still, normally strutting about. Electra was unwavering too, gaze set on him, like two towers watching over the valley.

"It is not easy, my Lady," Agimar murmured from behind them. "To make such a choice."

Electra didn't respond.

As I was pained by betraying Auria, she now bears the same burden. Driven by fate, the soul crushes itself beneath its own desires.

Pain glistened on the surface of her eyes—in their deeper facets, a growing softness.

The wind murmured in the trees.

Electra's hair rippled along the sides of her helmet as she took a deep breath into her chest, closing her eyes, setting her shoulders back. When she opened them again, she was calm.

"We have defenses to arrange," Electra instructed her officers, and they spurred into action. "Take your time," Electra said to Tazio. "But I forbid you from dying."

Tazio managed a chuckle.

"I'll enter through the waterfall soon. Can you find it?" Tazio asked.

"Yes."

Electra disappeared at some point as Tazio studied the horizon.

Sieg lingered for a few more moments, then he too turned his horse to disappear behind the crest of the hill.

To plot his vengeance. Another war I cannot avoid. A war I've provoked by my own rage.

Auria rested quietly under the dawn light. Tazio wondered what Zara and Alesso and Neri and Leone were doing. By now Aurian scouts would have been alerted of the tremendous change in fortune. Victory cheers would soon line the streets of Auria. But right then, the valley seemed to mourn. After so much bloodshed, Tazio understood the hills were haunting. But beautiful—the sun piercing through the clouds as if the heavens honored those who had fallen. The sea blowing like a whisper of comfort. And in it, Tazio felt his parents. And Aeon. And all those who'd passed before him. Their deaths the fire that drove him. Their love the light beside him.

"For what?"

The wind touched the river of tears that had begun to fall on his face.

"Vengeance?"

His soul ached. Empty from the lack of satisfaction that opened a pit he feared he'd never fill. A place for some poison to breed rage that would pollute his sense again.

It was not right to take this path.

"I had to," he whispered, remembering his parents.

He found himself gripping the reins of his horse with white-knuckled hands.

"How could I have known! Say something! Anything!" he screamed at the sky, rearing his horse.

Spotted clouds drifted by, and through one of the gaps, the sun cracked along the edge and glanced into his eye. The beauty of the golden light reminded him of his mother when they sat together in warmth for the final time.

"Tazio... you have to have the courage to do the thing you're afraid to do—even if you're afraid. We only discover the answer when we move into fear. Just know that no matter what you choose, we'll put the wind at your back."

"Mother?" he pleaded, falling off his horse, rolling in the mud.

Tears turned his vision into a blurry mess, but her voice soothed his haunting emptiness.

Too, he heard his father.

"Even at your age, people follow you, Tazio," his father's voice echoed. *"We need leaders. Especially talented ones."*

"I understand, Father, but I'm beginning to tire of tricks and wit," Tazio heard himself say.

"They're your gifts, boy."

"I'd rather not go into this now..."

Tazio saw the vision of his father's eyes cast to the ground by his petulance.

"I'm sorry," he heard himself say.

"I'm sorry?!" He screamed, thrashing in the mud, wanting to tear himself apart. "Those were my final words to my father?"

The horror of wanting to go back. To do anything different. To smile like his father smiled. To embrace him. To laugh. *Anything.* It all burned in his heart.

"Son, I'm not sure how to reach you," his pa's voice echoed. *"But know that I only want to help you. You'll just have to look for a way to get beyond yourself."*

Tazio screamed, unable to bear the searing shame. "I can't hear it! Enough!"

He pushed himself up from the mud, knowing that he could not go back.

I cannot forgive myself for what I've done. To all of them. Even Falkone.

Thunder rumbled overhead. Lightning crawled through the clouds that had thickened and sealed away the hopeful gaps where light spilled through.

"To Auria or Electra. Choose."

He looked toward Auria, where victory bells were singing. At least one good thing had come of the evil he'd done.

He mounted his horse and stared at Auria glistening in front of the sea, the gulls flying in joy above it. His horse huffed beneath him. Sorrow at leaving Zara and Alesso nearly pulled him in, but he turned his back on the Gran Parete, pushing toward the shadowed woods, feeling the earth beat beneath him. The morning air lashed him as he sank into the emptiness in his heart.

Perhaps that's all there is then. To be numb. Perhaps that, after all, is man's game. To live the pain of life and do the deeds you're driven to do. Deluded by our own reason, driven by our own passions.

Tazio's heart groaned as the forest blurred past. Knowing he'd suffered just to gain power. Killed and machinated and avenged only to be left barren.

Life is a fool's errand—full of tricks and wit even the cunning mistake for wisdom. All of us repeating its endless acts—and for what?

Tazio stopped at the gorge where the Thoracians had routed the Aurians just hours before. Corpses littered the banks like a cruel taunt.

"For this?" Tazio shouted at the sky, *draeda* surging through him.

Lightning tore down and struck the water, its force blasting Tazio off his horse. The river glowed blue with energy, like the threads in *Etria*. Tazio looked at the veins in his hands and arms, which glowed blue. "This power..."

"Are you alright?" Electra asked, emerging from some trees nearby. "Come. Unless you'd prefer to endure the storm."

Her loyalty made Tazio's heart swell, and he walked over and kissed her, feeling her flinch as the lightning in his veins flowed through her.

"What is this?" she asked, pulling away and looking at her glowing veins.

"Power, Electra. Now, *we* will be the storm."

ACKNOWLEDGMENTS

Thank you to my parents for planting the seed of possibility in me. Though dreams can breed unrest, *Jester* was born from the freedom to believe. Thank you to *the* family in Firenze who housed me. The real writing started there. To all my family and friends, the beta readers who provided feedback, and to all those who read *Jester*—thank you.

ABOUT THE AUTHOR

R.C. Allan is a lover of the epic, the ethereal, and the absurd—and especially the combination of them all. He graduated from the University of California, Berkeley, with a degree in Rhetoric and a minor in Theater. Originally from Pasadena, California, he lives on Planet Earth with his tuxedo cat, Bubba, in Nashville, TN.

Made in the USA
Columbia, SC
22 February 2026

79727246R00225